W9-ABC-165

1991

The
Distant
Kingdom

The Distant Kingdom

DAPHNE WRIGHT

 DELACORTE PRESS

Published by
Delacorte Press
The Bantam Doubleday Dell Publishing Group, Inc.
1 Dag Hammarskjold Plaza
New York, New York 10017

This work was first published in Great Britain by Michael Joseph Ltd.

Copyright © 1987 by Daphne Wright

All rights reserved. No part of this book may be reproduced or transmit-
ted in any form or by any means, electronic or mechanical, including
photocopying, recording or by any information storage and retrieval sys-
tem, without the written permission of the Publisher, except where per-
mitted by law.

Manufactured in the United States of America

First U.S.A. printing

Designed by Jeannine C. Ford

LIBRARY OF CONGRESS CATALOGING IN PUBLICATION DATA

Wright, Daphne.
  The distant kingdom.

  1. Afghan Wars—Fiction. I. Title.
PR6073.R47D5 1987   823'.914   87-15329
ISBN 0-385-29598-7

In memory of Catherine Wright

"God forgive me, but with the exception of the women, you were all a set of sons of bitches."

(Sir Charles Napier's marginal comment, 1843, in Vincent Eyre's *Military Operations at Cabul*)

One

Perdita Whitney was twenty-six when she went out to India to die. As she waited for her ship to sail, she had no doubt of the ultimate outcome of her voyage, but no resentment either. For as long as she could remember, she had felt herself to be a burden on her uncle and aunt, and now that there was no reason for her to live in their house, India seemed to offer her a chance to get herself out of their way forever.

During the last months of her mother's illness, Perdita had often sat looking down at that gray, pain-racked face, longing for her mother's sufferings to end but terrified of the exile her death would bring. Perdita knew that there would be no place for her at the rectory when her mother no longer needed nursing; but there was nothing else she could do and, she believed, nowhere else she could go. She had no means, no acquaintances, no friends.

It was not until two days after the funeral that her aunt told her that she was to be sent out to India to live with her father. At first the idea shocked and frightened her, but during the six weeks it had taken to get her a berth on a suitable ship, she had had time to think it over and realize that it offered a sensible solution.

Knowing that it was the Indian climate that had killed her three siblings in their infancy and broken her mother's health, Perdita did not once consider that she might survive it, however many other people managed to spend their lives out there. Her unknown father's continuing survival she put down in part to the fact that he was a man and in part to the well-known strength of the wicked. Although no one had ever actually described his crime, she had grown up with the knowledge that he had done something shocking to her mother.

More than once during her childhood, Perdita had wondered whether her own wickedness could have had something to do with him; for the very bleakness of her life had convinced her that she must once have done something dreadfully wrong. But the only time she had ever tried to ask her mother about it, Diana Whitney had silenced her by saying, "You hurt me very much by speaking of your father; he was not a good man like your uncle." Nothing must be done to hurt her mother, and so Perdita had never asked again, turning elsewhere for enlightenment. She believed that she had found it when one of the kitchen maids told her that the convulsions from which she occasionally suffered were a mark of the devil's possession. Relieved at least to have the answer, Perdita had gone to her uncle for help.

Shocked out of his habitual self-absorption by his eight-year-old niece's terrified shame, the rector had soon disabused her of the idea and had decided that he must do something to protect her against such ignorant superstition. He had taken her education upon himself and had taught her the classical languages that formed the basis of his own schooling; together they had read the military and political history of the ancient world, and as she progressed they had tackled the philosophers and some carefully censored poetry. It had often struck her uncle that she displayed great quickness of mind as well as considerable application, but when she was a child it had never occurred to him to tell her so, and later, when he found it so hard to keep his hands from her slender body, he was concerned only to hide the admiration he felt for her. She, knowing nothing of his real feelings and hating the way he touched her, assumed that he shared his wife's quite different assessment of her brains and character.

Standing on the deck of the great East Indiaman, looking down at the busy Southampton dockside, Perdita was aware of a new sadness. She felt no anger at her sentence of exile, just as she had felt none at the treatment she had suffered in Norfolk, but she did wish that her aunt had been able to show some signs of regret at their parting, if only to counteract the effect of the rector's frighteningly passionate farewell. But Mrs. Wallier had left the ship almost at once, saying only, "Well, Perdita, behave yourself and take care not to trouble Mrs. Flaxman. It is very good of her to have agreed to act as your chaperone; don't make her regret her kindness."

Perdita shivered a little and pulled her black shawl tighter around her shoulders against the April wind. As she and Mrs. Flaxman watched the other passengers board the ship, she was dreading the moment when she would have to meet the girl who was to share her cabin. It had been a shock even to discover that she would not have it to herself; but when she had been told that her companion was to be the Lady Juliana Blagdon, who was traveling out to India with her mother, the Countess of Beaminster, Perdita had been appalled.

It was obvious that they would have nothing to say to each other, for Perdita's only experience had been of household tasks and charitable duties around the parish, while Lady Juliana's must have been very different. Perdita might know all there was to know about the ancient empires of Greece and Rome, and more than a little about the Romantic poets, but she had no conversation. Once she had grown up and her uncle had begun to frighten her with his stroking and fumbling, the only beings with whom she had ever been able to feel at ease were the birds and animals she had watched in the countryside around Fakenham, and she did not think that Lady Juliana would be at all impressed with accounts of the nesting habits of the house martin or the appearance of the first cuckoo each spring.

There were few young ladies boarding the ship, but even if there had been dozens, Perdita would have had no difficulty picking out Lady Beaminster and her daughter when they eventually came. Not only were they accompanied by obviously superior servants, but by their carriage and dress alone they proclaimed themselves apart from all the other passengers. Perdita tried not to stare, but for one agonizingly embarrassing moment she caught the elder lady's eye and read unutterable disdain in it.

Her ladyship, who had been wondering whether the benefits of taking her daughter away from the unsuitable man who had caught her attention might not be outweighed by the disadvantages of introducing her into a place like India, which was apparently filled with the kind of people you might expect to meet in the company of your housekeeper, was surprised to find herself being inspected by a gawky young woman dressed in ill-fitting mourning clothes. Accustomed to sizing up the people she met, Lady Beaminster noticed that the younger woman's face was of a good oval shape and that her eyes, which were quite well spaced and large, were of a pleasing deep blue. But her pale brown hair was impossibly badly arranged, and her long hands were un-gloved and roughened, as though they were accustomed to laundry water. Lady Beaminster raised an eyebrow; the young woman blushed and turned to her companion with some remark. Her voice surprised Lady Beaminster, for it was low and well articulated, almost cultivated.

Trying to prolong the conversation with Mrs. Flaxman so that she would not have to face Lady Beaminster again, Perdita was struck by a sudden, wholly unexpected pang of homesickness for the rectory. It was one emotion she had never thought to feel and did not know how to deal with. Fortunately a string of shouted orders and the sound of run-ning feet distracted her, and she turned to see barefooted men clambering up the rigging toward the long bundles of furled sails. Other men were hauling at ropes, and Perdita could hear the clanking of a great chain.

"That's the anchor, Miss Whitney," said her chaperone. "We shall be off immediately. Come along to your cabin."

Perdita looked back for a moment, to see a gradually widening strip of scummy water appear between the ship and the harbor's edge. Whatever was to happen had begun. There was no going back.

In the early days of the journey the two young women looked askance at each other and hardly spoke. But quite soon the absurdity of behaving as strangers when sharing a cabin twelve feet by ten for a voyage that might last up to five months occurred to them both. And after Juliana Blagdon helped to nurse Perdita through a bad bout of sea-sickness, they became almost easy with each other, in spite of the vast differences between them. Once past the bay, Juli-ana fell prone to boredom and envied Perdita her rapt enjoy-ment of the sea.

Perdita would stand in the stern, feeling a sensation of escape that daily grew stronger and more intoxicating as the East Indiaman plunged southward into the sunlight. She buried the memories of Fakenham Rectory and the growing unpleasantness with her uncle in the glorious sight of the ship's great sails bellying outward with the wind and the green-blue water churning into creamy foam under her oak planks. Perdita could spend hours watching the rise and fall of the water and listening to the sounds around her. She knew that she was making herself conspicuous by her vigil at the rails while the other ladies worked at their embroidery in the shade of awnings, gossiping and flirting with the men who sketched or lounged around talking, but she could not care. Whenever she tried to talk to any of them, she was snubbed, and there was so much to see and enjoy around the ship.

When the weather was bad, she turned to books. Juliana lent poor Miss Whitney her illicit copy of *Jane Eyre*, the first novel Perdita had ever read. At first she devoured it, astonished to recognize so much of her own situation in that of the tormented child, but with the advent of the terrible Mr. Rochester her sympathies dwindled, and she found herself shocked that any woman could have anything to do with so monstrous a man. But, remembering the shame and fear that her uncle's kisses had aroused in her, she found herself thinking that all men must be monstrous in one way or another.

It was unfortunate that very soon after she returned the book to its owner, she found corroborating evidence of that thought. There was a long calm, and the great ship hardly moved for eleven days, reminding Perdita of "the painted ship upon a painted ocean." On one of the calm days some of the gentlemen on board had a boat lowered so that they could indulge in their favorite amusement.

Perdita watched, puzzled, as they emerged from their cabins below deck with guns over their arms. Laughing, calling friendly insults to one another, they handed their weapons down to the boatmen and clambered after them. She saw the boat pull away from the ship and waited with Juliana to see what they would do.

To Perdita's horror, she saw one after another of them stand up, brace himself against the rocking of the boat, take aim at the birds that had followed the ship so trustingly, and fire. She could find no admiration for the accuracy of their shooting and looked around, distressed, as she heard approving comments on their marksmanship from some of the other spectators. At intervals, the sportsmen sat back while the boatmen rowed around to collect the corpses that floated on the dark green surface of the sea.

By the time the men had exhausted their desire for sport and even the poorest shots had bagged enough birds, they had the boat returned to the *Jupiter* and unloaded onto the deck a slimy heap of wet, flaccid bodies: thirty pintados, two gannets, no less than seven immense albatross, and a Cape hen. But the real horror followed. As Perdita stood in a corner with Juliana trying to avoid the sight, the officers and gentlemen followed their take up onto the deck, bringing with them a wounded Cape hen as a curiosity. It was a large black bird, one of whose wings had been broken by a stray bullet. To Perdita's eye it was clearly in great pain and fear, furiously pecking at the strong, cruel hands that held it pinioned and wrenching forward as though to slash the legs of the spectators that circled around, screaming at them. One of the Lancer officers on deck had a small noisy terrier, which was frenziedly yapping at the bird. Lieutenant Smytham raised his voice over the cacophony to call to the dog's owner. "Let's fight them."

Cries of "Good idea!" "Start them off," and "Lay you a pony" followed from all sides. Smytham watched avidly as the bird was released to turn on its tormentors. The dog leaped toward it and bit deep into the wounded wing. The bird brought its sharp beak furiously down into the small dog's fleshy side, and Perdita was revolted to see bright blood welling up out of each creature on the white scrubbed planks. She whispered, "How can they be so cruel?" half to herself, half to Juliana.

Juliana answered, "It is horrible. Let's go away." But somehow they could not. On every face around them they saw fascination, and one young lady near them breathed, "Isn't it exciting?" as her little pale pink tongue flickered out to moisten lips grown suddenly dry.

The dog won in the end, tearing out the throat of the wounded bird, but not before the bird had ripped into the victor's flesh with its sharp beak and claws. Perdita turned, sickened, to go down to the cabin, and Juliana followed, almost equally upset. She burst out as the door swung to behind her, "That was vile. How could they do such a thing?"

Perdita answered slowly, "I can't imagine. And if they do that to animals who have done them no harm, what will they do to their enemies? It is barbaric. But perhaps all men are like that. It may be that they cannot help behaving cruelly."

"Oh, Miss Whitney, not all men. I—I—" She looked hesitantly at Perdita's gentle face and finally poured out her story, telling her first sympathetic listener of Andrew Sarum, the young scientist whose love for her had led to her exile from home. He was a man whose preoccupations were as far removed from those of the men of the *Jupiter* as possible. "And my elder brother, Augustus, too, is more interested in botany than in hunting and killing. That is one reason, I think, why Mama does not like him very much. I suppose," she added thoughtfully, "that Marcus must be very different. Mama loves him best, you see, although he has been in India for years now; and Lieutenant Smytham told me only last week that he had met my brother before his furlough and that Marcus is a 'fine fellow' and very brave. I expect that means he likes killing, don't you?"

Perdita could only agree and feel thankful that she was unlikely ever to meet him. As the days passed, she and Juliana became more at home with each other, swapping stories of their lives. Perdita tried to imagine a childhood of dancing masters, governesses, servants, and wealth in a palacelike house in the round green hills of Dorset, and she could hardly believe Juliana's careless references to the Prime Minister and other statesmen who had been part of it.

In her turn, Juliana listened, amazed, to Perdita's halting descriptions of life in Fakenham. Once she said doubtfully, "You mean that you never saw anyone except your mother and her relatives? Oh well, servants—I don't count them. How did you bear it?"

She seemed to find Perdita's story fascinating and asked innumerable questions about the rectory, wondering privately what it could be like to be part of a world where you lived like a servant and had no prospect of ever changing your situation. She could not really conceive of anything so far out of her own experience, but at least the effort made her own troubles shrink in contrast to what her companion had endured for so long.

One afternoon as the two young women lay sweltering on

their beds and the great ship approached the line, Juliana said, "It is like a book. You have had this terrible life, cold, uncomfortable, bullied by your aunt, and now you are off to India, where I expect everything will come right and you will meet a wonderful man who will marry you and make you happy ever after."

Perdita shuddered a little at the thought of the few men she knew anything about: either they were cruel and bloodthirsty like Lieutenant Smytham and Mr. Rochester, or they were like her uncle. The memory of the things he had done to her and the misery and disgust she had felt nauseated her. But Juliana was watching her, and she had to say something before the girl guessed what was the matter. Making herself smile a little, Perdita said, "I am twenty-six, Juliana. The time for any such thing is long past, and even if Jane Eyre fell in love and married, it won't happen to me."

"I don't see why not. You are very pretty, even if you are twenty-six, and as soon as you come out of those dreadful black clothes, all these horrid men will see it. Even now Lieutenant Smytham looks at you sometimes like that. Haven't you noticed?"

Perdita, who had noticed only the look of contemptuous pity on the young man's arrogant face, answered, "Juliana, I am sure your mother would not like you to discuss such a subject, and it is very wrong to tell lies, even out of a desire to be kind. Lieutenant Smytham looks at me as if he despises me, as I am sure he does."

"You sound just like a governess I once had. But I won't say any more, I promise. Oh, it's so hot: I can hardly breathe. If it were not for the shower bath, I should expire."

Lady Beaminster had at first looked on the growing friendship between her daughter and the odd young woman who shared her cabin with some disfavor; but there was very little she could do to prevent it. Nevertheless, she made several searching inquiries into Miss Whitney's antecedents, and in the end she was satisfied: even if she was sadly lacking in graces, she was perfectly respectable, had been decently brought up by a clergyman and his wife, and was distantly related to a family Lady Beaminster had once heard of. What was more, Juliana seemed prepared to accept some of Miss

Whitney's gentle suggestions for calmer behavior and the proper direction of one's thoughts, and for that Lady Beaminster was deeply grateful.

Perdita herself, once she had discovered that Juliana shared her disgust at the killing and torturing of the birds, began to shed some of her reserve and talked to Juliana more and more like the sister she had never had. She could not bring herself to talk of the things her uncle had said and done, but she did confess to the sense of awful foreboding she had had ever since the first albatross had been shot at the beginning of the calm. Juliana, who had never read *The Rime of the Ancient Mariner* and who had no particular objection to the shooting of defenseless birds for sport, tried to laugh her friend out of her fear and, once the calm broke, said gaily, "You see, your poet was wrong. Nothing happened after the death of that albatross. Cheer up, Perdita." And Perdita had tried to shake off the sense of doom, telling herself that perhaps Mrs. Flaxman was right and that she had indeed allowed herself to be too much influenced by what she read. But her attempts at self-regulation seemed doomed when, on one enormously hot afternoon while she was watching the sun flash off the waves, she felt the frightening hot and cold prelude to one of her convulsions. Gripping the rail, she closed her eyes in concentration as she tried to keep the horrible force at bay. But as always it was stronger than she. Just at the moment when she thought she was winning—as it tricked her by pretending to recede—she relaxed and it got her.

She was aware of nothing more until she opened her eyes to see Mrs. Flaxman's face, angry and embarrassed, close to her own. She said shakily, "Oh, I am so sorry. Did I—I mean, have I had a fit?"

"Hush, Miss Whitney. Not so loud. When Lady Juliana came running to me, I told everyone that you had fainted from the heat. I think they believed me, but you must not tell anyone anything different. Will you promise me that, at least?"

To Perdita, who felt as though she were floating peacefully through warm space despite the pain in her head and in her bitten tongue, Mrs. Flaxman's anxiety seemed absurd. But all her fears and anger had been dissolved for the moment

into the peaceful warmth, and so she only smiled and nodded. Then her eyes slid sideways and focused on Juliana.

"I am sorry, Juliana. You must have been very frightened.
I know it is horrible to watch."

The girl, who had been extremely frightened by what she
had seen and heard, particularly as Perdita had begun to
come around, said, "Yes, I was afraid. But you are better
now. Do you feel strong enough to come below? I think you
should get out of the sun and down to the cabin before any
people come along here."

"Very well," said Perdita, and pushed herself up off the
deck. She staggered a little as she worked out how to balance
herself again, but Juliana was there to give her an arm. Mrs.
Flaxman was relieved to see that she would not have to go
with them, but she did remind Juliana of her promise to say
nothing to anyone of what she called "the unfortunate incident."

Perdita kept to her bed for a week, during which a looming
storm passed away: the great dark clouds that had been
threatening the ship for days disappeared during one night,
and the sinister greenish tinge to the sky vanished into a
clear bright blue. The wind, which had been tossing the ship
around in a most unpleasant, nearly violent motion, seemed
to control itself and blew them strongly toward their destination. The sporting gentlemen were confined to the deck,
and with their guns stowed for the moment, they seemed to
revert to humanity. They took up their sketch pads again,
and their writing tablets. When Perdita at last emerged from
her cabin, she was astonished to see Lieutenant Smytham
himself sitting in the stern sketching with some delicacy the
very species he had been slaughtering so little time before.

Happily for Perdita, there were no more calms and no
further instances of cruelty, so that all she had to contend
with during the last two months of the voyage were boredom and loneliness. When they were alone together, Juliana
was happy to confide in her and listen to her, but in company she would smile at anyone, and when there was dancing on the deck by moonlight, Juliana was always surrounded by gentlemen clamoring for a turn with her.
Perdita, considering it very strange that Lady Beaminster

was prepared to allow her young daughter to dance under such circumstances, even under her strict gaze, would walk off into some dim corner so that she did not have to feel conspicuous in her partnerless state.

It was hidden in one such shadowed place that she overheard a group of Lancers, who had walked apart to enjoy their cigars.

One, whose voice she did not recognize, said, "Poor old Whitney's going to have quite a time of it with that woman in his house."

"Is that a brother? What does he do? Not army, surely?"

"No, her father. I've never quite been able to work out what he does. He certainly has some connection with the Company, but I suspect he is also in business on his own account—bit of a nabob, you know. And he lives rather a, well, sybaritic life."

Perdita was interested and would have liked to have come out of hiding to question the speaker, but she was too embarrassed.

"Not the man to be landed with a bluestocking daughter, then."

"No, indeed, but I don't suppose she will be with him all that long."

"What? You don't think she'll be married off, do you? Wouldn't fancy it myself, even if he is a nabob. All those books—and that morality!"

"Oh, I don't know," came another voice, which Perdita thought she recognized as Lieutenant Smytham's. "She's got a sweet face when she smiles. And a damned fine ankle, too." A burst of laughter followed, bringing a painful blush to Perdita's pale cheeks.

"You shocking rake. When did you see that?"

"Oh, one day when she was worked up about something and pacing up and down the deck, her skirts went swishing about, and I got a clear view."

"Look out, old boy, here comes the major."

Perdita waited in her corner, almost too humiliated to breathe. She tried to forget the terms in which Lieutenant Smytham had described her body to concentrate on the small particles of information she could add to the picture of her father. If he were a sybarite and a bit of a nabob, he

could not possibly be the careworn, fever-ridden, lonely administrator into whose life she could bring some comfort, which she had lately been imagining. Now she substituted for that comforting figure a rotund, yellow-complexioned merchant with snuff stains on his cheeks, who would despise her and make fun of her to his cronies, much as the Lancers had done.

By the time the ship reached the Bengal coast, she was in a pitiable state of nervous distress, which even Juliana could not penetrate. They had been at sea for one hundred and thirty-five days, and Perdita had been surrounded by strangers who seemed to despise her and whose preoccupations horrified her. She knew no one in India; Juliana and Lady Beaminster, the only people who had been remotely congenial to her, were due to travel up the country as soon as they landed to stay with Juliana's brother, and Perdita was terrified of discovering that she did not like her father or he her. She almost reached the stage of wishing she was a paid companion or a governess in rainy East Anglia. But when she found herself thinking such thoughts, she would take herself to task and walk slowly around the deck, looking out over the sea and trying to recapture the sense of freedom she had felt when they first sailed.

On the morning they reached the Diamond Harbor, the sea was as flat and gleaming as a newly polished silver salver; the pale lavender sky overhead was mistily pearled with heat; and from the direction of the flat, tawny shore drifted a most peculiar smell; not exactly unpleasant, Perdita decided, but definitely strange. She watched two small steam-powered boats come bustling across the shining sea toward the motionless East Indiaman and tried to rehearse words she could say to her father: words to placate him, to assure him that she meant to be no trouble, that if he did not like her, she would of course go straight back to England. But even as she said them over in her mind, she knew that they were not right. Then another thought struck her: What if he were not at the harbor to meet her? How would she find her way to his house in that town with the strange name? She had very little money and no knowledge of Hindustani. What if she were lost in this place full of wild beasts and savages? The rising panic was mercifully checked by one of the ship's officers, who saluted her and handed her a letter.

"The pilot's boat brought letters aboard, ma'am."

"Thank you," she said, taking it with slightly damp fingers. As soon as he had gone, she broke the seal and spread out the folded sheet to read:

My dear Perdita,

Welcome home. They tell me that passengers won't be disembarked until two o'clock this afternoon, and so I shall have to curb my impatience to see my long-lost daughter.

This last year must have been very sad for you, Perdita, but now that we are together, we will start again and rebuild a happy life.

Your devoted father,
Edward Whitney

As she went down to her cabin to finish packing, she passed Lieutenant Smytham, who was pleased to have confirmation of his estimate of her looks. When she smiled, she did indeed have a very sweet face. He touched his cap and said something civil, and he was amused to see her blush pinkly and hear her say breathlessly, "Thank you, Lieutenant Smytham. Yes indeed, it is a lovely day." And then she added in a rush, "I did not think I could ever be so happy."

Two

Edward Whitney turned out to be quite different, not only from her uncle and the men she had met on the *Jupiter*, but also from the harassed, ill, lonely administrator and the gross nabob of her terrified imaginings. Instead, he was a tall, loose-limbed man with an expressive face, eyes as blue as her own, and a kindness that led him to make her life as easy as he possibly could. His first words when they met at the Diamond Harbor were: "I had been expecting a little dark creature like your mother, not a golden beauty! My dear Perdita, I am so very happy to see you at last."

He took her to an enormous, white-pillared house, where they were to stay until January while she became acclimatized to some of the odder aspects of life in India and he sorted out his business affairs. As they climbed the broad, gracious steps to the front door, she whispered, "But, Papa, this isn't your house, is it?"

He laughed and said, "No, I sold my Calcutta house when I moved up country, but I am sure you will be comfortable with Macdonald and his wife. They're a friendly pair."

And so it was. They all three appeared not to notice her faux pas or her continual clumsiness, and when she conscientiously apologized for quoting something she had read, Mrs. Macdonald said warmly, "My dear Miss Whitney, please do not apologize. All I have to do here is ride out on our one watered road in the evening and write letters home or read. I am delighted to hear about Mr. Coleridge's poem, which has not come my way. Please tell me some more of it."

She took Perdita to visit the Miss Edens at Government House and frequently bemoaned the fact that Perdita's mourning made her ineligible to attend the dinners and balls that the Governor General and his sisters held there for Calcutta society. Perdita, however, was relieved. There were so many things she had to come to terms with that the idea of formal entertainments was a daunting one. Instead, she dined with her father and the Macdonalds, when they were not being entertained elsewhere, and the occasional guest who was received *en famille* in the vast, richly furnished rooms.

The heat was a trial to Perdita at first, and she suffered all the small agonies of prickly heat and insect bites. She discovered that the English considered no one properly healthy who did not suffer prickly heat, but she found that hard to believe; she learned to lie in her room with the blinds closed and the *punkah* going all through the day, too hot even to read or write, until it was cool enough to get up and drive out on the road that was kept watered to lay the otherwise choking dust. She learned, too, to call luncheon "tiffin," and she gradually absorbed all the slang and the Indian words that made up the private language of Anglo-India. She slowly became accustomed to never stirring without at least two servants trailing behind her, and even to the sight of the *durzee*—a most dignified man with a long beard—mending her underclothes in public on the veranda.

In many ways the whole experience of India was disturbing. With the sight of dreadful beggars in all the streets and corpses floating down the river daily, with the endless talk of the burning of widows and other strange native customs, Perdita could feel the closeness of death and corruption—a closeness that was oddly underlined by the comfort of the life she now lived—until her body ceased to seem part of herself as it always had, but became something outside her, part enemy, part fragile dependent, needing care and protection. She found the sensation disorienting.

But soon even that became familiar, and as she grew accustomed, she found herself enjoying the life she led, despite the awful poverty and suffering she glimpsed in the town. She began to volunteer remarks to her father and sometimes even to Mr. Macdonald. They both seemed to be interested in her point of view, although she could not make them understand her indignation over the plight of the sick and the beggars, and they would ask questions to draw her out. She questioned them, too, intrigued to hear about their business, which appeared to be based on the production and export of opium.

One evening as they were all four driving out to Garden Reach to visit Sir Charles Metcalfe, she asked Mr. Macdonald where all the opium went, puzzled that even a country as large as India could absorb the vast amounts they told her were produced each year.

"China, my dear. It goes to China to pay for the tea we all like to drink."

"But why do the Chinese want so much?"

"I'm not sure that they do, but we have made them so accustomed to the drug that they cannot support life without it, and so we have a market."

"But surely that is not quite right, Mr. Macdonald?" Perdita said a little nervously.

Her father intervened. "Possibly not, but it is the Chinese's fault for insisting that the Company pay for tea in bullion. If they would only take manufactured goods in exchange, we could slow down the opium trade. But their insatiable demand for silver almost ruined England, and the only thing they will pay silver for themselves is opium. Enough."

The unusually irritable note in her father's voice was enough to stop Perdita's criticism immediately, and she sat in silence, blushing furiously and keeping her eyes on the road in front of the carriage.

Kind Mrs. Macdonald hated to see her cowed for a matter so stupid as politics and said, "I have been thinking that it would be a good idea for you to buy silks and muslins for your new gowns while you are here. There will be little choice in the Hills, and my *durzee* is very skilled. He can make them up for you, and then when you put off your mourning, you will have plenty of suitable clothes. What do you say? Shall I send the *sirdar* to the bazaar tomorrow to bring back a selection of materials?"

"Good idea, Mrs. Macdonald," said Edward Whitney, relieved that she had successfully changed the subject. "You will need plenty, Perdita, and I can think of no one who could help you choose better than Mrs. Macdonald."

"Thank you both very much," said Perdita quietly.

When the time came to leave the amiable couple, her luggage greatly increased with all the things they had helped her to buy, Perdita was more reluctant than she could have believed possible. But the eight-hundred-mile journey north would mean her father's uninterrupted company for weeks, and that in itself was an attraction that quickly made up for losing the kindness of Mrs. Macdonald.

Perdita soon discovered that Edward Whitney was happy to talk to her on any subject except the production and sale of opium, and he seemed never to have heard of Mrs. Flaxman's innumerable rules for polite conversation or Uncle George's views on what females should think and say. Her father told her anything she asked. They talked of the countryside through which they were traveling with such enervating slowness, of the history of the Company and how the first piratical traders had laid the foundations for the modern army and administration that now controlled the presidencies of Madras, Bengal, and Bombay. He brought alive for her all the glitter and strangeness of the native states that he had visited on the Company's business—and his own—during the years he had spent in India alone while she and her mother protected their health in Norfolk. At times her heart ached when she thought of his terrible isolation. One evening at dinner, when she had gained enough confidence, she said something to him about it.

He laughed and said, "I was not without consolation, my dear." Then he stopped laughing and said seriously, "She had to go, Perdita. She was always ill, and there was your health to consider. She had lost all our other babies, and you were her only hope. She knew she could never have any more children."

"But I am as strong as a horse, except for my fits," she said, watching his kind blue eyes smiling at her in the candlelight.

"Then that must have been the good Norfolk air. You were a very sickly baby. And besides, there was nothing for her to do here, no one to visit; very few other white women lived here then, and she was afraid of the natives. She hated it when I had to travel: afraid to come with me to the native states, and afraid to stay alone."

"I can understand her fear," pursued Perdita, "but I can't see why she minded the lack of occupation. She did nothing at home that I can remember. Even before she became ill, I mean: a little sewing, some small charities in the village, a little reading—that was all."

"Did she never go to London or visit anyone?"

"Oh, no. We could not have afforded that. She and my

uncle and aunt used to dine at the manor sometimes, but that was all. It was a very . . . well, bleak life in Norfolk." Perdita was upset to see an angry frown distort Edward's classic features and rushed to apologize as usual.

He brushed her words aside, and his face relaxed as he said, "Well, I shall just have to try to make up for all that now that you are here with me. I am sorry that our mourning prevented you from enjoying all that Calcutta could have offered, but that will be over when we get to the Hills, and you shall have the girlhood she would not allow you."

"Could not, Papa; not 'would not.' "

He looked at her as though he were weighing a difficult problem before he said, "No. You should know that it was definitely 'would not.' I sent drafts to Childe's Bank with funds enough for you both to live in more comfortable circumstances; it was not much at the beginning, of course, but as my income increased, so did the drafts. But she would not accept them."

Perdita's shock must have been mirrored in her pale face, for he continued, "I am sorry to have to tell you this, but it is better that we are honest. She would not take the money."

"But why ever not? How could she have lived like that if she did not have to?"

"Because she thought my way of life was shameful, and the sources of my income evil." He paused for a few moments, waiting for the questions, but Perdita was unable to speak, and so eventually he gave her the explanation.

"My money comes from opium, and like you, she considered it wrong to make money from such a substance."

"So that was why she would never take any laudanum at the end. Papa, whatever she believed about the trade with China, I am sure she was wrong about that. To suffer so if you do not have to must be wrong." Then she smiled, trying to show him that she would not ask anything more, despite her deep conviction that he was wrong to profit from such a business.

One morning the following March, Perdita awoke from a sleep so deep that she felt as though she had been half buried in the yielding softness of her feather bed. As she dragged herself into wakefulness, she stretched languorously and felt a tingle of delight run through her body. She lay wondering a little at her happiness. For so long in England she had awoken to cold anxiety and fear, but now India had warmed her, and as she lay in the silver and yellow silken bed that had once seemed so barbaric, she luxuriated in contentment.

It was not just the astounding physical comfort of her new life, nor the army of servants to attend to her every want, nor the strange but delectable food, nor the delight of never feeling cold (it had continually amused her to hear her compatriots in Calcutta speaking of "the cold weather"), nor the wonderful absence of dizziness and fits. A large part of her happiness was centered in the person of Edward Whitney.

Soon her ayah would come in with the clothes she would need for her customary morning ride with him, but she had a few more minutes to enjoy her extraordinary sense of ease.

The room in which she lay was dominated by the bed. It seemed to be a symbol of everything that had made India such a revelation of delights. Ornately carved, its posts were covered in thinly beaten silver, and it was hung with yellow silk shawls from Cashmere instead of curtains. The dazzling color was echoed in the window blinds through which the sun was gleaming for once.

Perdita had been disappointed to discover that Simla was as liable to fogs, rain, and snow as Norfolk, but the loveliness of the place soon made up for that, and the generous aromatic fires that were kept burning in all the rooms every day insured comfort. She pulled the silk quilt up under her chin and allowed herself to dream.

She could almost feel herself a beautiful woman in this room. Her glance wandered over the luxuriously embroidered dressing gown that Edward had given her and the beautiful ivory brushes that lay on a silver table between the windows. The coarse matting on the floor was covered with handsome silky carpets that he had had sent down from Bokhara. Everywhere she looked, she saw something strange and lovely; only her sad black English clothes seemed to have any connection with the pathetic creature she had been or the miserable life she had once led.

The door opened and in glided her ayah with the intelligence that the *burra sahib* would expect her in half an hour. At least that was what Perdita thought she said, for the ayah's English was nonexistent and Perdita's own Hindustani still clumsy, despite the lessons her father had arranged for her. As she sipped the tea the girl brought, Perdita thought how much simpler life would be if she could only wear a pair of loose, comfortable white chintz trousers and a knee-length tunic like her ayah's, instead of the stiff, hideous habit and monstrous underclothes she had to put on. She thought she might even have been graceful if she did not have to walk around encased in whalebone and serge.

Suddenly shocked at her own immodesty, Perdita put down her teacup and scrambled up, thinking that perhaps lazing in that bizarre bed was responsible for making her think like a courtesan. She allowed her ayah to dress her in silence and tried to avoid the sight of herself in the looking glass. When she emerged onto the veranda, she found Edward already there, idly slapping his crop against his gleaming boots. She ran over to him, profusely apologizing for having kept him waiting.

"My dear Perdita, it does not matter in the slightest," he told her, once again furiously angry with his dead wife and her relations for turning his intelligent, beautiful daughter into this nervous, shrinking woman. When she first arrived, he had been appalled, and at moments during their months with the Macdonalds in Calcutta it had even crossed his mind that she was unbalanced. For the first few days she had hardly spoken except to apologize and had been absurdly clumsy, walking into chairs and tripping over small tables, her whole body apparently a mass of uncoordinated angles. But gradually she had begun to relax, to tell him something of her life, and finally to respond to his efforts to draw her out.

To his delight, he had found that she had a sense of humor and could make wickedly apposite comments on some of his acquaintances; and he had found that her isolation and lack of social savoir faire had at least left her mind uncluttered by the sort of secondhand judgments he heard all around him in Anglo-India. When he explained the political situation facing the new Governor General, she had asked some very shrewd questions and clearly understood all the implications of what he told her. As they had grown more used to one another, he had come to enjoy her and to have few regrets about being saddled with such an elderly daughter in his house. He would never have rejected her, believing firmly that it was up to him to make up to her for the miserable childhood she had suffered; but finding her such good company was a relief.

And the more he came to like and admire her, the angrier he became. If his wife had wanted to live in uncomfortable poverty for a scruple, that was her own affair, but in spurning his money she had condemned their child to a life of unending punishment, and that he found he could not forgive. He had only to watch Perdita change from the friendly, intelligent woman he had discovered into the stiff, gauche spinster in company to recognize the severity of that punishment. She was always pathetically grateful to be spoken to with the barest civility in other people's houses and had seemed to be overjoyed when she discovered that Lady Beaminster had brought her daughter up to Simla for the hot weather, as though unaware that they would never have spoken to her in England and that she was only invited to spend so much time with them because of the lack of suitable companions for the Lady Juliana in their restricted society.

Edward Whitney was under no such illusion, and he feared that when the son arrived to join them, Perdita's visits to her ladyship's bungalow would be severely curtailed. He decided that he must make plans to prevent the hurt that he foresaw for her.

The thought reminded him of something else, and as they moved off toward the hills he said, "Now that the heat is coming, I believe that you should relax your mourning. It would not be improper to wear some of the lighter gowns you had made up in Calcutta."

"But, Papa, it is hardly a year."

"I am aware of that," he said with a smile that went unanswered, "but it will not help her for you to make yourself ill in this climate by wearing unsuitable clothes. Even up here it can become uncomfortably sultry. If you are worried about the conventions, why not consult Lady Beaminster? I am sure she will agree. And would you not rather put off your blacks?"

"Oh yes, indeed," she said, and sighed.

"You must not grieve. You did what you could for her—far

more than you should ever have been asked to do," he said, bitterly angry all over again, "and now she is gone. It is time for you to live a little selfishly."

"But isn't that wicked? Sometimes I am so shocked when . . ." She paused, looked sideways at him, and, reassured by the familiar smile crinkling the corners of his eyes, continued, "When I realize that I am glad that she—that she . . ."

". . . is dead," he finished for her. "You would be a most unnatural woman if you were not, Perdita. You should never be afraid of acknowledging the emotions that you feel." He paused for a moment but then decided that it was too important to ignore and started again. "English people are taught that there is something shocking in every feeling except duty, family affection, and guilt, but there is absolutely nothing wrong with being happy. So long as you are not damaging someone else, you should enjoy whatever you can."

She rode on thoughtfully, obviously turning over what he had said in her mind. After a while she looked up at him and smiled more openly and serenely than she had yet. He was enchanted by her, and he wondered how he could tell her to smile like that at people she met instead of looking as though she expected them to strike her.

He said, "I believe that more firmly than anything else, my dear. It does no one else any good at all for you to be unhappy."

"Thank you, Papa. That makes sense," was all she said, but he thought that he had made some progress. They rode on at ease with each other again, through the flower-filled paths toward Jacko, the absurdly named mountain to the west of Simla.

It was one of her favorite routes, for it led quickly away from the town and its difficult inhabitants into a paradise of green valleys, tumbling torrential streams, and quite beautiful trees. There were the vast cedars, whose scent could transport her instantly into the chiefly imaginary world of her early childhood, enormous rhododendrons with fat piles of buds that were just beginning to show their color, and of course the flowers: tiny wild tulips starred the new grass in the upland valleys, and drifts of violets echoed the purple of the distant Himalayan peaks.

As she bent low to avoid an overhanging branch, Edward admired her increased confidence in handling the sturdy pony he had bought for her and taught her to ride. Even at the small compliment she blushed again, and again he was afraid for her. But she seemed to sense his momentary discomfort and banished it by asking him about the silver furniture in her bedroom.

"I found it in Lahore when I was there last year," he answered.

"Lahore in the Punjab? I did not know that you had traveled there. Was it for the Company?"

"You must have been studying my maps," he said, pleased. "Yes, I was asked to take the Governor General's compliments and messages to Runjeet Singh, the ruler of the Sikhs. They call him the Lion of the Punjab, you know, because he keeps his country very firmly under control. But I fear that there is going to be trouble with him."

"Trouble between him and the Company?"

"I hope not, but there is a tricky mass of tangled interests up there in the northwest, and someone is bound to try to cut through it."

Perdita looked at him, puzzled, and he tried to explain briefly the sources of the dangerous explosiveness of the frontier lands.

"Beyond the Punjab lies Afghanistan, which is ruled by three men. The most important to us is the Dost Mohammed Khan, who reigns in Caubul and who hates Runjeet. We need both of them, and it could be awkward if they should come to blows."

"But why do we need the Afghans, Papa? I know that the Company trades with the Punjab, but surely there is nothing for us in Afghanistan. I thought you told me that they despise trade."

"Yes, that's true, but they have men of other races to do their trading for them; and at some time we have to move up the Indus to find new markets for our manufactured goods. Then, too, the Afghans have some commodities that we want. But it is not so much for trade that we need their friendship. Afghanistan is all that stands between our sphere of influence and that of the Tsar of Russia. And if Russia were to conquer Afghanistan, there would be nothing to stop her armies from invading India. War between England or the Company and Russia must be avoided at all costs."

"I should have thought all war should be avoided."

"As Lord Auckland has said, my dear, 'The most peaceful policy is not always the most pacific.' Sometimes you have to risk a small war to prevent a greater."

"I suppose so, but to settle a quarrel between two states by murdering each other's people seems truly absurd—and cruel."

"Very likely. That is why we have to send an envoy to the Dost's court to try to keep him allied to our interests. But if diplomacy fails, war is the only way—and it is the natural way. You have only to look at an animal defending its territory or young to see that. But enough," he said, seeing that her face had taken on the strained, white look he remembered from the early days at Calcutta. "You asked about Lahore. Well . . ." And he went on to describe the city and its warlike people.

She listened, interested, and when he paused, she said feelingly, "How marvelous it must have been. I wish . . ." But then she paused, still finding it very difficult to express any desires of her own. He encouraged her, and she went on. "I wish I could travel and see some more of this country. Sometimes I feel as though I am still in England."

Edward laughed at that, and, stretching his arm in a wide circle that seemed to embrace the distant snow-turbaned peaks of the Himalayas, the towering rhododendrons with their massive flower buds, and the strange scents that were the only thing that she remembered from childhood, he said, "Anything further from the Norfolk of my youth I cannot imagine."

Perdita laughed, too, and said, "No, no, Papa. Not the countryside, or the birds or trees or any of the natural surroundings, but the way we live. Apart from the servants, I see no Indian people, and my life is one of visiting and being visited by these sneering English people, getting up sales of work and recitals like Lady Beaminster's for charity, discussing only English things and ignoring everything that happens outside our immediate concerns. For example, yesterday Mrs. Fletcher told me, as though it were of startling importance, that the Governor General's sisters have a small dog called Chance and that when she and Colonel Fletcher were last in Calcutta, she gave it a biscuit. And when I ask her some question about India, she looks at me as though I am mad, tells me what a terrible place it is, and changes the subject."

"Well, she is a thoroughly stupid woman, and her world is bounded by herself, the weather, and her children. One day perhaps I shall take you to meet some real Indians, but you must work at your Hindustani first."

"Of course, Papa," she said accepting a rebuke he had not thought he was making, "I am trying, but I find it very difficult."

He silently cursed his clumsiness and suggested they ride home to breakfast, adding, "What are your plans for today?"

"I am going to Lady Beaminster's after breakfast to practice for the recital, and then I said I would sit with Juliana and perhaps go for a drive later."

"Well, do talk to Lady Beaminster about your clothes. I'm sure she will agree with me."

The rehearsal went well enough, and Lady Beaminster began to believe that she might raise quite a large sum for the starving. On her journey to the Hills, she, like Perdita Whitney, had been severely shocked to see the effects of a famine that was raging from Delhi to Allahabad. Its victims lay dying by the roadside, untended and unhelped by the visiting English, who seemed hardly to notice them, or by the wealthy Indians, who appeared to care even less.

But it was the children that determined her to do something to help. She was not a sentimental woman, and she had strong views on the proper station of the lower orders. But the sight of those tiny, stick-limbed children with shockingly swollen bellies and frighteningly staring eyes, who begged monotonously for food in each of the towns and villages she passed, could not be ignored. Lady Beaminster had decided then to do something for them.

A musical evening had seemed the best plan; not only would it be quite different from the fancy sales that the other English ladies liked to hold, but it would also give Juliana an occupation and stop her thoughts from dwelling exclusively on the unsuitable man she believed she loved. She had an adequate contralto voice, and the doctor and chaplain were providing the bass and tenor parts respectively, leaving only a soprano to find. Lady Beaminster had disliked the various senior officers' wives, who might have been thought suitable but seemed to her to be both underbred and arrogant. Despairing, she had yielded to Juliana's persuasions to include Miss Whitney. The young woman could, it seemed, sing in tune and was properly grateful for the attention paid to her. She did not encroach, much to her benefactress's relief, and so she was allowed to continue the role she had taken on the *Jupiter* as a kind of honorary companion for the rebellious Juliana. In fact, Lady Beaminster had come to rely on Miss Whitney.

As they were drinking tea after the rehearsal, Perdita took advantage of a pause in Juliana's chatter to turn to her hostess.

"Lady Beaminster," she said hesitantly and then, on seeing a small smile of encouragement, continued. "Do you think it would be very unsuitable if I were to put off my mourning? It is not quite a year since my mother died, but—"

"I think it would be perfectly acceptable, Miss Whitney. The climate is becoming disagreeably warm, even up here, and I am sure it would be more suitable for you to wear some light muslins. It is a good idea."

"Oh, it was Papa's idea, not mine, but he thought I should consult you first."

"That was wise of him. Forgive me for speaking so frankly, but you have no chaperone up here, and so it is my duty: your father is in many ways an unconventional man, and it would behoove you to take care before you follow his advice."

Rebellion flared briefly in Perdita's face, but before her ladyship could be certain of what she had seen, the big blue eyes were veiled, and Perdita was saying, "I see. If you think it premature to put off my mourning, I shall of course—" But once again she was interrupted.

"That is not at all what I meant. I agree about that."

"That's good," broke in Juliana impetuously. "Then you can wear something splendid for the recital, after all. Since you are the best singer, it is only right that you should look the best as well."

Perdita's eyes became a little pink. It was so unexpected that a charming, aristocratic child like Juliana should be so generous with admiration of someone like herself, and so affectionate.

The reason for Lady Beaminster's remark about Mr. Whitney's unconventionality was in his arms at that precise moment. Aneila, daughter of a line of Rajput warriors, was also among the reasons why he had not retired home to England with the fortune he had amassed, unlike most of his companions from Calcutta, who had taken their riches back to build curious half-bred houses in the green valleys of the English countryside. Edward Whitney knew that even if he had been able to marry Aneila, he could never have uprooted her or transplanted her successfully into the cold, damp soil of England. And having no happy memories of the place himself, it would be no hardship if he never saw it again. Instead, he had removed both their households from Calcutta and installed her in a lovely house a few miles outside the town, well away from the prying eyes of the British.

Both of them had been prepared for a diminution in his visits after the arrival of his daughter from England, but once she had taken up her informal position as Juliana Blagdon's companion, he had resumed his regular visits to his mistress. He occasionally wondered whether Aneila resented the time he was prepared to lavish on his English child when he saw so little of his Indian sons, his care for them restricted to financing their education and easing their entry into the army and civil service. But she gave no sign.

He looked down at her heart-shaped face, thinner now but lovely still, and kissed her in gratitude for the years of affection she had given him. In the twenty-three years that she had lived under his protection, she had never complained about anything he had done or not done. She was not always happy, he knew, and it had taken her some time to become accustomed to separation from her family and the structure of her religion—both had had to be renounced when she went to live under the protection of a casteless foreigner—but she had never tried to involve him in her sadness, and as far as he could tell, she had not blamed him for any of it. For a moment he thought of the tight lips and angry eyes of his virtuous wife as she confronted him with evidence of one after another of his shortcomings and of the reluctance and disgust with which she infrequently allowed him to exercise his marital rights.

Aneila had taught him that there was more to lovemaking than the sharp, quick pleasure and sense of release that followed the spilling of his seed. She had shown him how to give her pleasure and in doing so increase his own; she had taught him, too, that the exercise of his rights had gentler names and purposes than those he had known. He had told her a good deal of his wife—most of which she found impossible to believe—and more recently of his daughter and what had been done to her. Aneila had been full of extremely sensible suggestions for her comfort and happiness, but he had been able to put only a few of them into practice. That particular afternoon, Aneila had asked him, "And how is it with Perdita? Is she becoming any happier?"

"A little. She seems to be very friendly with the Blagdon girl; but there's this confounded concert they're organizing."

"Confounded? It seems to me an excellent thing for a great lady from England to sing to make money for the starving people of Delhi."

"Yes, yes, very commendable; but what if Perdita makes a fool of herself? If she should break down or something, or refuse to sing at the last minute, or—worse—have a fit, she would never be able to face any of these people again."

"You have told me that she is very shy; surely she would never have agreed to sing if she did not know she could do it."

"Well, I hope to God you're right," answered Edward gloomily before taking her into his arms again and forgetting his myriad concerns. He smelled the musky scent of her dark hair and felt the softness of her delectable body through the fine, pale gold-colored sari. Desire flamed in him suddenly, and he picked her up and carried her out of the colonnaded room that bordered one side of her garden and into her bedroom.

Before he left her two hours later, she briefly touched his face and said, "Do not worry about the daughter so much. Show you love her, tell her what is good about her, and comfort her if she is not happy. Talk to her as much as you can and show her that she can tell you anything. All will be well. If she knows you think well of her, she will not be so nervous with others. They will like her if she does not make them so uncomfortable."

"Any sane person would, but these appalling English-women—who can tell what they will do? Oh, Aneila, you do not know how much I love you."

She stretched up to take his handsome head between her tiny hands and bring it down so that she could kiss him.

"Yes, Edward, I think I do. As you know that you are the lord of my life."

Three

By the time the last rehearsal was sung five days later, Perdita's new gowns had been extracted from the sealed tin boxes in which they had been protected from damp, heat, and insects, and Juliana's brother had arrived in Simla from his station. When Perdita drank a cup of tea with Juliana on the afternoon of the concert, she found the girl bubbling over with pleasure at her brother's arrival.

"I had expected to hate him," she confided, "but he is completely charming. When Mama and I arrived at the station, I could hardly believe that it was him, if you see what I mean. And he makes Mama so much kinder than she normally is. He is very handsome, too, and so brave: all the other officers told me so. He saved the life of his friend Captain Thurleigh in a skirmish once, and Capital Thurleigh told me that there's no one he'd rather have in what he called a 'scrap' than Marcus. I am sure you will like him; all the ladies at the station were in love with him. And I know he will like you."

Perdita was quite sure he would not. A young man as popular and successful as Captain Marcus Blagdon would have no time for someone like her. That in itself did not worry her at all, but she was afraid that Juliana might change her mind about "the big spin," as she had heard herself called, when she saw her brother's contempt. The girl's friendship had meant a great deal to Perdita and she would miss it. But the habits of a lifetime did not break, and so she smiled and encouraged Juliana in her happy anticipation. Nevertheless, by the time Perdita left Lady Beaminster's bungalow, she was very quiet, and as the *jonpauni* took her home to dress for the concert she began to wish that she had never agreed to make herself so conspicuous. After all, if it had not been for the concert, she never would have had to meet Captain Blagdon or risk his disdain.

Her father misunderstood the cause of her nervousness, and when she eventually emerged from her room in the new cream-colored silk gown, he took her hand and said with as much confidence as he could muster, "You need not be afraid, my dear. I have heard you sing in church, and there has never been a flat note." She turned her anxious face toward him, and he watched amusement banish the frown and smooth the deep crease from between her eyes.

"I am not afraid about singing flat, Papa."

"Good," he said, and wrapped her cloak around her shoulders. "And you look wonderful, if you will allow me to say so."

"Really? Papa, you would not be flattering me, I trust?"

"No, of course not, Perdita. I said when you arrived that you looked pretty, and that was in those dreadful black clothes. Now, in this delightful gown, you look very beautiful indeed. Try to smile at people, won't you? It is only when you frown that there is anything wrong at all."

"I will try, Papa. But all those people make me so worried."

"I know, but they need not. They are of no importance, and it is quite likely that you will never see any of them again. It is probable that I shall have to travel again for the Company, and I thought you might like to come with me."

"Where would we go?" she asked, interested.

"Lahore again, I expect. Reports from Caubul are causing some consternation in Calcutta and in London. And the Company will need to be sure of the Sikhs if there is trouble in Afghanistan."

He congratulated himself on the diversion as he saw her eyes liven in the milky dusk. It was a particularly lovely evening. The rain had held off all day, and the few clouds were like insubstantial puffs of cotton wool, washed pink by the declining sun and sailing quickly past the violet-colored mountain peaks. The air felt soft on his face as the carriage turned into Lady Beaminster's drive, and he smiled encouragingly at his daughter.

Her interest and pleasure survived their entry into the drawing room and the first encounters with her acquaintances. He escorted her to the platform that had been erected at one end of the long room and waited with her until she was settled next to Juliana in front of a large potted palm. She took up her music with gloved hands that scarcely shook, and he left her there hopefully, to find a chair next to a collector up on sick leave from his district near Agra. Mortimer Blandfield was a dull man, but at least a bachelor who liked India and did not consider his years there an exile.

"Charming, your daughter, Whitney. Quite charming," he offered by way of greeting.

"Why, thank you, Blandfield," answered Edward, surprised to hear a note of genuine admiration in the man's voice. He looked across the room to the dais where Perdita had risen to shake hands with the doctor and saw again how the gown Mrs. Macdonald had had made for her became her. She must have put on a little weight, he decided, for she did not seem nearly so angular, and above the low-cut corsage he could distinctly see the swell of her white breasts. In fact, she seemed to have a rather pleasing shape, after all, and with the light of a candelabra warming her pale skin and glistening on her hair, she did indeed look charming. Belatedly he realized that there was yet another danger from which he would have to protect her. Accustomed to overhearing disparaging remarks about her age and her gaucherie, he had planned to protect her from hurt when she discovered that everyone around them assumed that she was quite unmarriageable. But he had ignored the scarcity of English women in India and the likely supposition that his not inconsiderable fortune would go to her. Surprising an almost lecherous expression on Blandfield's face, Edward revised his plans hastily.

His thoughts were broken by the first notes of the piano, reasonably well played by Lady Beaminster, as the chaplain rose to begin the first recitative of the *Messiah*.

As she listened, Perdita wished, as she had so often before, that it had been written for the soprano part. The infinitely consoling words, a little mangled by Mr. Carswell's dramatic rendering, moved her and made her think sentimentally that perhaps even her mysterious transgression might have been forgiven and her iniquity pardoned. Happiness was not an emotion she knew much about, and the absence of misery and fear she now felt seemed almost miraculous. The feeling persisted and sustained her through her first two arias, so that when she finally rose to sing "I know that my Redeemer liveth," a new confidence and warmth rounded her always accurate singing into something approaching splendor. The two men who shared the platform with her exchanged amused glances, wondering what had happened to put poor Miss Whitney in such a glow. Her father thought she looked transfigured, and Blandfield kept wiping his hands on his handkerchief and shifting in his chair, while several of the newly arrived officers who had not had time to hear the town's views of the despised Miss Whitney were greatly taken with her.

Even those, such as Captain James Thurleigh, who took little interest in women were impressed with her voice. After he had greeted Lady Beaminster, he asked about her.

"Who was the soprano? I have rarely heard so magnificent a voice in India."

"Poor Miss Whitney. Yes, it was rather surprising, wasn't it? She is the daughter of a retired merchant, a Mr. Edward Whitney, late of Calcutta, who has some advisory position with the Company. She has become quite a friend of Juliana's, and so I expect you will become acquainted with her —" She broke off to greet her daughter. "Ah, Juliana, my love, that was delightful. Here is Captain Thurleigh telling me that Miss Whitney's voice is the best he has heard in India."

Juliana looked approvingly at the captain and was about to speak when she caught sight of her brother. She ran over to seize his hand and drag him away from the group to whom he was talking.

"Juliana, have a care for my dignity and for your own," he said, protesting, but it was kindly said, for he had taken a liking to his handsome sister and took pleasure in her ingenuous enthusiasms. "Do not be too surprised, Thurleigh," he said to his friend. "I expect my little sister has had a touch of the sun."

"Please do not listen to him, Captain Thurleigh. He likes to pretend that I am a baby for some reason. Oh, good," she said, her lively eye catching sight of Perdita, "here is Miss Whitney. Perdita, let me introduce my brother, and Captain James Thurleigh, who was just telling Mama how much he liked your voice."

Perdita blushed unbecomingly and stammered some disclaimer as Captain Thurleigh bowed over her hand. Lady Beaminster moved away to talk to the collector, and Perdita turned to Captain Blagdon, who said, "I know far less of music than Thurleigh here, but I very much enjoyed your singing."

The image she had invented of an arrogantly scarred hero waving broken hearts like trophies on a lance faded away as she took in the weary kindliness of his smile and the altogether undistinguished pleasantness of his square face. Although he had his mother's dark hair and eyes, he had none of the high-bred bony handsomeness she had bequeathed to her daughter. Perdita shook hands with him with far more composure than she usually displayed in company and said quietly, "I am glad you enjoyed it, Captain Blagdon. It has been a great pleasure to sing, hasn't it, Juliana?"

"Well, it has certainly been better than sitting in the drawing room doing embroidery or writing letters before driving out with Mama to call on these dreadful women, and for some reason we are not allowed to take part in theatricals here."

"Juliana, hush, please. All those ladies are here," protested Perdita, laughing a little.

"Oh, pooh. You know how terrible they are. And here is one now," she added in a whisper. Perdita was conscious of a sharp disappointment as she watched the approach of Maria Jamieson.

"Captain Blagdon," cooed the reigning beauty as she reached them, "forgive me, but Mama sent me to bring you to her." She put one of her plump little hands on his sleeve confidingly and smiled up at him. "She and I were very happy when Papa wrote to us that he had granted you leave. We always feel so unprotected in this place without you all."

He looked down at her, understanding the possessiveness of that hand on his arm and the message he read in her shallow eyes, which seemed to say, "These conventions are absurd. I find my husband immensely boring. You are rich and important. I am beautiful, the wife of your senior officer and the daughter of your colonel, and one day I shall have you." He withdrew from her a little and, determined to rebuke her for her too obvious rudeness to his companions, said, "Do you know Miss Whitney and my sister Juliana, who have come here from England?"

"Why, yes, of course. Miss Whitney, pray forgive me, I did not see you standing in the corner there. I must say how surprised I was to see your father here this evening. I did not know he knew Lady Beaminster. Good evening, Lady Juliana."

Juliana, who could not bear the woman, begged Captain Thurleigh to escort her back to her mother.

As they walked away, Maria Jamieson turned back to her victim to say, "Your singing was very sweet, Miss Whitney, but I thought—I know you will not mind my saying this, Captain Blagdon—that dear Lady Juliana had a little trouble with some of the high notes."

Perdita stood in her corner, silent and resentful as the evening's pleasure trickled away. She knew perfectly well that Juliana had been criticized while she had been praised only because she presented no threat to Mrs. Jamieson's supremacy. Emboldened by the compliments she had received earlier, she said more bravely than she had yet spoken to her tormentor, "I thought Juliana sang delightfully. Handel is, of course, rather a difficult composer to enjoy until one knows the music well." It was not true, of course, but she knew that Maria Jamieson was ignorant enough to believe it, and the amused smile Captain Blagdon sent her seemed to make the lie worthwhile.

Mrs. Jamieson, who was too set up in her own conceit to believe poor Miss Whitney capable of malice, merely looked coldly at her, turned to their companion, and said, "I promised Mama that I would fetch you. She wishes to ask you something."

"And we must not keep the colonel's lady waiting. Goodbye, Miss Whitney. We shall meet again."

She watched him go, already lost.

"Well," said an indignant voice at her elbow, "I hope he does not marry her."

"Oh, Juliana, how could he? She is married to Major Jamieson."

"Well, he might easily be killed, and Marcus must marry someone soon, and she is the right age, and so pretty; he seems to like her. Look at that!"

Perdita watched the beautiful Mrs. Jamieson touch his arm as he smiled down at her, and she wished that she, too, could have been small and rounded, with soft, black-lashed eyes and tiny white hands. Then her common sense returned, and she remembered that she would prefer not to think or behave as Mrs. Jamieson did, and if that was the price for looking like her, it was too high.

They saw Captain Blagdon kiss her hand, turn for a moment or two to her mother, and then saunter off toward Captain Thurleigh.

"Perdita, do you think that perhaps we should go?"

Perdita turned her head to smile at her father. "Perhaps we should, Papa. I shall just go and say good night to Lady Beaminster, and then I shall come. Juliana, shall I see you tomorrow?"

"Yes indeed."

Driving back through the small town in the softly scented moonlight, Perdita regained some of the serenity that Mrs. Jamieson had destroyed. Edward took her hand in his and told her of his pride in her and relayed as many of the compliments he could remember, adding, "Even I did not know that you could sing like that."

"It is my one talent, Papa. Uncle George taught me, though Aunt Mary always thought it a shocking waste of time."

"What did she want you to do instead?"

"I am not certain, but she seemed determined that I should never learn to enjoy myself."

She said it without bitterness, and it was a moment before he could bring himself to say, "And your mother?"

"I don't know. For so many years she was ill and needed me to do things for her, but she used to seem pleased when Uncle George taught me things."

"You must miss him now." The moon, which was full that night, shed almost as much light as the winter sun in England, and by its illumination he saw a strange expression of disgust pass over his daughter's face like a sharp wind riffling the surface of a still, deep lake.

He might have asked her about it, but she prevented him by saying luxuriously, "Isn't that moon wonderful? There is so much here that is beautiful that I cannot understand why so many people dislike it."

"Unlike you and me, Perdita, they cherish happy memories of England, and for every sight, sound, and scent that is different from those they knew in Buckinghamshire, they hate this country. They can find no value here and live defensively, trying to surround themselves with as much of Buckinghamshire as they can. It is very sad. Tell me," he went on in a different tone, "did you enjoy this evening?"

"Beyond anything I have ever done, Papa. I always like singing, of course, but tonight so many people were kind. Not Mrs. Jamieson; that would be too much to expect! But nearly everyone else I talked to—even Juliana's brother."

"Delightful fellow, I understand, but rather strange. Don't lose your heart to him."

"Do not be absurd. I am not a girl," said Perdita as the extraordinary possibility first presented itself to her. "I have always known that there would be nothing like that for me."

"Now it is you who are being foolish. Be careful. Captain Marcus Blagdon is not a man for you. But there are plenty of others: Mortimer Blandfield could hardly take his eyes off you this evening."

Perdita blushed, shocked at the crudity of her father's thoughts, and said as soon as she could compose herself, "Please Papa, do not. You sound as though you wish to be rid of me. You must not expect it. Even if I had not already known that I should never be married, I would have discovered it by now." She saw that he was about to expostulate, so she continued calmly. "On the ship I overheard Mrs. Flaxman talking to another lady, who said, 'I sympathize with you; Miss Whitney will be very difficult to get married off, *even in India.*' And you see, Papa, I would so much rather not try. I have been very comfortable with you."

Rather impressed by her dignity, he patted her hands and said briskly, "As far as I am concerned, I would be delighted if you were to stay with me forever, but I thought all young ladies wished to be married. There, let us leave this topic."

"You are good to me, Papa," was all she said, while the image of Marcus Blagdon rebuilt itself inside her eyelids.

Over the next few weeks, as she came to know Captain Blagdon better, she often had to remind herself of her father's warning. He continued to behave delightfully, escorting Juliana and herself on rides and flower-collecting expeditions in the hills around the town, and still she found him kind. There seemed to be no meanness in him: melancholy, perhaps, and an uncertainty beneath the charm, but nothing else. He showed no desire to criticize other people's short-comings, unlike the other English she had met, or any fear of exposing his own. He was even prepared to confess to a bit-ing, paralyzing fear during a tiger hunt with Captain Thurleigh the previous year. The captain, who had been with them at the time, had laughed at that and told Miss Whitney not to believe a word of it; Blagdon had bagged the beast with no trouble at all. Dutifully, Perdita had laughed with him but did not revise her opinion of Captain Blagdon. She found him admirable as well as charming, and could sense no threat in his manner of the kind that made her avoid Mr. Blandfield whenever she could.

Edward Whitney watched the quartet with foreboding be-cause he was afraid, in spite of Perdita's denial, that she might lose her heart. But Lady Beaminster had no such fears: of all the women at Simla that year, she would have chosen Perdita as a companion for her children; there was no possi-bility that Marcus might form an attachment to her. She even watched complaisantly as Juliana made Marcus teach poor Miss Whitney to dance one morning in her drawing room.

Lady Beaminster had decided to follow up her recital with an evening party, to which Perdita had received an invita-tion. She had confessed to Juliana that she did not know how to dance, and the girl had insisted that she must learn. Pro-testing that it would be impossible, Perdita nevertheless watched Juliana and Marcus, followed, and eventually learned the steps they demonstrated, finding considerable pleasure in making her body obey her. But when Juliana told her to practice with Marcus, Perdita found herself tripping over her own feet, bumping into her partner, and generally reverting to the clumsy, heavy-footed creature she was used to being.

Marcus, who was always rather touched by Miss Whitney, took enormous trouble to calm her embarrassment and grad-ually persuaded her to try again, talking to her throughout so that she could not concentrate on her shortcomings. When he decided that she had gained enough confidence, he made Thurleigh partner Juliana and asked his mother to play for them so that Perdita could practice dancing in a set. She was perfectly sure she would never dare to participate in a real dance, but she was profoundly grateful to them and added extraordinary kindness to the list of Marcus's virtues, which seemed to grow every day.

Perhaps the attribute for which she was most grateful was that he never made her feel uncomfortable in the way her uncle and Mr. Blandfield had done, and she responded to that by talking to Marcus as freely as she talked to her father and trying to banish the sadness she detected at the back of his eyes.

Captain Thurleigh, on the other hand, could wither her with a single glance or a contemptuous word, and she wondered more and more why the two men were such friends. The one was all gentleness and weary kindness, the other a frightening mixture of harshness and puzzling joviality. He would occasionally address jocular remarks to Perdita, and she usually found that her fear of him prevented her from understanding them. The words he used were familiar, but the meaning almost always escaped her, and she would look at him with a sickly smile on her lips, fear patent in her expression while she tried to make a suitable reply.

Juliana watched, saddened that Captain Thurleigh's initial admiration, engendered by Perdita's singing, should have dwindled into contempt. She herself found him amusing and admired his flashing, dark eyes and strong, arrogant face. He looked magnificent on a horse, his seat excellent and his control of the animal absolute, and she could well believe some of the tales she had heard of him at the station. His men would follow him to hell, one young gentleman had told her, and she had only been excited when an older officer muttered, sotto voce, "And they have all too often." To her, he seemed a very suitable friend for her brother: brave, celebrated, dashing, and just very slightly brutal. He seemed the epitome of manhood. But she knew that Perdita did not like him, and so she tried to control her admiration. Just occasionally, she thought that if she were not already in love with her botanist, she might fall victim to this handsome soldier.

Had she but known it, if she had evinced any signs of such a thing, Lady Beaminster would have cut short their stay in the Hills immediately. Her ladyship disliked the captain and had been seriously displeased when she learned that the colonel had granted him leave to accompany her son on his furlough. The ostensible reason was that Captain Thurleigh had suffered several bad bouts of fever and needed to recover in the more clement air of the Hills, but Lady Beaminster could see no signs of illness in his clear brown skin, flashing eyes, and boundless energy. She thought him a dangerously unsuitable friend for her son.

Four

Perdita and her father dined alone on the night of the ball, and he was pleased by her increasing assurance. She sat opposite him in her low-cut ivory gown; a string of pearls he had given her glowed gently around her neck, her golden brown hair curled around her oval face, and at last there was a gleam of happiness in her fine eyes. He was afraid that it had been put there by Blagdon's attentions and wondered how he could stop her from erecting false hopes on an impossible foundation without destroying what she had gained.

In fact, he need not have worried; Perdita had no expectations of Juliana's brother. She was merely lost in delight at knowing that she loved him, for that was not something she had ever expected to feel. When she awoke in the early morning, she might lie in her bizarre silver bed imagining herself eighteen and well born, receiving his love, but she always knew the absurdity of her fantasies and had no trouble remembering that she was in fact twenty-six-year-old Perdita Whitney, daughter of a merchant. She sometimes chided herself for the absurdity of her dreams, but she could not resist succumbing to their novel and delectable pleasure.

She told herself very sternly that she was not to expect him to dance with her, and so she was only a little disappointed to find that he was not present when she and her father arrived in the ballroom of his mother's house. After greeting Lady Beaminster properly, Perdita turned to Juliana, who was looking enchanting in a pale pink muslin gown that was lavishly trimmed with lace. It was more modestly cut than Perdita's, as was suitable for a girl who would still have been in her schoolroom in England, but no one could have denied its elegance or the fact that it became Juliana far more than some of the extravagant toilettes did the other guests.

Edward Whitney was pleased to see that Juliana seemed genuinely glad to see Perdita and that her apparently sincere compliments brought some pleased color into his daughter's cheeks. Determined that she should enjoy herself, he made

her dance the next country dance with him, although dancing was a form of exercise he found irritating in the extreme.
As soon as he led her to a chair at the edge of the room when
the music stopped, he was greeted by his old acquaintance
the collector, who begged the honor of a dance with Miss
Whitney. Perdita, who had just caught sight of Marcus arriv-
ing with two friends and looking quite exceptionally magnificent in his regimentals, for once smiled happily at the
plump little man at her side and rose to take her place in the
set with him. She was more nervous dancing with him than
with her father, but she did not make too many mistakes, and
when it was over and he offered to take her to the veranda
for a breath of air, she went willingly.

When he led her away from the lamps and a group of
other guests chatting by the long windows, she was disconcerted, but the moon was shining and she told herself that
not even Mrs. Flaxman could have seen anything improper
in walking a little apart with so elderly a gentleman. In fact,
Mr. Blandfield was in his late forties and considered himself
a bit of a dog, handsome don't you know, and good with the
ladies. As soon as they were hidden from the other guests, he
took one of her cool hands in his own unpleasantly warm
clasp and said, panting slightly, "My dear Miss Whitney, I
have something to ask you."

Perdita, who had been looking entrancedly at the mountains and thinking how lovely they looked swathed in star-
light and how strange that the shadows should be deep violet
rather than black, tried to pull her hands away and said as
politely as she could, "Yes, Mr. Blandfield?"

"Now, don't tease. You have been so very encouraging until now. And you know quite well what I want." He rubbed
the palms of her hands with his thumbs, and she tried to pull
away. His hands tightened, and she was reminded sickeningly of her uncle. Mr. Blandfield gave up waiting for her to
speak and said, "You know that I have a deep regard for you,
Perdita, and you have been so sweet tonight that I can't wait
to ask you to be my wife."

Horrified, Perdita tried once more to pull her hands out of
his but felt the strength under the sweaty plumpness that
gripped them. She wanted to scream at him to let her go, but

her embarrassment was such that she said only, "Mr. Blandfield, please don't."

He lifted her hands, one after the other, to his full red mouth and planted a wet kiss on each. She wrenched them away at last and was frightened to see in his face the expression that used to distort her uncle's, compounded of anger, pleading, and something else she could not define. She tried to speak but could think of nothing to say. She felt one of his hands grip her breast as the other reached around her waist and saw his wet lips open as his face came down toward her own. Revolted and very much afraid, she pushed at his chest violently and backed right against the wall of the house, saying breathlessly, "I think you must be ill. Don't touch me. Don't touch me."

She saw his hands coming at her yet again, and before he could close in on her, she turned away and ran into the house to find her father. Lost in her dreams of Marcus, she had hardly registered the attentions of her father's corpulent acquaintance; the knowledge that she could have aroused in him such beastliness by her vague courtesies filled her with shameful horror. She half turned and believed he was pursuing her. She blundered back into the ballroom, looking desperately for her father, and was badly jolted when she heard a quiet voice say, "Miss Whitney, you are distressed. Is there some way I can help?"

She turned to see Marcus Blagdon, as gently calm and civil as usual, and said, "No, I do not think so. But thank you. I was just looking for my father, but I cannot find him."

"No. I believe that he is playing cards in the smoking room. I shall fetch him for you in a little while, but why not walk with me for a moment on the veranda? It will help you to recover." He watched in consternation as her blue eyes dilated, and he said softly, "Something has frightened you. What has happened?"

"Nothing," she said, and then added absurdly, "I don't know. It was all a mistake. I do not know what to do. Oh, where is Papa?"

"Tell me what happened. Come." He escorted her into Juliana's small sitting room where he said, "I cannot allow one of my mother's guests to suffer so without helping. Tell me."

And so she told him exactly what Mortimer Blandfield had said and done. She allowed her own horror to escape and the shame she felt at having aroused such frightening passion without even knowing that she was doing so.

He was extremely angry and did his best to comfort her despite the waves of fury that beat through him. It was intolerable that this shy, worried woman should have been so exposed to Blandfield's importuning, and he determined exactly what he would say to the wretched man. In the meantime he talked quietly to her of how men are sometimes driven by their natures to do things that they instantly regret, and he assured her that she had never behaved with the slightest impropriety. Gradually he had the satisfaction of seeing her grow calmer and soon judged it time to restore her to her father's care. He took her back into the drawing room and left her with his mother while he went off to the card room.

She had told Lady Beaminster that she had a headache, and so when Edward came up to them to take her home, their hostess saw nothing amiss, although it was still early.

He did not mention what had happened until they reached his house, when he took Perdita into the drawing room, made her sit down, and gave her a glass of wine.

She shook her head, but he said, "Drink it, Perdita. It will help to calm you. Blagdon told me what happened, and I can understand that you found it very unpleasant, but you must not exaggerate. The poor chap only tried to kiss you, I gather." She shuddered at the memory but obediently took the glass from him and sipped some wine.

"It was not so much what he did as what he said, that I— that I had encouraged his advances. And I did not, Papa. I am sure of that. What is it about me that makes people behave so?"

"Do you mean that it has happened before?" he demanded.

"Not really," came the answer, "at least not like that." She raised her eyes to his face and was reassured by the steadiness in his expression. "But Uncle George used to kiss me like that. I had thought he was angry with me because he always looked accusingly at me, and then he would hold me and kiss me, and I could not breathe. I always tried to push him away, but he would go on and on, and then once, when I thought I should faint, he stopped and started to weep. It was horrible. He begged my forgiveness, but then as I was trying to think what to say, he changed and told me that it was my fault. It was just like tonight. Papa, what am I to do?"

She shrank from the blaze of anger in his eyes. He came to her chair, took the glass from her hand, and, kneeling in front of her, put his hands on her shoulders. He said, "You must not think of it. That uncle of yours sounds quite appalling, and if he were here, I would give him the thrashing he so clearly merits. Blandfield was a little different: he wanted to marry you. That was reasonable, even if you would not have accepted him. The thing is that you are far more beautiful than you realize, and if you look pleadingly at men, they may well become inflamed by you, especially out here. After all, my dear," he added in an attempt to make her smile, "the poet did write:

" 'What men call gallantry
    And the gods adultery,
    Is far more common when the climate's sultry.' "

She looked away, inexpressibly distressed that even her father should joke about such things. When she could command her voice not to tremble, she said, "I expect you are right, Papa. I think I shall go to bed now. Good night."

Over the next few days she tried to put the horror out of her mind, but she did not succeed. The only thing that could banish the memory of those gross, wet lips and groping hands was the knowledge of Marcus's kindness. He and Juliana had called on her the day after the ball to inquire after her health and, if she had recovered from her headache, to persuade her to ride with them. She had gone—anything was better than sitting doing nothing but remembering—and she was passionately grateful for their friendliness. Naturally, neither mentioned Mortimer Blandfield, but Marcus showed his solicitude for her in innumerable little ways, and she was able to look at him, knowing that she would never see in his dark eyes the look that spelled such vileness.

When they returned to her father's house, as usual laden

with flowers to press and sketch, he left her and Juliana in order to keep an appointment. He had been so relieved to see the extent of Perdita's recovery from the shocking distress that as soon as he reached Thurleigh's bungalow, he said, "She seems a little better today, but I am afraid that it will take some time before she entirely forgets last night's scene."

Captain Thurleigh, who was standing in front of a small fire warming one of his booted feet, looked across the room, his handsome face dark with anger.

"Are you talking about that Whitney woman? What business is it of yours if she flirts with some damn fool of a collector and gets more than she bargained for?"

Marcus stopped halfway across the room, his eyebrows contracted together. He said slowly, "None of my business, perhaps, but I found her in great distress, and I was sorry for her. I know what it is like to be pawed like a piece of matrimonial meat by people who seem to think that the touch of their repellent flesh is what one desires above all else. I was sorry for her," he said again.

"Well, I can't understand why you should cherish such a fondness for a poor miserable thing like Miss Whitney."

Marcus did not care enough to argue, and he hated scenes. He dismissed the subject of Miss Whitney and called for two *burra* pegs from Thurleigh's bearer before sitting down in one of the old brown chairs and stretching his booted feet toward the fire.

They were talking happily as they waited for the other guests, and James had just leaned forward to refill their glasses when the bearer came back bringing a note for Marcus. The handwriting was strange to him, and he opened the folded half-sheet curiously. There was a single line: "Please come at once to your mother's house. She needs you. Perdita Whitney."

He handed it to James, who said, "That woman again! Must you go?"

"Yes. Whatever you think of her, you must do her the justice of believing that she would never write such a note if my mother were not in need of me." He clasped his friend's hand briefly and strode out of the room, calling for his horse.

Ten minutes later he walked up the steps of his mother's house, to find Perdita waiting in the hall. She said to him urgently, "They are in the drawing room. I shall be in Juliana's room if you should need me." He looked after her, puzzled, but went quickly to find his mother lying back on a sofa, her feet wrapped in a dark shawl and her eyes uncharacteristically reddened with weeping.

He knelt beside her, patting her hands, and listened, appalled, as she told him that the overland mail had arrived that afternoon, bringing a letter from her lawyers with the news of his brother's death from typhus. Her hands seemed terribly cold, and he could hear Juliana gulping behind him, but he could think of nothing to say. He understood at once that the news was catastrophic, and he tried to flog his mind into a proper regret for the elder brother he had hardly known, but he could not. He could not even be sure if it was his mind or his mother's voice that spoke the sentence, "You will have to sell out now, at once, and come back to England."

He sank forward until his forehead was lying on her lap. She lifted one of her hands and smoothed the hair back from his broad brow, over which the skin was stretched so tight. She said quietly, "I know that you want to stay in this country, but it is your duty to leave. Augustus had no children; you have no heir yet. You must return to Beaminster."

He could not speak.

It was many days before Perdita heard from any of the Blagdon family. Although she had written a letter of condolence to Lady Beaminster as soon as she had heard the news, she was not at all surprised that she received no acknowledgment; but she wished that she could have done something useful for Juliana at least, who must have been devastated by what had happened.

When Juliana did emerge from seclusion to seek comfort from Perdita, she poured out stories of the late Lord Beaminster's goodness, his virtues, the way he had filled her world. Perdita, understanding that he had been more of a father to her than the old statesman, felt poignantly for the child in her misery and tried to comfort her. But Juliana was inconsolable.

Her grief had been exacerbated by her mother's endless arguments with Marcus. She told Perdita that Lady Beaminster was determined to make him return to England with them, while he was equally determined to stay in India.

"Now that he has inherited, he has responsibilities, you see," confided Juliana tearfully. "It would be different if we had any other brothers. She says he has to come home; but he could never take Guster's place, and he says he hates England. He wants to live here, and he won't say why. I don't see why he shouldn't if he wants it so much, but Mama does not accept that life in England can be just as dangerous as out here. She gets so angry when Marcus reminds her that he is still alive and Guster, who never risked this climate, is dead, and she says such terrible things. Oh, Perdita, what is going to happen?"

Perdita could not answer and was aghast at the selfishness of her unspoken protests. Overriding even her sympathy for Juliana was a rebellious question that returned again and again. "Must I lose these two friends, the only ones I have ever had, just because some stranger contracted typhus thousands of miles away?"

The answer to both questions came dramatically a week later, when Marcus Beaminster came to Whitney House to ask Perdita to marry him.

Almost dizzy with incredulous delight, Perdita stood in her father's library looking at Marcus, searching his face for some sign that he really had said the words she thought she had just heard. She thought he seemed unhappy, and in wondering whether she ever would be able to banish the look of strain from his dark eyes, she forgot her early-morning fantasies of just such a scene and all the things she had once longed to say to him.

He watched her, too, in gentle surprise that she did not answer. Then he kissed her hand and repeated his question. Perdita could feel a hot, disfiguring blush pouring into her face, but her voice was nearly steady as she said, "Of course I will, Marcus . . . if you truly wish it."

The humility of her answer touched him, and the tenderness in her expression seemed to assuage part of the hurt his mother had dealt him. Remembering some of the things she had said to him as she tried to force him to accept his new responsibilities, he closed his eyes for a second or two.

Perdita watched a deep line appear between his dark brows and misinterpreted the source of his pain. Thinking that he was grieving for his dead brother, she touched his hand and tried to help.

"It is only so bad for a little time, Marcus. Sorrow eases, and I shall help you all I can. Please do not let it hurt you too much."

Hearing her low, tranquil voice, so different from his mother's, Marcus forgot that Perdita could have no idea of the accusations his mother had made. The bitter words she had flung at him had left him aching for the comfort that Perdita seemed to offer. For that moment it hardly even mattered who she was. He walked forward into her arms and felt one of her hands stroke his hair.

"It will pass, Marcus, I promise you. Everything will be all right."

Five

Perdita's short engagement was a time of indescribable happiness shot through with moments of devastating anxiety. She had never expected anyone to marry her, and it seemed miraculous that a man like Marcus Beaminster should want her. At first it was not the disparity in their worldly positions that preoccupied her, although as the wedding day approached and Lady Beaminster subjected her to a course of rigorous instruction on the obligations and duties of her new position, she became more and more aware of her lowly status. In the beginning the contrast had seemed to be between her solitary position looking in at the world from outside and his secure place in its center. She had only her father; Marcus had friends throughout India and always would have, no matter where he went. He was at ease everywhere; she, only in the protection of her father.

But once she was married, she knew it would be different: there would be no more excruciating shyness or terrifying loneliness. She would be Marcus's wife, part of the world. In marrying her, he would be putting her once and for always beyond the reach of the things that threatened her.

Wherever she went, whomever she had to meet, she was able to forget her fears because Marcus was with her. They were rarely alone together, but to see him smile at her across a dinner table could illumine a whole evening; feeling the softness of his lips on her hand as they parted seemed to be a code to remind her of the time when he had stood with his head on her shoulder, his arms around her, his heart beating against her breast.

It seemed impossible that he should love her as much as she loved him; but that did not matter. He cared enough to want to make her his wife, and she knew that she would never be able to repay him for what he was giving her. She felt that she had reached the end of her journey. She would be able to rest now, secure in the knowledge that she would never have to struggle again.

Her father watched her flower and was aware of an emotion that was almost jealousy. He laughed at himself for it and hoped that it was not the reason why he was suspicious of Beaminster's motives. The proposal had been so startling that Edward had not been able to help wondering what lay behind it. It was easy to see why the new earl should feel he had to marry, but not why he should have chosen someone so unlikely. Edward's first thought had been of his money, but he was quickly able to discard that suspicion; the extent of the lands and fortune Beaminster had just inherited would have satisfied the most extravagant man, and he was not that.

Unlikely it might be, but Edward had to fall back on the idea that Marcus Beaminster had discerned beneath the shyness and gaucherie Perdita still displayed in company the qualities he himself admired. And yet, he would ask himself, what man in Beaminster's position ever married a woman of such an age for her intelligence, honesty, and courage when he could have had youth, fashionable prettiness, gaiety, confidence, and suitable breeding? Even in India there were plenty of such girls, any of whom would have given her eyes to marry him.

Edward concealed his thoughts from Perdita, determined that they should not impinge on her delight, and he reminded himself that whatever Beaminster's motives for the marriage, there was no doubt that as his wife, Perdita would be secure in a way she never could be as plain Miss Whitney. Grateful for that at least, he discussed dowry and settlements with Marcus and made arrangements for a suitable wedding with Lady Beaminster.

They agreed that in view of the groom's mourning, the marriage itself should be a simple service held at Whitney House with a formal reception afterward for only the most important of Simla's residents. There was to be no music at the service, no extravagant display at the reception, and immediately afterward Perdita was to go into half mourning for the brother-in-law she had never known.

Lady Beaminster had fortunately already purchased several lengths of silk for herself in muted grays and lavenders that could be made up for Perdita to wear in the evenings, and the Simla bazaar provided plenty of muslin for morning dresses. Lady Beaminster was able to assure herself that the bride would at least be suitably clad for all occasions, even if there were no guarantee that she would behave as she should. But at least her mistakes would be made in India, where they would not matter very much, and by the time Marcus came to his senses and returned to England, she would probably have learned enough to pass.

His mother never put such thoughts into words, but she did not hide them as well as Edward Whitney hid his, and Perdita was well aware of them. At first they did not matter at all: if Marcus cared for her, what did it matter what his mother thought? But the obvious disapproval began to awaken Perdita's imagination, and she started to invent wild anxieties. The first time she wondered whether she had misheard Marcus's proposal, she mocked herself, but as the wedding day came nearer and nearer, she managed almost to convince herself that he had never asked her at all and that only his undeniable chivalry had prevented him from pointing out her mistake. When she forced herself to think rationally and recreate in her mind the day when he had proposed to her, she knew her anxiety was fantastic, but she could not get it out of her head that there was something wrong.

Marcus had never shown that kind of emotion again or taken her into his arms even when they were alone, and she wished that he would so that she could be sure. Perhaps then she could tell him of her silliness and they could laugh over it together. Instead, he treated her with all his usual gentle civility, shielding her from the intrusive curiosity of the Simla ladies, doing his best to see that she was not overpowered by his mother and giving her not only endless small presents but also a lovely, delicate necklace of pearls and diamonds—as a token of his esteem, he said.

Edward saw the slow diminution of her radiant happiness and wondered what it was that was worrying her. He wished he knew how much she understood of the physical aspect of marriage and whether she was frightened of that, but he did not manage to broach the subject with her. He hated the thought that she might be going to Beaminster ignorant of the meaning of physical love, but with the memory of her reaction to Mortimer Blandfield's very mild advances in his mind, he could not think of any words that would not shock her. In any case, he believed that only a woman could tell her what she should know, but the only woman he could have asked—or trusted to tell her the right things in the right way—was Aneila, and she could not do it. As she had explained to him when he talked to her about it, if Perdita were as innocent as he feared, she would never be able to accept advice on such a subject from a stranger, and a foreigner at that.

In the end he had decided that he would have to trust Lady Beaminster to include that lesson in all the others that she was delivering, and he comforted himself with the thought that at least the boy seemed gentle enough.

But there was one day when he almost broke his silence. He found Perdita walking aimlessly around the garden one morning, occasionally bending down to pick some of the violets that grew in fragrant purple pools under the trees. He watched her for a while as she stopped beside a large carved stone urn that stood against a background of cypresses. She made a charming picture there, tall and slim in her pale gray gown, with one hand resting in unselfconscious grace on the stone and the other holding the violets by her side, but he was worried by the pinched frown on her face. She looked almost as though she were rehearsing a speech; then a blush welled up, and she covered her face with her hands. At once he went to her.

"Perdita, tell me, are you unhappy about something? If there is anything you want to know, you will tell me, won't you? Are you having doubts about the marriage?"

Perdita tucked the little bunch of sweet-scented flowers into her lace-edged corsage and turned her head.

"How could I have doubts, Papa? Lord Beaminster is charming, very kind, and I . . . I have a great affection for him." At her father's questioning look, she revised her cautious statement and said in helpless truth, "I love him, Papa. Don't you like him?"

"Of course I do. He is a splendid fellow, and a very good match as they say, but—"

She interrupted with a small, wise smile. "But you wonder why he should have chosen me. So do I."

"Believe me, my dear, if he has come to know you as well as I know you, he has shown the best of good sense in choosing you." He stroked her warm cheek and liked the way she leaned toward him. Perdita took courage from his obvious approval.

"It is silly, Papa," she said, at last expressing her most constant fear, "but I cannot get it out of my head that he asked me by mistake; or that he never really asked at all. Perhaps I misunderstood what he said to me that day."

Edward laughed kindly as he said, "If that is all that has sent you out here in such a melancholy state, I need not have been so anxious. No, I can assure you that you did not mistake his intention. He spoke to me quite clearly when he asked my permission to speak to you."

She seemed so relieved, and her face took on some of the happiness she had shown before, that he decided once again not to try to talk to her about the consummation of the marriage. In fact, it had never occurred to Perdita to worry about that, in spite of Lady Beaminster's elliptical and vaguely threatening instructions. It was the fear that Marcus might have changed his mind about her, or that she would disappoint him or destroy whatever feeling it had been that had driven him into her arms, that tormented her.

But even when she was most nervous, Marcus had only to look down at her, smile his familiar smile, and call her "my dear" for her to forget every doubt and fear in a spring of delight that welled up in her. At such moments she was entirely happy and longed only for the day when she would be his wife and be able to talk to him about anything.

The day of the wedding was clear and bright, and when Perdita first awoke, she lay peacefully in her barbaric bed, thinking of nothing but Marcus: the sound of his deep voice, the things he would say to her when they were alone, and how she would answer. They would become so familiar with each other, she thought, that it would soon cease to feel strange to be alone with him. She would learn to know him so well that she would be able to read his thoughts and, in loving him, take away the sadness she had so often seen in his brown eyes.

It was not until her ayah was putting her into her wedding gown that Perdita's mood was disturbed. She began to think that as she and Marcus became better acquainted, he might dislike what he found out about her. After all, they were still almost strangers to each other, and he knew nothing about her.

Edward, coming into her room to escort her to the dining room, where Mr. Carswell waited with the Beaminsters, was shocked to see that his daughter was trembling and very pale. He put an arm around her waist and asked gently, "My dear Perdita, what is it?"

She shook her head as though she could not speak but then managed to say, "Oh, Papa, what shall I do if he does not like me?"

Stumped for something comforting and convincing to say, Edward led her to the sofa at the foot of her bed and made her sit down. Then he sent for a glass of very weak brandy and soda and made her drink it as though it were medicine. When she had obediently finished it, shuddering at the unfamiliar taste, he took the glass away from her and said, "That's better. Of course he will like you. He wants to marry you. Now, don't you feel better?"

Perdita was not at all sure, but she nodded and stood up to take his arm. He could feel her trembling slightly and hoped fervently that her composure would survive the actual service.

He was glad to see that Beaminster turned at the sound of their entry into the room and smiled warmly at her. But it was not until she stood beside him and felt his shoulder touch hers for an instant that she ceased to shiver.

The tiny physical contact allowed her to become calm enough to speak her responses clearly, although she wished her hand were not so damp when she had to put it into Marcus's. He did not make any sign that he had noticed and pushed the ring onto her finger, saying after Mr. Carswell, "With this ring I thee wed, with my body I thee worship, and with all my worldly goods I thee endow."

Perdita smiled shyly up at him, confident at last that he meant every astonishing word of it.

After the quiet of the simple service, walking beside him into the drawing room where her father's guests were assembled was like going before a convocation of hostile inquisitors, but Marcus was beside her; she was his wife; she knew that she would be able to face them. Their repetition of her new title as they greeted her began to convince her that, unlikely though it might be, she really was the wife of the Earl of Beaminster. Nevertheless, as she watched Captain Thurleigh walking toward her through the crowd, tall, dark, and arrogant, she hoped passionately that she would not say something stupid and shame Marcus. His friend raised her hand to his lips.

"May I wish you joy, Lady Beaminster?"

His words were simple and very conventional, but they seemed kindly meant, and so she was able to answer appropriately and smile as she watched him move on to grip Marcus's hand. No one else would be able to make her feel as uncomfortable as Captain Thurleigh once had, and his affability seemed to have set some kind of seal on her marriage. As soon as she could, she left Marcus's side to find her father. She had to wait while he talked to Mrs. Fletcher and another lady whom Perdita had not yet met, but as soon as he saw that she wanted him, he extricated himself and came to draw her aside. With the understanding kindness she was used to hearing in his voice, he said simply, "Well, dear?"

"It is going to be all right, Papa."

He took both her hands and looked down at her oval face, lovely now in its happy certainty.

"I know it will, my dearest girl," he said, bending to kiss her.

Several guests who saw him smiled to see his obvious affection, but Maria Jamieson, who had already found plenty of disagreeable things to say, thought it very unbecoming to show such feelings in public and said so to her big husband. Major Jamieson did not answer, and so she went on. "And she really should not wear her corsage *en coeur* like that. She simply hasn't the figure for it."

Her own half-high gown of *citron gros-de-naples* was richly trimmed around the back and shoulders with lace, and she was proud enough of her curving shape to have dispensed with the old-fashioned pelerine that was still considered de rigueur in Simla. She found it pleasant and satisfying to know that she was so much more richly dressed than the bride, and she tossed her head a little to set her glossy ringlets dancing as Lord Beaminster came to greet her. As he bowed gracefully over her hand, she was aware of Jamieson's usual jealous supervision and smiled even more warmly. But when the bridegroom moved on, a discontented expression banished the pleasure from her face. Her full lips settled into a pout, and her husband, who had once been captivated by her prettiness and vivacity, waited for the complaint that he knew would come.

"I feel so sorry for him. I cannot imagine what they will have in common, and it will be so hard for her to learn our ways. Poor Miss Whitney. We shall all have to help him when they get back to the station."

The major said nothing, wondering unhappily just what form his wife's help was likely to take and feeling sorry for the new Lady Beaminster. His knowledge of her was small, but he thought she seemed amiable enough and would probably make his junior officer a good wife once she got over her shyness. He watched them come together by the empty fireplace and hoped for several reasons that the marriage would be a happy one.

Perdita, whose back was beginning to ache with tiredness, hoped that they might be able to leave, but Marcus had been given very strict instructions by his mother and explained that they must stay a little longer.

"But it will be quite soon now. Why don't you sit down for a while? You look very tired."

Perdita shook her head, unable to explain that it was not rest she wanted as much as a chance to be alone with her husband, to tell him some of the things she felt and feel him close to her. She braced herself to endure for as long as she had to, but it was only about half an hour before Lady Beaminster signaled that she had done enough and took her away to change.

There had been no suitable houses left for Marcus to hire, and so they would have been reduced to going into tents until his mother left and handed over hers if Captain Thurleigh had not offered to vacate his bungalow and lend it to them. It was one of the most secluded and in many circumstances would have been ideal for a newly married couple sharing their first few days together.

When Marcus and Perdita reached it, they found the candles already alight and Captain Thurleigh's bearer waiting to greet them. Marcus was relieved to discover that his wife's servants were already installed with all her baggage un-packed, and he suggested that she might like to lie down for a while before changing for dinner. Perdita was surprised but, anxious to do anything he wished, said nothing and fol-lowed her maid to the room that had been prepared for her.

Marcus retired to the smoking room and sent for brandy. He would have liked to smoke a cigar with it, but he was afraid that Perdita might dislike the smell and did not want to upset her or make her ill. Vaguely thinking about her, he sat down in one of James's comfortable old chairs and picked up the latest *Delhi Gazette;* but he could not concentrate on its gossipy articles and eventually stopped trying to read and thought about what he had just done.

Until his brother's death he had never even considered the idea of matrimony. Since the news had come, he had thought of his wedding only as a way to pacify his mother and to insure that he could stay in India with his regiment. He knew that she was right—he had to produce an heir. But now that the wedding was over, he started to think of it all from Perdita's point of view and began to wonder if he had been very unfair to her. He had always been sure that she would cause no trouble or ever complain about anything he did, but for the first time he began to think that that was not enough. Feeling unaccountably guilty, he resolved to take no more advantage of her ignorance and inexperience; he would tread warily and make sure he did not force himself on her until she was more accustomed to him.

When dinner was announced, he joined her at the table and did his best to entertain her. She followed his lead as well as she could and put off the idea of telling him anything that mattered until the servants had left. But almost as soon as the last white-uniformed man had gone, Marcus smiled in a reassuring way and said, "It has been a dreadfully exhaust-ing day, hasn't it, my dear? I expect you would like to retire now."

Perdita, remembering the exact words with which her mother-in-law had told her to obey her husband, no matter how distasteful his demands, hastened to rise from her chair and agree. She found that her voice did not work properly and so she merely nodded, hoping that she would be able to do whatever was wanted. When he offered her his arm, she took it and allowed him to lead her across the hall to her bedroom door. He opened it and, having kissed her hand, said again, "You must be very tired. I hope you will sleep well. Good night."

Surprised and rather distressed by his formality, Perdita watched the door close behind him. Her ayah, who had been waiting as usual, said something consoling, which Perdita did not quite follow, and proceeded to undress her. When she was alone, she lay back against the pillows, pretending that she did not mind Marcus's having left her like that and trying to remember just what it had felt like to be embraced by him: the weight of his head on her shoulder; the softness of his hair against her neck; the way their bodies had seemed to cling to each other for one lovely instant. She told herself that it would happen again soon, that everything would be different once he had become accustomed to being married to her.

But over the next few days Perdita began to wonder why the idea of marriage had seemed so momentous. Her life had hardly changed. Marcus was always a delightful companion, but he did not spend very much time with her and each night merely kissed her hand and left her alone. More and more she wondered why he never touched her and what it was that she could be doing wrong.

One afternoon as she was driving out with Juliana, the girl criticized her brother for leaving his bride to spend so much time without him, and Perdita was tempted to speak frankly and ask her advice. But Juliana was an unmarried girl and Marcus's sister; it did not seem possible. Once again Perdita buried her anxieties and said reproachfully, "You should not say such things, Juliana. Don't you remember your brother explaining to us weeks ago when you wanted him to spend more time with you, that when you have fought beside a man and faced death with him, that creates a bond stronger than any mere family connection? You must not think he neglects me; and you cannot expect him to drop all the friends with whom he has such a bond merely because he is married."

Juliana tossed her head rebelliously and said, "Well, I should be very angry. You are a deal too patient and forgiving, Perdita. One day you will have to stand up for yourself, or you will be very unhappy."

"Well, that day has not come yet, Juliana. I am very happy."

She used to tell her father the same thing when he came to visit her almost every day. He was not convinced, and once or twice he asked questions about Marcus, to which Perdita invariably replied, "He is charming to me always, Papa. I cannot imagine a kinder or more careful husband," with which he had to be content.

In most ways it was true. After Marcus managed to forget the difficulties and embarrassments of his wedding day, he behaved to his wife with complete courtesy, trying to entertain and amuse her whenever they were together and making no demands of any kind. If she were not as much at ease with him as with her father, that would come, she told herself, and she began to forget her fears.

The only discomfort that remained was her feeling that she was not really his wife, that her complete inadequacy for the position would become as obvious to everyone else as it was to herself, and that she would be removed. She knew that she was in fact indissolubly married to the Earl of Beaminster, but she began to pine for the reassurance that their one moment of physical contact had given her.

Day after day she found herself longing to touch him, to feel his head on her shoulder once more and hear him say, "Perdita, I need you." One evening, when he had punctiliously escorted her to her bedroom door as usual, she freed her hand from his cool clasp and laid it gently on his cheek. He stood very still for a moment and then moved away, making no acknowledgment at all. She was left with her hand stupidly held in the air, the blood pouring in her cheeks, and a feeling of sick humiliation in her mind. He said good night stiffly and left her.

It was only a few days after that that the dowager was due to leave Simla with Juliana, and Perdita and Marcus to move into her house. Trains of camels had already been loaded with the dowager's trunks and had set off on the long journey down to Calcutta when Marcus escorted his wife to bid her good-bye. Old Lady Beaminster was gracious to her, but

Juliana hugged her childishly and even wept a little as she said, "I hate leaving you. You must make Marcus sell out and come home to Beaminster. It is lovely there, and we shall need you. Make him come soon, before any of the dreadful things they talk about happen here. I shall be so unhappy with only Mama, worrying about you two."

"Hush. You must not say that, Juliana. I shall miss you very much, too. But we can write to each other: you shall tell me all your doings so that I can imagine myself being with you, and I shall do the same. You will be happy enough when you are presented next year."

She watched the mulish expression creep into Juliana's strong face and wished passionately that she were not leaving. Without Juliana, she would be left friendless again, for in a disturbing way Marcus had ceased to be a friend when they were married. They talked often but never of things that mattered. Sometimes Perdita thought nostalgically of the evening of Mortimer Blandfield's proposal when she had first discovered Marcus's gentleness and she had been able to speak to him freely. She began to imagine herself obviously ill or troubled in some way so that he would again talk to her as herself and not, as she believed he viewed her now, as a tedious guest who had to be kept content.

With her mind so engaged, she did not try to hide her sadness from him as the dowager's caravan left, but he looked irritated and said only, "I am glad you spoke so sensibly to Juliana. She is apt to become overemotional and say things she does not mean. She will be perfectly happy at Beaminster with my mother."

Perdita ordered her voice to obey and succeeded in saying, "I know, but I fear that you and I shall miss her and your mama very much."

"We shall indeed. Now, my dear, if you will go in, I shall instruct the servants to bring our trunks so that Thurleigh can repossess his own house."

"Of course. Poor Captain Thurleigh." She made herself smile at him and walked into the long, white-walled drawing room, to sit doing nothing but think of herself more than ever as an impostor in her mother-in-law's house.

That night, for the first time since the wedding, she ate alone. After dinner, she sat in an uncomfortable upright chair, pretending to read a novel Juliana had left for her, until she felt she could go to bed, wondering where Marcus was and with whom. When at last she lay between the cool sheets, unwatched by any of the servants, she allowed pent-up tears to slide out of the corners of her eyes. In the halcyon days of her early love for Marcus, she had imagined that marriage to him would constitute the greatest possible human happiness; it had not occurred to her that, married, she could be so lonely.

Some two hours later, she felt herself slipping over the edge into sleep when she heard him returning. His voice sounded odd as he spoke to the bearer, thickened and somehow rougher. She lay listening to his steps crossing the hall, walking past her door to his own. The hot, slow tears began to gather once more. At least he had always wished her good night before. She tried to tell herself that he believed her to be asleep and would not have wished to disturb her, but common sense did not help her distress. She was turning her face into the pillow when he came back, and so she did not hear anything until he stood in the doorway, saying in that strange voice, "Perdita?"

"Yes; what is it? Are you not well?"

He looked at her as though she were half hidden in a fog and said only, "It is time."

She did not understand anything except that he was not happy, and so once more she stretched out a hand to him. He came toward her, touched it briefly, and then drew back the bedclothes.

The smell of brandy on his lips was almost nauseating, and his face, so close to hers, seemed to be that of a stranger. She shut her eyes, saying over and over again to herself the words Lady Beaminster had said about her duty.

What followed could not have taken more than ten minutes, but it left her feeling battered, ashamed, embarrassed, and longing for comfort.

She was not completely ignorant of the mechanics of copulation—no one brought up in farming country could be—but she had never thought of the ugliness and brutality of agricultural mating in connection with herself; still less with the civilized, quiet, infinitely superior man she had married.

She kept her eyes shut to block out his unfamiliar face, but when he started to groan frighteningly, she opened them again, shocked and worried. After a moment or two the sound ceased, and he flopped forward to lie still at last, his head near her shoulder. Very concerned, she said quietly but with urgency, "Marcus, what happened? Are you all right? Marcus?"

He did not speak, but she could feel him breathing, so that her first panicked fear that he had suffered some fatal seizure was calmed. She waited, not daring to move or speak, for whatever was to happen next, embarrassingly aware of a trickling sensation between her legs. She hoped he had not noticed it, but she was very afraid that he must have. She would have liked to apologize for it but could not have spoken of such a subject if her life depended on it. She started to wish that he would move away from her.

Almost as though he had sensed the thought, Marcus pulled himself up and away. She averted her eyes once more, anxious to see nothing of him. When he had extricated himself and stood beside her, adjusting his dressing gown, he said in a voice from which all roughness and brandy had been choked, "I am sorry, my dear."

At that she opened her eyes again and saw in his a reflection of her own unhappiness. She tried to smile as she said, "I too."

He dropped his hand onto her shoulder in the gesture she had seen him use with his friends, and he squeezed hard for a moment before he left her. With that brief clasp she was a little comforted.

She longed to wash and change her frilled white nightgown, or at least have clean sheets put on the bed, but she could not have borne to call her ayah to witness what had happened. She eased herself to one side of the bed and lay in sticky discomfort, worrying about the servants' reaction in the morning, about facing Marcus again, and about the horrid ache in her back and whether something inside her had been damaged. She slept very little.

When Edward came to visit her the next afternoon, he found her languid and hollow-eyed, and as soon as they were alone, he asked if something had happened.

"Nothing that I should not have expected, Papa," she said.

He left his chair and went to sit beside her on the sofa, patting her clammy hands.

"Was it very bad?"

"No," she said, laying her head on his shoulder and feeling the grateful warmth of physical kindness for which she was so starved. It seemed that he understood, for he held her close for a moment before he said, "I think you need some diversion, now that you have lost Juliana. Will you let me take you to visit an Indian lady of my acquaintance tomorrow? I often drive to see her in the afternoons, and I am sure she will be delighted to see you."

Perdita sat up, immediately interested, and said, "But, Papa, my Hindustani is not yet good enough."

"No matter. Aneila speaks English. I cannot take you today, but tomorrow I shall collect you at two o'clock. She lives a few miles outside the town, but we shall be there soon after four."

Then they talked of other things, and after he had left her, she was able to greet Marcus and Captain Thurleigh with reasonable composure when they returned from their afternoon's ride. Captain Thurleigh shook hands with her politely, and for the first time in days Marcus smiled at her instead of at the air to one side of her face. With real concern he asked her how she was feeling. Seeing the surprise in his friend's face, she hastened to say, "Oh, my headache is almost gone, thank you. I shall be better after dinner. I do hope that you will be staying, Captain Thurleigh."

"Thank you very much," said Thurleigh politely. He added, "Perhaps you would sing for us later." Her frightening sense of aloneness began to ease.

Dinner that evening seemed friendlier, and Perdita found herself responding to Captain Thurleigh's conversational overtures with less fear than usual and, she believed, making slightly more intelligent replies. After dinner they sang a duet, an old English ballad both had learned as children, while Marcus watched them, his beloved features gradually relaxing in the candlelight as the two voices mingled and answered each other.

When their guest had finally left, Marcus returned to the drawing room and said, "That was very good of you, my dear, when you must be so tired after your headache."

"Not at all, Marcus. I like to sing, and you must know that I shall always try to please you, to be the kind of wife you want me to be."

She watched him withdraw into his formal courtesy to say, "You are very good."

When he left her at her bedroom door again, she thought with relief that the previous night's visit was not to be repeated, but later, when the servants had disappeared, he came again to her room. This time was not quite so bad; she knew what to expect. But again she kept her eyes closed until she felt him leave her and heard his sad apology. Once more she tried to reach him, and once more she was left rebuffed and alone.

The following afternoon Edward arrived to take her for the promised drive, and at first she was happy. They did not talk much, but once more she felt herself to be in the hands of someone who could help her cope with life.

Although most of the sky was obscured with heavy white clouds and there was no direct sunlight, the drive out of Simla was pretty. Perdita soon lost her languor in looking around her at the deep precipitous valleys below the bumpy road, the sudden glint of water through the dark trees that filled the ravines, and the colorful birds that flashed and darted past the carriage.

Edward was pleased with her reawakening and did his best to answer her questions about the things she noticed, but he was lamentably ignorant of natural history and could not identify the birds that were unfamiliar to her or name the gigantic climbers that hung in curtains of delicate flowers from the trees they passed. At one moment she turned, laughing, to say, "Why, Papa, how can you live surrounded by all this and not care to know the names of the plants and creatures?"

He took his eyes off the road for a second to smile. "My dear Perdita, I have always thought it enough merely to enjoy the beauty of the scenery without troubling myself with its scientific components."

"Well, I think it decidedly shocking," she answered, and he was pleased to hear the mischief in her voice.

In mock solemnity he answered, "I shall endeavor to improve my mind."

He was glad to see that she had some color in her cheeks again and a sparkle in her eyes. Her carriage dress of lilac jaconet, *en pelisse*, was becoming, and her big creamy leghorn bonnet made a charming frame for her face. She looked happy once more, and he thought that if only Aneila could help her over the trickiest hurdle of any new marriage, she would be all right.

They drove on through a small Hill village, admiring the picturesque dress of the women and ignoring the menacing expressions of the narrow-eyed men at their sides. As they left the squalid little houses behind, Perdita asked, "Is it much farther, Papa?"

"Not very. About another twenty minutes. You will probably see the house once we have rounded that corner, there. Look up to your right."

She followed his instructions and saw the outlines of a modern bungalow clinging to the top of the hill above the road.

"It must have a spectacular view," said Perdita.

"Yes. Aneila has always liked to 'see out,' as she puts it."

"Have you know her long, then?"

"Yes, for many years," answered Edward, wondering whether to explain his relationship with her to his innocent and so easily shocked daughter. If he had not at last decided to marry Aneila, he might have given in to her doubts about this meeting, but he thought Perdita would find it impossible not to like Aneila, and he could not think of anyone better qualified to tell his daughter the things she ought to have learned from her mother before she had ever had to suffer at the hands of her husband.

He turned his horses into the steep path that led up to Aneila's house, pointing out the fine specimen trees she had had planted in her large garden and trying to stifle his sudden doubts. Englishwomen were so damnably distorted by their wretched upbringing. He reminded himself caustically that that was precisely why he had brought Perdita here, pulled his horses to a halt, and handed her out of the carriage.

Aneila was welcoming, and Perdita found herself enchanted both by the house and by its mistress. She was tiny, not much more than five feet tall, with bones as delicate as some tiny woodland creature's under her ivory skin. Her sari was of grape-colored silk, most beautifully embroidered in gold. Perdita decided that she had never seen a more graceful or lovely woman in her life.

She summoned up enough Hindustani to apologize for not being able to converse properly, and Aneila clapped her hands and exclaimed that few English people made such progress, and that she should not be ashamed. Then she rang a small brass hand bell and called her servants to bring tea, saying something to Edward that Perdita could not quite catch.

He rose and told his daughter that he would return soon, adding, "Our hostess tells me of a matter which she wishes me to attend to for her. I shall not be very long." He hurried out, hoping that Aneila would be able to do as he had asked in spite of her reluctance.

But when he returned a little less than an hour later, he realized that the attempt had failed. Perdita was sitting stiffly by the window, gazing out unseeingly at the distant bluish-purple hills, with the familiar white distress on her face, and Aneila's expression of shame told him much. He said quickly in Hindustani, "I am sorry. I see that I was wrong. I shall take her away now, but I shall come back as soon as I can. Do not be sad."

And she answered, "It is I who should beg forgiveness. I have dishonored you in the eyes of your daughter." He stroked her face briefly and walked toward Perdita.

She started at his touch but pulled herself together enough to rise, thank Aneila formally, and follow her father out of the house. Once in the carriage, however, she rounded on him and, with a passion he had never seen in her, said, "How could you? Why should you do such a thing to me?"

He waited, unsure of precisely how to answer her.

She went on. "That woman was, is, your . . . Oh, I cannot say it."

"I am glad of that at least," he answered in a biting voice she had not heard from him before. "Aneila is a woman I have loved for many years. She has borne my children." He ignored Perdita's angry look. "And now that I am free, she has agreed to become my wife. I see that I should have told you all this before, but I assumed your good manners would prevent what you have just done; and I wanted you to know her before I told you she was to become your stepmother."

"Now that you are free of a tiresome daughter, you mean?" Her angry voice shocked him into replying more truthfully than he might have done.

"I had not thought of that. It is true that I should not have married her while you were living in my house, because there is no doubt that having an Indian stepmother would have made your life difficult with the memsahibs. But I really meant that now that your mother is dead, I am free to marry."

The hurt of it silenced Perdita. It was as though whenever she felt secure in her affection for someone, that person would change and become quite different: Uncle George, Marcus Beaminster, and now even her father. As though he understood a little of what she felt, he said more gently, "Aneila and I care for your happiness, my dear child. I asked her to explain to you some things that could make your marriage easier and help you to be happy with Beaminster. She did not wish to, but because she knows that I love you, she was prepared to try. I gather that you did not let her."

"What she said was disgusting. It is bad enough that marriage should entail what it does, but to behave like that . . ."

"I hope one day that you will know something of the great happiness that Aneila has brought me." He was silent for a few yards and then said carefully, "Relations between men and women can so easily plunge them into hell that deliberately to refuse to learn to avoid that is stupid." His voice changed into the brisker one she knew. "I hope that you will write apologizing before you leave for the Plains."

Marcus was surprised to see her face so drawn when he returned to the house just before dinner, and he asked, concerned, "Did you not enjoy your drive?"

"Not very much." She looked at him, thinking that at least he had none of the coarseness that seemed to infect even the best of other men. Whatever happened between them at night, during the day he was always as gentle as she could have wished. She asked with some difficulty, "Are you dining out?"

"Not if you wish me to stay with you."

She smiled at him gratefully but shook her head.

"I shall be all right. I am just tired. If you have an engagement, I shall go to bed, I think."

"Very well, my dear," he said, relieved, and went off to dine with James Thurleigh and Major Jamieson.

Six

By the end of August, the thought of leaving Simla without making peace with her father had started to torment Perdita, and so she called at Whitney House one morning about three weeks before she and Marcus were due to leave for the Plains.

Edward greeted her kindly enough and watched in some sympathy as she struggled with her apology. When she had blurted out some clumsy words, he patted her hand and said, "It is as much my fault as yours. I should have told you more about Aneila before I introduced you to her. I am sure if you came to know her, you would understand a little more."

"I'm sure I should, Papa. I am sorry."

He brushed her reiterated apology aside and said, "She understands. I hope that when you come up next year, you will be able to be friends with her."

"I hope so, too, but I don't suppose I shall be here. Surely Marcus won't be able to have so much leave again so soon?"

"Probably not, but that has nothing to do with it. It would be very bad for you to swelter in the Plains just because he has to. As I told you, I may not be here myself, but the house is at your disposal whether I am or not. I am sure Beaminster will see the propriety of your coming up here. If you like, I'll have a word with him."

Perdita smiled gratefully, and as she saw the familiar crinkling at the corners of her father's blue eyes, she felt herself forgiven. Nevertheless, his words had roused a latent anxiety, and she said, "Is there still danger up north, then?"

"You mustn't be anxious, Perdita. Any government expects trouble on its frontiers. It may still be possible to sort this out peacefully," he said reassuringly. Then, seeing that she was not convinced, he went on, "But whatever happens, it will not touch you. Any fighting will take place hundreds of miles from here, and even if Beaminster were to be involved—and there is no certainty of that—I should take care of you while he is away."

Perdita paled at the thought, but looking up at him she

was reassured by something in his smile and said, "I hope it will be arranged diplomatically, but, Papa, please be careful. It would be worth not having you here next summer if you can stop them going to war . . . but I wish I knew that I would see you then."

"My dear child, it is not I who can decide on whether there will be a war or not. I only take messages. But you know that if I can be here, I will, and in any case, I will arrange things with your husband. I am sure I can persuade him to let you come up."

In fact, he had no difficulty. Marcus knew quite well how tiresome English women found the heat, and he had always expected to send her to some Hill resort or other. He was only relieved that she would be able to go to her father's house instead of to some strange place where she would be lonely.

Edward watched the sudden lightening of his son-in-law's eyes as they spoke and wished he could be certain of its cause. Yet again he wondered why Beaminster had married Perdita. He appeared to be treating her properly, but he did not have the air of a man in love. Then, suddenly impatient with his anxieties, Edward tried to push them away; the thing was done now, and provided he always kept an eye on her, he had done all he could. Nevertheless his worries kept recurring.

"If only," he said to Aneila a few days later, "she looked as happy now as she did on the day of his proposal."

Aneila, listening patiently as always, did her best to comfort him and explained that all women took time to become accustomed to leaving their father's house for their husband's.

Perdita told herself the same thing day after day as she struggled with her continuing desire for some sign of Marcus's affection. She soon learned to hide her needs, for she saw how they irritated him, and she tried to appear content. But that in itself became a Herculean task when he took her away from Simla to his station several hundred miles to the south.

The house he had leased for her was squat and dark, and although it was in a pleasant situation close to the parade ground, it was ugly and full of depressing, uncomfortable furniture. Perdita hated it. She knew that if she wrote to her father, he would have rugs and furniture sent down to her at once, but she could not make the effort to write. Marcus, too, would probably have given her anything she wanted, but he did not seem to understand how much she detested her new surroundings, and she found she could not tell him.

While they had been in Simla, she had hardly registered the fact that he was a soldier, but at the station, hearing him speak of his men and the patrols and maneuvers they carried out, she could not escape the knowledge, and it made him seem more than ever a stranger. When she understood at last that his reason for being in India was to fight, that he was trained to lead his men to death, her father's words came back to her with increased significance. The idea of war began to obsess her.

One afternoon soon after their arrival, she had lain down on the lumpy sofa in the drawing room and called a boy to pull the *punkah* to dispel some of the stuffy heat that was so tiring. She turned her face up to the expected draft as the clumsy contraption began to creak and swing, but all she felt was a cloud of gritty dust, and then, horribly, the corpse of a lizard that had made its hot-weather nest in the folds of cloth. To her shame, Perdita screamed. When the *khitmagar* came running, she ordered him to have all the *punkahs* in the house replaced, but that was the only improvement she made.

Everything seemed a fearful effort, and she was always tired, with a nagging pain in the small of her back that made it doubly hard to seem content. Small things irritated her more and more, and she began to feel aggrieved that Marcus had not noticed her malaise and that he spent so little time with her even when he was not on duty. But one morning when he had returned from his usual early ride, he asked if she were ill. She made an effort to stifle her crossness.

"No, Marcus. I expect that it is just the change of climate; I felt very strange when I first landed in Calcutta last year, and this is almost as hot. I shall be better as soon as I become accustomed. And when I become more used to life in cantonments."

"Is it so different from Simla?"

"Yes," she answered baldly, and then, seeing the surprise

on his face, she searched for an unexceptional comment to add. "I find it so difficult to enter into the interests of the ladies here, and they know nothing of mine. You see, I do not know—or care very much—what things cost, and that seems to be their chief preoccupation. And I know no scandal about the people they discuss all the time." She laughed a little to drive the frown from his eyes. "I expect I am a sad disappointment to them."

Marcus laughed, too, genuinely amused at that, and said, "I can imagine that their conversation is dreadfully dull, but as soon as you have recovered your health, you will join us riding in the mornings and get away from them for a moment each day."

That "us" made her wonder, not for the first time, with whom he spent his time. He spoke often of Captain Thurleigh and the other officers she knew, but she could not help thinking that he must also be seeing Major Jamieson's wife. If it were she who shared his morning rides, Perdita decided that she would never join them. Even so, she smiled at Marcus and told him she looked forward to it.

He left her then to the mercies of Maria's mother, Mrs. Fletcher, who had called dutifully to inquire about her health and to invite them both to dine. Perdita nearly always felt better by the evening, and the opportunity of getting away from her depressing house was too enticing to refuse.

Pleased, Mrs. Fletcher settled down to tell Perdita how important it would be for her to make a good impression on the other guests, and she explained carefully how she should behave, warning her of the kind of entertainment she could expect.

"Of course I shall not have any card tables, so you don't need to worry that you can't play. Lieutenant Smytham will be coming, and the colonel wishes to keep him away from cards as much as possible."

Wondering whether he could be the same Smytham she had known on the *Jupiter*, Perdita asked a few questions. It became clear soon that he must be the same man, and she blushed at the prospect of meeting him again. It was hard enough to live cheek by jowl with Mrs. Fletcher and her disagreeable daughter, who had seen her translation from despised spinster to young countess, but to have to face a man who had known her only as the black-clothed misery she had once been was daunting. And he had probably heard about the fit she had had and might tell people about it. Now that she seemed to have grown out of her affliction, she hated the thought of anyone knowing about it.

When she saw Marcus again at luncheon, she asked him about the lieutenant's position at the station and was very surprised to hear that he was in trouble.

"I hadn't realized that you knew him," said Marcus. "I don't think you will see very much of him here. He's been behaving very foolishly, playing far too deep. And now the *shroff* has refused him any more credit."

"What is a *shroff*?"

He looked dumbfounded for a moment at her ignorance of what every griffin learns on his first or second day in India, but then, remembering how new she was to the country, he collected himself enough to say, "A fact of life for young officers, I am afraid, my dear; a moneylender. One's pay is so little, you see, that one goes first to borrow for a horse, perhaps, then for a hunting trip or a second horse or more servants, and perhaps for card debts. And then before you know where you are, you are borrowing to pay the interest on the first debt; and so it goes on. One foolish cold-weather's spending can put a man in bondage for the rest of his life. Smytham has run through his own money already. He's a fool—and still losing."

"Can't anyone do something to help him?"

"A friend might. Don't look at me like that, Perdita. I didn't mean that only a friend would take the trouble to try, but that he would listen only to a friend, and he won't have any here. I believe the colonel has tried to talk to him, but he seems determined to crash."

"Poor man."

"Yes," he answered curtly, and Perdita decided that it was time to change the subject.

But knowing that he was in trouble lessened her nervousness a little as she went to dress for the Fletchers' dinner. Determined not to give Maria Jamieson the satisfaction of seeing her appear clumsy or ill dressed, she spent some time trying to select the most suitable of the dinner dresses her mother-in-law had had made and eventually chose one of supple tigrine in a delicate Esterhazy gray, which was to be worn with a white crepe hat decorated with a curling ostrich feather. The pearls her father had given her at the beginning of the year would be suitable, and she could wear the diamond-and-pearl drop earrings that had been his wedding present.

She was still bothered about her appearance when Marcus led her into the Fletchers' house, but once she could examine the other ladies' gowns, she was able to relax. As far as she could see, hers was no different except in its obligatory lack of color, and her jewelry was second to none.

Her confidence was just bringing a nice color into her face when Mrs. Fletcher introduced her to Lieutenant Smytham. Looking up into his bleak face, she was relieved to detect no signs of recognition and greeted him with equanimity.

In fact, he had recognized her almost immediately and in a detached way wondered at the change in her. The promise of good looks he had once discerned in her seemed to have been fulfilled, despite her obvious exhaustion and uncertain color, and he would have liked to talk to her. But he was too far into his own private hell to be able to make any real contact with anyone. He addressed a few civil inanities to her, but as soon as she was joined by her husband, he moved away.

Later in the evening Smytham thought he saw Perdita looking at him with sympathy and something very like affection, but he dismissed the fancy, unaware that by then she had been told every detail of what had happened to him.

It was Maria Jamieson who had painted in all the background to the picture Marcus had sketched for her. Over a glass of warm, sickly lemonade, Mrs. Jamieson said with satisfaction, "Oh, yes, he was *jawaub'd* all right."

Perdita looked blankly at her.

"I am sorry, Mrs. Jamieson, but I don't know what that means."

"How silly! I keep forgetting how little you know of our ways here in India," answered Mrs. Jamieson with a kind of pitying pleasure. "It means 'refused.' And because of it, he is going to the devil. Miss Fuller is beautiful, of course, but that was not why he was so determined to marry her. She has thirty thousand a year." The sharp voice deepened in respect. "But her guardian saw what was happening and dismissed him, and now no one will allow him near her daughters unless they are so poor and plain that any husband would be better than none. I should not be saying this, except that I know you would never repeat it."

Perdita looked at her in distaste and said, "Certainly not. But are you quite sure that you are not doing Lieutenant Smytham an injustice? I expect he cared deeply for Miss Fuller. I do not think you should say such things."

It did not occur to Perdita that her attitude to Mrs. Jamieson had changed, but the difference in her behavior struck the beauty with considerable force. Accustomed to Lady Beaminster's timid acquiescence, or at the least silent disagreement, Maria Jamieson was distinctly resentful of the outspoken criticism, and when she found herself standing next to the Resident's daughter after dinner, she described not only Lieutenant Smytham's latest excesses but also the disagreeable airs the new countess had put on and how little they became her.

"After all," she added with a little laugh, "Major Jamieson is vastly senior to dear Captain Blagdon. Oh, how silly of me, dear Lord Beaminster. I do think someone should give her a hint; she should be told that it will harm his prospects if his wife insults the wives of his superior officers."

"I do not suppose that he will mind that very much. I can't imagine that he will stay for very much longer in India," replied her companion dryly, putting her finger on one of Mrs. Jamieson's many resentments against Perdita. The Jamiesons were trapped in India, utterly dependent on the Company and ultimately facing an impecunious old age in some provincial town in England, while Perdita Beaminster had the money and position to go home whenever she chose.

The result of the dinner was hardly what it was supposed to have produced. Far from insuring that Perdita became part of station society, it achieved the opposite, for Maria Jamieson was not alone in her dislike. After a few weeks of sharing their jealousy and criticisms of the woman who had so sadly failed to fill the position she had unaccountably won for herself, the ladies of the station ceased to pay calls on her. That suited Perdita very well, and had it not been for the tedium of her life and the continuing symptoms of ill health, she would have been almost content.

The only thing that kept boredom at bay was the letters that Juliana sent from all possible points on her overland journey home. They tended to come in batches of four or five and kept Perdita amused for hours at a time. Occasionally Juliana lapsed into forebodings about living with only her mother, retired at Beaminster, or she wrote sadly of Augustus, but in the main her letters were full of fun, and Perdita would search for amusing things to write in turn so that she gradually found herself seeing the funny side even of the ladies who could make her feel so uncomfortably inadequate.

Marcus watched her slow acclimatization with relief, and he blessed his little sister when he understood how much her letters lightened his wife's mood. He wished he could do something similar himself, never realizing that all she wanted from him was the kind of casual gesture of welcome and comfort that he and his friends exchanged without thinking whenever they met. Marcus knew that his wife hated, and felt humiliated by, his visits to her room as much as he, and he tried to avoid touching her at all other times. He had no conception of her yearning to lay her head on his shoulder and feel his arms around her.

He worried, too, about her health, noticing her increased pallor and disinclination for meals, which had not disappeared as she became accustomed to the changed climate. Indeed, the weather had become almost cool, yet she still suffered. He eventually asked the regiment's doctor to call on her.

That evening, when Marcus returned to cantonments after leading a patrol to investigate some reported trouble in a neighboring native village, he found her lying on her sofa, an expression of half-secret pleasure on her face. She held her right hand tightly over her left, afraid that she might upset him by holding them out to him, and said as quietly as she could, "Dr. Pooley says that I am with child."

Thoughts poured through his mind; he wanted to respond adequately to this gift she was bringing him, to the reprieve from distasteful duty that was implicit in her pregnancy, to the rare happiness on her face, but he did not know how. He smiled worriedly and tried to speak. Then he moved toward her; noticing that she squeezed her hands still more tightly together, he stopped himself from laying one of his own on them and finally found some words.

"I am very glad, but I hope that you are not too uncomfortable."

She tried to match his tone of distant courtesy as she said, "Oh, no. And Dr. Pooley says that in a few weeks I shall no longer feel so nauseated in the mornings. He tells me that the child will be born in April, and he thinks it is excellent that I'll be back in the Hills by then."

"I see. That is good. I shall write at once to Mama; she will be so pleased. But should you not be in bed?"

"Dr. Pooley said that I must rest in the afternoons and retire by eight o'clock, but that I should not fancy myself to be ill."

"I'll speak to Pooley, but you must tell me of anything that you need or anything you would care for to make you more comfortable."

She looked up at him for a moment. "All I need is more books to read, but they will come soon. Juliana has promised me all the latest publications she can find when your mama takes her to London."

He said nothing then but resolved to write urgently to Calcutta, where it was possible sometimes to purchase English books.

It was almost six weeks before the rumor of Lady Beaminster's pregnancy drifted round the station and aroused the other wives' interest in her once again. Several of them invented reasons to call on her so that they could verify the news and tell her all about their own confinements, but Mrs. Jamieson was the first. She arrived with her mother, full of a story of her little daughter's cleverness in tricking her unfortunate nurse in some game they played.

But all thoughts of little Susie were driven out of her head at the sight of the Countess of Beaminster, looking extraordinarily healthy and really quite beautiful, actually on her knees on the floor unpacking a large box of books.

She scrambled up as they were announced. Dust and scraps of rush from the matting clung to her misty-gray muslin gown, and loosened wisps of hair curled around her rosy face. She shook hands and apologized for the mess.

"Beaminster has sent all these for me from Calcutta. He knew that I had read all my existing books too many times, and so he has done this. Is it not charming of him?"

"Yes, indeed," answered Mrs. Fletcher politely. "I thought they must have come from England."

"Oh, no," came the innocent answer. "This one seems to have been printed in Calcutta, and this, *Lady Annabella*, in America."

The polite smile on Mrs. Fletcher's crumpled face shrank as she said, "I know that is not your fault; you are still very ignorant of life in India, Lady Beaminster, and you may well have heard some teasing talk when you were in Calcutta, but it is very wrong to buy Indian or American versions of English books. Several people have told me that the Governor General's sisters are purchasing the Indian printers' illegal editions of *Pickwick* as it comes out, but I cannot believe such a thing. They know as well as I do that it is our duty as English people in India to stand out against these pirates."

"But I am told that the English *Lady Annabella* will not be available here for at least another year, and then it will cost twenty-two shillings instead of the three rupees Beaminster paid for this edition." Perdita was rather proud that for once she could discuss prices as all the other English ladies did, but it did not help her.

"I am afraid that this is a case where your sense of duty must conquer your desire for pleasure, Lady Beaminster."

Perdita was about to reply crossly, but she suddenly remembered a piece of advice her father had given her right at the beginning when he had first explained to her about the memsahibs, and so she said, "I understand now. Thank you so much for telling me."

The response so pleased both Mrs. Fletcher and Maria that they stayed for another hour, regaling Perdita with all the tittle-tattle of the station.

The most interesting subjects were the increasing possibilities of what they described as an exciting war in Afghanistan, Lieutenant Smytham's continuing progress toward ruin, and the fascinating news that the Governor General, Lord Auckland himself, and his two sisters would be stopping at the station on their stately progress up through India to Simla. The gubernatorial caravan, they told her, included over eight hundred camels and one hundred and forty elephants besides twelve thousand people, stretched out for at least ten miles on the march, and raised dust clouds that could be seen throughout the surrounding country.

"And they have a full orchestra," added Maria Jamieson. "So it has been decided that the station should hold a ball for his lordship and his sisters—the Miss Edens, you know—and they will lend us their musicians. It will be wonderful to be able to dance properly again." She achieved a sigh that was supposed to indicate how much she missed the sophisticated season of a capital city, which she had never in fact enjoyed. "But how cruel of me. Of course you, dear Lady Beaminster, will not be able to dance. You must forgive me."

"Willingly. But I never really cared for dancing, and so it will not matter that by then that I shall be too cumbersome to do anything but watch."

Perdita's acknowledgment of her condition allowed Mrs. Fletcher the opening for which she had been waiting, and she proceeded to give her advice on the management of a confinement. Then she felt sure that Lady Beaminster would like to know how brave Maria had been with each of her three children. But she must not allow herself to worry: India was not as dangerous as people said; after all, she herself had lost only two children and Maria none yet.

Before very long the catalog of horrors and warnings had driven the healthy color out of Perdita's face, and she was beginning to wonder desperately how she could make her visitors be silent, when Mrs. Fletcher gathered up her gloves and rose to go, saying, "But you must not allow yourself to be afraid. As it happens, I shall be going to the Hills again myself next season, and so I shall be at hand. Good-bye, dear Lady Beaminster."

Once they had left, Perdita reprehensibly told her butler that if anyone else called, she was not at home, and she went back to her sofa with one of her new books. As usual, she lost herself in it completely, so that when she was finally brought back to her own world by Marcus's return, she was restored almost to the morning's bloom.

Nevertheless he looked searchingly at her and said, "You look tired, Perdita."

"Perhaps I am a little," she said, pleased that for once he had used her name instead of the impersonal "my dear," which had once seemed so affectionate. "Mrs. Fletcher came to visit me with Maria, and they stayed rather a long time."

"Prattling all the time, I suppose, of the Auckland visit."

"Mostly, and of poor Lieutenant Smytham." Perdita was surprised to see a frown on his face and, suppressing an impulse to lean up and smooth his wrinkled forehead, said, "He must be so unhappy."

"I am sorry that you should have heard any of it, and knowing the gossip of this station, I suppose you have heard the lot; I know you have a kindness for him. I don't think he is unhappy precisely, but he is certainly behaving foolishly. I only hope he will pull himself together before Auckland arrives. If there really is to be a war, Smytham could damn his chances of getting into it if he makes a fool of himself then."

By the time the Governor General's spectacular caravan approached the station, Lieutenant Smytham had resolved his difficulties. Perdita, who felt herself to be enormous and was disinclined to leave the house, was probably the last person to hear the denouement of his pathetic little tragedy.

Marcus had insisted that she attend the private dinner to which they had been bidden by the Resident, with whom Lord Auckland and his sisters would be staying, although he had agreed to carry her excuses to all the other festivities. It was after dinner there that she discovered that Smytham had lost again, heavily. With no money, no more credit from the *shroff*, and no prospect of redeeming his notes, he had shot himself the day before the station's ball.

It was the all-knowing, all-telling Maria Jamieson who had enlightened Perdita as they stood chatting to Captain Thurleigh after dinner. Perdita looked at him for confirmation, and he said, "What, Smytham? Yes, damn fool. But there was nothing else to be done once he was in so deep."

"Nothing else? But to kill yourself over a game of cards! That cannot be right."

James Thurleigh looked down at her and felt all his clamped-down resentment surge to the surface of his mind. He found the palpable evidence of her fecundity revolting, and he said, averting his eyes from her swollen figure, "It is not something a female could understand. The cause of his death, Lady Beaminster, was not a game of cards but honor." Perdita tried to ignore the note of brusque contempt in his voice.

"Of course I understand the principle, Captain Thurleigh, but I cannot accept that such a principle is more valuable than a man's life, even a man in debt."

"Then you must be very stupid," he answered without thinking, and then, seeing the consternation in both their faces, apologized curtly and left them.

As he walked away from them he resolved to keep his temper better in the future. The truth was that young Smytham's suicide had shocked him. Officers in India should not embroil themselves with respectable women, he decided. Take whores if they must, but only trouble could follow from involving gently bred English ladies in a life that was fitted for men alone. Good God, they were here to subdue and rule an alien country. They should not have to be bothered with the destructive games of bored and flirtatious young ladies. After all, even Smytham had been a decent officer until he fell victim to Miss Fuller.

"Ah, Thurleigh," came a voice, interrupting his angry reverie, "I want to present you to Mr. Macnaghten, His Excellency's political secretary."

James Thurleigh hastily pulled himself together and exerted himself to make a good impression on one of the most influential men in India.

They spoke among other things of the threat in Afghanistan and of the possibility of going to war over it, and Thurleigh was pleased to find his views well received. A leading question from Mr. Macnaghten opened the way to a discussion of the proper way to neutralize a hostile country, and Thurleigh began to forget his irritation in the absorption of his professional interests.

The political secretary was so impressed that later in the week he spoke to Lord Auckland of the young captain's vigor and good sense. His lordship, never the most vigorous of men himself, was pleased and quickly acceded to Macnaghten's suggestion that they add Captain Thurleigh to the already enormous entourage. It did not occur to either of them that he might prefer to remain with his regiment. It was well known that only a transfer into the political branch could bring influence and the chance of wealth within the reach of young officers, and this one's family could not help him. Mr. Macnaghten had gone out of his way to find out about Captain Thurleigh and had discovered that his father had a lowly position at East India House in London. The young man had risen as far as he could on his merits; a little influence would not be unwelcome.

Colonel Fletcher, who had provided the information, was equally aware and was therefore very surprised when his officer expressed the strongest reluctance to leave his regiment.

"You must be the only man in India who would turn down such a chance, Thurleigh, and I am not sure that you can. I am glad, of course, to know of your loyalty to the regiment, but there is very little you can do here at the present, and a spell with these political fellows will do you no harm. If we do go to war over this fuss in Afghanistan, as they're beginning to suggest, we shall probably get you back. I think you must go. Tell me, why are you so reluctant?"

The only answer to that question was one he could not give, and so he had to fall back on, "I am a soldier, sir, and I have no wish to spend my time being polite to a lot of old women who sit behind desks and write letters."

Colonel Fletcher, who privately approved of the sentiment, had to deliver a reprimand and order the insubordinate officer to report to the political secretary forthwith.

Captain Thurleigh saluted smartly and left to spend the rest of the morning with his new master. They had luncheon together, and it was not until well into the afternoon that Thurleigh was free to go in search of Marcus Beaminster.

They had often discussed the merits of a transfer to the political but had come to the conclusion that each was more suited to the camaraderie and sport of regimental life than to the lonely political responsibilities of some remote district. They had served together for the entire fourteen years of Marcus's life in India, sharing quarters, organizing cold-weather hunting trips together, racing their horses, pursuing an amicable rivalry in the matter of their careers, and becoming fast friends. Marcus was the best of fellows, and

James Thurleigh, who did not make friends easily and was often avoided for his abrasive manner and caustic tongue, was annoyed at the prospect of perhaps several years stuck serving Macnaghten hundreds of miles away, surrounded by weak-kneed civilians. He walked angrily over to the mess in search of Marcus and, not finding him, felt his temper going. Half an hour later, he ran him to earth at home.

The servant who showed Captain Thurleigh into the drawing room had not announced him as he was such a frequent visitor, and he walked in to find Marcus sitting beside his wife's sofa, reading to her. To many, it would have seemed a charming scene, a model perhaps for a painting entitled *Domestic Happiness*, but it provoked no such gentle thoughts in Captain Thurleigh. He greeted Lady Beaminster formally enough before turning unceremoniously to Marcus to say, "Have you forgotten our appointment? We were to ride to the river this afternoon."

Marcus, about to express surprise, caught sight of Thurleigh's expression and substituted an apology to his wife. She was disappointed but at the same time pleased to realize that Marcus had been content enough in her company to forget to ride out with the most bellicose of his friends. It seemed like a triumph over the warmongers, and she smiled happily up at Marcus. She was rewarded with a rare caress. As his hand left her arm, she looked across the room at Captain Thurleigh and was childishly pleased to see a frown contracting his heavy black brows. She felt suddenly much better and wished him a pleasant ride in a voice designed to provoke him. It did, and he left the room.

A week later Thurleigh rode off with the Governor General's staff, determined to rejoin his regiment as soon as he could arrange a transfer but consoling himself with the knowledge that he would at least be working close to the Commander in Chief. If there really were any fighting to be done, it would be he who chose which regiments got the chance to do it, and James Thurleigh was determined to do all he could to make sure that the 121st was one of them.

Seven

The Beaminsters, who were also going up to Simla, would travel about four times as fast as the Governor General's monstrously large procession, and so they did not leave the station for another six weeks, in good time to reach the Hills before Perdita's confinement.

The last few weeks in the Plains were almost all pleasurable for her. She had put the horror of Lieutenant Smytham's death behind her, telling herself that however great his misery must have been before he shot himself, at least his death had freed him from it, and she was no longer seeing his shattered head in her nightmares. She wondered from time to time whether anyone had thought to write to Miss Fuller before the inevitable gossip of Anglo-India reached her guardian's house in Meerut: even if she had not cared for him, she would probably have been distressed to hear of his suicide. Perdita thought briefly of writing herself but then dismissed the idea as an impertinence and tried to concentrate on preparations for her coming child.

She had had to give up collecting flowers for Juliana when Dr. Pooley became concerned at the swelling of her ankles, and she missed being able to drive out of cantonments to the countryside, which to her surprise she had found appealing. The golden flatness of the plain could never compare with the loveliness of the Hills, of course, but it held its own attraction, especially in comparison with her ugly, dark bungalow.

Lying amid the clumsy furniture day after day, Perdita had come to rely on her books. She tried to ration her reading so that Marcus's novels would last longer than a few weeks, but she had found the self-discipline difficult until she took up needlework. Then she could read for half an hour, sew for two, and pick up her book again. But among the forty-three servants she and Marcus employed was a *durzee* who expected to do all the sewing required by the household, and he had been seriously affronted to discover that the lady-sahib intended to make clothes for her child herself.

An impending revolt among the servants was quelled only by Marcus's asking the *sirdar*-bearer to explain to the rest of them that the doctor-sahib had decided that it would calm their mistress's mind if she were to take up sewing, and he ordered the *durzee* to make up a piece of valuable silk from China into a dressing gown for the lady-sahib to wear after the birth of the child.

But it was not only the servants who considered that the sight of the countess laboring over the seams of bonnets and nightgowns was unsuitable. The resident's wife caught her at it one morning and begged her to desist.

"I realize that it is difficult for you to understand your position" was how she began her explanation. "But by doing a servant's work like this, you are lowering yourself in the eyes of your servants and therefore lowering the standing of every Englishwoman in India."

"By occupying myself with embroidery on a bonnet for my own child? Surely you are exaggerating," protested Perdita, for once genuinely astonished to find herself at fault.

"If it were only the embroidery, that would be different, but you are actually making up nightgowns and other clothes, I hear."

Searching for support for her own position, Perdita said, "Well, Catherine of Aragon embroidered and made shirts for her husband, and she was Queen of England."

Mrs. Malwood's sharp nostrils contracted, and the corners of her mouth turned down into an expression that had become familiar to Perdita as the face of English disapproval and that she privately called "the bad-smell-under-the-nose expression." Mrs. Malwood said, "That is quite different, as you very well know. It is to be hoped that we have progressed sufficiently over the last three hundred years to make any such comparisons absurd."

"I beg your pardon," said Perdita pacifically, putting her work down on a small table.

After that visit, she took to hiding her stitchery under a cushion whenever she heard a visitor approaching the bungalow. She also apologized to Marcus when he came into her drawing room unexpectedly one afternoon before she had time to put the scrap of linen away. He stood looking down at her and said in a warm tone she rarely heard, "My dear

Perdita, you do not have to apologize to me ever. If you wish to sew, you shall do so, whatever the servants think." He then went on, with some difficulty. "I know that our life is sometimes hard for you here, and I have wanted to say for a long time now . . . to tell you how grateful I am for the way you have endured so much."

She smiled shyly up at him and said, "I am afraid I upset you too often, and I know that I do not behave as I should, for Mrs. Fletcher and the others frequently tell me so, but I do try."

"I know you do. Now if you would care for it, I could read something to you while you work. Have you finished *The Vicar of Wakefield* yet?"

"No, but it will be very boring for you to read without knowing what has gone before."

"Well, you must tell me first, and then I shall read." And so she told him, describing the characters as though they were people she had met, whose actions were dictated by reality. He was struck as he watched her expressive eyes by how much of herself she kept hidden from him in the normal way. It was as though in trying to do nothing to offend him, she blotted herself into insignificance. He began to want to know more about her, and when she had brought the narrative up to the point at which she had last closed the book, he asked questions about it, trying to draw out of her some opinions of her own. They led her on to comparisons with other novels and, indeed, to real people she had observed. Marcus listened, asked, and contributed his own ideas.

Perdita found herself arguing vehemently with him over the importance of reading novels. Her work lay forgotten in her lap when dinner was announced, and she realized how much she had enjoyed herself. Marcus, too, seemed happier than usual, and they continued to talk animatedly as he helped her up off the sofa and escorted her to the dining room. A little hesitantly she began to ask about his own tastes, and as the evening progressed, she felt that they had recaptured some of the friendship they had enjoyed before their marriage. When she eventually rose from the table, much later than usual, he said to her, "I have kept you up so long, talking too much, but I have enjoyed it too much to regret. I hope you are not too tired?"

Her smile took on an unaccustomed brilliance and, as she passed his chair, she said, "It has been the happiest evening I have spent for a long time, Marcus. There is nothing to regret, except that Dr. Pooley orders me to be in my bed by eight o'clock. Good night." He took her hands and kissed them.

The next morning she was afraid that their new friendship might not have survived, but there was no change. During the next few weeks she felt something of the sensations of a child who goes to bed each night desperately afraid that the weather will have broken by the next morning and made some promised treat impossible, only to awaken each day to find the sun pouring in through the half-drawn curtains.

Marcus and Perdita became increasingly easy with each other and began to talk as she had once talked with her father. She gradually lost her exaggerated respect for her husband's knowledge and opinions, and if he said something she regarded as nonsense, she would tell him so. In his turn, he began to forget that she was female and therefore not a fit recipient of confidences or speculation on serious matters and talked to her of the increasing possibilities of war in Afghanistan and of his own doubts about it. One evening she told him of her father's view that a war with Russia must be avoided at all costs, and he said thoughtfully, "I would agree with that, but I am afraid the cost might be very high."

She answered, "You sound almost reluctant. When I spoke to Captain Thurleigh once about the possibility, he said he thought it would be 'excellent sport.' "

"He was joking."

About to contradict Marcus, for she was certain he was wrong, Perdita saw the openness of his smile shrink a little and caught herself in time, saying merely, "Oh, I see."

Marcus heard the old submission in that small phrase and was sorry.

Despite that temporary stiffness, their new friendliness was still with them when they made their journey to the Hills. Colonel Fletcher had been unable to grant Marcus leave for the whole season but thought it quite proper for him to take his young wife to Simla and stay with her until the child was born. She was in no condition to travel alone, and his own wife and daughter, who might have served as an escort, were setting off to visit relations in Delhi on the way and could not take her there with them.

Marcus was concerned for Perdita and would have been reluctant to send her away alone whatever his colonel thought. Traveling in India was an uncomfortable business even for those in the best of health; for a heavily pregnant woman, it could be disastrous. He decided that a palanquin would be the safest conveyance for her, and on hearing it said that the hot weather was likely to be early that year, he arranged to leave a week earlier than they had planned.

Accordingly they set off on March 15, Marcus riding and his wife lying behind the curtains of her palanquin, carried by teams of bearers and followed by the buggies and bullock carts of servants and luggage.

They traveled mostly at night to save the bearers from the growing heat by the light of the *messalchi's* torches of rag and flax fed from a skin bottle of oil, moving at about three miles each hour through fields and jungle, across rivers or through the dirty streets of native towns. Often Perdita would open the curtains of her palanquin to watch and was amused to see the flashes of countryside revealed by the intermittent light of the torches.

One night she had been asleep and was awakened only by a change in the motion of her chair. She pulled aside one of the curtains to see what had caused it. All around her she could see a broad expanse of water, so smooth and clear beyond the ripples that every star was reflected. The moon was nearly full and drenched the whole scene in thin, beautiful light; but not until they reached the farther bank did she realize that her bearers, coming to an unbridged river, had swum across, carrying her palanquin on their heads. As so often before, she was horrified at what native servants did for their white employers apparently without a second's thought.

But five days later she felt them dump her chair unceremoniously onto the filthy road in the middle of nowhere. She pulled aside the curtains and was summoning up the severity necessary to call crossly to her *chuprassi* when she saw what the bearers had seen: a huge Bengal tiger crouched at the edge of the road amid the long, drying grass. The words died, and she watched in horror as her bearers scattered; even the *chuprassi* left her side. The sudden movement excited the animal, and it sprang fully eight feet across the road to catch one of the running men.

Perdita had never known his name, but she always recognized him, for he was the youngest in either of the teams and used to greet her with a cheerful if half-insolent smile. She watched in cold terror and shame as the creature's powerful claws rasped the clothes from his back and great strips of flesh with them. His screams split the quiet of the night, and in between she could distinctly hear the vile crunch as the tiger's teeth hit bone. When the animal finally killed the wretched man, it dragged his body back across the road and into the jungle. In the suddenly harsh moonlight, Perdita saw the red flesh and sharp ends of white bone where the man's shoulder had once been. She watched as the tall grasses closed behind them and sat upright, shivering and unable to speak.

By the time Marcus returned, surprised that her bearers had taken so long to catch up with him, she had recovered enough composure to call to the *chuprassi* and beg him gently to round up the surviving bearers so that they might proceed. When Marcus understood what had happened, he berated the men for their cowardice at leaving the lady-sahib, swearing at them and telling them that the young man's death was a fit punishment for his lack of courage. He stopped only after Perdita called out, "Marcus, no, please stop."

He dismounted then, angrily thrust the reins into the *chuprassi*'s hand, and came to stand by her in the moonlight. He saw that she was trembling violently and took her hands in his, saying, "My poor dear, forgive me."

She shook her head, unable to speak, and he signed to the bearers to start moving. He walked beside her for the rest of the way, never letting go of her hand. It was not much more than a mile to the *dawk* bungalow, and she was soon lying down on the uncomfortable bed provided, afraid to close her eyes in case she dreamed of the scene she had just witnessed. Marcus insisted on their remaining at the rest house the following day as well, so that she could recover from the shock.

He refused to believe her assertion that she would rather get away as quickly as possible from the place.

But they moved off at last, and he took care to ride at her side. Toward the end of that night's march she began to feel queasy but put the symptoms down to the swaying motion of her palanquin and the remaining effects of the shock. She told herself that a decent night's sleep would make her feel better.

They stopped for their next halt at the house of acquaintances of Marcus's mother, where they planned to stay that day and the following night. Now that they had reached the hills, the air was cool enough to travel during daylight.

Their hostess greeted them warmly, then took one look at Lady Beaminster's face and said, "It is so disagreeable, Lady Beaminster, to travel in such a condition. You must come and lie down at once. Are you sure that you would not prefer to stay here for a few more days to recover a little?"

"Thank you, but no," answered Perdita. "We have only one more day's march, and I would like to reach Simla as soon as possible."

"Well, you must know best, but if you should change your mind, I hope you will tell me. Now come along and lie down."

She showed Perdita to a large airy bedroom with the most comfortable bed she had had since leaving Simla the year before. She slept for nearly fourteen hours and was able to assure Marcus that she felt perfectly strong when they met at breakfast.

But when she took her place in the palanquin, she began to wish that she had accepted the invitation to stay. She felt thoroughly unwell and was aware of a great reluctance to travel any farther. But it was too late to go back, and the nagging discomfort gradually eased as the morning drew on. She subsided into a kind of doze, occasionally aware of glimpses of the hills and green, green trees through the swinging curtains, sometimes catching a glimpse of her *chuprassi*'s turban or Marcus's straight figure riding beside her whenever the road was wide enough.

Toward midday she fell into a real sleep, only to awaken less than an hour later from an unkind dream that she could not quite remember. About to call to the *chuprassi* to ask him whether the lord-sahib had ridden on ahead, she felt a piercing pain in the small of her back. It quite knocked the breath out of her for a moment or two, and she lay back against the cushions, trying to regain her breath. It crossed her mind that perhaps the pain had something to do with her child, but she dismissed the thought; it was not due for several weeks. She sat up once more and drew back the curtain.

To her relief, it was her husband and not the *chuprassi* who answered her call of "*Koi hai!*"

"What is it, my dear?"

"Nothing much, Marcus. I felt a curious pain, but it has gone off now. I just wanted to see you." He leaned down from his horse and took one of her hands in a comforting clasp, saying, "Tell me if it happens again. I shall stay beside you now."

After that she left the curtains open so that she could see his dear, distant figure riding beside her. The sight of him was so reassuring that for a time she was able to ignore the pain that kept gripping her, but after a few hours its increasing violence left her in little doubt that it was caused by the child, and she had no alternative but to tell her husband.

"What the devil am I to do now?" he asked. "Oh, I beg your pardon. I did not mean to blaspheme, but there will be no English doctor between here and Simla, and it will be well after six before we get there."

He looked so distraught that she found herself comforting him, and they agreed that it would be better to go on as fast as they could and hope that nothing happened before six. Then Perdita remembered the woman her father had taken her to see.

"Could we not go to Aneila?"

"Who is she?"

"My father's . . . a friend of my father's. I believe they have just been married."

"I see. I did not know you knew her. Will she help us? And do you know where she lives?"

"Yes. And her house is at least one and a half hours nearer than Simla. I think she will help me, although I was vile to her. I think—" She broke off, too shaken by the pain to speak for a moment.

He saw her trouble and said decisively, "We must pray

that she has not gone away. Tell the *chuprassi* where she lives." And he urged the bearers to greater speed.

One hour and twenty minutes later, Marcus saw to his relief the lights of the house, and he rode ahead to warn Aneila. Far from refusing to see Perdita as he had feared, Aneila came immediately out of her room and said, "Poor Lady Beaminster. She must be so frightened. When did it start?"

Marcus hardly noticed her Indianness as he said, "I am not quite sure. She first mentioned a pain four hours ago, but then she said nothing more until about an hour ago. But it must be very bad: you have only to look at her face to see that."

"We shall see. Here they are." She ran down to the palanquin to hold both Perdita's hands in her own and say with great calmness and confidence, "Do not worry. All will be well. I know what must be done, and we shall do it together. Lord Beaminster, please come and help me bring your wife inside."

He picked his wife up in his arms and carried her into the house. Catching a glimpse of his square face in the dusk and seeing real anguish in his eyes, Aneila thought that perhaps Edward was wrong and the marriage was based on love. No man could be so worried by the pain of a woman for whom he cared nothing. He carried his burden indoors and laid her as carefully as he could on the bed. Aneila then hustled him out so that their ayahs could undress Perdita and make her as comfortable as possible.

"I am going to die, aren't I?" she said as soon as Marcus had gone, looking up at the bunched white muslin curtains above the bed.

"No, of course not. People die only if they are ill, and you are not. You are bearing a child like thousands of other women."

"But I am too old."

Aneila sat on the edge of the bed and wiped the sweat off her stepdaughter's forehead with a fine cloth and said, "No, you are not. I am ten years older than you, and I am going to have another child. I am not afraid, and you must not be. Do not fight, Perdita; this is natural. Later you must push, but now you should do nothing."

As she stood up, Perdita said anxiously, "Don't leave me, please."

"I will not. I go just to tell your husband that all is well. I will be only one moment."

Marcus was waiting outside the flimsy door to Perdita's room, and he said as he saw Aneila shut it behind her, "Come here to the veranda." When they were out of earshot of his wife, he continued. "Are you sure she will be all right? Is it not taking far too long?"

"First babies always take a long time. It is true that she is old to be having the first, but I think all will be well unless she bleeds."

"Bleeds?" he repeated, horrified.

"Yes, I do not know the words in English." She launched into a stream of Hindustani, which he understood well enough.

"I see. I shall ride on to Simla, then, to find the doctor."

"Very well. And please tell her father. He is at Whitney House, and he should be here." She left him then to go back to Perdita, who had heard the sound of Marcus's horse clattering down the steep road. She clutched at Aneila's hand in sudden fear.

"Marcus! Why is he leaving?"

"He is going to Simla to fetch your father and the doctor." She smiled slowly. "It seems that most Englishmen believe that women do not know enough about the bearing of children to help each other without a doctor. But don't be afraid. I remember well what it is like." She wiped Perdita's forehead again and sat down by the bed to wait.

The pains came at closer and closer intervals, and Perdita's fear sharpened with each one. She clung to Aneila's wrist and cried out in terror, "It is breaking me open!"

She felt her head stroked and heard Aneila's voice saying softly, "Nothing will break. All babies are born thus. Wait, and you will see."

She repeated the advice and offered comfort throughout the four hours it took for Perdita to move into the third stage. Aneila said, blessing the benevolent gods, "I can see the baby's head, Perdita. Now you must push—push down as hard as you can."

Perdita, terribly tired and almost beyond fear, tried to

obey. She kept her eyes fixed on Aneila's black ones as though she might find there the extra strength she needed. The contractions sped up until they merged into one indistinguishable challenge. She longed to give in, but there was nothing to which she could surrender. She tried to push through that tearing sensation, as Aneila begged. Then, at nearly half past ten, through a worse pain than she had yet felt, she vaguely heard Aneila's voice, which had sustained her through so many hours, saying, "It is coming now, Perdita. That is good. Push once more." She tried to obey and suddenly felt the pain and the burden leave her. In exhausted relief, she closed her eyes and felt nothing until Aneila put a small, white bundle into her arms.

"You have borne a son, Perdita. You should be very proud."

Perdita opened her heavy-lidded eyes at last and looked down at the tiny squalling creature in her arms. She had never seen so young a baby before and was sorry that hers was ugly, but he was hers. Surging up through the exhaustion and the pain that remained, she could feel the beginnings of triumphant joy. Her arms closed around her son, and she knew then and forever that all the difficulties of her married life, all the fears and anxieties she had ever felt, and all the pains of the last few hours had been worth suffering for this. This child of her union with Marcus would redeem them both.

Aneila stood at the foot of the bed watching the superb smile that lit her stepdaughter's face and the tenderness with which she held the child against her and was glad. Perdita looked up and impulsively took one hand from her child to reach out to Aneila.

"Later I can say it properly, but now . . . I want to tell you that I am very glad it was you who was here."

Aneila came around the bed to touch her cheek. They were still holding hands when Marcus arrived with the doctor and Edward.

Eight

"Not at all, dear Lady Beaminster. I always feel that I am in loco parentis with regimental wives, and I wanted to see how you did after that terrible confinement. I should have come before, but Dr. Drummond told me that you were not to have any visitors."

The doctor had insisted that Perdita keep to her bed for a month after the birth of her son, and when she had confided something of her dread of visits such as this one from Mrs. Fletcher, he had said with a very understanding smile, "I will do what I can to keep them off you."

Partly because of that, the month had been a good time for Perdita. She saw Marcus only rarely, but when he was with her, he seemed kind and concerned for her and their son, and he often brought her flowers. Sometimes she wanted to ask how he spent the rest of his time, but the nearest she could come to that was to ask for news of the other officers she knew were in Simla. Marcus always answered readily with some anecdote or other or passed on kind inquiries they had made about her health. Perdita soon understood that he had renewed all his old friendships, and she tried not to feel excluded. It seemed sad that the last few weeks at the station, which had been so happy and satisfying to her, should have made no difference to him and that he should have relaxed so easily into the violent world of sport, guns, and killing that the other officers represented. Perdita knew that they were all in Simla because of the possibility of war in Afghanistan, and she felt their presence to be threatening. But, she would remind herself, looking around her magnificent bedroom at Whitney House, here at least they have no place. Here Marcus is mine—gentle, kindly, and my son's father; this world at least is not plagued with war fever and excitement.

Her own father, too, was a crucial figure in her private world. Until he had had to leave Simla for Lahore on his expected mission for Lord Auckland, he had come every day to sit with her. Several times Perdita had tried to tell him how much Aneila had helped her, but it was difficult to find the right words, and she always stumbled over her gratitude. Nevertheless, as Perdita spoke, Edward understood her genuine admiration for Aneila and was pleased.

Before he had to leave Simla, he asked her to visit Aneila sometimes, and she said with her old, sweet smile, "How can you ask, Papa? I should visit her for my own sake in any case. And I owe her too much to leave her alone for so long."

Edward bent forward to kiss her smooth, pale forehead and said, "My dear, I am glad that you can be friends with her. Take care of yourself and the boy, too."

"Of course. By the way, we have decided to call him Charles Edward."

She laughed at the quizzical expression on his dear face. "No, not because we are secret Jacobites. Charles was Marcus's father's name, and Edward for you."

"Thank you, Perdita. I am very touched. Now I must go. I hope to be back here before you leave in September, but I shall write in any case. Good-bye, my dear."

When he had gone, she was sad for a while, but the fascination of small Charlie banished unhappiness. When she held him in her arms, when she fed him and felt the imperious tug of his gums on her tender breasts, she was filled with an overwhelming emotion she knew to be love. To her father and her husband she was always grateful that they should notice her and trouble to be kind, but with Charlie there was no such sapping obligation. Since his birth, she felt herself at last a whole person like other people. It was as though in bearing Charlie she had somehow, miraculously, joined the human race.

Mrs. Fletcher's loud voice brought her back to the present. She looked at her visitor with some sympathy mixed with dislike. The older woman must once have looked very like her pretty daughter, but the years in India, with all their anxieties, resentments, fevers, and disappointments, had made her face sag and wrinkle. Her complexion was sadly yellowed, and her brown eyes were lackluster. She made great efforts to repair the ravages of time, and her caps and bonnets were always adorned with false ringlets, but her own hair had not been as dark and glossy for many years, and the contrast was nearly as sad as the bitter twist to her lips. Perdita smiled at her.

"I am really much better now, thank you, Mrs. Fletcher. Dr. Drummond is even allowing me to take a little exercise. He says it is beneficial. But you really need not feel responsible for me. After all, quite apart from my husband, I have my stepmother close at hand." Perdita watched in some amusement as Mrs. Fletcher arranged her face into an expression of deep concern. She smoothed the ends of her handsome barège mantlet, obviously admiring its thick green sheen, unaware that the color only accentuated her sallowness, and said, "That puts me in mind of something I meant to say to you. We—that is, I—do not believe that it would be wise of you to see much of, er . . . Mrs. Whitney."

"I do not know what you mean. She does not go out into society, but there is no reason for me to avoid seeing her. After all, my husband need not go, though when we were all together, naturally she met and spoke to him and did not seem to mind being unveiled in his company."

"So I understand. It was all very unfortunate, but I am quite sure Lord Beaminster would agree that you should cut the connection now."

Perdita had been lying on her daybed under a soft pale yellow silk quilt, under instructions to keep calm for the good of her child, but at this example of monstrous prejudice she sat up angrily.

"Mrs. Fletcher, let me make one thing quite plain: Aneila Whitney is my father's wife. Without her, I do not know how I should have survived Charles's birth. How could I cut such a connection?"

"Well, please promise at least that you will not greet her in public?" pleaded Mrs. Fletcher. "It would give such a bad impression."

"Mrs. Whitney does not go into public places. I shall visit her quite privately, as she prefers. But if it will make you feel any better, I shall undertake never to mention her to the ladies of other regiments."

"I do think that would be wise, but please do not excite yourself so much. I am sure you should lie down. Now, that is better. Let us talk of more pleasant things. Will you go to the Governor General's ball next week?"

"Yes, I believe so. Dr. Drummond has promised to release

me soon, and we shall probably be there. Tell me," she went on, her good nature demanding that she make some kind of reparation for shocking her visitor, "who else is here this season?"

"Well, naturally Maria and the children. She is the only one from our station, but there are plenty of others; and of course all the Governor General's suite. And then I believe that there is a gentleman from America staying here. I have not met him yet, though I understand he is quite respectable —and often received by Miss Eden."

"What is he doing in India?"

"I cannot imagine, my dear. Oh, yes, I think I heard someone say that he is a writer and that he is making a grand tour, or something of the sort, though it sounds quite absurd, I know. I really did not listen."

"Well, he sounds more entertaining than the usual convalescent officers up here to recover from their excesses in the Plains."

"Lady Beaminster, sometimes I wonder whether you quite appreciate the difficulty of life out here for most of the Company's servants."

Perdita's ayah saved her from having to answer by opening the door to usher in Dr. Drummond, whom her mistress greeted with relief.

Seeing her expression, he smiled understandingly before turning to her visitor to say, "Good afternoon, Mrs. Fletcher. I trust you are well?"

"Yes, indeed, Dr. Drummond. Apart from my back, which as you know, is always torturing. Yester—"

"You are always very brave," he said, bowing urbanely. "And now I am afraid I must break up your tête-à-tête with Lady Beaminster."

He moved over to open the door for her, and reluctantly she rose, saying as she passed Perdita's sofa, "I know you are too sensible to forget our little discussion, my dear." She averted her eyes ostentatiously from the flamboyant silver bed and nodded to the doctor as she walked out the door.

He was too polite to say anything about her, but his narrowed eyes were full of mischief as he came back to Perdita's daybed. He shook her hand and asked how she was feeling.

"Very well. It seems fraudulent to be taking up so much of your time when there is nothing wrong with me."

"It is always a pleasure to see you, as you well know. But I do think you have been remarkably lucky."

"I had very good nursing."

"So it seems. I have just come from Mrs. Whitney. Your father asked me to look in on her now and then."

"Oh, how is she? I have longed to see her, but until you let me out of here I cannot; she will not come here."

"So she told me. And I said to her that I would allow you out today. I am a little worried about her. She tells me that she has had all her other children with great ease, but I understand that that was all some time ago. She seems rather low, and I think it would do her good to see you."

"Of course I shall go. But Dr. Drummond, please tell me what it is you fear for her. Is it serious?"

"Please do not agitate yourself, Lady Beaminster. There is nothing particularly alarming, but as I said, she seems low, and she has a small fever. But I shall keep an eye on her. Now tell me exactly how you are."

But Perdita had nothing to report, and after a brief physical examination he told her that she was fit enough to get up.

"Though you should not ride just yet. But you will definitely be well enough to dance at the ball at Auckland House next week."

"I am glad. I have been looking forward to it."

He looked surprised, and Perdita remembered that she had told him of her dislike of the constant round of dreary entertainments at the station. Now she laughed a little and said, "Ah, yes, but this one will be different. I want to meet Miss Eden again. I only spoke to her briefly, but she was so much more interesting than all those vapid women."

Dr. Drummond, who had a huge admiration for the Governor General's elder sister, was pleased to see that his good opinion of Lady Beaminster was well founded. He smiled with the twinkle that made him so engaging and agreed, telling her of many of his heroine's exhibitions of humanity, of how she rescued two unfortunate orphans, of the money she gave for the starving, of her untiring devotion to her brother's support, although, he went on, "Like you, she very much dislikes the ceaseless dinners and balls. I am sure you will find her most agreeable. She . . . But I must not go boring on." He stood up to leave. "Your husband will be happy to know that you are completely recovered. He has been very worried about you." Perdita flushed, and a small, wistful smile widened her lips, which made the doctor wonder a little; but speculation about his patient's marital affairs was outside his province, and so he said nothing.

Soon after he had gone, Marcus came in and stood by her side, looking at her somberly. She smiled warmly up at him.

"Isn't it wonderful, Marcus? Dr. Drummond says I am well again and can get up."

"Yes," he answered curtly, thinking of the pleasure of his renewed friendships while she had been confined to her room. He and his fellow officers had been so much easier together when he did not have to worry about protecting Perdita from their sarcasm or his friends from the boredom some of them quite obviously felt in her company.

Perdita lowered her eyelids in disappointment. Guiltily aware of having hurt her yet again, Marcus knelt down on the floor by her sofa and took both her hands in his.

"My dear, I am truly glad." But it was too late, and the unshadowed trust with which she had looked at him was gone from her eyes. She smiled politely at him now and gently withdrew her hands.

"I am not allowed to ride yet, but he says I may visit Aneila if you have no objection."

"Naturally not. You must do as you wish, always. But I hope he will allow you to ride again soon. I have something for you. Come."

He helped her up, smoothing the huge white cashmere shawl around her shoulders, and took her over to the window. There he showed her a groom standing outside in the garden holding a stocky gray mountain pony. Perdita smiled, for some reason amused by the hairy little beast.

"Marcus, thank you. You should not give me so many things."

He was standing close behind her with one hand still under her left elbow when he said, "Why not? I know how much you have missed riding Moti, and you have given me so much."

Perhaps he was just shy of me when he first came in,

thought Perdita, and Dr. Drummond was right that he has been concerned. If he can say something like that, perhaps he does care, after all. And so she leaned back just a little, so that her body was brushing against his, and said, "Have I, Marcus, truly?"

"But of course, my dear," he answered, stiffening and withdrawing from her. "Not least a son."

Again she felt shriveled by his coolness and embarrassed to have tried to touch him when he clearly found it distasteful. He seemed so different from the man who had carried her into Aneila's house and who had walked beside her palanquin holding her hand. She moved away from him, determined not to give way again to her impulses to reach him.

"I should dress now. Would you send ayah to me?"

"Certainly. I have to ride with Thurleigh this afternoon, but I shall see you at dinner."

She had to exercise all her self-control to prevent her dislike of Captain Thurleigh from overcoming her. She and Marcus had been so much happier together once he left the station, but now that they were back in the same town as he, they seemed to have lost the easy warmth they had shared, and try as she might, she could not help blaming his friend. However, provided she kept her intercourse with Marcus at a polite but restrained level, they would do well enough.

Her resolve not to burden him with her desire for warmth between them lasted well into the next week, and when she went to her room to dress for the Governor General's ball, she felt that they were in remarkably good accord. That and the pleasure she took in her new gown helped banish much of her usual nervousness.

The gown had been made from a piece of white satin embroidered with delicate gold threads that Mrs. Macdonald had sent her in a parcel of silks from Calcutta with a letter.

The white satin is called "Amy Robsart," which seems sadly inappropriate. But I hear it is all the rage in England, and I have bought the only lengths to have arrived here, so you will be very modish when you wear it.

Perdita had immediately liked the rich-looking material, but she had been afraid it would be too magnificent for any occasion Simla could offer until she had received the invitation to the Auckland House ball. Then she had called for her *durzee* and given him firm instructions to copy a picture in the latest *Ladies' Magazine* her mother-in-law had sent.

The result was a magnificent creation with a very full skirt that made the most of the delicate white flowers framed in gold on the gleaming satin. The corsage was cut very low, and the sleeves were daringly short, set close to the shoulder with several lace falls hanging gracefully from them.

With her hair becomingly dressed and one of Marcus's presents, a delicate diamond necklace, adding the finishing touch of elegance, she felt enough confidence to stand in front of the long pier glass in her bedroom. For the first time in her life, she could look at her reflection without embarrassment and even smile at it. She was surprised to find that she liked the look of herself; but she also felt a kind of recognition and wanted to say something like, "Oh, so there you are at last."

When she emerged into the hall where Marcus was waiting, he said involuntarily, "My dear Perdita, you look delightful. That is a new gown, isn't it?"

She smiled at him and did not find it necessary to brush away the compliment with some self-denigrating phrase as he had half expected. All she said was, "I am glad you like it." But she carried her head high and, looking at her, he believed she would play her part that night without shrinking.

Nevertheless, he watched her covertly as they drove to Auckland House and as they entered the ballroom, where she was introduced to many strangers. He was pleased to see that she greeted them adequately and smiled as they spoke to her, and he enjoyed the surprised and admiring glances she aroused. Quite soon he felt able to leave her with the colonel's lady while he went to pay his respects to Mr. Colvin, His Excellency's private secretary.

Mrs. Fletcher directed Perdita's attention surreptitiously to a group of colorfully dressed Indian men seated around the Governor General and said in a loud whisper, "Is it not shocking that there should be natives at our ball? I for one will not dance tonight, and you would be well advised to do the same. What Miss Eden can be thinking of I cannot imagine!"

Perdita looked down at the squabby little woman, unbecomingly dressed that night in deep maroon figured satin, and tried to hide her revulsion. She said as politely as she could, "I do not see why we should be shocked. The boot will probably be on the other foot, as my husband would say; I gather that Sikhs are like Hindus and find it shameful that we English ladies should dance in public at all."

"What nonsense! You must not make too much of native superstitions. Ah, here is dear Maria."

Perdita suddenly remembered a promise she had made to Mrs. Macnaghten, who had called on her the day before, and moved off with as much grace as she could muster. She was quite determined to avoid the petty malice of Maria Jamieson, who, she had heard, had been telling as many people as she could all about "poor Miss Whitney, who so extraordinarily managed to snare dear Lord Beaminster."

As she walked across the room toward Mrs. Macnaghten, Perdita looked appreciatively around her. Like all the rooms in Simla except her father's, this one had plain white walls, but they had been embellished with red patterns stenciled around the cornice to match the unusual curtains that seemed to have been made up of alternating strips of red and white cloth. At either end of the great room, fragrant wood fires burned merrily, their comforting crackle mingling with the orchestra's playing. Towering vases of magnificent rhododendrons flamed against the white walls, and festoons of red muslin decorated all the doorways.

The visiting Sikhs, thought Perdita, far from blighting the ball with their contaminating presence, added greatly to the evening's entertainments. They were dressed in brilliantly colored satins, and their jewels were far more lavish than any of the ladies'. Watching them, Perdita envied her father his mission to their ruler's court and wished that she could talk to them instead of exchanging suitable conversation with the English guests. Marcus came up to her as she stood near the Sikhs' cushions and persuaded her to join a quadrille that was forming.

Perdita still found the complicated dance difficult but

managed not to make any very obvious mistakes. Marcus's expression of amused pleasure told her that he understood both her doubts and her determination to overcome them, and at the end of the dance they walked off the floor together in obvious accord.

Several of the ladies who had not been in Simla the year before and who had not yet met Lady Beaminster decided that little Mrs. Jamieson's tongue had run away with her. The new countess behaved with perfect propriety, they decided, and was obviously on the best of terms with her interesting husband. Her happiness pleased the more generous of them, and several of them looked forward to making her acquaintance.

They were not at all surprised later in the evening to see her claimed for the waltz by Mr. Colvin. As Lord Auckland's private secretary, he was an important man in Simla, and it seemed fair that he should choose to dance with that glowing creature. And, of course, it meant that Lord Beaminster would be free to stand up with one of them.

Perdita was delighted that Miss Eden had yielded to the blandishments of her brother's aides-de-camp for a waltz, which she found much easier to dance than the difficult quadrille, and she liked Mr. Colvin, who had been introduced to her earlier by his wife. But as they whirled into the throng of dancers, neatly avoiding Sir Henry Fane and his daughter, she was suddenly afraid she would not be able to think of anything to say to him. Looking around for a subject, she saw the gorgeously dressed Sikhs and said something to him about the ill-concealed surprise on their faces.

Mr. Colvin answered, "It has been explained to them that it is the custom for English ladies to dance at gatherings such as this, and that you are not what they call 'nautch-girls,' but I think they find some of our customs hard to understand."

"So I believe. I heard from my father that some years ago the King of Oude believed that a group of ladies had been dancing for his entertainment and waved them away when he was bored. It must have been rather difficult."

"I had not heard that. But these fellows would never do anything like that. They are very polite, you know. They told his lordship that roses bloomed in the garden of friendship and that nightingales were singing in the bowers of affection sweeter than ever." He laughed.

Perdita felt that he was mocking the Sikhs in a way he would never mock an Englishman, however absurd, and protested. "But, Mr. Colvin, don't you think those are rather pretty conceits? Just imagine having nightingales singing to one in a rose bower of affection. I think I should like it very much."

"If only one could take them seriously, Lady Beaminster. But these emissaries will say anything. Why, only the other day at the *durbar* Lord Auckland told them that he hoped they had not suffered too much during that awful rainstorm, and they said—I think I have this right—they said that the canopy of friendship had interposed such a thick cloud that their tents had remained quite dry. Torrens and I went along to see, but do you know, they were wet through."

"Yes," answered Perdita, "I suppose even affection and friendship are useless against natural disasters. But never mind. I shall cherish the roses and the nightingales."

"They say you are a bit of a nightingale yourself, Lady Beaminster," he countered with a smile. "Perhaps Beaminster will bring you to our picnic next week at the falls, and you could sing to us. I know that you have received an invitation. Do say yes. It would be a capital end to the fête."

"You must ask Beaminster. I do not know what his plans may be; but for myself, how could I refuse so charming an invitation?"

He was about to answer when the waltz ended.

"Ah, what a pity. Well, at least I can look forward to next week. Shall I return you to Beaminster now?"

"Please," she said, taking his proffered arm.

They walked across the room toward one of the long windows, where Marcus could be seen in animated conversation with a group of officers; but on the way they were stopped by Mrs. Fletcher, who had been talking to a young man who stood with his back to them. As he heard Mrs. Fletcher greet Mr. Colvin, he turned, and Perdita found herself face-to-face with him. At first she thought his bony, clean-shaven face and cool, gray-green eyes looked dauntingly severe, but his sudden smile changed all that, and she found herself smiling in return. He held out a well-shaped hand and introduced himself in an accent that was strange to her.

"Charles Byrd."

She looked at him with interest, wondering whether he was the American Mrs. Fletcher had mentioned and what he could possibly be doing in India. He seemed quite different from the English civilians, whose languid arrogance and automatic performance of the conventional social duties made them difficult to know. Perdita liked the way this stranger inspected her before deciding whether or not to smile; it seemed to make his friendliness worth something.

"Good evening," she replied, not sure how to tell him who she was. Fortunately, hearing her talking reminded Mrs. Fletcher of her obligations, and she performed the necessary introduction. Mr. Byrd registered Perdita's title with a little bow of such amused irreverence that she nearly laughed, and when he asked if she would dance with him, she accepted with far more alacrity than she usually showed.

They stayed talking to Mrs. Fletcher and Mr. Colvin until the opening bars of the next waltz, when Mr. Byrd took her away to dance with him. He was only a little taller than she and slightly built, but when he put one arm around her waist and took her hand, she had an impression of formidable strength. As they circled around the floor, he murmured outrageous descriptions of some of the other guests they passed, displaying all the freedom of an outsider who cared nothing for their shibboleths—or for their approval. Perdita listened and laughed guiltily and enjoyed herself as never before. She was sorry when the music ended. He led her to the edge of the room as far from Mrs. Fletcher as possible and said warmly, "Lady Beaminster, I have enjoyed this dance as I never expected to enjoy anything in Simla."

Her lips curved again, and her eyes seemed to sparkle as she answered, "I have the feeling that I ought not to have let you make me laugh like that, Mr. Byrd." She stopped there but then could not resist adding, "But it is wonderful to hear someone say all those things I have been afraid even to think."

Mr. Byrd lowered his voice and said with an ironic smile, "One should always tell the truth, Lady Beaminster, and no one could pretend that that young Mrs. Jamieson is not exactly like a wasp. She behaves as though she has to try to sting as many people as she can find before her poison is exhausted. Not that I imagine it ever will be; she seems to have an immense supply."

"I had thought I was its only recipient," said Perdita, serious for a moment but nevertheless noticing the way his greenish eyes narrowed as he smiled at her, and the fine lines that radiated from them.

"Oh, no. I have overheard her delivering nicely judged doses to several people tonight. What a pair she and her mother make! This India of yours seems to do something very strange to women—or are most English ladies like the ones I have met out here?"

"I would not know. I knew hardly any in England and none who were at all like anyone I have met in Simla."

"Thank God for that. But now, tell me, how do you come to be out here? You are much too young to have come out with your husband."

"Don't tell me that you have not heard the whole story," she said, and instantly regretted allowing her hurt to sound in her voice. The slight bitterness interested him, and he looked closely at her.

"I have heard nothing about you. I assure you that my question was not meant to distress you. Let's talk of something else."

Ashamed of herself and wanting to bring the crisply curving smile back to his lips, Perdita said quickly, "No, no. I am sorry. It is just that I have been treated to so many versions of what has been said about me that I forgot that you are a stranger here and leapt to an unjust conclusion. Will you forgive me for thinking you were like them?"

"Willingly. I take it that some of these women are involved?"

Perdita ignored that and gave him only the briefest outline of her history. Charles Byrd was intrigued to know why any of what she told him should have provoked Simla malice, but he decided that he enjoyed her engaging company too much to risk losing it by forcing her to tell him more than she wanted. He had been in British India long enough to suspect that by birth or behavior she must have broken one of the inflexible codes that alone seemed to make Indian exile sup-

portable for the English memsahibs. He could imagine, too, that they found it difficult to assimilate anyone as different from themselves as this woman.

It was not easy to pinpoint exactly why she seemed so unlike them. Of course, she was far more intelligent than most of the rest, and she could laugh, which he had already discovered was a rare talent, but there was more. He thought it might be worthwhile to know her better, and for the first time he was glad that Simla was such a small, intimate town. It ought not to be too hard to become acquainted with her husband so that he could see plenty of her.

"And you, Mr. Byrd, what has brought you here?" Her appealingly low voice, conscientiously trying to fill the gap in their conversation, brought his plans and speculation to a halt.

"Well," he said slowly, watching her with pleasure, "I had a small difference of opinion with my father, who wanted me to live in Virginia and become a mirror image of him, while I wanted to pursue some line of my own."

"And?" prompted Lady Beaminster.

Mr. Byrd smiled. "And so I told him I wished to write a book analyzing the rise and fall of empires, which gave me a splendid opportunity to travel a long, long way from Virginia. He didn't believe me, and so he told me not to come back until it was finished."

"How long will that be?" asked Perdita, but before he could answer, they were interrupted by her husband, who had come to find her to take her home. He greeted Byrd pleasantly and waited while he said good-bye to Perdita before taking her off to make their farewells to Lord Auckland.

Later, when they were driving home through the bright moonlight, Marcus said, "You seem happy tonight."

"I am. So many good things seem to have happened. Aneila is better from her fever; Dr. Drummond has said that I may ride with you tomorrow; Miss Eden was just as interesting as I remembered her; I managed to avoid Mrs. Fletcher for most of the evening—just as you did—and I think I have learned to make conversation. Oh, and I do not think I said anything I should not have tonight."

"I am sure you did not," he said warmly.

"Well, I almost asked Mr. Colvin about what was happen-

ing in Afghanistan and what would happen if the situation worsened, but just in time I remembered your dislike of my talking politics on such occasions."

Her humility touched him, and he wanted to tell her that she should talk any way she pleased, that he had only asked her not to display her antagonism to the probable war one evening when James Thurleigh was expected to dine, but he found he could not.

"Thank you, my dear. I can tell you, however, that we have a man in Caubul now, Alexander Burnes, who has written that there really is a Russian intriguing there already and apparently well received by its ruler. A man called Ivan Vicovitch. We have some of his letters here, I'm told."

"What have they shown?"

Marcus flushed slightly in the cool moonlight and answered, "It is not yet known. There is no one here who can read Russian. Copies have been sent down to Calcutta, where there is thought to be an Armenian who can translate them."

"Who will perhaps find that Mr. Vicovitch is writing to his masters that there is a man in Caubul by the name of Alexander Burnes who is intriguing for the English."

"Quite possibly. But that has nothing to say to the matter. By the way, when you were dancing with Mr. Byrd, did he talk of any of this?"

Perdita shook her head.

"Good. It is merely a precaution, but I should be glad if you would not speak of the matter to him. As far as we know, he is perfectly honorable, but it is not so long since England was at war with his country, and he should not learn any private details of our affairs."

"We talked nonsense most of the time, but I promise I shall not tell him anything about Persia or Afghanistan or Russia, even if I have the opportunity, which is unlikely," she said, hoping that was not true. Charles Byrd was the most amusing person she had yet spoken to, and his irreverent comments on the people and customs that had caused her so many hours of shame and anxiety were as refreshing as water in a desert.

Nine

But she did meet him, the following week at Mr. Colvin's picnic. The Beaminsters, like all the other guests, sent their tents and servants down to the falls to be ready for their arrival at half past eleven. Marcus had tried to persuade her to make the short journey in a *jonpaun,* a curious coffin-like carrying chair, but she insisted on riding her new pony.

They went with Mrs. Jamieson and James Thurleigh. Perdita tried not to irritate him or give him an opportunity to say something cutting but disliked the intimacy with which he and Marcus talked. Sometimes she felt as though they used a private language that she was forbidden to learn, made up of jokes, allusions, and half-expressed memories. She often had to remind herself of her rebuke to Juliana the year before and Marcus's old explanation of the bonds forged between men who have fought side by side and faced death together.

She forgot the small frustration when they arrived at the picnic place, though. It was perhaps the most beautiful part of the country around Simla, and she had not been there before. It was a small valley, "rather Swiss" as Mrs. Jamieson called it to pretend that she was well traveled in Europe, with a bright noisy river splashing through it and cascading over tumbled rocks at each end. The grass of the valley floor was bright green, sprinkled with wild tulips and tiny scented irises and ringed with huge cedars that were almost as dark as the recesses in the rocky walls by the waterfall. Immense purple and green swallow-tailed butterflies settled on the starry flowers in the grass and even on the ladies' skirts, as though they were giant flower petals.

It was an enchanting place, and Perdita found it easy to forget the tiresomeness of people like Maria Jamieson as she wandered along the edge of the little river toward the falls, delighting in the sparkle of the water and the scents of the flowers and trees. She was watching a particularly fastidious butterfly landing on flower after flower until he found one to his liking, where he stayed basking in the sunlight, when she was joined by the American.

He said, "Pretty, isn't it, with that white water falling against the blackness of the cave under this bright blue sky?"

"Yes, indeed. But I think I like the butterflies most of all; so many of the flying creatures here cause such trouble that to see lovely ones like these that do not bite or sting or crawl is refreshing."

Charles Byrd laughed and held out his right hand.

"It is very good to see you again, Lady Beaminster."

She took his hand, once again noticing its shapely strength, and smiled in greeting. He walked on with her to the end of the valley, talking easily, and she was conscious of a distinct irritation when they were joined by other strollers.

Throughout the day she kept catching his eye and all too often read in his expression the amusement or contempt she felt as she watched the games of battledore and shuttlecock or listened to the vapid conversation all around them. And when he came strolling toward her after luncheon, her eyes lit up in pleasure. He looked quite different from the other gentlemen, and not only because of his clothes, she decided. He moved with an easy suppleness that was quite foreign to the languid civilians and much more graceful than the kind of healthy athleticism displayed by young officers like Captain Thurleigh. Perdita looked up as Mr. Byrd reached her side, shading her eyes from the sun.

"They're setting up the butts for some archery now. Will you let me take you to watch?" he asked.

"Thank you very much," she answered, and allowed him to help her up from her camp chair. As they walked toward the row of butts beyond the tents, he asked whether she was going to shoot. She smiled ruefully as she said, "No. It is not something I have ever learned, and I am so clumsy that I expect I should either drop the bow or shoot the arrow into one of the spectators."

"Having waltzed with you, Lady Beaminster, I can tell you that I think it very unlikely." He was surprised to see her blush at such a small compliment, and he began to wonder just what she had felt as she danced in his arms. A rather pleased smile tweaked at his lips, and he said, "I did not feel you miss a single step or even falter as I held you then."

Her half-suppressed gasp seemed to confirm his suspicion, but tantalizingly she turned her head away and made some polite remark about the first of the toxophilites, who was just raising his bow at that moment. Looking at the back of Lady Beaminster's charming leghorn bonnet, Charles Byrd decided that life in Simla might have some possibilities after all. But he would have to move circumspectly until he was more sure of his ground. He answered her remark appropriately and suggested that they join Miss Fane and Mrs. Jamieson, who were standing only a few yards from them.

For once Perdita was prepared to talk to Mrs. Jamieson and managed to recover her complexion and composure in time to fulfill her engagement to Mr. Colvin.

As she moved into the shade of a large rock in front of a row of chairs, she saw a surprised expression on Mr. Byrd's face, which changed to one of intent attention as she started to sing. She had chosen Marcus's favorite song, "Look Where My Love Lies Sleeping," an Elizabethan sonnet that had been set to music, and she looked toward him as she sang the last line. She was pleased that he raised his glass to her and smiled approvingly, and she smiled happily back before bowing shyly to the others, who were clapping politely. Mr. Colvin came over to thank her and his wife to beg another song; in the end she sang three more.

The sun began to sink behind the hills before the Beaminsters left, and so it was in the soft, delicately scented dusk that Charles Byrd came toward her once again.

Having greeted Marcus and Captain Thurleigh, he said to Perdita, "Lady Beaminster, you must allow me to tell you how much I enjoyed your singing. If I did not want to sound rude to my hosts in this place, I should say that once more you have provided me with a chink in the curtains of boredom that closed about me some weeks ago."

"Thank you, Mr. Byrd, but you must not exaggerate."

"I do not," he said briefly. He rode back with them, and as he was careful not to alarm her any more, Perdita found it pleasant to have so lively a companion to talk to while the others discussed a hunting expedition they planned to make during the next cold spell.

Life continued in its dawdling Simla way, with visits to the Europe shop, needlework sales, dinners, a few balls, endless calls, and several plays put on by different groups of their small society. The whole European population that year amounted to one hundred and fifty, and many of them were not the sort whom Perdita was allowed to know. She began to recognize the all-enveloping boredom of which Mr. Byrd had complained.

Her newfound ease in social occasions remained, although whenever she saw her husband talking to Maria Jamieson or dancing with her, Perdita would feel an unpleasant mixture of jealousy and fear, and her face would take on a strained, wistful expression that Charles Byrd found rather appealing. He was evidently persona grata at Auckland House and was consequently in demand at every other house in Simla, and Perdita grew accustomed to meeting him at most of the dinners she attended. He always sought her out, and as she talked to him her eyes lost their anxiety and glowed with a kind of confident happiness.

She had no idea that she was falling in love with him. To her the two sides of love were the striving hero worship she felt for Marcus and the all-enveloping protectiveness that their son aroused in her. She knew only that in Charles Byrd's company she was happy and herself. She never tried to hide anything from him, and they talked with rare freedom about anything that occurred to either of them. He found her amusing, critical but always gentle, thoughtful, touching, and very beautiful. He began to hope more and more that her apparent devotion to her noble husband might be nothing more than an effective mask.

Somehow the happiness Perdita found with Charles began to spill over into the rest of her life, and she even tried once more to get on terms with Marcus's friends, particularly Captain Thurleigh. For a long time he proved elusive, but she worked at it under Aneila's instructions.

"You are jealous of them all; that is the trouble, Perdita," her stepmother said to her one afternoon. When Perdita protested, Aneila had added, "Yes. You want your husband to put you first, before anyone else, and he does not. Why should he? They are old friends; they shared many things before you ever came to India. You cannot become a friend like that to your husband, but you have other weapons to fight with." And she went on to tell Perdita all the things she had tried to explain over a year before. This time, still shocked, Perdita listened, but she could not imagine herself doing any of it. Marcus had not resumed his visits to her room since the birth of Charlie, and she wondered, sick and ashamed of her suspicions, whether it was because he and Maria Jamieson were lovers. The idea hurt her, but it frightened her, too. Aneila saw her shiver and asked what the matter was, but even to Aneila she could not speak of that particular fear.

Nevertheless, she tried to put the rest of the advice into practice and found that Captain Thurleigh did indeed seem less contemptuous and unpleasant when she allowed him to thrust her into the background. When he paid any attention to her, she confined herself to topics such as sketching, or the work she was doing for Miss Eden's fancy sale in June, or the picnic in Annandale that she had planned with some of the other ladies. Each time she had to make conversation with him, she felt Mr. Byrd's curtains of boredom closing around her, but it seemed worth it to keep Thurleigh's contempt at bay and win Marcus's approval.

She often smiled to herself when the truth of one of Charles Byrd's shockingly apt phrases was brought home to her, and she tried to describe him in one of her weekly letters to Juliana. When she had finished a paragraph, she sat at her writing table looking out over the magnificent view of Jacko.

The mountain's look of rugged strength pleased her almost as much as the frothy flowering shrubs that grew on its lower slopes. It seemed to put the difficulties of her life with Marcus into perspective. As she gazed out the window, she had a peculiar notion that the mountain offered a reflection of her marriage. While she had been at the edges of acquaintance with Marcus, she had found endless small pleasures like the flowers that turned Jacko's slopes almost into a garden, but as she had come to know more about him, it was as though she had had to climb higher and higher up the mountain, leaving those easy joys behind. It was a hard climb, and the higher she went, the fewer flowers she found, but perhaps when she reached the top she would feel the splendid solidity of the bare rock beneath her feet, the struggle would be over, and she would be free in the uncorrupted air of the summit.

At that thought Perdita laughed at herself. It was ridiculous to make such a parallel, and in any case, there would always be other higher peaks to reach.

She picked up her letter to reread it.

He is not tall. In fact, he is almost small beside Marcus or Captain Thurleigh, but he is very charming. I find him by far the most entertaining person here, and almost the only one I can talk to about anything other than the weather, the price of Mrs. Fletcher's new bonnet, or our children. For some reason he and I share many ideas and jokes. There was a terrible moment last Sunday, for instance. We were all in church listening to the new clergyman preaching. It was the thirteenth, and so perhaps there is something in the superstition after all. He suddenly decided to give us a demonstration of the raising of Lazarus from his tomb and positively *shrieked* the words the Lord is supposed to have used to call the corpse forth. I tried so hard not to laugh and had almost succeeded, when he became a trumpeting angel and flung his arms around so that the sleeves of his gown flapped like moth-eaten black wings. It was too much for me! I had to turn my head away in case he saw me laughing. Alas, Mr. Byrd was sitting behind our pew, and I caught his eye. His expression so exactly mirrored my feelings that I had to take refuge in a fit of coughing. Happily, though, we were not the only ones affected. Even Sir Henry Fane, who is the Commander in Chief, was laughing when we eventually escaped.

He, by the way, has done me such a good turn. . . .

Perdita picked up her pen again, dipped it into the square glass inkwell, and went on to explain to Juliana that Sir Henry had decided, in the face of worsening news from Afghanistan, that it would be absurd to send able-bodied officers down country and had commanded Marcus to remain at Simla until further orders were received. All the same, she dreaded the prospect of his going to war.

Unlike Perdita, most of the English in Simla that year were exhilarated at the possibility. They felt as though they stood on the edge of great events. By May, Lord Auckland had decided that he would have to send troops into Afghanistan to sort out the dangerous quarrels, and by July, his decision was known to almost everyone.

The Russian Czar, who had been steadily moving his armies southward toward India, extending his empire yearly, was known to be suborning the Shah of Persia from an old alliance with England. The Shah's new and perhaps more powerful ally had persuaded him to cross the frontier of Afghanistan and lay siege to the city of Herat. It was frighteningly obvious to Lord Auckland in India, no less than to Lord Palmerston in London, that the siege was the first step in the Czar's battle for India, and they decided that he must be stopped.

But he would have to be stopped in such a way that his altogether friendlier dealings with the English in Europe were undamaged. Therefore, Lord Palmerston could not seem to be involved at all. What must be done in Afghanistan must seem to be done by Lord Auckland alone and to have nothing to do with Russia. It was the Governor General who had to find the excuse, and the means, not only to stop the Russians but also to turn them back and to effect the permanent removal of their envoy from Caubul.

To that end he had sent Mr. Macnaghten to Lahore to negotiate a new alliance with the Sikhs of the Punjab, which lay between British India and Afghanistan. Without the Sikhs' support any expedition across the Afghan frontier would be doomed. And it seemed likely that the Sikhs' leader, Runjeet Singh, could also furnish an excuse for it.

Some years earlier he had seized the city of Peshawar from the Dost Mohammed Khan, and since then several raids had been made across the border to retake it. If Auckland could negotiate a satisfactory treaty with Runjeet, he might be able to justify moving his troops up to Afghanistan as an effort to protect the territory of an ally.

The next problem would be how to act once the troops were established in Afghanistan. Lord Auckland therefore summoned to Simla Alexander Burnes, whom he had previously sent to Caubul to assess the character and loyalty of its ruler, the Dost.

Burnes had been much impressed with the Dost, and he believed that there would have been no question of Russians in Afghanistan if the English had been more generous in their support of its ruler. But when Burnes reached Simla in July, he discovered that Auckland and Macnaghten had decided that the Dost was too dangerous to English interests and would have to be removed.

Their excuse for this piece of meddling in the affairs of a country over which they had no rights was to be Shah Soojah-ool-Mulk, once king in Caubul but who had escaped unharmed to Lahore thirty years earlier.

Most deposed Afghan kings had been killed—or simply blinded—by their successors; indeed, the Shah's own brother Zemaun had had his eyes put out before he, too, had reached the sanctuary of the Punjab. But Soojah had retained all his faculties and could be presented to the Afghans and the world (or as much of it as was interested in the machinations of the English) as a monarch, unjustly thrown from his kingdom, being returned to power by the disinterested generosity of a third party.

He would be indebted to the English both for his restoration and for the large subsidy they promised him, and so he would be far easier to control than his cousin, the Dost. But just in case he should waver in his loyalties, there would have to be plenty of English soldiers in Caubul to stiffen him. The Shah was to be provided with English officers for his own army and some regiments of the Company's to help him control his country.

Many of the subtleties of Lord Auckland's position escaped the notice of the English in India, but all were agog at the thought of a magnificent foray that would display their invincibility and provide ample opportunities for advancement and fame. There was hardly a political or military officer in the whole country who was not intriguing for a place on the expedition.

Charles Byrd, a detached spectator in Simla, probably saw further into the background of the picture than most of the English. He was both a political historian and an outsider, and to him at least it was clear that the government in London, who gave Lord Auckland his instructions, would have to tread very delicately to avoid disturbing Count Nesselrode, the Czar's envoy in Europe.

The American, like others, waited with interest to see how the difficulties would be resolved, and he eased the tedium of life in Simla with his pursuit of Lady Beaminster while he waited.

They met at one of the innumerable picnics held in late May before the rains came to put an end to outdoor life.

After luncheon, Perdita left the chattering party behind to wander slowly through the valley, allowing the tranquil beauty of the place to soak into her. And it was beautiful: the water of the stream was the clear, hard, greenish blue of aquamarines, except where the rocks churned it into white foam. The white cedars scented the air with their pepperiness, which mingled seductively with the gentler scent of the wild white dog roses that wreathed and tumbled through the big dark trees. Looking up for a moment, Perdita was enchanted with the sight of one spray smothered in small white flowers. Arching against the translucent blue of the sky, the flowers curiously echoed the small, soft, pearl-colored clouds that drifted idly by at the edges of her vision. Birds sang to each other, and the long-tailed butterflies flipped past her to settle for a second or two on the honey-rich flowers before tossing themselves into the air again.

She was far enough away from her companions for the sound of their voices to be drowned in the birdsong, and she thought to herself that heaven, if there were such a place, might look and smell and sound rather like that valley. She paused in the shade of an immense tree to reach up and smell a spray of roses, a smile on her half-parted lips and the glint of happiness in her blue eyes.

Charles Byrd had followed her and stood watching her with pleasure. His own taste had previously been for the vapidly pretty, whose shallow minds and conventional chatter promised satisfaction without the threat of emotion. He was surprised to find himself so intrigued by this virtuous creature, however charming her perfect oval face and increasingly alluring figure. He longed to touch her, and occasionally as they waltzed in one or other of Simla's larger houses, he had believed that she, too, felt the first small shivers of desire. He watched her as she stood oblivious to him and thought about how to break what he felt was a half-spun web of enchantment that was threatening to enmesh him completely. She sighed, and he said her name quietly.

Perdita turned slowly, almost languorously, to see him standing quite close to her with the sun glistening on his fair hair. His greenish eyes were narrowed against the glare, but his delicately cut lips were relaxed and smiling. It seemed as though he were part of the world in which she had lost herself. As she smiled back at him, his hands started to stretch out toward her in an involuntary movement, which he checked before saying formally, "Forgive me for disturbing you, Lady Beaminster."

She blushed, which amused him, and waved his apology aside. "You do not."

He smiled again and searched for something acceptable to say to control his sudden desire. "How is your son?"

"Well, I think," she said, but her face lost some of its happiness.

Charles said gently, "What is it that troubles you about him?"

"Oh, I don't want to bore you with my maternal prattle."

"You could never bore me."

She looked up quickly as he spoke, and then laughed. "I am very sure that I could. But since you ask, I am troubled at the way the servants treat him. Not only do they keep telling him what a brave warrior he will be when he is older, but his ayah always addresses him as *chota rajah* or *bahadur,* and the other day I heard her say, 'When you are grown you will be a great man and beat all the black men from the Ganges to Attock.' "

Charles felt the moment of intense emotion relax and said more easily, "Oh, I shouldn't let that worry you. All children's nurses say absurd things to them, and presumably you will send your son back to England before too long. Or at least when it is time for him to go to school."

"I suppose so. But he will have a terrible time if he goes straight from being a king here to being an ordinary small boy in an English school. Tell me, Mr. Byrd, what would your mother have done in such circumstances?"

His eyes danced as he said, "Now I shall bore *you.*"

She shook her head and indeed listened in genuine interest as he told her more about the woman who, he had already made it clear, was at the center of his heart.

But soon he checked himself and, despite her protests, refused to tell her any more about his childhood. But he did say, "I wish you knew her. She would like you so much."

Perdita felt herself blushing once again and tried to stop it by saying, "Would she? It is charming of you to say so."

"Yes, she would. She admires the English. And you are like her: gentle and yet as strong as anyone."

"You are being very kind but quite wrong, I'm afraid. I am not strong at all. In fact, I am the most shocking coward. Almost everything frightens me."

She did not understand why he smiled at her in just that way, but she felt enfolded by his obvious approval. Then he said, "I am afraid that I have made you conspicuous by seeking you out like this. Perhaps I should walk on for a while to let you return alone." He put out his hand. "Until we meet again."

Perdita took the hand and liked the firm clasp of his long fingers. She watched him walk away, surprised at his concern for the conventions they both found absurd. But when she returned to the chattering, bustling party, she caught several inquisitive glances and was glad that he had not returned at her side. She wished that Charles were one of Marcus's particular friends so that she could see as much of him, undisturbed by the curiosity of people like Maria Jamieson, as of the men of her husband's regiment.

Ten

Neither of the Beaminsters saw Charles Byrd again until a dinner on June 14, given by the Colvins. The weather had been disagreeably hot in the meantime, and the heaviness of the air heralded the rains, as did the incessant plague of fleas. Everyone agreed that the more you had your rooms cleaned and agitated, the worse the beasts became, and at times it seemed that their bites would bring social life to an end even more quickly than the wet. It was said that at least one lady would faint at each dinner from the torment of bites that she could not scratch.

That particular evening no one actually lost consciousness, but Perdita herself was feeling too unwell to sing and for once refused her hostess's request. She could see irritated disappointment on Emma Colvin's face and understood the cause: meeting each other almost every day, the guests had very little left to say, and without some diversion the endless parties tended to flag after dinner.

Mr. Byrd strolled over to where Perdita stood and said quietly, "I hope you are not ill, Lady B."

"Not at all. Only so very warm. I do not think I could sing tonight; I am so sorry."

"Never mind. It means that you and I can talk. Let me take you to that sofa." As they walked away to the edge of the room, Mrs. Colvin exchanged smiles with little Mrs. Jamieson. Lady Beaminster's predilection for the American's company had not passed unnoticed, even though it caused some surprise. He was so insignificant compared to dear Lord Beaminster.

Perdita, completely unaware that she was providing scandal for her bored acquaintances, said as they sat down, "Do you know, Mr. Byrd, I am surprised to see you still here. I thought you would have escaped weeks ago."

"Alas, I fear I gave myself away to you when we first met. It's true that this town is probably the most tedious spot on earth, but interesting moves will be made here soon, and I would not want to miss them."

"Interesting for your book?"

"Partly. Lord Auckland is providing me with some first-rate material on the management and extension of conquered territory, but there are other things that keep me here." He smiled as he spoke, and Perdita found herself smiling in return.

"I cannot imagine what. You do not like mountains, you hate English ladies, you are homesick for Virginia—"

He interrupted her. "Not Virginia. I know I told you that I sometimes long for home, but it is my mother's house that I miss, not my father's."

"Tell me about it," she said with the warmth of genuine interest.

"Where to start?" he asked, laughing. "It is not like this place at all, although it is her summer home—at the Cape. I suppose it is the color I miss most and the space. Unlike the sickly pink and gray and green of these hills, the Cape seems to be entirely blue and gold, blazingly so in the sun, and the dunes stretch flat for miles. You never feel shut in there. It is the right setting for my mother, too. Like me, she is happier there than in any other place in the world."

"Does she not like Virginia?"

"No," he said curtly, and Perdita hastened to apologize, suppressing a question about why he was not at this Cape if he liked it so much.

He stopped her apology, saying, "Please don't. You can ask me anything you wish. That is just a difficult subject for me to talk about. But I'll try. My mother was born in Boston, and she always found Virginia strange and almost uncongenial, but she lived there as best she could until a few years ago, when she went back to Boston. My father did not understand."

In her desire to comfort him, Perdita said, "It is difficult to see how our parents behave sometimes. My mother left my father in India and took me away from him to a horrible life in England. They had been married only nine years, and she never saw him again."

He understood her motives for speaking as she had and thought it strange that the British could never be direct in their sympathy. He looked at her as she sat beside him, wearing a gown of watery green silk that seemed to suit her quiet beauty, and it struck him for the first time that he would have been bored if she sat in silence, despite her appealing face and figure, which was quite the opposite of his usual reactions to women. He remembered with wry amusement how he used to sit in Caroline Endlesham's carriage in Calcutta wishing that she would just be quiet for once so that he could admire her undistracted by the appalling, stupid things she said. He watched Perdita's face change slightly, and the enveloping kindness in her face shrink into a half-nervous smile of welcome, and he knew that her husband was approaching them. He rose.

"Ah, Byrd," came the cool, pleasant voice of Captain Lord Beaminster. "Hot, isn't it? I do not wonder that you would not sing, my dear. You must be tired."

"A little, but Mr. Byrd has been telling me about America, and I have been diverted from the temperature."

"Indeed. And shall you be returning soon, Byrd?"

"To America? I doubt it. My father believes it would be better if he does not see me for some time, and in any case I am pledged to complete my book on the management of empires before I return."

"I see. Are you taking India as your model? It has not been precisely an empire since the days of the Mahrattas."

"Nevertheless, it provides interesting sidelights on the problems. My chief subjects are the Roman and Venetian models, and since the Venetian was primarily a trading empire, I find the comparisons with your Company useful."

"I see. How interesting. I am sorry we haven't more time to talk now, but I must take my wife home. Perhaps you would dine with us one day next week. My dear?"

Perdita, pleased that they should begin to be friends, smiled and endorsed the invitation. Charles Byrd agreed to come the following Saturday.

Long before Saturday arrived, Perdita had forgotten almost everything, including her growing delight in Byrd's company, in her anxiety over her stepmother. Dr. Drummond had continued to call on Aneila, and it had soon become clear to him that she was suffering from more than a difficult pregnancy. But it was some weeks before he became convinced that his fears were justified.

On the afternoon of Perdita's visit on June 17, he was just leaving the house as she arrived. He tried to banish the concern from his face, knowing how much Lady Beaminster cared for her father's wife and, unlike many of his compatriots, finding that admirable.

She shook hands with him happily before going in to Aneila, whom she found sitting in her favorite chair by the big window in her drawing room. Perdita was immediately struck by how well Aneila looked. Her face was too thin, of course, but it had been so all year, and for once there was some rosy color in her cheeks and her eyes sparkled. She stood up with an effort and said in her fractured English, "You look beautiful, Perdita. You must be very happy."

"Yes, I think I am. But you should not be standing like that. Come, sit down. Was Dr. Drummond pleased? I have not seen you look so well for weeks."

"I do not know. He always tells me to take care, but this time he said very little else. All I have is a small chill that makes me cough."

Resolving to interview the doctor to make him tell her more, Perdita changed the subject by asking for the first time about Aneila's sons. She talked proudly of them and happily, interrupted only by a brief fit of coughing. When Perdita saw the tiny flecks of blood on the fine handkerchief Aneila pressed to her lips, she knew at last what Dr. Drummond feared; and from the way Aneila tried to conceal the handkerchief, she understood that she knew, too.

Later, Perdita was not sure how she had managed to carry on talking peacefully as though nothing mattered very much until it was time for her to leave. She was horrified to realize that Aneila was seriously ill, frightened for her, worried for Edward miles away in Lahore, and passionately sad for herself. She tried not to think selfishly, but it seemed very hard that she should have had only a few short months to know Aneila, who had turned out to be so much more of a mother than her own. Forbidden resentment flooded her mind at the thought of the implacable fate that seemed to rule the lives of everyone for whom she cared. She wanted to throw herself onto the floor by Aneila's chair and lay her head in Aneila's lap and weep and beg her to say it wasn't true.

Instead she controlled herself, pretended not to have noticed the bloody handkerchief, and talked on about the unimportant things that Aneila seemed to enjoy hearing. But she watched her carefully, and when Aneila's eyelids seemed to grow heavy and her breathing labored, Perdita rose to go, promising to return the following day.

Once in her carriage, she told the driver to take her directly to the doctor's house, while she tried to organize in her mind all the questions she had to ask him and all the things she would have to tell her father in her next letter to Lahore.

Dr. Drummond gave her the confirmation she had sought but dreaded, telling her gravely that quite often a pregnancy could exacerbate tuberculosis.

"It is possible, though unlikely I am afraid, that she will bear the child successfully, but I am afraid there is little chance that she will recover."

"Why did you not tell me sooner?"

"Because you can do nothing for her except continue to give her the illusion of life. Grief will come to you in the end, but I did not want you to burden her with unhappiness in her last weeks. Come, Lady Beaminster; you must not give way. Mrs. Whitney must not suspect that you know of her condition."

"But why does she look so much better?"

"It is one of the cruel illusions of the disease. At this stage the cheeks usually take on such a hectic flush and the eyes sparkle, but it is with the fever and not returning health."

"I see. Thank you for telling me now. I must write to my father at once; it will be a difficult letter." She blotted her eyes and left, resolving to do as he said and keep up the pretense that Aneila would recover, however difficult that might be.

As her buggy rounded the corner by Stirling Castle, she saw Mr. Byrd riding up from the direction of Auckland House. He waved to her, and she asked the driver to stop. While she waited for the American to come up to her, she thought how odd it was that the very sight of him brought comfort. He swung himself down from his horse and came to take her hand, looking carefully into her face.

"What's up, Lady B?" he said. "You don't look happy."

It did not occur to her to pretend to him, and still clinging to his hand, she told him.

He listened in silence until she had finished speaking and then said, "That is very hard. Is Drummond certain?"

"I believe so. He thinks the consumption will develop soon, and there is nothing he can do. And he is not even sure that the child will survive."

"I did not know that there was a child. I don't think you told me that."

"No. It is to be born in October. I begin to think that all this is my fault." He waited silently for her to explain, but when she could speak again, she said only, "I am sorry to have held you up like this, but I am very glad you were here."

"I am glad, too. You know, if you should ever need me and I do not happen to pass by, I hope you will send for me." As he heard himself speak, he was shocked back into self-consciousness. The words could have been understood as a declaration of devotion that he would never have made. It was true that he liked her, admired her, and preferred her company to that of anyone else in the town, but he had long ago determined never to allow flirtation to assume serious proportions. He withdrew his hand and raised his hat formally.

"Good-bye, Mr. Byrd, and thank you," said Perdita before ordering the buggy driver to take her home.

Unfortunately Maria Jamieson and her mother had been driving past the crossroad and had seen the urgency with which the American spoke to Lady Beaminster and the warmth with which she held his hand. They watched avidly until their carriage had passed the interesting couple, whose absorption in each other was such that they never even looked to see who was driving by, and looked at each other in pleasure.

"Poor dear Lady Beaminster," said Mrs. Jamieson. "She cannot know of his reputation. Even so it was not very wise of her to hold his hand in the open street."

"No. But we must not forget that she was never taught how to behave in that peculiar upbringing of hers."

"I think it is your duty, Mama, to tell her." Mrs. Fletcher, remembering the reception of her last piece of advice, disagreed and suggested that a friendly warning from someone her own age might be more acceptable to the erring count-ess.

"Oh, Mama," protested Maria, "you know that she is years older than I." They drove home in conspiratorial silence, and each looked forward to telling her particular circle of friends what she had seen. Maria also looked forward to the opportunity of telling Lady Beaminster just exactly what Mr. Byrd had been doing on his progress up-country.

She called the following day while Perdita was feeding Charlie and had to wait, bored and supercilious, in the draw-ing room while Perdita gave her son his customary time at her breast. Not for anyone would she have cut short her time of physical closeness with the child, and particularly not for Maria Jamieson. But eventually the hard sucking ceased, Charlie's hand relaxed and dropped from her breast, and she realized that he was asleep again. Reluctantly she freed her-self and handed the milky baby to his ayah. Then she tidied herself and walked toward the drawing room, determined not to let her tiresome visitor get under her skin again.

Perdita did not apologize, as she would once have done, for keeping Mrs. Jamieson waiting, and she listened in de-tached silence to her views on the harm that feeding one's child wrought to one's figure and her advice on ways for Perdita to disguise the damage that was already so obvious. Allowing herself only the mild comment that her child's well-being was of more importance to her than retaining a fashionable shape, Perdita watched the superior smile on her visitor's face and hoped yet again that her horrible suspi-cions were wrong. Quite apart from her own humiliation, she hated to think of anyone as kind as Marcus being taken in by Maria's hypocrisy. She was careful never to criticize her in his hearing, and she tried not to watch them or specu-late, but Maria always spoke of him so possessively that it was hard to take no notice, and Perdita could not forget that even Juliana had been afraid that Marcus might one day fall in love with Maria.

She wondered very much why she was being treated to this visit as she listened to the usual stream of information and comments on their friends, and she dreaded the moment when Maria might speak of Marcus. Then she stopped for a second, leaned forward slightly, and said, "There is something I feel I ought to tell you."

Perdita waited in growing misery.

Mrs. Jamieson read her frozen expression as disdain and went on vengefully. "I have recently received a letter from my godmother in Calcutta, telling me about Mr. Charles Byrd, and I think it my duty to tell you about him."

Perdita heard her out in silence, almost unbearably relieved but hating the pious voice almost as much as the malice that hid behind the sugared smiles and shallow, dark eyes. When she was sure that the tale of seduction and adultery and desertion was over, she said, "Maria, do you never tire of seeking out human weakness and unhappiness? Why does it give you so much pleasure to tattle like this?" Mrs. Jamieson blushed, but whether in shame or anger Perdita could not tell, and after a moment or two she said sanctimoniously, "It gives me no pleasure. On the contrary, it saddens me to see people behaving so badly, but I had to tell you. It would not have been fair, knowing what I do of Mr. Byrd's reputation, to have allowed him to continue to take advantage of you."

"I cannot imagine what you are talking about. Mr. Byrd is a friend of my husband's, to whom I very much enjoy talking. What he has done or will do is as little concern of mine as it is of yours. And now, if you will forgive me, I must change. My husband is expecting me to ride with him in half an hour."

Ruthlessly dismissed, Maria Jamieson had no option but to leave with as much dignity as she could muster, thinking that both she and her mother had underestimated Lady Beaminster. Perdita herself was left almost shaking with dislike. The intelligence about Charles Byrd had shocked her even though she found it almost impossible to believe that a man who talked to her so intelligently and never made the kind of advances she had once suffered from Mortimer Blandfield could be a rake. But it was the desire to hurt, which was clear in Maria Jamieson's disclosures, that distressed her most.

Marcus knew that something was wrong as soon as he saw her. Hoping that he had not brought that look back into her eyes, he asked what had happened. She could not speak to him of Maria, and so she said, "Only that I have had some visitors this afternoon who told me that Lord Auckland is supposed to have said he would burn Herat if he could. It seemed to bring nearer all the terribleness of what might happen if you are sent to this war."

To her astonishment, Marcus came to hold her hands as he said slowly, "You must not be afraid, Perdita. All that is going to happen is that we shall march into Afghanistan with a few Sikhs for appearances, fight a skirmish or two, and escort Shah Soojah to his capital." He looked down at her very kindly. "Would you prefer to go away? Juliana has just written me another wailing letter pleading with me to sell out, or at least send you and Charlie back to England. And there is no doubt you would both be safer there."

"Oh, no, Marcus, please don't send me away. Juliana told me what she was doing in her letter to me, and I wrote back at once that neither of us wants to leave India."

"Do you like it so much, then? I have sometimes thought you were not very happy." She looked at him, wondering what had prompted such uncharacteristic questions. Then she answered him as honestly as she could, ignoring both the war and Maria Jamieson. "During those years in Norfolk I sometimes used to think that one day I might be free of fear and unhappiness—and those horrible convulsions. I never thought I should be as healthy or as positively happy as I am now. Because of you, Marcus. If I seem nervous at times, it is caused by particular things, such as the war or Aneila's illness, but never by the life I lead here with you. Don't send me away. Please."

He stood in front of her, wanting to give her something of the openness she gave him, but he could not. The only thing he wanted to tell her would smash that open trust in her smile, and she would hate him, as he was coming to hate himself. He saw her smile waver and knew he must say something. So often she tried to reach him, and so rarely could he bring himself to meet her. All he could manage was, "Good. You at least have a right to be happy."

The bitterness in his voice stung her, and she said, "And are you not happy?"

"I? Oh, well enough. The ponies will be chilled if we leave them much longer. Will you come?" She recognized the finality in his voice and knew that she must tread no further, and so she picked up the skirt of her fashionable dark blue dress and preceded him out of the house.

The air seemed even more oppressive than usual, but the sky was magnificent: half the blue of recent weeks and half angry, dark clouds from behind which the sun blazed, turning their edges to quicksilver. Marcus looked up suspiciously and said, "Would you rather stay at home today, my dear? I do not like the look of those clouds."

"Oh, no. I should like to ride; I seem to have had no exercise for days. Ah, here he is. Good afternoon, Captain Thurleigh."

"Lady Beaminster. It almost looks like rain at last."

"I do hope so. If it does not come soon, this stuffiness will become unbearable. And it will be good to see the valleys green again. It always seems so odd that they should dry out so fast."

"Yes, indeed," he answered, making what Perdita recognized as an effort to be civil. They rode on together, leaving Marcus to bring up the rear, out of the town toward Jacko.

They had hardly been out for half an hour when the storm began with a single immense crash of thunder. There was an eerie stillness for a full minute afterward, and then the rain began, not lightly at first but in one tremendous downpour. They turned back at once, but Perdita was quickly drenched. She found it very difficult to see through the curtain of water. A lightning flash startled her surefooted pony and made it shy. It could have been very dangerous, for the path was narrow just there and the slope below steep and very rocky, but she was riding on the outside of Captain Thurleigh. He whipped his hand across to grasp the reins just above her pony's bit, bringing it to a standstill with rigid strength. Through the sudden nausea that took her, she heard Marcus's anxious voice.

Thurleigh answered for her. "No harm done, old fellow, though I dare say Lady Beaminster is shaken."

"Yes," said Perdita, trying to control her chattering teeth and deep inward rigor. "But I shall be all right. Thank you, Captain Thurleigh. I am most grateful to you. But I think we should go back as fast as we can." Her face was drained of all vestiges of color, and her eyes looked almost as dark as her dress. Marcus, who had dismounted and come running up to her, grasped her shoulder and said, "Do not be afraid, my dear. I shall lead you back. Hold on."

She was going to thank him when she caught sight of an expression of revulsion on his friend's face and was silenced. She thought later that she must have misread it, for when they eventually arrived back at the house and she thanked him once more, he was wearing his usual mask of arrogant civility. He told her again that it was nothing, bowed, and rode off, leaving her and Marcus to go in.

They discovered immediately that the rain had brought down the ceiling of their dining room. The house was in an uproar, with the *khalasses* carrying silver and furniture out into the hall, workmen yelling like monkeys on the mud roof as they tried to repair the damage, and the old butler trying to control them all, apologize to the lord-sahib, and call the lady-sahib's ayah all in the same breath.

Perdita could only laugh. Marcus looked worried and said he thought she must be overwrought and should lie down.

"I am not hysterical, Marcus, dear. Not quite, at any rate. Well, we certainly won't be able to have guests to dine to-night. Will you send a note to Mr. Byrd while I get these wet clothes off and see what can be done?"

She went away and returned a short time later to take charge, calm the *khitmagar*, organize the *khalasses*, and ask Charlie's ayah if he had been upset by the commotion. Marcus had not known how much progress she had made with her Hindustani and was almost as impressed with that as with her newly acquired decisiveness.

"After that horrid shock this afternoon, I expected you would be prostrate, not organizing the household like this."

"Well, someone had to," she answered, surprised at his questioning anything so obvious. "If we had left the servants to themselves, they would have been running around in circles for half the night."

"You continually surprise me, Perdita."

Eleven

The rains continued almost without ceasing until the end of August, putting an end to the entertaining of early summer. There was usually half an hour's pause before dinner each day, and then Marcus and Perdita joined the rest of the Simla residents on their ponies for a quick canter, reveling in the fresher air and the glorious sight of the mountains freed for a moment or two of their burden of cloud and silvery pink in the setting sun.

In spite of the dreadful weather, Perdita never failed to visit Aneila, even though she often became disagreeably soaked on the drive. She and Dr. Drummond had both hoped that the cooler temperature brought by the rains would give his patient some relief, but it was not so. During August her face and hands became thinner than ever until the bones around her eyes showed starkly through the skin and gave her once lovely face a monkey-like look.

Edward had written both to her and to Perdita telling them that he was trying to get away from Lahore, but it seemed that Runjeet had taken a liking to him and invented pretext after pretext for keeping him; he could not jeopardize the alliance by offending the old ruler. But he wrote encouragingly whenever he could and tried to calm Perdita's fears about what would happen. By the end of August she had almost forgotten that there was to be a war as it became obvious that Aneila was fading fast. She wrote to Edward to tell him of what seemed like a race between approaching death and the birth of the child.

In the end, the child, a fragile tiny girl, was born alive on October 1, the day the Governor General made public his plans to invade Afghanistan.

Perdita had just heard Marcus read out the first paragraph of Lord Auckland's manifesto when Dr. Drummond called to give her the news and to tell her that Mrs. Whitney was as comfortable as could be expected. She wanted to leave at once, but as Marcus pointed out, she could hardly have reached the house before dark, and there was no reason for such haste. She recognized the sense in what he said, and when the doctor had left she sat down again and tried to concentrate on what he read to her.

The Right Hon. the Governor General of India having, with the concurrence of the Supreme Council, directed the assemblage of a British force for service across the Indus, his Lordship deems it proper to publish the following exposition of the reasons which have led to this important measure.

But Perdita's mind was too taken up with thoughts of Aneila and her child to understand half of what Marcus read. By the following morning all she could remember of the Governor General's reasons for going to war were: that the Dost Mohammed Khan had made an unprovoked attack on Runjeet Singh; that he was actively engaged in promoting Persia's designs, which were wholly at variance with its alliance with Great Britain; and that the Governor General had decided to reconcile the differences of all parties by escorting some other Afghan chief to Caubul to reign in the Dost's stead.

It made little sense to Perdita, and when she arrived at Aneila's house, the sight of her almost transparent face put it right out of her mind. Aneila's eyes glittered with a sinister brilliance, but the hollows beneath them were like dark pits, and in her thin hands the veins seemed almost like ropes.

Perdita sat down by her bed, trying to keep up a confident smile as she talked quietly to her stepmother, but her lips trembled once too often. Aneila saw her distress, and said, "You must not be sad, Perdita. It is karma."

"How can I not? So many people need you, and you . . ." For a minute or two she could not continue and turned her face away from those sunken eyes that saw so much.

"You do not need me, Perdita. You are stronger than you know. And Edward will be sorry, but he will be all right. My sons are men now, and so it is only my little daughter who needs me. Will you take her?"

Through her tears Perdita said, "Of course I shall, and I shall try to teach her to be like you: forgiving, loving, and brave." She would have said more, but a deadful paroxysm of coughing shook Aneila and left her too exhausted to talk.

Dr. Drummond came again in the afternoon and told Perdita that she should not be there.

"It can be only a few hours now, and you can do nothing to help. You have your child and your husband to care for."

"I must stay, Dr. Drummond."

"Have you ever seen anyone die? It is not a pretty sight."

"My own mother. I know what to expect."

"But not of consumption? No? Then you cannot know. This is not an easy death or a silent one. As Mrs. Whitney becomes progressively weaker, she will be unable to cough, and as the fluid collects in her throat she will begin to drown." He saw horror in Perdita's eyes and said, "I am sorry to be brutal, but it is as well that you should be prepared."

"I will stay nevertheless. How could I leave her alone now with only servants?"

"She won't be alone. I will be here." Perdita felt deeply grateful to the man who, in spite of being in the train of the Governor General himself, was prepared to watch at the deathbed of an Indian woman who was despised by almost all the Europeans who were his other patients.

They returned to the bedroom and sat on either side of the huge, white-curtained bed as the sun drained out of the sky.

Aneila's was indeed a horrifying end. Perdita ached to do something, anything, to relieve the laboring figure who lay propped up on the lace-edged pillows struggling to breathe through the blood and mucus in her throat. At one moment Perdita could not bear to sit doing nothing and stood over her to help her up, hoping to ease the breathing, but Aneila gasped. "Don't. Your breath is like ice on my skin."

Perdita went sadly back to her chair to watch. Aneila's hair had been cut short to relieve the fever. Perdita thought she had never seen a sadder sight than Aneila's face, beaky now and as pale as any Englishwoman's, lying with the feathery streaks of black hair across it. Her eyes were open and conscious throughout the sixteen hours she took to die. The sound of her terrible breathing was echoed by the sad cries of her child, who had been whisked out of the sickroom at the instant of her birth and was being cared for by the servants.

Eventually, just as dawn was breaking in a pale gold over the mountains outside the window, Perdita saw the figure on the pillows relax, and for one blessed moment she thought she was asleep.

Dr. Drummond waited for a moment and then came around the bed to lift Perdita from her chair. Her knees buckled, but he held her firmly, took her out of the room, and called for her carriage.

"There is nothing you can do here now, Lady Beaminster. I shall arrange everything, and you must get home."

She seized his hand and said, "But I must take the child. I promised her I would look after the child."

"Not now. She will be adequately cared for by the servants here, and I do not think Lord Beaminster would be . . . I believe you should consult him first."

"Dr. Drummond, that baby is my sister. I cannot leave her in a house like this with only servants. Unless you believe that she could communicate the disease to my son, I must take her with me."

It would have been easy for him to lie, but his powerful integrity would not allow him so easy a way out of the dilemma, and so he said, "I can see no signs in the child of the disease, and there is no reason to believe that she could take it to your household. But I must counsel you to think very carefully before you take her."

"I have thought of little else all night. My father cannot take care of her, and Mrs. Whitney was estranged from her own family. There is only I. My husband will understand."

In the face of her determination there was nothing for the doctor to do but acquiesce, although he felt sure that Lord Beaminster would find a way to repudiate the child. What serving officer in India could afford to allow a half-caste child, one as good as illegitimate at that, in his son's nursery?

But Marcus was not like other officers in the Company's service. He had all his mother's disdain for the opinions of the mob, and although he had, and voiced, certain reservations about allowing the child to be brought up with his son, when Perdita said, "We have to. She has no one else, and without Aneila, Charlie and I would probably be dead," he could only agree. He had done her too much damage to deny her that.

Lady Beaminster's latest eccentricity passed almost unnoticed in the excitement over the Simla Manifesto, as it came to be called, and the news that came down from Herat. By October 7, the English were alight with chauvinistic pleasure to hear that the Persians were in retreat from Afghanistan, fought off entirely because of the bravery of a young English soldier, a Lieutenant Pottinger, who had happened to be in Herat and had organized its defense. (In fact, the men who had sent him there secretly were also quite pleased with the way he had carried out their instructions.)

To Perdita the news of the Persians' defeat seemed to remove much of the justification for the Simla Manifesto and Lord Auckland's proposed invasion of Afghanistan. But she had learned not to speak of such things, and she listened in dissenting silence to the fiery excitement of those around her.

At one of the last parties before his lordship's departure for Ferozepore in the Punjab, where he and Runjeet Singh were to review their armies, she danced once more with Mr. Colvin, who said to her, "It is a golden opportunity, Lady Beaminster. If we press on as we have been doing, we shall have a footing across the Indus and in Central Asia that will consolidate our power in India for another century."

"I can understand that, Mr. Colvin, but is there not some risk? Sending all those men into a hostile country, I mean?"

"You must not worry over such things. We are not going to conquer, merely to restore to the thrones of Caubul and Candahar a previously deposed monarch who happens to be better disposed toward us than the Dost. All will be well. But I should not be boring you with such subjects. I hope you will sing for us once more before we go."

Later his request was echoed by many others, and Perdita yielded to them. Her heart was too full of mourning for Aneila (which she could not show conventionally) and of fear for the future to sing the cheerful songs they preferred, and so she chose "The Last Rose of Summer," a plaintive lament that Juliana had recently sent her in a parcel of books.

As always she sang to Marcus, who was standing in a group of gentlemen beside the fireplace. But it was of the man at his side she was thinking as she sang the last verse.

> So, soon may I follow
> When friendships decay,
> And from love's shining circle
> The gems drop away!
> When true hearts lie withered
> And fond ones are flown,
> Oh, who would inhabit
> This bleak world alone?

As her voice died into silence on the last note, her eyes looked across the room directly into Charles Byrd's, and at last she understood. All the companionship of the last five months, all the happiness and interest and warmth, had sprung from her dealings with Charles Byrd. To her utter dismay, she knew then that she loved him.

His own eyes widened in recognition, and a smile of complete intimacy illuminated his face for a moment or two. Mrs. Colvin, walking forward to thank the singer, came between them, and Perdita tried to pull herself together.

A little later she saw him strolling casually toward her. Still rocking from the shock, she evaded him and soon persuaded Marcus to take her home. He thought she looked worried and said, "I had not heard that song before. It is beautiful but so sad."

"I know. Juliana sent it to me, and I could not have sung a cheerful song tonight." She turned to him and impulsively put her hands on his. "Marcus, I wish you didn't have to go to this war."

He made an effort to leave his hand where it lay under his wife's and said as gently as he could, "I can understand that, but you must not worry too much. It is for this that I became a soldier; and we shall be back very soon. I know you will be lonely here, but I expect Whitney will return soon now, and it is not as though you will be alone. All the wives of his lordship's staff will be staying here when we march, and I imagine Mrs. Fletcher and—and the others will stay, too.

There would be little point in their returning to the station when the regiment marches north."

Perdita withdrew her hands and said, "Yes, I know. I did not mean to fuss. And there will be no loneliness with little Charlie and Aneila."

The apology she had felt obliged to make emphasized the difference between her dealings with Marcus and those with Charles Byrd. With Mr. Byrd she never felt the need to excuse or explain anything she said; she knew that he understood her. She valued his good opinion, but she had never felt that she needed to perform tricks to win it. When she was with Marcus, she always found herself trying to anticipate his moods and his reactions to what she did or said, and yet she never felt she really knew him. Charles Byrd knew her, and she him.

Unaware that most women spent their lives trying to feel as she felt for Charles Byrd, she tried to banish the thought. Marcus was her husband, and whether or not he was faithful to her, she could not but feel that her love for Charles was the extreme of disloyalty. Suddenly she wanted to do something for Marcus to make up for it, but all she could think of was to press herself more than ever into the background of his life during the few days before he was expecting to leave.

Had she been able to read his mind, she would have known of his gratitude for her restraint; but she could not.

She tried also to keep out of Charles Byrd's way, afraid that he would guess what had happened to her if they talked. But it was inevitable that they would meet in so small a town. They encountered each other riding out to Jacko one afternoon. Perdita was with Marcus; Charles Byrd, alone. Marcus called out to him to ride with them, and he brought his chestnut alongside.

His first courteous words to Lady Beaminster were courteously answered, but then she dropped behind so that he was left conversing with her husband, unable to look back without rudeness.

He was disconcerted. The day after the last ball, he had sat contentedly on his veranda smoking a cigar and pondering on the possibilities the evening had presented. Too experienced in his dealings with women not to understand the expression in her eyes while she sang to him, he felt as though he might after all be able to settle the unlikely and tiresome desire he felt for her.

He had been given permission to join the Army of the Indus on its march to Ferozepore, from where he would ride on alone, except for his servants, to Persia and on to Russia and Europe. It would seem therefore the ideal moment for a consummation and settlement of his feelings. There could be no lingering, disenchanted diminution of attraction; only a sharp parting before the glow faded. They could both, he thought, enjoy the ache of deprivation that way and keep the memory of "love" undamaged for as long as they chose. Carefully stubbing out his cigar, he leaned back in the long, cushioned chair, looking out toward the valley and thinking of ways to overcome the practical difficulties.

Lady Beaminster was not experienced in intrigue, he was sure, and so it was more than usually important that all should go smoothly and in guaranteed privacy. Any nervousness on her part would quite ruin the bittersweet moment of fulfillment and loss that he planned.

Looking up at the moon, a thread of a crescent in the black sky, he felt a faint stirring of the disgust that he had thought long conquered. An image of his father's activities slid into his mind like a scar, and the memory of his mother's pain opened it again.

Reminding himself that he had no wife to hurt and that Captain Lord Beaminster was manifestly not in love with his, Charles Byrd resolved to proceed, only to be foiled by his quarry's determined evasion.

He called several times unsuccessfully and began to wonder yet again whether she had been treated to gossip about him. After her coolness when they met out riding, he was sure of it. The ache he felt had none of the elegiac pleasure he had wanted.

The army marched on November 6, and Charles Byrd was disturbed to realize that his disappointment was caused not so much by his failure to seduce a beautiful woman as by his suspicion that he had left her thinking badly of him.

For her part, Perdita felt a regret so sharp that it was not assuaged even by the knowledge that she had not betrayed her shameful feelings for him.

Twelve

With the army went the Governor General, his sisters, all his officers and political advisers—everything, in fact, that had made Simla such a fount of gaieties for the season. The wives and daughters who were left behind faced a bleak six months: there could be no parties or dinners; picnics, even walks, were impossible as the snow began to fall; and with the expense of going to war, many of the husbands had had to retrench and pack their wives together like plums in a bottle. One small house was stuffed with five wives and their assorted children, all expected to share the same drawing room.

Perdita, visiting one of them one morning early in December, could only feel grateful that she had the freedom of her father's house. She was nearly sure that Marcus would never have condemned her to quite such an ordeal, but nevertheless she was glad that she had not had to put her trust in him to such a test. During one pause in the conversation she murmured something sympathetic to her hostess, who said, sighing, "Yes, Lady Beaminster, it is a little difficult. But so far we have not quarreled once, and it is a comfort to know that the expenses are being shared in this way. After all, the costs of this war are very high."

"But why? I beg your pardon, but surely the Company pays for the war." A pitying smile greeted Perdita's absurd ignorance.

"The Company does not pay for its officers' horses or personal servants, and each of them, you know, was expected to take a minimum of ten. Then there were all the other things, such as soap and cigars and linen—everything that makes a campaign supportable. Surely Lord Beaminster took servants and equipment with him?"

"Oh, yes, I believe so. It is just that I never really thought about it. He said so little of his preparations, and—well, since I am living at Whitney House, there are all my father's servants as well as my own. I had not thought about it."

The familiar expression of disdainful superiority crossed

the woman's face, and Perdita took her leave as soon as she could, wondering when, if ever, she would be accepted by the other wives. Too often she felt that their company was insupportable and that becoming like them would be like surrendering to despair; but at the same time she hated to feel disliked and excluded and tried again and again to do and say the things they all thought were right.

When she heard that her father was to return to Simla in time for Christmas, she felt as though she had been reprieved from some dreadful punishment. When he actually arrived, on December 20, she stood in the hall, her hands held out to him and joy shining in her eyes.

"Papa."

He ignored the servants, the baggage, and the packet of letters he had brought for her and walked quickly to take both her hands and kiss her cheek.

"Perdita, my dear child. You look wonderful, so different from the poor, pale creature of last April. I have missed you."

"And I you, Papa. Come, come in and sit down while they unpack for you."

He dropped one of her hands and led the way into the large beautiful drawing room into which, for once, the thin winter sunshine was flooding. He looked around, as though reminding himself of the place, and then led her to a striped sofa near the crackling fire.

They sat down, and a sudden shyness caught Perdita by the throat. There was so much she wanted to say to him of Aneila and her child, but somehow she could not start. He seemed to understand, for after a little time he broached the subject himself.

"My dear, thank you for your letters. It helped to know that you were with her. It must have been difficult for you, remembering your mother's death as you must have."

"Papa, please. I wanted to tell you . . ." She paused, and then taking courage from his warm clasp on her hand and the affection in his clear eyes, she went on, choosing her words with care. "I wanted to tell you, in all the letters I sent, that I understood why you cared for her so much. When I came to know her, I, too, saw how different she was. I wanted you to know that I understood."

"Thank you, Perdita." Something in his voice or face made her look away from him into the fire. She watched the pale orange and blue flames that leapt and died among the fragrant pine boughs, and after a few minutes, in a firmer tone, he changed the subject. "Tell me about your boy. Is he well?"

"Yes." Perdita looked back at him, smiling. "He and Annie both. It is a very selfish way to think, but I cannot help being glad that we have had to stay up here. I dread to think what effect the Plains would have had on two such young children. Although," she added, "I do wish it had not been a war that kept us here."

"Don't fear for Beaminster. They are unlikely to see much fighting if all goes according to plan. But read his letter. I am sure he will tell you all that has happened. There is one from an American gentleman as well. I gather that you all became acquainted here."

Edward was interested to see a faint, camellia-pink blush well up into her cheeks. To save her embarrassment he said, "They will have unpacked my boxes now. I shall go and change."

Alone in the light, golden room, Perdita picked up the two flat packets. The one addressed in unfamiliar writing was much fatter than her husband's. She wanted to know what it contained and yet felt a strong reluctance to break open the shell she had grown around her feeling for Charles Byrd. She laid his letter down and broke the seal on her husband's.

It was a brief, kind inquiry about her health and that of the children and went on to give a few bare details of the army's march. Disappointed but not much surprised, Perdita took up the other letter. With an odd dryness at the back of her throat and a slight trembling in her long fingers, she opened it and read.

Ferozepore, November 30

I was distressed to leave without bidding you good-bye, for I believe I must have offended you in some way. We were so comfortable together that I found your coldness hard to understand when I met you riding that day. If I have offended you, I must beg you to forgive me, for I value your good opinion.

Please believe me when I write that I am your most obedient servant.

Charles Byrd

Postscript: On the next pages you will find the letter that I would have written to the Lady B. I thought I knew.

Conscious of a curious tingle of pleasure and a little ashamed by the sensation, Perdita turned to the other letter.

My dear Lady B.

The Army of the Indus! The grandiloquence of its name has been matched only by the absurdity of its ceremonies. There seems to be an extraordinary hysteria about this camp and an idea that some momentous benefit is about to be conferred on mankind. Only yesterday I was told by one of your politicals that "this will be the first time the flags of a civilized nation will have flown across the Indus since the days of Alexander the Great."

But will they ever get to the Indus, let alone across it?

They seem to make difficulties for themselves wherever they can, and to the shame and horror of the commander it has been discovered that the Sikh Army has better discipline and can carry out its maneuvers far more efficiently than the Army of the Indus. They console themselves with an unfounded belief that the Sikhs would run away if they faced a real battle! No one seems to have tried to discover whether perhaps the Afghans, too, may have such unsuspected talents. They are all too busy telling each other that history is being made here "on the banks of the Sutlej."

The first great review was held a couple of days ago, on the twenty-eighth. It was to be the formal meeting of the two most important leaders in India: His Lordship the Governor General and the Lion of the Punjab. Imagine the excitement!

Well, the Lion turned out to look like a one-eyed,

whiskered shrew, and such was the excitement and the pushing and shoving that the ceremonial greetings turned into a circus. Picture it for yourself: the Lion/shrew dressed in coarse red cloth, rather dirty, squatting on his huge, gorgeously caparisoned elephant, rode in the center of a line that moved ponderously toward the Durbar tent just as His Lordship and Sir Henry Fane, similarly mounted, urged their *mahouts* forward. The inevitable happened: the two lines collided. Sikhs rushed forward to protect their maharaj; English officers dashed up to see the fun; *mahouts* cried out and pulled helplessly on their *ankuses*. Eventually, amid all the running around and yellings, Lord Auckland simply leaned forward out of his *howdah*, very neat in his dark blue and gold, and, with one hand, plucked the little red Lion off his plunging elephant. As you can imagine, the Sikhs took a very sideways glance at all that, until they saw their king splendidly protected by Sir Henry, who is about three times his height and weight.

Unfortunately their fears were not quieted for very long. It seems that when the Lion was escorted into the tent that had been set aside to display the Company's gifts to him, he was so excited by the sight of two very modern, very splendid, nine-pound howitzers that he fell over a pile of shells and prostrated himself in the dust before your guns. Not a good omen, thought the Sikhs. Though I expect Sir William Macnaghten was pretty pleased. He does not seem to care for them at all.

Perdita was still laughing when Edward returned. He was intrigued to know what had brought such a sparkle to her face.

"Beaminster much to say?" he asked casually.

"I beg your pardon?" she said, looking up from the pages. Then, as the sense of what he had said triumphed over the words she had been reading, "No, not very much. This one is from Mr. Byrd, a most diverting account of the camp at Ferozepore and all the spectacle. I almost wish I had been there to see all those elephants and horses and gold and scarlet. It sounds magnificent and absurd at once."

"It certainly had its moments of absurdity. Tell me about

this American. I met him only once when I dined with your husband."

"He is the friendliest creature, and very good company. I miss him sometimes." She caught her father's sardonic eye and blushed again.

"I see you do. Well, be careful."

"Papa, please don't be absurd. I doubt if I shall meet him again, but he writes an amusing letter."

"Shall you answer it?"

"I do not know." She wanted badly to talk to someone about her feelings for Charles Byrd, and Edward would be the ideal confidant: trustworthy, sympathetic. But somehow she could not bring herself to do so. She changed the subject. "Shall we go to the nursery? You will want to see Annie. We have called her that so that when she is a little older, she will not feel strange when she is with other English children."

"I see. But, Perdita, you will not want to keep her now. It was very good of you to care for her, but you and Beaminster cannot be saddled with her all your lives. I can arrange a household for her."

"With you away for months at a time and with no one to mother her? Papa, it would be cruel. Let her stay with a real family. I do not mean to take her from you, but she will be happier in a nursery where she is not alone. I shall take the greatest care of her, I promise."

He looked searchingly at her, trying to see if she was sincere or forcing herself for duty's sake. At last, reassured by her open smile, he said, "I have no doubts on that score."

"You see, a girl needs a mother. It was not until I came to know Aneila that I understood how much. I would like to do for Annie a little of what Aneila did for me."

Edward could not say any more, and so they left the subject there, although later Perdita discovered that he had settled a small fortune on the child for her education and expenses.

That evening at dinner, Perdita found herself talking and talking, as though she had been marooned for months on some uninhabited island. Edward watched her, entertained and amused to see how she had changed in the months he had been away. He wondered a little whether the difference was due to her marriage and motherhood or to the influence of the friendly American. One day he would ask her, but for that evening he was content to listen and enjoy her vivacity.

Once she said, "Papa, this is so comfortable. To be with you again, I mean. It is a little like that first hot weather, only better, because I know so much more."

"About what?" he asked, interested to know how she viewed her transformation.

"Everything. Myself, other people, you. And it is so good to have someone I can talk to again."

"Since Beaminster left, you mean?"

"Not exactly. We talk of course, but not like this. I often feel that he is trying to make conversation at me, instead of telling me things he wants me to know, or asking because he wants to know about me. I was really thinking of Mr. Byrd." She stopped, but Edward prompted her with a smile that told her how much he already understood. It gave her enough courage to continue.

"It was not until I became acquainted with Charles Byrd that I understood what it all means. I'm sorry, that is not very clear."

"Never mind. Go on."

"Well, I loved Marcus because he was kind, because he did not frighten me. I admired him for all sorts of reasons, and when he wanted to marry me, I felt as though he were offering me a sort of armor. I thought if I were his wife, I should never be afraid again. And that seemed to be love."

"Yes?"

"Then I began to know Aneila, and it did not seem strange anymore that you should love her, because there could be no one kinder or more gentle."

"But that was only part of it," said Edward, looking at her with eyes so naked in their sorrow that she wanted to put her arms around him and rock him as she rocked the babies.

"Papa, dear, I know that now. And it was Charles Byrd who taught me."

"What precisely?"

"That loving someone does not consist in gratitude for comfort or for protection. It comes from knowing them and being known; wanting the same things; finding the same things funny or important; being able to talk as freely as you would talk to yourself; not worrying about whether he agrees with you or not, because you know that he will understand why you think as you do." She was silent for a moment or two, trying to sort out exactly what she did mean, and then she found some words.

"I suppose it is recognizing that when you are with him, you become whole."

"And so what did you do?" asked Edward, moved by both her experience and her words. She laughed a little bitterly.

"I tried to pretend that it had not happened. And I thought I could make it happen with Marcus now that I understood. But, Papa, Marcus doesn't want me to know him." She turned away so that he should not see how close she was to tears. But he heard them in her voice.

He said very gently, "And what will you do about Charles Byrd's letter?"

"I will answer it."

But she had no time before Christmas. With Edward back in the house, there seemed to be none of the aching, empty hours to which she had had to become accustomed. He knew that the children were too young to understand, but he was determined to celebrate Christmas in as dramatic a way as possible, and that involved her in a lot of work.

On the day itself he presented Perdita with a glorious necklace of emeralds interspersed with big pearls, telling her, "Runjeet gave it to me when I left Lahore, and I would like you to have it."

"It is lovely, Papa," she said sincerely. But there was an odd look of anxiety about her eyes.

"What is the matter, Perdita? I know there's an old tale that green is an unlucky color, but I can't imagine even the most superstitious of people taking that as far as emeralds. Or don't you care for them?"

"Heavens, no. I think it's the most wonderful piece of jewelry I have seen. But . . ." She paused and blushed. Then she said quickly, almost stammering, "It is only that I have heard that all such gifts have to be passed on to the Company. I am sorry, Papa. I do not mean to offend you." She looked shyly up at him and was both disconcerted and relieved to see that his lean face was amused. His blue eyes were narrowed in laughter.

"My dear innocent. Don't you think that after nearly thirty-five years I know the Company's rules? I bought it back."

"Bought it?" she echoed, looking down at the fabulous jewels in her hands. There were eight large drop emeralds, each separated by ten perfectly matched pearls. Although she knew very little about precious stones, Simla conversation had taught her enough to know that this was worth more than a few hundred pounds.

At last the meaning of several snide remarks she had overheard became plain. She raised her eyes again and said, "Then we are rich?"

Her tone of astonished awe struck him as being very funny, and he bellowed with laughter. When he could speak again, he asked, "How did you suppose we could have lived like this if I were not?"

She looked around the drawing room, for the first time really noticing not only that it was calm and beautiful but also that it was at least as large as the rooms of Auckland House, that the carpets were more luxurious than any others she had yet seen in India, and that everything from the curtains to the wall shades was of the finest quality. She, too, started to laugh as she recognized her full absurdity.

"Oh, Papa, it is too silly. I just thought that housekeeping in India must be much cheaper than it is in England. And I never thought about why people like the Fletchers live in such horrid surroundings compared to these. Oh, dear, no wonder they dislike me so much."

"You sound almost relieved," he said, surprised by her tone.

"I am. It always seemed that there must be something very wrong with me to make them all so critical, and I have really tried to do everything that they want, however foolish it seems, but it did not seem to change them. I never thought they might be merely jealous. Oh, dear, now my present to you is going to seem very frugal."

She handed him the black velvet slippers she had embroidered in gold thread for him and smiled when he kissed her.

"Frugal or not, Perdita, they are very handsome, and I

shall wear them with pleasure. Now, where are those children?"

Five days later she was sitting down to write a reply to Charles Byrd's letter when Edward came into the morning room. He paused in the doorway, thinking what a charming picture she made in her pink-and-white-striped gown, with her loosely dressed curls catching the morning sunlight. He dreaded having to tell her that he was to leave for Calcutta at the end of the week, and so when she looked up, he put off the moment.

"That is a lovely box. It does not look Indian. Where did you find it, Perdita?"

"Lady Beaminster sent it out to me when she wrote to us after Charlie's birth. I think it was meant to say something like, 'Well, at least you have produced a son; this is to express my modified approval of you.' "

Her glinting smile took any bitterness out of the words, and he laughed with her.

"I am glad that you can find her amusing."

"It helps, I find. One day, perhaps, I shall find other things amusing, too, and then there will be nothing to fear."

He decided not to ask her to explain that elliptical but all-too-understandable sentence. Instead he said, "Perdita, I shall have to leave you again. His lordship has written, telling me he wants me to go back down to Calcutta."

Her head drooped a little, and she said shakily, "I do not find that so very amusing."

He felt wrenched for her. Accustomed to traveling on his own, he could still understand something of her loneliness. He said, "If I could take you and the children with me, I should, but you know I cannot. And what would Beaminster say if the army were to return and he found you gone?"

She stiffened her slender neck and brought her chin up to say, "Of course, Papa. We will do very well. But I will miss you."

"I, too. But life here won't be so bad once Auckland and his private staff are back in the spring; although I am not sure how society can be formally pursued with forty-odd ladies and only about twelve gentlemen."

"Yes, we shall be unique in the history of Anglo-India, but

I expect Miss Eden will contrive something." She smiled carefully and went on, "You must not worry about me. I ought not to have said what I did. We will do well enough. I have my books and letters to write, and the children are too young to know what they lack."

Nevertheless, when the day came, she clung to her father as they said good-bye, and he could feel her trying to control herself. He folded his arms about her and rocked her slowly against his chest without speaking. After a while he said gently, "It is not for very long, Perdita, and I'm sure Beaminster will be back soon."

She lifted her head and unlocked her hands from around his neck, sniffed childishly, and said, "I know. I am behaving like a baby. I am sorry."

He brushed the goldish-brown hair from her smooth white forehead, kissed it, and said, "I like it. But I must go now. I shall write to you, and I hope to be back before the next cold spell."

"You will have all the heat in the Plains."

"I know. But it won't hurt me. I'm an old India hand." He smiled and was gone.

Resisting the impulse to collapse onto a sofa and howl like a masterless puppy, Perdita picked up her pale green barège skirts and walked briskly toward the nursery, thinking of all the tasks she had to accomplish and all the entertainments she should attend once the season started in April, trying to suppress all thoughts about the two short weeks she and Edward had spent together. The one she could not quite ignore was the question that returned again and again: *How could my mother have wanted to live apart from him? He is the best company I have known and the kindest man. And how could she have left all this luxury for that dreadful, cold little house in comfortless Fakenham with her sanctimonious brother and his bitter wife? How could she?*

He, meanwhile, riding toward Sabathoo on his way down-country, was wondering about his son-in-law and hoping that his daughter's mixture of unfailing sweetness and sometimes sinewy intelligence would bring Beaminster closer to her once they were together again. For himself, he would have found her irresistible, as the young American clearly did. He wished he had known something about their dealings while he was in Ferozepore so that he could have found out about the man.

So they thought about each other as the distance between them lengthened. Then other concerns gradually drove their personal preoccupations into the background.

Thirteen

Apart from the serious shortage of gentlemen, that season in Simla was much like any other. Gossip and flirtation, balls and picnics, the whole round of time-passing occupations began to speed up after the opening ball at Auckland House on April 17. Perdita, still desperately worried about what might be happening to Marcus, had avoided that, pleading a slight chill, and did her best to get out of all the large formal entertainments that she was afraid would be a severe ordeal without his support or Charles's.

But she went several times to dine en famille with Miss Eden, her brother, and Miss Fanny Eden, finding them entertaining and a better source of intelligence than anything else available. Mr. Macnaghten, now Sir William, had stayed with the army to be official envoy to the court at Caubul once the new king had been installed, but Mr. Colvin had returned with the Edens and could always be relied on for comforting little bits of news.

And they were needed, for it slowly became clear to the waiting wives that all was not well with the army. Despite the enormous number of private servants and baggage animals that the officers had with them and the crates of wine, cigars, soap, and jam, there was little food. The commanders had expected the troops to live off the land through which they marched, but a severe famine and the internecine struggles between the commissariat officers of the Bombay and Bengal divisions of the army, not to speak of the depredations made by bands of Balooch plunderers, had combined to bring the officers and men close to starvation. Rations had to be cut and cut again. Innumerable camels died, and the loads they carried had to be abandoned. Before the column reached Candahar, their first objective, the men were said to have been reduced to eating sheepskins half cooked in blood.

They were in no condition to win what had to be a decisive victory for Candahar if the expedition were not to be a failure before it had hardly begun. The city was under the control of two of the Dost Mohammed's brothers, who ruled there by his favor. They had to be overcome, and the city secured and garrisoned, before the Army of the Indus could move on to its next stage on the road to Caubul.

Sir William Macnaghten was perfectly certain that the Sirdars who ruled Candahar would not resist and said as much at every opportunity; but as he was a political man, the military commanders, Sir Willoughby Cotton of the Bengal Division and Sir John Keane of the Bombay Division, were not so sanguine, and their subordinates had still less respect for the envoy's military judgment.

On April 19 the great army camped outside the walls of Candahar, and it was reported that a force of some fifteen hundred Afghan horsemen was preparing to attack. The hungry and exhausted English waited, but nothing happened. That evening Keane held a pleasant relaxed dinner party in his tent for some of his favored officers.

The following morning some horsemen did ride into the camp from the city, but they turned out to be deserters, ready to join Shah Soojah and his English supporters. They proved to be a good omen when, two days later, the Candahar Sirdars fled the city before the English had fired their first shot. The people then sent embassies to the approaching Shah, and he was eventually welcomed into Candahar with salutes, *feux de joie*, and flowers. And the fields, gardens, and granaries of the place were opened to the starving troops.

The news reached Simla just in time to make the Queen's birthday ball on May 24 a double celebration. Perdita had always been afraid that she would have to attend that ball even if she avoided every other, but once it had been transformed to honor not only the girl queen but also the success of her valiant troops, Perdita was glad enough to go.

The ball was to be held in a series of tents in the valley of Annandale. Once the quite unseasonable rain had stopped just three days earlier, the organizers proceeded to transform the valley. They erected a temporary hall and two large tents where the guests could dine, and they laid a dance floor in the open air between the tents. Then they hung huge signs in as many of the surrounding trees as would bear them, saying VICTORIA and CANDAHAR in wreaths of flowers. Flowers also edged the dance floor and decorated all the tables in the tents.

Perdita, hearing of all the splendor from Maria Jamieson, knew that she should make an effort with her dress and appearance and decided to wear Runjeet's emeralds. She had had a new gown made to wear with them from a piece of heavy green satin sent up by *dawk* by the indefatigable Mrs. Macdonald in Calcutta. The color was so striking and the necklace so spectacular that Perdita resolved to have no trimmings on the gown at all—rather to the distress of her *durzee*, who thought an evening gown without lace an impossibility. But by asking after his progress and reiterating her instructions daily, she got what she wanted.

Once her ayah had dressed her and fastened the jewels around her throat, Perdita examined her reflection critically but with confidence in a long pier glass that stood by the silver dressing table.

Her hair had been dressed in the loose curls Edward had admired, and the green satin seemed to accentuate the golden lights in it. The necklace fitted perfectly; its large pendant emeralds lay on her white skin just above the low-cut green satin bodice. The great stones seemed to catch all the light that fell near them and flash it back in sharp brilliant bursts.

When she arrived at the valley, rather late, she saw that the ladies outnumbered their possible partners by nearly five to one. She made her way over to a group of chairs where Emma Colvin was sitting with her sister, Harriet Beadon. They greeted Perdita with all the friendliness she had come to expect from them and enviously admired her jewels. Mrs. Colvin, who was wearing a modest string of pearls, said, "It is quite beautiful. Tell me, where did Lord Beaminster find it?"

"Oh, it is not from him. My father gave it to me. I believe it comes from Lahore; it was a farewell gift from Runjeet Singh." The charming smile on Mrs. Colvin's face froze, and she looked sadly toward her sister. Perdita dryly added, "And my father bought it back from the Company for me."

Mrs. Colvin had the grace to blush, but the awkwardness of the moment was dissipated only when her husband came to take her and Lady Beaminster into dinner. Perdita was seated on his right, and when he turned to her with a courteous remark, she smiled and congratulated him on the army's success. He would not accept her accolade for himself, but he did say, "It is very gratifying. We have laid the foundations for reorganizing the entire Afghan nation. It will be something in afterlife to have been in some sort a sharer in such important events."

"Yes, indeed. And I am so glad that the army will be able to rest for a while and eat properly now."

His face contracted, and she regretted her instinctive remark. He said coldly, "I see that the grumblers have been writing to you, too. I find it hard to believe of Beaminster."

"My husband has written very little of military matters, Mr. Colvin, but you must know that everyone in Simla has been concerned by the reports that say the soldiers have been close to starving and persecuted by Balooch bandits on their march."

"Soldiers expect hardship, madam, and marching through a country that has suffered a famine is bound to entail some privation."

He changed the subject by asking if she had heard anything of the fireworks that were to be lit after dinner. She had not and allowed him to talk of them until a change of course let him turn to his other neighbor.

They ate their way through the sumptuous dinner, and Perdita wondered if she were alone in thinking of the incongruity of a hundred and fifty Europeans set down in a heathen country where large numbers of people starved to death each year, eating salmon sent from Scotland and sardines from the Mediterranean. But a little later she caught an amused glance from Miss Eden and after dinner discovered that her thoughts were shared.

They were standing together by the flower-edged dance floor watching a quadrille when Maria Jamieson came up to them on her way into one of the tents. She greeted Miss Eden simperingly and then walked on past a group of blanket-wrapped Hill men who had come down from their poor villages to watch the cavortings of the foreigners. They bowed down to the ground as Mrs. Jamieson walked by, unseeing. Miss Eden whispered to Perdita, "I sometimes wonder they do not cut all our heads off."

Perdita could only agree and found that her few moments with the astringent and intelligent great lady helped to control the dreadful boredom of the rest of the evening. It was with enormous relief that she called for her carriage at midnight.

By then she had danced with most of the officers there and once with Dr. Drummond, who had looked down at her as the music ended and said, "Lady Beaminster, you must allow me to tell you how happy I am to see you looking so well. You had such an unhappy time last year."

Her lovely eyes seemed to glitter in the lamplight as she smiled up at him. "But there were good things, too."

"I am glad of that." As he bowed over her hand, he gave it a comforting squeeze. "Well, adieu, Lady Beaminster. I trust that having emerged from your seclusion on this occasion, you will not spurn my hospitality next week."

"Oh, Dr. Drummond, I do not really like to go out while Beaminster is with the army."

"I can quite understand that. But it won't help him, you know, for you to mope yourself into a decline just because he is seeing a little fighting. And the news is good. Please consider it."

Perdita promised she would, but when the time came, she succumbed to temptation and sent her apologies. She spent the evening at home writing letters and rereading the ones she had received from her husband and Charles Byrd. Both were well, if their letters did not lie, and Marcus's description of the joys of reaching Candahar were almost enough to wipe out the picture Perdita had formed of the starving army making its way painfully through a barren country to face a savage and intractable enemy. Marcus wrote of magnificent rose trees and delectable fruits and of the enthusiastic welcome the people of Candahar gave to Shah Soojah, and he told her comfortingly that "this business" would soon be over.

Like all the other wives, Perdita passionately hoped that he was right, and like them she waited for news. They soon heard that the army had left Candahar for Ghazni, a supposedly impregnable fortress that stood squarely between them and Caubul, on June 27.

By the next *dawk* came letters from Lahore announcing

the death of Runjeet Singh. The politicals left in Simla were worried about the effect this news might have on their treaty, for without the active support of the Punjab, or at least a guarantee of open lines of communication between Afghanistan and British India, the army would be in serious trouble. But most of the ladies were more interested in the news of his obsequies.

They heard that the old man had spent his last few hours on earth distributing his unrivaled collection of jewels to shrines around the city to insure that the priests prayed for him in perpetuity. Only the wailing protests of the *sirdars* gathered around his bed had prevented the legendary *koh-i-noor*, the light of the universe, from disappearing into a holy shrine forever.

The old Lion's determination to secure a favorable reincarnation was echoed by some of the *ranees*, his wives, who announced their determination to share his pyre in spite of the protests of their stepson, Kurruk. Simla was partly horrified, partly thrilled by the news, and when the minute guns were fired there (one for each year of Runjeet's life), there were few who did not shiver at the thought of the pyre.

Soon eyewitness accounts began to filter down to Simla in letters from friends, relatives, and fellow officers stationed at Lahore, and the full horror was passed from person to person. Perdita learned of the details in a letter from Charles Byrd, who had stayed on at Lahore with old General Harlan, a compatriot of his, when the army moved on toward Afghanistan. She found herself at once admiring the courage of women who burn themselves alive for love and disgusted by the waste and cruelty of the custom.

Parts of Charles's description of the occasion stuck in her mind and fueled nightmares for months. Almost the worst was his account of one of the *ranees* walking unveiled and barefoot to her torturing death, preceded by a man walking backward and holding up a looking glass so that she could assure herself that she showed no fear. Drums rolled, and the young queen walked forward, intent on keeping her feelings out of her face. She was followed by three more, carried in palanquins, and then by the old man's female slaves who were to burn with him. Some of them were as young as fourteen; for them, at least, the fate could not have been voluntary.

"It seems rather unfair," added Charles, "that his boys are excused by reason of their sex from the fate when they have shared everything else with these unfortunate women." Perdita did not quite see the point he was trying to make, but it did not seem very important compared with the rest.

But soon there was good news to chase the rest into the background of her mind. In early August came the announcement that Ghazni, too, had fallen. Sir John Keane had carried it with a brilliant surprise attack at night. The Army of the Indus lost only seventeen men with about one hundred and fifty wounded, but the defenders had been taken entirely by surprise, and nearly five hundred of them were killed. Simla considered the result to be very satisfactory and its sequel even more so.

Afzul Khan, one of the Dost Mohammed's sons, had been watching the fortress from the safety of the heights above it. When he saw the colors of the 13th Light Infantry hoisted on the citadel on the morning of July 23, he rode hell-for-leather with his thousands of horsemen to Caubul to inform his father of the invaders' invincibility.

The Dost then tried to surrender to the English, but Sir William Macnaghten refused his conditions. He fled northwest to Bokhara while the Army of the Indus then fought its way up through the Khyber Pass to Caubul and was able to escort Shah Soojah into his ancestral city unopposed.

The deserted wives hoped that this success would mean the swift return of their husbands, but they soon heard that only half the army was packing its traps for the long march back to India. There had been some consternation when rumors had begun to circulate that the army had been raised not simply to escort the new king to Caubul but also to garrison his city for him and indeed to help him administer his whole territory. It quickly became clear to even the most sanguine that some occupying force would be necessary.

But no one wanted her husband to be part of it, particularly once the news of poor Colonel Fletcher's death arrived. It seemed that he had been set upon on the road between Caubul and Candahar and butchered.

When Perdita heard that, she made herself ignore her dislike of his wife and daughter and hurried to the house they shared to give them her condolences. She found Mrs. Fletcher lying in a darkened room, sniffing at a vinaigrette and entertaining Lady Macnaghten and Emma Colvin. She received Perdita's regrets graciously but turned straight back to her other guests to say, "But if I do go home to my sister, as indeed, Lady Macnaghten, I long to do, poor dear Maria will be left here on her own. I expect that Jamieson will take over the regiment from my dear departed husband"—her eyelids dropped in reverence for the dead for a moment— "and she will have no one to help and advise her. It is not easy to be the colonel's lady."

Lady Macnaghten patted one of the brown-spotted hands that plucked so nervously at her handkerchief and said warmly, "Please do not distress yourself, Mrs. Fletcher. I shall be here to advise Maria. As soon as the countryside around Caubul is settled, Macnaghten has promised to send for me, and if the 121st is to form part of the garrison, well, then Maria can travel up to Caubul with me." She caught sight of Perdita sitting silent on the other side of the sofa. "And you, too, of course, Lady Beaminster."

Perdita smiled briefly and hoped fervently that Marcus's regiment would be sent back to India soon. She asked civilly after Maria, and then, seeing that the two elder ladies were bored with her, left kind messages and went home to wait for news.

Fourteen

As soon as it was safe to do so, Sir William sent a young cousin of his, Edward Conolly, down to Simla to fetch Lady Macnaghten, and Marcus Beaminster and Major Jamieson took advantage of the opportunity to send for their own families. The party left Simla in February and set off toward Ludihana and Ferozepore, where they would cross the Sutlej into Afghanistan.

They had over seven hundred miles to go, but it seemed that they could never travel at more than a snail's pace. Two of the ladies rode, but Mrs. Jamieson was frequently unwell and had to be carried in a palanquin like the children and their ayahs. Then there were the hundred or so camels bearing all the baggage and furniture they were taking to insure reasonable comfort in their new homes.

Marcus had written to Perdita describing the house he had taken for her in the newly built cantonment, and this time determined not to put up with ugly and uncomfortable surroundings, she had brought much of the furniture Edward had ordered for her when she told him of the station bungalow. Then there were carpets, hangings, china, wall shades, and shawls as well as all her own and the children's luggage. She was afraid that her twenty-five camels might be excessive for the march and camp life on which she had embarked until she saw the numbers belonging to the other ladies.

The camel drivers were forever quarreling with the banghy men and with the ladies' domestic servants, many of whom fell ill or moaned about the dangers of the country to which they were going. Sometimes Perdita would see an expression of exasperation cross the face of young Conolly. His sepoys were well trained and could be depended upon to break up the physical fights between the various different bands of servants, but it was to the lieutenant they looked for justice in their squabbles. She believed that he found some difficulty in sympathizing with the Oriental mind.

She was often tempted to intervene when she overheard the angry altercations but always stopped herself, knowing how little he would appreciate her help and in any case doubting that her understanding was much superior to his. She was, however, shocked that he could hardly address a word to a native without adding, "Damn your eyes" or some other curse, and she did her best to keep her children out of his way.

The long hot trail across the Punjab tried all their tempers, and Perdita at least felt relieved when they reached the Indus and saw the savage slopes of the Khyber Pass ahead. She knew that once into the pass they would be entering enemy territory, but to her the mountains were exhilarating: so different from the misty purple, pine-clad hills around Simla. Something in the sight of the steep, granite rocks towering up over tiny fertile valleys pleased her. The torrential rivers ran cold and clear, and every foot of cultivable land was crammed with fruit trees, vegetables, and wheat crops. The villages through which the party rode consisted generally of a small, dilapidated fort that protected a group of mud-walled houses with flat roofs and small, defensive windows.

The travelers watched picturesquely dressed tribesmen working their fields with their mysteriously veiled women beside them, and they decided that they had rarely seen so well formed a race. The men were mostly tall, with fine dark eyes and prominent noses, and they rode their horses and shaggy ponies with superb grace and control. Perdita was especially taken with the children, laughing beauties with huge, speaking eyes and pale brown skin. The little girls gave some indication of the probable good looks of their veiled mothers.

To Perdita, watching in relief as the Afghans waved peacefully at the English children who rode in camel panniers and palanquins with their ayahs, the life in these villages seemed very appealing: to grow crops and herd animals in scenery of such splendor, unworried by social or political upheavals, seemed ideal—infinitely preferable to life in Simla or Calcutta. She said as much to Maria Jamieson, who did not even bother to reply. All she said, twisting her full, pink lips in disdain, was, "I had always supposed the tribesmen to be dangerous, but here they are herding sheep like any other peasants."

Perdita answered, "Well, they are all armed. I daresay they would not be so peaceful if they resented our army."

Lady Macnaghten, riding on ahead that morning, misheard and edged her horse back nearer to Perdita's to say, "But we are not their enemies, Lady Beaminster, and they do not resent us. My husband has written often to explain that the people of this land are happy to have their rightful king restored. They came to detest the Dost when he started to ally himself with those dreadful Persians. It is no wonder that these farmers watch us ride peacefully through their villages. They know that we are their friends." She waved toward a group of little girls playing in the dust outside a squalid-looking house. They flashed their irresistible smiles and waved back. "It is gratifying to know that we have been able to bring peace even to so turbulent a country as this."

They reached cantonments at Caubul late one afternoon in May, very stiff, tired, and argumentative. Behind them straggled the long caravan of camels bearing their baggage. The children were fractious and tearful, and Perdita had found herself growing more apprehensive with each mile they advanced farther into Afghanistan. But even so, she was relieved when they finally reached their destination.

Marcus was looking remarkably well, she thought, and he was very solicitous when he saw how pale she was. He made her leave the unpacking and go to lie down, while he attempted to wring some kind of order from the two parties of servants and the mountains of baggage.

She was still asleep when he went into her room dressed for dinner, and so he wrote her a note of explanation and concern for her health and sallied forth to Alexander Burnes's house in the city, where he spent a convivial evening with a mixture of political and army officers. One or two of the unmarried men were wondering aloud whether the arrival of the memsahibs would circumscribe their amusements, but Sir Alexander waved their fears aside with a plump hand and described in exhaustive detail the charms of his latest Afghan inamorata.

Marcus listened in growing disgust and was not surprised when Colonel Robert Warburton took the first opportunity to slip away. But one of the other guests asked what was up.

James Thurleigh, as one of Sir William's peripatetic political officers, knew all the details and said breezily, "Haven't you heard? The old fool is well and truly caught. Unlike our host here, who understands how to treat these women, he is going to marry one."

"Good God, an Afghan?"

"Yes. I cannot imagine why, except that she is said to be a niece of the Dost and perhaps he thinks he'll reap some political advantage, or perhaps, like Beaminster's esteemed father-in-law, he *loves* her."

Marcus winced inwardly at the heavy sarcasm his friend laid on the word and moved away to talk to another officer whose expression of disagreement suggested that he, too, would prefer to discuss another subject.

James saw the withdrawal and once again silently cursed the English ladies for the complications they always brought with them and the divisions they always drove between their husbands and old friends. He went over to Marcus later in the evening to make amends by asking, "Do you go to the cockfight tomorrow, old fellow?"

"I hope so. I expect my wife will wish to rest, but if she does not, I think I shall have to ride with her, show her something of the country." He saw James frown and said, "After all, she has crossed India to come here. I can't carry on now as though I were a bachelor."

"I suppose not," answered his friend, forbearing to ask, as he would have liked, "And why the devil did you send for her?"

Marcus would have found the question difficult to answer. He did not admit, even to himself, that he had missed her presence in his life.

She was still tired and pale when they met at the breakfast table the next morning, but when he suggested that she might like to spend the day in bed, she said, "I don't think so. There is nothing so boring as lying idle when there is so much to be done, however tired one may be." She saw his look of surprise and smiled in some amusement. "Nothing that need concern you, Marcus. I merely want to see this house arranged and all the furniture I brought up properly disposed. You don't mind, do you, if I have things changed around?"

"Of course not. This is your house to do with as you please. But I had hoped you would ride with me. The plain looks at its best now with the fruit trees in blossom and the worst of the rain over for the year. And the city is interesting."

Perdita thought she heard real disappointment in his voice but quickly told herself that she must have been mistaken. Then, just in case the miracle had happened, she modified her plans and said, "Perhaps we could ride later this afternoon before we dine, if it is really safe."

"Of course it's safe. I have to report to General Cotton this morning"—he looked down at his watch—"in about forty minutes, and if you will be busy, I will go on into the town. I may not be back until four or five, but we can ride then. Please don't exhaust yourself while I am gone." She promised and watched him go, feeling slightly encouraged.

As she went about her self-imposed tasks that morning, making the servants lay the carpets she had brought and rearrange the new furniture until she was happy with the result, she thought about her husband. In the light of his apparently genuine desire for her company, not to speak of his sending for her when he could have left her in Simla, it began to seem to her that she had misunderstood him in the past; that perhaps it was her unworthy suspicions that had caused the lack of ease in their dealings. Perhaps she had expected too much of Marcus in their marriage, just as Aneila had told her. Standing in the newly arranged drawing room with part of her mind occupied with what to put on the half-round side table between the windows to lighten the blank wall, she resolved to change herself, to be the sort of wife Aneila had tried to teach her to be. Then perhaps she would learn how to find in her husband the kind of friend she had had in Charles Byrd.

And she resolved not to write any more letters to the American, deciding that it was as much her concentration on him as anything else that had prevented her from getting on better terms with her charming but difficult husband. After all, before she had met Mr. Byrd, Marcus had been much more affectionate and ready to talk to her than he became as they went about in Simla society after Charlie's birth.

At much the same time Marcus Beaminster was standing with his friends in the crowded courtyard of Mohammed Ali Khan's house near the Char Chouk in Caubul waiting to watch a pair of black fighting cocks tear each other to pieces. Marcus felt rather uncomfortable. He much preferred the Afghans' partridge fights, which were contests of skill only, and always stopped before either of the birds damaged the other. But he was ashamed of his squeamishness. To distract himself, he looked around the tight-packed circle of men and young boys. He was quite surprised to see how few facial differences there were between the English and the Afghans. The tribesmen were a little darker of complexion, of course, but not really as much as he would have suspected, and it seemed to him that if they were cleaned up and dressed in European clothes, some of them would have been almost indistinguishable from many dark-eyed Englishmen. For some reason the idea filled him with a vague disquiet.

A new tension shivered through the close-packed crowd as the birds were brought into the improvised cockpit. Marcus knew that they were trained to fight, and having heard some of the methods that were used, he leaned forward to look curiously at them. Edward Conolly, standing on his right, said, "I fancy the old champion. What about you, Thurleigh?"

"No, I've faith in the challenger. I'll bet you. How much?"

"Ten guineas."

"Paltry. Never mind. Beaminster?"

"What? Oh, all right, I'll stake the same."

The birds' turbaned owners opened their large wicker cages, and the two cocks strutted out, their black feathers gleaming and their tiny eyes glittering. The atmosphere in the courtyard was tense and already rived with violence. Not only were the birds to be fought to death, but the men watching them and laying bets on their battle were enemies, too. They might admire each other's skills and manliness and be quiescent for the time, but the English had invaded Afghanistan, occupied it, and planted on it a ruler of their choosing and were treating it very much as their own. They had built their houses on the Caubul plain and sent their officers to gather the new king's taxes, settle his people's disputes, and pull recalcitrant clans and villages into line. Some of them had dishonored the wives and sisters of the Afghan men, and now they had made it clear that they were planning to stay by bringing their own wives and children up from Hindustan.

More than one of the bearded faces in the crowd were blazing with anger and defiance that had nothing to do with the morning's entertainment.

The two birds circled around each other for a while, feinting this way and that. Then the old one succeeded in distracting his adversary long enough to land on his back and latch in his spurs for a second or two before the younger, pecking furiously and using his strong wings like paddles, dislodged him. Both birds were soon bleeding, but they fought on with courage and skill. For several bouts it was not clear which would triumph, and each time they separated and retreated to regather their strength, the watching men raised their bets. The fight must have lasted for nearly nine minutes when Marcus heard James Thurleigh's voice, hoarse and breathless, "Look, the champion's tiring. It won't be long now."

The two English officers who had backed him watched in regret as they realized it was true. He wrought one more savage gash in the other's left wing before he was finally beaten to the ground. There was complete silence in the crowd as the men waited for the victor to kill the loser. He took his time, and the elder bird tried to push himself up off the dirt floor. But his strength was gone, and with a pathetic flap of his wing, he sank back. The new champion trampled on his body and raked sharpened spurs deep into his neck. As they saw the blood spurt out, the Englishmen knew it was over.

The men of both races who had backed the winner shook hands and slapped each other on the back in friendly congratulation before turning to demand their winnings from the rest. The shifting crowd released the pressure on Marcus, and he turned to face James Thurleigh to pay his debt.

"So you were right, after all. Who would have thought that the victor of thirty fights would fall like that?"

"You had only to look at the new one's pedigree. I talked to Mohammed Sharrif earlier, and he told me that none of this one's line ever liked to be beaten—and he's young and full of hate. I was sure he would trounce the old black. Besides," he said with a smile that demanded acknowledgment, "I am always right."

Unusually, Marcus did not respond to the mockery in James's smile, and he was annoyed to see an inward, calculating look in his friend's clear brown eyes. Unaware of any tension, Conolly answered gaily, "Of course he is, Beaminster. What political officer was ever wrong?"

"That sounds remarkably like a sneer," said James, who remembered all too vividly the loathing of most regimental officers for the better paid politicals, who took precedence over them whatever their actual seniority.

"God forbid. Only a small joke, old fellow. Are you going back to cantonments for luncheon, Beaminster?"

"Why not both come back with me?" said James, and when they had agreed, he elbowed his way through the crowd toward their host to say good-bye in his newly acquired and very sketchy Persian. The three of them rode back together through the narrow, dirty streets of the bazaar to Thurleigh's lodgings at the foot of the Bala Hissar.

It was nearly three hours before Marcus put down his glass and picked up his coat.

"I must go. I promised my wife I would ride with her."

James looked at his averted head.

"Well, then, I shan't see you for some time. I'm off to the south in the morning, and I suppose you will dine at home tonight."

"Yes. How long will you be gone?"

"Only a few weeks, I expect."

"Come to the house when you get back. I know my wife will want to see you."

"I doubt that. And I—"

"Don't say it, please," Marcus interrupted. Then he said good-bye and left, calling for his horse.

He found Perdita in the room she had allocated for the nursery, on her knees playing with his son while Aneila was concentratedly ringing a string of temple bells her father had given her. Perdita looked up as her husband came in, and he was struck by how happy she looked, a little disheveled and panting from the boisterousness of Charlie's favorite game. She picked herself up off her knees and said, "We shall play again tomorrow, Charlie, but now Papa and I are going to ride."

"Me, too," he shouted. "Me, too!"

"That is his new phrase," said Perdita, "that and 'Mama, I want it,' but I do think soon we should find him a quiet pony. Look how tall he is becoming."

"So I see. It is strange. He was just a baby when I left. And do you see how like Mama he is becoming in spite of his fair hair?"

"Yes," said Perdita shortly, and then laughed as she caught sight of his quizzical smile. "And just as determined, I am afraid. Well, we shall leave him with ayah now," she added, smiling at the Indian woman who had been sitting in the corner out of the way until she was wanted.

They walked away to the sounds of Charlie's furious yells, punctuated by the sweet chiming of Annie's Tibetan bells.

"Where shall we go?" asked Perdita.

"I thought I would show you the town. I think you will find it interesting."

They rode off across the plain, crossing innumerable streams that irrigated the small square-sided orchards toward the city, which was dominated by its medieval citadel and dwarfed by the mountains that reared a thousand feet up behind it.

"That is the Bala Hissar," said Marcus, pointing to the battlements, "where we were quartered when we first arrived."

"It looks menacing and rather uncomfortable."

"Not so bad, really. And more sensible for an invading force than open cantonments would have been. Until we could be sure that the country would not rise and reject Soojah, it would have been foolhardy to live in a place that would be so difficult to defend."

"But are you sure now?" she asked, thinking of the children.

"I do not think the envoy would have sent for his wife if there was any risk, do you? Besides, we have found these fellows very friendly," he added, ignoring the evidence of hostility he had momentarily sensed at the cockfight. "We introduced them to racing, and some of the fellows have even tried to teach them cricket—though that was a bit of a failure. But I like them. They've far more pride than the Indians; you'd never catch an Afghan behaving like that grain *bunnya* last year at the station. And they are splendid horsemen, and very strong. We turn right, up that alley there."

Perdita looked warily around her as they entered the city. It seemed very foreign and sinister. The houses on either side of the narrow street presented blank mud walls, occasionally pierced by wooden rainwater pipes and small doorways projecting from under the first-floor eaves. When she asked why they were so small, Marcus said, "I suspect so that the houses may be easily defended. These families are forever feuding, and their minds run rather on attack and defense. Their motto seems to be 'blood for blood.'"

The surface of the road had been worn away and would have been impossible to drive over. As it was, their horses had some trouble picking their way over the irregular ruts and loose stones, constantly impeded by the dense crowd. At one moment Perdita looked back and was frightened to see that their grooms had been kept several yards behind them by the press of men wearing coarse turbans and stinking sheepskin coats over their long gowns, and she whispered to Marcus, "Isn't this rather dangerous? Should we not go back?"

He smiled reassuringly and said, "Good heavens, no. The bazaar is not far now. You should not worry about the crowd. It is always like this."

He urged his horse forward, shouldering its way through the crowds, until they reached the great covered bazaar that was the pride of the city. Perdita had supposed that they would dismount and walk through the place, but Marcus rode on, and she saw that other horses, as well as donkeys and even camels, were being ridden through the avenues of shops.

They passed stalls of *poshteens*, the sheepskin coats that were so badly cured and smelly, and pottery, and teahouses, and small caverns where blacksmiths were sharpening their blades in a shower of sparks. Marcus told her at some length about the excellence of the swords, of how the steel of which they were forged was said to improve with age, and how they were tested for balance and purity with water. He saw Perdita's expression of polite incomprehension and explained with pleasure, "You see, on a true blade the water falls straight, like a skein of silk. If the stream bends or turns, you can tell that there is a fault in the steel. And they are sharp. One day I shall get one of the men to test one for you. The two tests are that the blade should cut through bone but also through a silk handkerchief thrown up in the air."

Perdita shivered, and, looking at the sea of unfamiliar dark faces all around and the shadowed, glittery shops with their dangerous merchandise piled up to the roof behind their keepers, she longed to be outside again riding toward the mountains, where she knew she would find flowers and hear birds and breathe free air. Feeling foolish, she said breathlessly, "Marcus, please may we return? I find this place rather oppressive."

"We'll have to ride on to the end of this lane, because we'd never be able to turn the horses here." She realized that he did not understand how frightened she was, and so she twisted the reins in her coldly slippery fingers and concentrated on controlling her mare.

At last they reached the farthest gateway and swung around to return through the town to the plain. The crowds were just as thick, and the blank outer walls of the houses seemed to press together, but at least she could see the sky if she tilted her head back, and occasionally she could see the top of a mulberry tree showing above the walls of some rich man's house.

At the junction of two of the filthy alleys they passed a group of women, quite hidden in their full-length white *chadris*, and nearly ran into a grass seller, whose laden donkey took up most of the alleyway. They could not turn their horses, and he refused to move. Perdita felt her knees trembling as she saw the fury on his face, but Marcus seemed unconcerned and shouted roughly for him to back his beast so that they could pass. The man yelled something as they forced their way past him, and Perdita asked, "What was that he said?"

"Roughly, 'Is Dost Mohammed dead that there is no longer justice in the streets of Caubul?'"

"Doesn't that worry you? Lady Macnaghten kept telling

me on our march that all these people were glad to have Shah Soojah on the throne instead of the Dost."

"There are always some malcontents, but that phrase is one they have used for years, according to Burnes. He heard it first when he was here before, long before there was any question of the Dost's removal."

"I see."

Eventually they reached the city gate, and as they rode out, Perdita took a deep breath, enjoying the sight of the blossoming fruit trees and the sparkling irrigation canals that divided one man's fields from another's, and she resolved never to set foot inside the city again.

In fact, she had to break her resolution several times over the next months to attend dinners at Alexander Burnes's house, but she avoided it at all other times. Instead she would ride out to the hills, sometimes with Marcus but more often with only her groom. After one expedition Marcus came back to the house to find her surrounded by sheets of blotting paper, arranging flowers for pressing. They seemed to be a mixture of tall spires of lilylike flowers and huge purple balls of blossoms that smelled oddly. He wrinkled his nose and said, "Those violet-colored things smell exactly like onions."

Perdita looked up, smiling. "Yes, well, they are onions, I think—what the botanists call allium, but magnificent. This flower head must be six inches across. I hope Juliana will be pleased when she adds these to her collection."

"I am sure she will. How is she? I have had no letters from her since we left Simla."

"Well, I think, although she finds the life she has to lead rather unsympathetic. In fact, your mother has written asking me not to encourage Juliana in her childish rebellions."

"Yes, Mama always wants everyone to do exactly as she wishes. And she never really understood any of us." He shook his head as though to free himself from some constraint and seemed to change the subject. "Does that nice American still write to you? He rather formally asked my permission while we were all at Ferozepore, and I told him I thought you'd be delighted to have letters from him."

Perdita laughed a little ruefully.

"Actually, yes, he does. But I stopped replying to them because I thought you might not like it."

To her astonishment he touched her cheek with one of his fingers.

"That was silly."

Emboldened by his tone, Perdita took the opportunity to air an anxiety that had been pressing on her. "In his last letter he told me that he thought of coming back to Caubul soon."

"Yes, I believe he said something of the sort before we left the Punjab last year. I must go now, my dear, or I shall be late."

As he left, Perdita sighed in relief. She had been dreading the moment when Charles Byrd arrived and might have betrayed the fact that she had been corresponding with him, and yet to confess it to Marcus at that stage could have given unnecessary weight to an innocent pastime. Now she could look forward to Charles's arrival unafraid.

By July, with the temperature hovering around eighty degrees most days, almost all the married officers had brought up their wives from their stations all over India, and life became the familiar round of calls, gossip, flirtation, and dinners. One Friday afternoon Perdita went to luncheon with Lady Sale, the wife of the commander of Marcus's brigade under Sir Willoughby Cotton. Florentia Sale was a formidable woman, regarded with terrified awe by most of the junior wives, but Perdita rather liked her, and they shared an interest in horticulture.

After the meal Perdita was taken to admire the new garden the Sales had made. It seemed to her both surprising and admirable that Colonel Sale, who was considered the hero of the action at Ghazni, should care so much for gardening, and she said as much as she admired the neat rows of edible peas, potatoes, cauliflowers, artichokes, and turnip radishes he had planted. His lady replied carelessly, "Sale has always had a *shoke* for gardening, but he prefers to grow vegetables while I cultivate the flowers. Look at those geraniums; they have been much admired by the Afghan gentlemen who come to call."

"I, too, prefer flowers, but I must confess, I am more interested in those that grow wild in the hills. Unfortunately I came too late to see the tulips, which I hear were particularly fine."

"Well, we shall certainly be here next spring. Sale does not believe it will ever be possible to leave Shah Soojah here without a European garrison."

"I am resigned. Although I hate the city, I prefer this country to Beaminster's old station; the climate is infinitely to be preferred and the scenery splendid, don't you think?"

"I regret Agra, Lady Beaminster. We were comfortably situated there with a fair garden and even a bathing pool. They tell me," she added abruptly, "that you are learning Pushtu."

"Yes, it gives me something to concentrate on so that my mind does not entirely atrophy, but in many ways it is more difficult even than Hindustani, and that was bad enough."

"Nevertheless, Lieutenant Sturt, who dined with us again yesterday, thinks it excellent that you should be making the attempt. He is worried that so few of us are employing Afghan servants, and yet without Pushtu, or at least Persian, how could we ever make them understand an order? I myself shall be employing a man from the city, and Sturt promises to help me with him. I advise you to think about it, Lady Beaminster. We need to be on terms with the people here."

Perdita, thinking that gossip had not lied when it said that Emily Sale must be about to become affianced to Lieutenant Sturt, murmured, "I think we have all the servants we need at the moment, but I shall certainly remember your advice."

Perdita left soon after that, finding Lady Sale's overwhelming manner tiring, and rode back to her own house, hoping that Marcus would be back from the racetrack. She had not accompanied him that day, partly because of the heat but also because there were to be races for the Afghans, and they always tended to become violent and were not considered suitable for the English ladies.

When her *khitmagar* opened the door for her, she asked him if her husband had returned. He nodded and told her that the lord-sahib was in the drawing room with another gentleman. Assuming that it was one of the politicals, Perdita went quickly into her room to spruce up before going to them.

They both rose when she came in, and Marcus said, "My dear, we have a visitor."

Perdita turned slowly and took Charles Byrd's outstretched hand, remembering the feel of his firm fingers as she shook it. She was trying to find something to say that would betray neither the intense sinking pleasure she felt at seeing him again, nor the almost equally intense dismay it brought in its train. Still holding her hand, he said, "Lady Beaminster, it is a real pleasure to see you again." She had forgotten just how his deep slow voice used to affect her; to hear it transported her back to the happiness of their sunlit meetings in the valleys around Simla. She withdrew her hand gently.

"How good of you to call. Are you staying long in Caubul?"

"I am not sure. But it seems as good a place as any to get on with my writing, and I have several friends with your army."

"Where are you staying?"

"With Johnson, the paymaster, who lodges in a house next to Sir Alexander's. It is a charming place, with a large compound and several shade trees. I hope Lord Beaminster will bring you to see it one day."

"You will find, Byrd, that my wife dislikes the city. She never goes there if she can help it. My dear, Mr. Byrd has brought you this from Persia." He handed Perdita a package containing a superb shawl.

She shook it out, saying, "It is quite lovely. But surely it is from Cashmere?"

"I imagine so, but I found it in the bazaar at Teheran. I am glad you like it."

"Who could dislike it?" she asked as she let its fine silky folds run through her fingers.

She wore it when they next went to dine with the Macnaghtens and was pleased with the compliments it won. The evening turned out to be far more enjoyable than she had expected, for Mr. Byrd was a fellow guest and had been placed on her left at the dinner table. Since Sir William, on her other side, was fully occupied with Lady Sale during the first course, she was free to talk to Charles Byrd. She asked some question about his travels but hardly listened to his answer, so happy was she to see him, to hear his voice, and to read the pleasure in his eyes.

During his absence she had tried to make herself believe that their friendship had been nothing out of the ordinary and that it was only the image of him built up in her lonely months at Simla that had made him seem so different from Marcus, so much easier to talk to and to know. But now she knew that her memory had not lied, and after dinner, when Lady Macnaghten as usual asked her to sing and he begged for "The Last Rose of Summer," she recognized her feelings for what they were.

So she smiled at him and said, "I don't think so; it is far too sad." Instead she sang one of Marcus's favorites and forced herself to sing it to him and not to Charles. Marcus seemed pleased, and Perdita tried to think it would have been better if Charles had not returned. She and her husband had been happy enough since she had arrived in Caubul, and she did not want to have to acknowledge how insignificant that quiet content now seemed.

But there was no avoiding the knowledge. Charles called on her often, as he called on several of the others, and she could not escape meeting him out riding or at the races. Then, too, Marcus seemed to have a liking for him and was forever asking him to dine, sometimes with James Thurleigh, sometimes on his own. Unlike the early Simla days, when Perdita had hoped every evening that he would be invited to whichever house she was going to, she now wished that she could avoid him. He had only to smile at her or say in his irresistible voice, "What a pleasure, Lady B!" when they met unexpectedly, for her to feel irrationally, dangerously delighted.

He helped her teach Charlie to ride the small pony Marcus had found for him and collect flowers for Juliana in the mountains. He seemed to have remembered everything she had ever said to him, and he asked questions about her father, the dowager, and Juliana as though they were his own family, too. He talked, when he was alone with Perdita, about things she had written to him and seemed to make it clear by every word, every gesture, even every glance, that there was more between them than mere decorous friendship. The more she tried to keep him at bay, the closer he seemed to come to her.

She wished that Marcus would give her more opportunity to be a wife to him, but he hardly ever came to her room in those days, and she had not plucked up the courage to try out any of the skills Aneila had described to her. But one evening toward the middle of August, they had been to dine at Sir Alexander's and were driving back across the plain by moonlight, admiring the heavily fruiting trees and the starry reflections in the small intersecting canals. He took her hand, and she felt herself blush. She turned her hand within his to clasp it. To her surprise and pleasure, he did not immediately withdraw, and so when he came to her later, she forced herself to touch him and to try to do all the things Aneila had told her a woman should do. She could not quite bring herself to open her eyes, though, and so she did not see his expression of half-stifled disgust. Nor could she feel that her interventions had had the desired effect, and she soon reverted to her usual statuelike inertia. But for once he did not apologize when he left her. She tried to think that at least she made some progress.

She learned the truth some six days later when she was lying down on her bed, feeling unwell, in the early afternoon. She had told Marcus that she would be having luncheon with Mrs. Jamieson, and so he must have supposed her to be still out when he came to the bungalow with James Thurleigh just after one o'clock. Thurleigh had returned that morning from an expedition to Ghazni with messages from Sir William, and they had not seen each other for almost a fortnight.

Marcus ordered the meal and called for a bottle of claret while it was being prepared. Perdita, who had been awakened by their arrival, heard the bearer take the wine into them and then leave, only half closing the drawing room door behind him. It quickly became clear that the two men were in the middle of a quarrel.

As soon as the bearer had gone, Perdita heard Captain Thurleigh say with considerable bitterness, "You have no feeling left for me. You spend all your time with that woman and your son, and I never see you. You wouldn't have behaved so to any friend in the old days, let alone to me. You have forgotten everything."

Then she heard her husband say in a voice she would hardly have recognized as his, "James, my dear, don't say that. You know that you are more important to me than any woman could ever be."

Lying stiffly, wishing that she could not hear and yet unable to block her ears, Perdita heard Captain Thurleigh say angrily, "But you're plugging her again, aren't you?" The word meant nothing to Perdita, but he went on to make its meaning all too clear. "You obviously enjoy her now, and soon there'll be another brat, and then another. By God, you have changed."

Then came the other voice, low now and almost choked with anger or emotion. Much of what it said was mercifully too quiet for Perdita to hear, but snatches of it carried across to her.

"You don't understand, James. . . . I married to . . . in India with you. . . . You never listened when I tried . . ." Then the voice rose, and she heard it all. "God damn it, of course I care for you. And if you think I enjoy . . . If you must know, her body revolts me. I can hardly bear to touch her. It wasn't so bad at first; she just lay there, but now—"

"Don't tell me, Marcus. I'm sorry. You are right, I didn't understand. Oh, don't look like that, my dear. Come here to me."

If Perdita had not known that those words were spoken by James Thurleigh, she would never have recognized the voice as his. It was so full of gentleness; so different from the harsh, arrogant tones she knew as his. He spoke again. "You should have told me, Marcus. I promised you once that nothing could hurt you while I was with you. Don't you remember?"

"I think I remember everything, James. But marriage seemed to be something I had to cope with on my own. I can't think why, because nothing ever goes right when I'm away from you. James, thank God you're here."

It was the kind of voice she had always longed to hear Marcus use with her: full of warmth, sureness, love. She had dreamed of it too much to misunderstand it now; but she had not known that men could love each other like that. Bitterly humiliated to remember her stupid, irrelevant jealousy of Maria Jamieson and her efforts to awaken such a love in Marcus, Perdita lay still, tears of shame and horror pouring down the sides of her nose. She could not wipe them away for fear that, moving, she would make a noise that would alert the men to her presence.

Their voices murmured on, too low now for her to distinguish the words, and she was left to think horribly of what they must have said to each other since the time of her marriage, what they must have thought of her clumsy demands on Marcus. Her mind could not encompass thoughts of any physical expression that their love might take; it was the idea of complete trust and openness between them that hurt her so much—that and the knowledge that they must be able to give each other what she had wanted, and been forbidden, to give to Marcus.

After what seemed an eternity she realized that they had had their meal, and she heard them leave. Appalled at the idea of meeting either of them, she gave them half an hour to get clear of the house, and then, without even calling for her ayah, she dragged one of her riding dresses from the wardrobe and pulled it on, sobbing with frustration at the tiny buttons on the shirt and reaching agonizingly behind her to hook up the tight-waisted skirt. At last she was dressed and hunted for boots. Finding a pair, she thrust her foot down and tried to pull the boot up. Her thumbnail bent back sickeningly and cracked. The small pain made her cry out, and she sucked the mutilated nail for a moment or two. Then she tried again to pull up the heavy leather. At last her heel slipped down into the boot, and she wrenched on the other one, stamping her foot to force it on. Forgetting her hat in her determination to be gone out of the house where she had heard such things, she ran out and around to the stables where, ignoring the surprised looks of the grooms and grasscutters, she waited impatiently for her mare to be saddled. Eventually, just as she began to think she could control herself no longer, the groom brought her over.

Perdita thought vaguely that the man looked rather ill, but she had no wish to draw his attention to her face, and so she did not speak. She turned her back, mounted, and rode off, looking straight ahead and praying that she would meet no one she knew.

It was not until she reached the edge of the plain at the foot of the Seah Sung hills that she was hailed. She had not noticed the horseman riding toward her at an oblique angle from the direction of the Bala Hissar, but she recognized his voice at once. She did not stop, but he soon caught up with her and, taking one look at her face, waved his own groom and hers back and said urgently, "Lady B, what's up?"

She said drearily, not expecting to be believed and not much caring if she were, "Nothing."

She urged her mare forward, up the steep path toward the little plateau where the foxtail lilies grew tall and white in the dusty brown earth. He followed silently, but when the path flattened out and he saw the flowery stretch ahead, he told the two grooms to remain where they were and rode forward to her side. She let the mare walk on to the farther edge, where a dry stream bed broke the little plain. Then he caught her reins and brought her mount around so that she faced him.

"Tell me what has happened. I have never seen you so unhappy. Tell me."

"I could not," she said, ashamed partly at the too obvious state of her face and partly at what she had learned.

"You can," he said. "You know that you can say anything to me." And he leaned forward over his horse's neck to take hold of one of her gloved hands. "Come, whatever it is will not be so bad if you tell me about it."

And so she did. All the pain and difficulty of her unreturned love for her husband came pouring out, culminating in one despairing phrase. "It seems that I would disgust any man."

The anger he felt shook Charles Byrd with its force. He dismounted and made her join him on the ground. Having loosely tethered their horses' reins under a rock, he took both her hands in his and said gravely, "Perdita, any man who is a man would do anything to sleep in your arms."

At that she raised her swollen eyelids and said, "It is very hard to believe."

He pulled her gently toward him and said into her hair, "I wish I could prove it here, but people ride this way."

"I know," she said, and drew back from him a little. But he kept his hold on her left hand and peeled back the tight leather glove until it was covering only the tips of her fingers. Then he turned her hand over, holding it in both of his, bent his head, and kissed the palm.

Perdita looked down at his head and felt his warm lips on her skin. Her heart seemed to be beating twice as loudly as usual, and there was a strange, half-pleasurable ache in her legs. She touched his hair with her free hand and suddenly wanted, almost unbearably, to put both her arms around him and hold him to her.

Charles raised his head and said gently, "You see what we could mean to each other."

Perdita said nothing, and he started again with some difficulty. "I never expected to say such a thing to you, but I want you to know how desirable you are. I want you. Yet more than that, I want you to know what you are and to value it." He waited, still holding her hand, and then, when she did not speak, went on. "And I want to know that you care for me."

"But you know that already. You have known it ever since I sang to you that night."

His smiling green eyes lit a trail of warmth right through her. He touched her face briefly.

"Ah, Perdita, I did not think you would admit it so easily."

Fifteen

All the way back to cantonments, Perdita prayed that Marcus would not choose to dine at home that night, thinking that it would be unbearable, impossible, to pretend to him that nothing had happened. As she rode silently beside Charles Byrd, down from the hills and across the plain, past the Afghan forts to the Caubul River, she wondered if she would be able to speak to Marcus again.

The shame was still there, but now she felt anger, too, furious anger that he should have put her in such a position. It was true, she reminded herself, that he had never said that he loved her, but to marry any woman feeling as he seemed to feel was a cruelty of which she would not have thought him capable. Charles Byrd's voice broke into her thoughts.

She turned her head to look at him, and his smile caught her unaware. She smiled back at him.

"I am sorry, I did not hear what you said."

"I asked only if you would like me to come back to the bungalow with you."

Her smile faded. "Thank you, Charles. But no. Here's the road to the town. We had better say good-bye here."

"Very well, but send for me whenever you need me."

"I will, Charles. I am glad you were here."

He kissed her hand formally and rode away, his groom following him. Perdita watched him for a moment or two before spurring her own horse forward. She was still trying to decide how she would greet her husband when she eventually walked up the steps to the front door.

But when she opened it, all thoughts of the afternoon's emotions were driven from her mind by a sharper shock. Charlie had fallen off his pony, and when Perdita entered the house, she found his ayah stanching a frightening flow of blood from a cut high on his scalp.

Perdita quickly sent a groom running for Assistant Surgeon Brydon, whose quarters were nearer than any of the other doctors', and took the howling child on her lap, replacing the ayah's reeking towel with a pad of fine linen from her work basket. He kept rearing up in her arms, saying between screams, "Let me see! Let me see it, Mama! Bring a looking glass!"

But she was afraid that the sight of the gash and the matted, bloody hair around it would frighten him even more than the pain and the stickiness of the now clotting blood, and so she ignored his frantic requests and tried to reassure him. She herself hated the tackiness of the blood drying between her fingers and under her nails, and she was disgusted and frightened by his pain.

When the doctor arrived, he said the cut would have to be stitched, and so Perdita held her son's head clamped against her shoulder while the man dug needles into his scalp. Submerged in what was happening to him, she did not notice that small Annie had crept into the room and was standing behind her shoulder, silently watching everything that was done to her foster brother. But when it was all over and the cries had blessedly stopped at last, Annie was sick all over the floor.

The servants clustered around, clucking reproachfully, telling her that she was an owl to add to the terrible trouble of the *chota rajah*'s hurts. Why could she not have kept out of the way as befitted a girl child? they asked.

But Perdita saw the marbled look to her skin and the dazed fear in her eyes and stretched one of her arms to the child, saying, "Annie, come here, my love. See, poor Charlie is better now. But it was frightening, wasn't it?"

The little, pale-faced, dark-haired child crept forward into Perdita's embrace and was held warmly until Charlie, either by accident or design, kicked her face.

By the time Perdita had calmed them both and stayed with them in the night nursery until they slept, she was exhausted, fit for nothing but her own bed and quite unable to face the thought of dinner. She scribbled a note for Marcus to tell him about the accident before she went to her room, desperately hoping that it would prevent his feeling that he must overcome his disgust and come to her. She did not think she would ever be able to accept him into her bed again.

It was easy to avoid seeing much of him in the following weeks, for like most of the other officers he was sent on frequent missions around the country. Sir William Macnaghten chose to think and report to Calcutta that the Afghan nation was at peace and the people happy under the benevolent rule of their new king and his English advisers. But it was not so.

They were hardly a nation in any case, being divided into three great tribes: the Dourranis, to which Shah Soojah belonged; the Barukzais, who were the Dost Mohammed Khan's people; and the Ghilzais, who held the eastern and western passes between Afghanistan and India. Each tribe was subdivided into smaller clans named after the areas in which they lived—Kohistanis, Khyberis, and so on—and even within the clans individual families pursued blood feuds to the ultimate point. Fiercely loyal, taking revenge as a matter of principle, these people could also change their loyalties in an instant, impelled by anger, hatred, greed—or honor. They were governable only by strength and cunning.

The English could no doubt have supplied an adequate measure of both; after all, it was their strength and cunning that had brought so much of India under their hand. But they had embarked on their hazardous Afghan adventure as an exercise in influence, not conquest. In Caubul they spent themselves to try to turn the Shah into their own ways of government. They persuaded him not to execute his enemies or even blind them. They sent their young political officers to persuade and cajole any rebellious chiefs who looked askance at the Shah, and they resorted to force only when they could see no other way.

But Shah Soojah-ool-Mulk was not an Englishman, and he wished to govern in his own, traditionally Afghan way. His affairs were in the hands of a much-hated and incompetent tyrant named Mullah Shikore, whose savage taxation raised the fury of his countrymen. The English disliked what was done, yet had to support it and to chastise those clans and villages that resisted.

Sir William had to be seen to be the Shah's friend, not his master. He had to walk a tightrope slung for him by his government's policy between weakness and overinterference and, despite his own tremendous confidence, the rope kept slackening disastrously and threatening to throw him off.

He had to divide his forces dangerously, too; part of the army had had to be left at Candahar and Ghazni under the command of General Nott, an acerbic man who had risen in the Company's army, to keep the south of the country pacified. The main force marched on to Caubul, and the political officers were spread about all the neighboring states. Among them were young Lieutenant Loveday at Khelat-y-Ghilzai, working to keep its unpredictable ruler allied to the British interests so that their southern lines of communication were not broken, and Colonel Stoddart in Bokhara, attempting and so far failing to impress the mad Nasrullah, who alternately supported and hindered the Dost Mohammed Khan.

Within Afghanistan there were two prime threats to the stability Macnaghten was trying to insure: Shah Soojah's nephew, who ruled in Herat and who had little love for his uncle but great ambitions; and the Dost himself, who soon managed to escape from Bokhara, whence he had fled before the invading army. Both were interested in fomenting rebellion against the Shah, and the Dost was raising an ever-increasing body of irregular troops. Macnaghten and the military commanders were bombarded with reports of his presence in villages all over the north of the country, and they sent force after force to chase after him. But so far they had not succeeded in engaging him and had to fall back on punitive skirmishes against the clans and families that openly supported him.

It began to seem to Perdita that the English were surrounded by an almost entirely hostile population, but she spoke of her fears to no one except Charles Byrd. He said one morning when he had come to call, "Yes. Your people need to get hold of the Dost. While he is at large causing trouble, you'll never be able to keep the chiefs quiet."

"But as far as I can understand," protested Perdita, "we cannot subdue even one small chief without losing thirty or forty men. What happens when they meet the Dost himself?"

"Perhaps, then, the force will be led by an experienced officer for once, instead of these gallant, thoughtless lieutenants. Are you afraid?"

She looked at him and said simply, "Yes." Then she added, "I cannot help seeing how easy it would be for any attacker to break into cantonments. The other day I saw an officer back his horse up the ditch and over the wall. And those are our only protection against intruders. I do not mean to complain, but what if the chiefs unite and decide to besiege us? The stores are all in the commissariat fort, and the ammunition is outside as well. How could we live if they took those?"

"I wish I could take you away with me."

A sudden fear almost nauseated her, but she tried to keep her voice calm and social as she asked, "Are you leaving Caubul, then?" She looked at him, which was a mistake, and then tried to pretend that she had not seen the understanding in his eyes.

"Only if you will come with me, Perdita."

Her longing and her love nearly overwhelmed her, but with a huge effort she stopped herself on the brink. After a little while she said as quietly as she could, "Charles, I regret more than I can tell you that you found me that day and that I told you what I did. There is nothing for you and me. I could never go away with you. It would be better if you left Caubul. If you stay, we can only make each other unhappy."

"Is that true? Really true? Is my presence here making your life worse than it would otherwise be?"

She stood up and walked toward the window to look out. He followed her and put both hands on her back. She ached to lean against him, and when his hands moved slowly, compellingly, over the thin muslin of her bodice, she gasped.

"It isn't true, is it, Perdita? Look at me." Obedient as always, she turned to face him. A feeling that was more than pure desire teased him. His hands gripped hers.

"It should be true."

"How like you! I shall stay, then."

She wished that she could suppress the relief she felt, but it showed in her eyes and in her carriage. He knew that in a week or two he would try again.

By September it was bruited around cantonments that the whole country was up in arms against the British all the way from Caubul north to the Oxus River on the border with Bokhara. Riding into the city, the English would discover that more and more shops were shutting in the bazaars, as though in preparation for violence in the streets. It became very clear that some of the Caubul chiefs, as well as those in the north, were supporting the Dost, and news of his successes led the married officers who were quartered in the city to move their families into the Bala Hissar on the assumption that their houses were no longer safe.

When Charles did not call for three days in a row, Perdita became more and more afraid. Like everyone else, she had heard that his hostess, Mrs. Johnson, had been moved into the citadel, and she worried about his safety. When he did come, she could scarcely wait for the *khitmagar* to leave before taking Charles's hands and saying, "Thank God, you are all right."

"My dear, of course. Have you been worried?"

"How not? I heard that Mrs. Johnson moved into the Bala Hissar, and since then none of us has seen you or Captain Johnson." She watched a slight smile cross his face.

"Did it not occur to you, my dear anxious love, that if two foreigners had been assassinated or even abducted, you would all have heard the news?"

"Yes, but everyone says that the city is ripe for insurrection. Why did you stay away?"

He looked at her, trying to say something noble about wanting to spare her pain, but for a reason he did not understand he told her the truth.

"Because I wanted you to worry and to fear, so that when I asked you to come away with me again, you would find it harder to refuse."

Something in his self-revealing frankness stopped her protests. "But you are not going to ask, are you?"

"I suppose I am not."

When he left her half an hour later to ride back to the city through the sullen, obstructive crowd, he wondered how he had come to such a ludicrous pass: so attracted to a virtuous woman whom he had failed to seduce that for her sake he was living in a dangerous city, volatile as a gunpowder factory, in the middle of a war that was no concern of his. The folly of it was not even amusing, he decided as he rode up from the Lahore Gate straight into a party of English officers.

"Afternoon, Byrd," called Lord Beaminster, riding beside Captain Thurleigh. "Coming to the cockfight?"

"I think not, thank you. I have some work to do."

They laughed at his seriousness and rode off. He was left wishing that her husband was more like Thurleigh so that he would have had no compunction in forcing her to leave him.

"I like that fellow," said Marcus as they rode down toward the gate, "don't you?"

"Well enough. But I do not trust him. What is he doing here, an American? I can't help thinking he must be in communication with that shocking American mercenary, old Harlan in the Punjab. Now that Runjeet is dead, things are rather ticklish in that area. Byrd could well be intriguing with factions here to ally them with Lahore. Why else would he stay?"

"God knows, but I'm sure you are wrong. He probably does not fancy riding south while the country is so unsettled. Wouldn't myself. But when we've got the Dost and pacified the tribes, he'll go."

"When. But with all this bungling and driveling, God alone knows when that will be. If only the Governor General would make up his mind that the only way to settle this damnable country is to send up at least six more battalions, organize the place properly, hang the rebels, and stop pretending that the Shah is in charge! But what happens? We send individual officers with insufficient troops all over the country to negotiate with all these treacherous chiefs and amirs. With what result? There's Stoddart in the mad Nasrullah's dungeons in Bokhara, poor Loveday in Khelat with the almost equally mad Balooches, and everyone in just as much danger from any crazy, treacherous Afghan chief whose territory he is sent to fix up."

"I never thought to hear you complaining, Thurleigh," called Lieutenant Conolly. "Anyway, my brother Arthur's been sent up to Bokhara to get Stoddart out. And we'll get the Dost this time, you'll see."

But they did not even manage to confront him until the end of October. On the twenty-seventh he broke ground at last, and two days later Marcus and his men marched in pursuit.

In spite of her hurt and anger, Perdita had found herself

becoming afraid of what might happen to Marcus. Now, knowing that he was facing a full battle with the Dost, she could not help thinking of the effects of the *jezails* that would be aimed at him and the swords, of which he had once been so admiring. In the light of the dangers he faced, her feelings paled, and she began to remember the affection she had felt for him.

Marcus's troops found the Dost unexpectedly on a beautiful morning at the beginning of November in the Purwandurrah Valley. The crisp autumn air was invigorating and reminded more than one of the Englishmen of home, where one could breathe without swallowing the dust of India and walk in the sunlight without fear of sunstroke.

The valley trees were as golden as autumn leaves in England and made a fitting background for the triumph all the officers expected. They marched forward with confidence to make an end to the trouble and rebellion caused by their enemy.

But they failed. Many of their native troops fled in the middle of the battle, leaving the officers to charge alone into the steadily advancing Afghan horsemen. Two young lieutenants fell, and there was almost no one who did not suffer saber cuts or bullet wounds. Marcus himself received a glancing slash across his cheekbone; the sword missed his right eye by only a whisker. He killed the Afghan who had struck him but was soon half blinded by the blood that seeped into his eye. He tried to rub it away but succeeded only in making it worse, and one of his men urged him to the rear.

By the end of the day the Afghans were the unquestioned victors. But the Dost appeared to have no wish to press his success and, astonishingly, withdrew. The English were left to fall back on Caubul, to have their wounds dressed and to start to plan how to recover their lost prestige and superiority.

It was clear to practically everyone by then that Shah Soojah was unpopular with his people and that the Dost was a hero to them. His generalship was demonstrably superior to the English in the wild and difficult country he knew so much better than they, and he seemed to be playing with them.

There were simply not enough English troops in Afghanistan to police the whole country and subdue the Dost's supporters completely, even if they had been allowed to do so. The only way to achieve the necessary support for the Shah was by bribery. Sir William Macnaghten's expenses were running at nearly one million sterling, and yet the tribes seemed as ever to be on the brink of rebellion.

The day after the humiliating defeat at Purwandurrah, Sir William was taking his customary evening ride, trying to flog his exhausted brain into considering how to escape from the disastrous mess into which his army of occupation had fallen, when an Afghan horseman rode toward him. To his astonishment, and indeed to that of everyone else who heard the story, the Afghan turned out to be an emissary of the Dost. He announced that his master was at hand. In a few minutes the Dost himself rode up, dismounted, and handed his sword to Macnaghten in surrender.

Relieved almost to the point of euphoria, the English treated their late enemy honorably and took him to the Residency compound, where he was accommodated as comfortably as possible in a tent pending his removal to India. He proceeded to impress practically all the Europeans who saw him or spoke to him, and they began to compare him all too favorably with the puppet king they had imposed on Caubul. But Macnaghten could not change horses in mid-race, and the Dost was duly packed off before the weather broke and snow closed the passes to India, soon to be followed as far as Jellalabad by Sir William, the Shah, and their staffs to escape the worst of the coming cold.

They left the rest of the occupying force in some idleness, filling their time as they chose with shooting, skating on the frozen lakes around the city, and any other amusements they could invent or adopt from the Afghans. Marcus, in particular, had time on his hands, since James Thurleigh had had to escort his chief to Jellalabad, and so he turned once more to his wife.

For her part, Perdita discovered that most of her hostility to him had dissipated as she nursed him through a bad fever that was the result of his wound. As she sat by his bed day after day, she had come to remember his gentleness and his care as much as the bitter hurt he had unknowingly dealt her. And so, when he came to find her one morning in December to cajole her into a ride with him, she greeted him with a smile and an outstretched hand.

But he thought she looked worried and said, "Tell me, Perdita, what is the matter?"

"Nothing very much. The *sirdar*-bearer has just told me that my groom is dead. Apparently it was pneumonia, which is rife in the city."

"Well, never mind that. We can certainly find you another. There must be many spare servants after all the actions in the autumn. I'll have a word with Johnson."

"Please don't trouble, Marcus. Lieutenant Sturt has told me of an Afghan, an excellent man, who would make a good groom. I have already engaged him."

"I think you should get rid of him, then. A Hindu would be much safer. I would not like the idea of your riding among these hills with a tribesman."

"Lady Sale thinks we should all be employing Afghans. She believes, or rather Sturt believes, that it is the only way to show these people that we are not their enemies and to learn what they are really like. Sturt thinks this man trustworthy—and he is certainly a far better horseman."

Marcus said uneasily, "Well, I think I'd better have a word with Sturt."

They left the subject then and agreed to ride into Caubul, where Perdita wanted to buy trays and new cutlery for the house, as well as some of the least stinking sheepskin coats she could find. The weather had turned very cold, and she was afraid that it might make the children ill.

Whenever they went out of doors, she saw that they were well clothed, and she told their ayahs to wrap strips of coarse cloth around their boots as the Afghans did. The other English ladies mocked her, and Maria Jamieson often said carefully within her hearing that the little Blagdons looked like bazaar brats.

Marcus laughed at her, too, sometimes, but kindly. He used to tell her that she was making them all soft, wrapping them up for outdoor amusements as though they were heading for the North Pole. She always answered him seriously, one morning reminding him, "You have only just recovered from a bad fever; there is a lot of pneumonia about; Annie's lungs are probably weak, and I could not bear her to contract tuberculosis like her mother. I think it is important that I keep you all warm." Then she went on. "Sometimes I wish that you were on Sir William's staff so that we could winter at Jellalabad with him and the king."

"Never mind. From what Thurleigh writes, it is not so much warmer there."

"Have you heard from him, then? Has there been any news of Lieutenant Loveday?"

His face tightened, and his eyelids dropped. Perdita knew then that the gallant young man must be dead. She waited for details, but all Marcus said was, "When our people reached the fort at Khelat, they found his body."

He turned away so that she would not ask any more, knowing how she would hate the knowledge of what had been done. He himself would rather not know that Loveday, a brave and very generous man, had been starved to the point of complete emaciation, chained naked to a camel pannier, and beheaded, apparently only hours before the relief force marched in.

Perdita knew that her husband did not want her to say anything more, and so she changed the subject by asking if he would escort her to the lake where most of the English practiced their skating. He had nothing to do now that the country was virtually pacified and Thurleigh was ninety miles away in Jellalabad, and so he shook the memories of Loveday out of his mind and agreed to go with her.

They rode off together, enjoying the bite in the air and the look of the snow-covered country. It was a clear day, and the sun beat down all around, sending sharp, intense light into their eyes. More than one of the English suffered from snow blindness before they learned to take precautions against it, and Perdita often found herself dizzy and almost nauseated by the brightness. Once or twice she even wondered if she might be going to have a fit, but she gradually became accustomed. And she enjoyed the winter; the snow seemed to gentle the mountains and, in whitening the forts and softening their edges, made the plain seem less sinister. The white covering also gave the city itself an illusion of cleanliness.

The lake was about six miles from the cantonment, toward Istalif, and the Beaminsters rode there on strong yaboos that

Marcus had bought a few months earlier from an itinerant horse dealer. Aktur, the new groom, rode with them, for Marcus had taken a liking to him and had come to accept Perdita's wish to get on terms with at least one Afghan. He had been a little worried a few days earlier when one of the chiefs said to him, "We wish that you had come among us as friends, for you are fine fellows one by one, though as a body we hate you."

But as they reached the lake, he shrugged the thought aside and helped Perdita dismount. He buckled on her skates and his own, and they skimmed off across the ice together.

The cold brought color into Perdita's pale cheeks, and she smiled happily as he wheeled toward her, taking her attention off her feet just at the moment when her leading skate hit a bumpy ridge in the ice. She staggered and fell toward him. He slid quickly forward to catch her, and she landed in his arms. To her surprise he held her there for a few moments longer than he had to before helping her to stand up once more.

Neither of them noticed Charles Byrd arrive at the lake with Lieutenant Sturt and his wife, Lady Sale's daughter. They skated off again to the far edge of the lake, hand in hand. Charles stood on the edge of the ice looking after them in dismay. Jealousy was a new emotion to him; if one of his flirts had ever shown any signs of turning to someone else, he had always been able to shrug and think himself well rid of her. But this time, this woman, was different.

It was several days before Charles Byrd rode over to the cantonment to visit Perdita once more. He found her warming her long hands at one of the charcoal stoves in the drawing room. She looked up as he was announced and said with a smile that he found enchanting, "Why, Charles, where have you been? I have not seen you for days."

"I know, but I have seen you."

She looked puzzled; the smile faded at the anger that was all too clear in his voice. She said, "Where?"

"At the lake. I saw you and Beaminster, but you were so engrossed in each other that you did not notice me." He tried to sound lightly bantering, but it did not work.

"You sound angry. Please don't be."

He looked at her, cursing himself for his absurd folly. He said, "It is very hard not to. He has behaved abominably to you, made you painfully unhappy, and yet he has only to smile at you, and you forgive him everything."

She held out both her hands to him. "Charles, I have to. I have told you—"

He interrupted, taking her hands in a painful grip. "I know, I know. And I am a fool. I wish I had never come here —or at least left when you first told me to. But I can't go now. The passes will be impossible until the snow melts. They say it's a foot thick. But my love, tell me one thing." He stopped, and she waited, hoping he would not ask her, but he did. "Tell me, just once, whether you meant what you said to me that day."

She looked at him honestly and said, "I have never lied to you, Charles." But he pressed her, and in the end she said quietly, driven to it by his persistence, "Yes, of course I love you. But it does neither of us any good to say it. There is nothing I can give you, and if you are going to be hurt every time you see me on reasonable terms with my husband, our lives will be intolerable." She tried to pull her hands away.

But he kept them, bent to kiss them, and then said, "Well, it is good that I did not imagine your feelings, I suppose."

"Please don't be angry," she said again.

He let her hands go then, and said more gently, "Only with myself, Perdita, for being such a sentimental fool. I can't promise to leave you alone, but I shall do my best not to worry you with demands."

She asked him then about his work and rang for some tea, so that when Marcus returned home forty minutes later, he found them decorously discussing the justification of civilizing savage peoples for commercial gain. Marcus joined them politely and, when Mr. Byrd left, said to Perdita, "Interesting man, Byrd. I hope he makes a success of that book of his."

"So do I," she said, smiling, "but he told me just before you arrived that he finds too many distractions here and cannot make himself sit down for the requisite number of hours each day. He thinks he ought to leave here and go somewhere where he knows no one."

"I doubt if that would work. He seems far too gregarious

to be solitary. Besides, he'd be a fool to leave now. No one in his right mind would travel through those mountains in winter. There's bad news again, I'm afraid."

"Oh, no! What now?"

"In spite of the Dost's surrender, the Dourranis are agitating. Nott is said to be putting down their revolt, and then the politicals will have the tricky task of pacifying them once they're beaten."

"Well, that ought to be all right. You told me that General Nott is a good soldier, and he has plenty of Indian experience."

"I've no doubts on that score. But there is some suggestion that the revolt was instigated from Herat."

"I begin to think there will be no peace in this country until whoever rules in Caubul is also chief of Herat."

"That's what James says. But we haven't the men to take it or garrison it properly afterward." They were silent until he burst out, "It's this wretched business of the pretense that we are here merely to support the Shah. We have to allow his people to ruin the balance we might have achieved by tyrannizing over some of the tribes. We cannot administer the province as though it were our own, but we are stuck here in expensive support because alone he would be helpless. I ought not to say this, but I wish to God it was the Dost we were supporting. He at least knows what he is doing and has some strength of character. I am sorry, my dear, to fuss so. Do not let it worry you."

"Very well," she said, thinking, How can it not worry me? Here we are in the middle of an intractable country, endeavoring to pacify a people that has never known peace in centuries. Our interference is resented, and we would be entirely at their mercy if there were to be an uprising. I have two small children to protect, and we are living in cantonments that could be taken by a determined assault in less than half an hour. The garrison would hardly be adequate even if it were all based at Caubul.

She went away then to visit Lady Sale, who at least would never ask anyone to stop worrying. In fact, she went so far as to criticize openly everyone from the envoy and the Governor General to the young officers who, she believed, were making her husband's task next to impossible. Then she started on the new Commander in Chief, General Elphinstone, who was making his painful way up to Caubul from Calcutta. Perdita knew nothing of him and asked who he was.

Lady Sale answered pithily, "No Indian service; no Hindustani or Persian; very bad gout; very charming. Useless for Caubul and nearly seventy, I should think."

"It seems a pity that General Nott should have been considered ineligible. After all, he knows this country and has been very successful in action."

"There is more to this appointment than plain soldiering, Lady Beaminster," came the tart rejoinder. "And the trouble with so many Company officers like Nott is that they are sadly lacking in the skills and graces of diplomacy."

Belatedly remembering that as a Queen's officer, Colonel Sale would not have a very high opinion of General Nott even if they had never quarreled personally, Perdita said nothing more.

The new general, who was in fact barely sixty, arrived with the spring and better news from the south. The military campaigns against the Dourranis and the western Ghilzais had been successful, and Sir William Macnaghten rode back to Caubul from his winter quarters to a reasonable welcome from the garrison.

The rain poured down most days, and the melting snow turned all the mountain streams into voracious torrents. But toward the end of April, the storms were interrupted, and outdoor amusements became possible once again. Like most of the officers, Marcus spent a good part of his time going after snipe and duck at the lake, while Perdita tried to keep the children amused out on their ponies. The birds Marcus shot made a useful variation to their tedious diet of mutton, poultry, and preserved vegetables, but that did not compensate Perdita for the loss of his company once more.

She had hoped, without really expecting it, that perhaps this time when Captain Thurleigh returned, Marcus might still spend some time with her. But it did not happen. Almost as soon as the court returned from Jellalabad, he began to dine out three or four nights in seven and to spend less and less time at home with his wife. Even when they were together, he hardly spoke. Perdita began to feel bitter again and to look forward more than ever to Charles Byrd's visits.

He called one clear afternoon at the end of April to ask her to ride with him to the tomb of Baba Shah. She had nothing to do; it was a week or more since she had seen him; and so she agreed.

He seemed much quieter than usual and hardly smiled. Perdita worked hard at making him talk as they rode across the plain, asking him at one moment whether he had been away.

He said, "Yes, I went with Burnes for some shooting in the Kohistan. We got over forty-five different species of duck."

"Marcus would be very jealous of that. Did you enjoy it?"

"Not really." He turned his head to look at her and said, "I find myself thinking of you whatever I am doing: riding, shooting, trying to read or work. I cannot get you out of my mind." She did not know how to answer the harsh tone in his voice, and they rode on in silence until they reached the tomb, where he made her dismount and give the pony's reins to her groom.

The tomb was a place they both liked—quiet, beautiful, and rather sad. The monument itself was an elegant white marble structure with the wide, pointed arches typical of the best Islamic architecture, and it was surrounded by graceful shade trees, walnut mostly, with some mulberry.

They walked through the trees and up the first flight of steps to discover that the tomb was empty. There was not even a disapproving mullah praying, and so Charles took her hands. Looking down at them, he said slowly, "Perdita, I cannot go on. I understand now that you won't ever leave him, but I cannot stand back and watch anymore. I have got to go away where I can be free of you. At the moment I can't work. I can't do anything except think about you, when I am going to see you next, what I should say to make you see why we ought to be together, what you will answer. . . . I have to go."

Standing so close to him, her hands imprisoned, Perdita was shocked by the pain his declaration brought her. She had never intended to go with him and was completely sincere in her determination to make the best of her life with Marcus Beaminster, but the knowledge that even if he did not want her, Charles Byrd did; that Charles was there to help, amuse, and comfort her had made it easier. She said painfully, "I think I have been very selfish."

"Ah, no, love. Not that. You did not ask me to stay. I wish —" He stopped, looked up at her at last, and said, "I wish that I could be to you all the things that he will not. But I understand now why I can't. And so I have to go. You do understand that, don't you?"

"Yes, I understand. It will be better for both of us," she said, thinking, How shall I bear it? Why don't I say, take me with you? If Marcus prefers to spend his time with Captain Thurleigh, let him, and I shall go with you. But instead she asked, "Where will you go?"

"I don't know. I'll leave here by the Koord-Caubul and on to Jellalabad and Peshawar and then decide. Perhaps home. I don't know."

"Will you write to me sometimes, Charles?" she asked hesitantly. "It would make it less—less terrible if I knew that you would write. What I mean is, then I would know that nothing terrible had happened to you."

He saw how much she minded his going. He started to speak, stopped, and then said only, "Very well. And now good-bye, my love."

"Now?"

"Yes. I won't come back with you. You will be all right with Aktur, and I do not want to see you there again. Out here under the walnut trees, you are Perdita who loved me and was not afraid to show it. There you are Lady Beaminster, with duties, obligations, and civility." He leaned forward, and she felt his cold lips on her forehead while his hands gripped hers so tightly that they hurt. "Good-bye." Then he left her.

She waited, shivering, alone by the white marble tomb, until she heard his pony's hooves on the uneven road. Then she walked slowly back to her waiting groom. She was about to ask him to help her mount when she felt the ground lurch and the waves of heat churn through her. Dismayed, she recognized the signs and gripped her nails into the palms of her hands, trying to stop it, working desperately not to succumb to the overwhelming force that tried to pull her down.

In one gap she saw Aktur's puzzled face and managed to say in Pushtu, "Wait, all will be well."

But the switching of her concentration was disastrous, and she felt herself go.

The next thing she felt was something soft under the bruise on her head; then the pain in her lower lip, which felt as large as a cricket ball. She tasted blood in her mouth and knew that she had had another fit. She felt too tired to remember where she had been when it happened or who she was or even who was with her. She closed her eyes.

Sixteen

It was dusk before she awoke fully and tried to get up. A peculiar smell seemed to surround her; she soon traced it to the filthy *poshteen* on which she was lying. Some memory returned, and she said, "Aktur?"

"Yes, lady-sahib, I am here." She looked across in the direction of the voice and saw that he was squatting at the foot of a mulberry tree watching her, an expression in his dark face that she had not seen before. He looked awed. She dismissed the thought impatiently and held out one hand for him to help her up. When he had adjusted her stirrup and handed her the reins of her yaboo, she thanked him and asked him to tell no one except the lord-sahib what he had seen. Slightly to her surprise, he agreed fervently.

When she reached the house, she found Marcus waiting for her in a fret of impatience. As soon as he saw her and took in the mud of her skirt and the blood on her lip, he said angrily, "Where have you been? What has happened?"

"I am sorry, Marcus. I rode with Aktur to Baba's tomb, and then I had one of my fits. I thought I was cured. I am truly sorry, but I cannot stop them. I did try."

"My dear, forgive me," he said at once, "but I was so worried. Lieutenant Flecker was fired at this afternoon by a party of tribesmen, and I was afraid something had happened to you. Come and sit down."

"I had better wash first, I think, Marcus. I am sorry you have been anxious."

He said no more then, but later he asked her not to ride outside the cantonments without his escort or that of another British officer. She agreed hesitantly but was unable to ignore the good sense of his prohibition. It made no difference, though, for the next few days, because the aftermath of the convulsion left her feeling weak and suffering from an unpleasant nagging headache that she could not throw off.

When she eventually got up again, recovered but still very pale, the fading bruise on her head felt like the memory of Charles's farewell: an ache reminding her of the past that she could not ignore. But both dwindled as the months continued and present anxieties took over.

Feelings among the occupying army were running high. General Elphinstone, charming though he might be, was despised by most of the senior English officers, especially by his second-in-command, Brigadier Shelton, and the government paid no attention to his various suggestions for improving the garrison's situation. They even refused his offer to purchase, out of his own funds, some land near the perimeter of the cantonment to make it more secure.

He had been selected for the post at Caubul because he seemed likely to conciliate Sir William Macnaghten, who had seriously disliked his predecessor, Sir Willoughby Cotton. But Macnaghten's temper was becoming shorter and shorter, and even Elphinstone's charm did little to help. It was well known, even among the most junior officers and their wives, that the envoy would brook neither criticism nor any suggestion that the country was in a dangerously volatile state, or admit that the cantonments were the worst situated and worst defended that any soldier would ever see. It was also known that Sir William was being badgered by Calcutta to reduce the expenses of the occupation.

Perdita hoped that that might mean its being abandoned, with the regiments being sent back to Hindustan. Like many others, she could see no good coming of it; the delights of the climate and scenery had come to seem insignificant in comparison with the hatred she could now feel all around and the knowledge that there were only two possible routes out of the country, both in the hands of wildly resentful tribes.

The only Caubuli who did not exude hatred, Perdita sometimes thought, was her own groom. But one morning when she had ordered him to bring her pony around to the front door, even his face was tight and his eyes cold with anger. She was shocked enough to ask him if there were something the matter, but he only stared at her and made some remark about the *feringhees* that was incomprehensible to her except in its tone of loathing. She pressed him in her slow Pushtu, and eventually she grasped the fact that his sister had been dishonored by an English officer. It took Perdita some time to understand exactly what he was telling her, but in the end she understood that the girl, aged fifteen, had been seized by an English officer and raped.

Perdita was disgusted, and although her first instinct was to ignore what she had learned, she soon knew that she could not. Quite apart from the political implications of such crass behavior at such a time, she felt a horrified sympathy for the unknown Afghan girl.

She asked Aktur if he knew the name of the man involved. He did not, but he knew enough to describe him as a lieutenant in Marcus's regiment with fair hair that waved and blue eyes. There was only one man who fit that description, Lieutenant Flecker, and Perdita could well imagine him behaving in such a way.

Telling Aktur that she had no wish to ride out after all and that she would speak to the lord-sahib about the officer, Perdita went back into the house, certain that Marcus would see the necessity of punishing the man. But when she had told her husband the story, he was unhelpful, explaining that there was nothing he could do and, worse, showing all too clearly that he was shocked that she would raise such a subject.

"But, Marcus, that young girl has been criminally used. Something should be done."

"No doubt, but if he paid her some compensation, that would be an admission of guilt, and we would be in a hell of a mess. I am sorry, my dear, but you will have to leave it alone. There is nothing to be done."

"Pay her?" repeated Perdita, shocked. "How could money make up for something like that?"

"All Afghans love money. Besides, why should punishing the man make what she says happened any better?"

"Of course, it would not. But it would at least deter him and others from doing any such thing again. And it would demonstrate to her and her family that we do not condone what happened, that our shame and disgust equal theirs."

"Well, we cannot. Any admission of guilt would be wrong. And I must ask you not to refer to the subject again. It is not fit for you to speak about such things."

Perdita looked at him, angrily thinking of all the things men can do to women. She said, "It is too important to ignore. If you will not help, I shall go to Major Jamieson, and if he will not, then to the colonel. If necessary, I shall go to General Elphinstone himself. I mean it, Marcus. No woman could stand by knowing that another has been raped and do nothing."

He saw that she was in earnest and, despite his dislike of the matter, said, "Very well, if it will calm you, I shall speak to the major."

Perdita never asked what he had said or if he had had to argue, but one afternoon he came back to the house and told her that Lieutenant Flecker was to be transferred to Candahar. Marcus said, "I must stress to you that this is no kind of punishment. The colonel considered that if an Afghan family was accusing a British officer of such a thing, it would be safer for him to be elsewhere. Do you understand?"

"I believe so. But, Marcus, tell me why he is not to be punished," she said in as neutral a voice as she could achieve.

He understood that she was not arguing in order to score points, and so his sense of fairness would not let him ignore the question. He said, "Because that kind of thing never happens to a completely innocent female, and it would not be possible to punish one man for what many did when the army first arrived." Seeing that she was angry and about to speak, he went on. "This is a most distressing subject. The lieutenant will be leaving with his company on Thursday, and you must leave the matter there."

"As you wish," she said, wanting to say furiously, What do you mean, not innocent? She was fifteen and never went outside without a *chadri*, and he abducted her. But she recognized the finality in his voice, and she did not want to jeopardize the careful equilibrium of their relationship by forcing through it. All she could do was to tell Aktur as gently as possible that his sister's assailant had been found and was being sent away.

He looked at her with passionate gratitude and spoke rapidly in Pushtu. She thought he said something like, "You have made it possible for my family to regain their honor," but she could not be sure and did not want to prolong the painful interview by asking him to repeat what he had said.

She dismissed him by asking him to bring the ponies to the

front door and went to the nursery to collect the children for their ride.

Both children were at ease in the saddle now, although Annie was less ready to tackle obstacles than her foster brother. At three and a half, Charlie was tough and adventurous. His frightening rages seemed to be more controlled, but he was still apt to hit out or roll on Annie if she got in his way. To Perdita's surprise the girl seemed to take it all in good humor and followed him everywhere she could. She often told Perdita admiring stories of his exploits and, if she did not want to do something, would use his words as apparently irrefutable support for her point of view. "Charlie says" became a phrase that always made Perdita smile.

They were happily riding races between the houses one day when Perdita was greeted by Maria Jamieson. They had seen very little of each another during the occupation, since Major Jamieson had spent several months at Candahar, but he had recently been summoned back to Caubul, and Perdita encountered his wife day after day. As usual, she was full of complaints and scandal. Almost her first words were, "Have you heard that Lord Auckland has resigned?"

"No. But how can you know such a thing?"

"Most of the *senior* officers know, and I expect all the spies. It is obvious, really, to anyone who knows anything about government circles. When the Whigs lost the general election at home, Auckland was bound to go. I expect he thought it better to leave than be recalled."

"I wonder what that will mean to us," said Perdita, more to herself than to Mrs. Jamieson.

Nevertheless Mrs. Jamieson answered, "Who can tell? Jamieson thinks that it will probably mean less than Macnaghten's departure." She saw from Perdita's expression that that, too, was news, and a pleased smile spread across her plump pink and white face as she said, "Oh, yes. He has been appointed Governor of Bombay, and poor, dear Sir Alexander will become envoy at last. He has waited long enough for it."

"I wonder if he is old enough—I mean, experienced enough—for the task," murmured Perdita.

"Well, he can hardly do worse than Macnaghten," said

Mrs. Jamieson tartly. "And at least Sir Alexander has some knowledge of the Afghan people."

Perdita could not help thinking of a remark of Lady Sale's she had heard a day or two before, that it was easy to tell how affairs stood in Caubul because when the skirmishes were being won and peace seemed possible, the envoy and his wife were referred to in cantonments as "Sir William and my Lady"; when things seemed black, they were "the Macnaghtens."

"It must be trying, though, to keep pressing on against the tribes, persuading the king into civilized ways, organizing the administration when every *dawk* brings letters up from Calcutta demanding retrenchment."

"Sir Alexander will think of ways of achieve it. He is so charming, I find. Don't you?"

The syrupy voice irritated Perdita, but she said in her normal voice, "I do not think I would trust him very far. He seems too volatile to me, too partisan in his judgments. But, perhaps," she added, wanting to be fair, "that is because he hasn't really got a job to do. Oh, forgive me, Maria, I must get the children indoors. Charlie! Annie! Come here, please."

After a respectable show of rebellion, Charlie cantered up, soon followed by Annie, looking breathless and pink but very happy. Perdita made them say good afternoon politely to Mrs. Jamieson and then took them away.

Perdita soon discovered what the news meant for her. Marcus's regiment was to form part of the envoy's escort. They would march through the eastern passes to Jellalabad, winter there, and then leave Afghanistan completely in the spring. She had never thought that she could look forward to returning to the station, but the prospect of exchanging its ugly dullness for the glittering terror of Caubul seemed inviting. As she started to make her preparations for departure, she was happier than she had been since Charles Byrd had ridden away from her. The only flaw in her pleasure was Marcus's fear that the force might have to fight its way through the passes.

That fear strengthened into conviction as news flew among the English that Sir William had at last found a way to cut the expenses of the occupation, which were rumored to have reached nearly one and a quarter million pounds a year. He had decided to halve the subsidy paid to the eastern Ghilzais, who were in control of the passes, thus saving about forty thousand rupees. In view of that, the plans for his return to India had to be modified.

For once Perdita shared Captain Thurleigh's views. He came to dine one night at the beginning of October and said irritably to Marcus, "He says he chose them because they have been so peaceful compared to the western Ghilzais. Why does he think they have behaved so well? Because they have been paid for it, with eighty thousand rupees per annum."

"But didn't some of you protest?" asked Marcus.

"Of course we did, but that idiot is so determined to leave for Bombay that he hardly cares what he's doing anymore. He and his doddering poodle, Elphinstone. At least that fool has done the decent thing now and resigned on the grounds of his health. You know that the date has been set now? For the twentieth?"

"Yes, we've had our orders. We are being sent to clear the Koord-Caubul pass with General Sale's brigade. He has arranged for Lady Sale and Mrs. Sturt to follow on with the envoy's party, and my wife will stay until then and go with them."

"But if the whole of Sale's brigade and the 121st leave, doesn't that mean that the garrison will be seriously depleted?" asked Perdita, as worried at the prospect of having to stay behind even for a few days as she was for Marcus's safety in the passes.

"Well done," said Captain Thurleigh sarcastically. "But the envoy believes that since the countryside is 'quiet from Dan to Beersheba,' there will be no risk. By the way, Beaminster," he went on, turning back to Marcus, "have you heard about poor Flecker?"

"No. Don't tell me he's got it?"

"Yes. He was set on just the other side of the Koord-Caubul. Two of his sepoys managed to escape and rode on to Jellalabad with the news. We've only just heard it. And those thugs are the sort Macnaghten thinks are so peaceful!"

He happened to look at Perdita at that moment and wondered why she was so pale. But he said nothing, and Marcus appeared not to notice. She rose, shaken to the depths of her being, and made some excuse to leave the dining room. She remembered with horrible clarity her groom's dark eyes glittering as he said to her something that had sounded like, "You have made it possible for my family to regain their honor," and she wished passionately that she had said nothing to him until the lieutenant had reached his destination. However much she hated what he had done to Aktur's sister, however much she had wanted him to be punished, the news of his death appalled her. And she blamed herself for it.

She also worried desperately about Charles Byrd. She had had no word from him and had no idea whether he had yet reached the safety of the Punjab. Horrible visions began to torment her of his body, broken and bloodied, lying among the rocks of the inhospitable Afghan mountains.

Marcus arranged for Captain Thurleigh to take over his house in cantonments once Perdita and the children had left, and with worsening news from all quarters, he asked his friend to move in as soon as he had to leave, to give her some protection. Thurleigh had all his necessities brought out from the city in time to join the Beaminsters' last dinner together.

His presence added the final touch that turned the meal from an unhappy occasion into a nightmare for Perdita. Marcus was to march the following day into a probably murderous fight to clear the pass; he was likely to be wounded once more and ran a real risk of death. There were so many things she wanted to say to him and ask him before he went that Thurleigh's presence was almost unbearable.

As she sat at the foot of her elegant dining table with Thurleigh on her right discussing absurdly unimportant topics, she could hardly eat. She watched the two men and wondered whether they felt the same, whether their determination to dress as usual and go through all the other absurd rituals of the dinner table was a mask to hide anxiety and desperation that matched her own.

"Won't you try some of the fowl, my dear?" Marcus's kind voice so startled her that her hand slipped from the stem of her wineglass, which crashed onto the edge of the table and splashed its contents over the immaculate white tunic of the hovering servant.

Averting her eyes from the spreading red stains, she said shakily, "I do beg your pardon. So clumsy. No, no fowl, thank you." She tried to stop there, but the act of speaking seemed to have smashed her inhibitions, and she burst out, "How can you be so calm? Tomorrow may bring terrible disaster, and you both sit here discussing fowls and claret."

She saw Captain Thurleigh look at Marcus and then snap out an order to the servants. They left the room, shocked at the break in routine and at the lady-sahib's uncharacteristic, raucous voice. Marcus stood up and came around the table to her chair. He took one of her hands, and in the warmth of his she realized how clammy hers was.

He said, "Perdita, we have to behave like this. If soldiers discussed everything that might happen to them before a battle, it would be impossible to go out and do what must be done. Do not think about it. You must think instead of the benefits of getting the children away from here before the cold becomes severe. You will like wintering in Jellalabad before we press on to India. James has very pleasant memories of last winter there. And then in the spring we will all go back to the station."

She put her other hand on top of his and looked at him. She said, with difficulty, "I am sorry to have fussed. But there are so many things I need to say to you before you go."

"Not now. Tell me in Jellalabad." He smiled at her almost tenderly and said, "You are very tired, dear. Come, forget the rest of dinner and go to bed."

Ashamed and unhappy, she could not force herself on them, and so she rose and left them.

Later, lying in bed unable to sleep, her imagination took her back to the dining room to witness all kinds of intimacy and trust between the two men, and truth and frank admissions of fear and danger. Angry with herself for her jealousy, she turned over, beating the pillow as though trying to make it softer. Five minutes later she turned again, and then once more.

Sometimes she slept for a while, but then she would dream that she was awake and desperately trying to lose consciousness. When she heard the servants moving around the next morning, she felt frighteningly tired, resentful, and almost ill. She waited until she could see light around the edges of the curtains and then rang for her ayah.

Thirty minutes later, dressed and outwardly serene, she was about to go out into the hall when she heard the men's voices.

"Do your best to keep her from worrying, and make sure they all get off on the twentieth, whatever has happened. If necessary, they can go to her father."

"Of course, old fellow." There was a pause, and then a choked voice she could hardly recognize as Thurleigh's. "Until Jellalabad, then."

"Jellalabad."

"Oh, God, why won't they let me march with you? Marcus, take care."

There was silence. After a few moments Perdita opened her bedroom door and joined them. Marcus, shocked at the deep black crescents beneath her big blue eyes and the almost transparent pallor of her complexion, said, "You should not get up. You need rest."

"I had to see you off, Marcus."

He hoped that she would not become emotional. The veneer of calm over his own turmoil was so thin that the smallest load would crack it.

Almost as though she understood, his wife said only, "I had to wish you Godspeed, and to tell you that I shall be praying for you all."

He smiled tightly, gripped her shoulder, looked once more at James, and walked away.

Seventeen

Bad news became almost commonplace while the garrison waited in Caubul. First came the announcement that Sale had been wounded and had lost nearly sixty men in the Koord-Caubul Pass. They had been fired at from behind every rock in the precipitous, narrow pass by Ghilzai tribesmen: sixty of them according to the first report, two hundred according to Lady Sale, who dismissed the first paltry number as an insult. Perdita could not see that higher numbers of enemy made the situation any better, except for English pride. What was very clear was that the road to Jellalabad was blocked by the "peaceful" Ghilzais.

In the intervals of trying to contain her fears for Marcus, Perdita consoled herself with the thought of the southern route back to India. But then came the sad story of a Mrs. Smith, the wife of a collector, who had been traveling with a small guard through the southern Bolan Pass toward Candahar when her escort was attacked. The guards fled, and Mrs. Smith apparently got out of her *palkee* and ran as fast and as far as she could before she was caught and killed with a knife.

Perdita listened to the story in dismay. Neither route could be guaranteed any longer. More and more people were saying openly that the occupation had been a failure and that the Caubul chiefs, and probably the Shah himself, were behind all the insurrections and assassinations of the past few months. Few of the English would admit it, but to most of them their cantonment seemed to be a trap from which there was no escape.

Day after day toward the end of October, Sale's guns could be heard from Caubul, and the envoy's departure was postponed again and again. More and more wounded were brought back with news of attacks and treachery in the pass. To Lady Sale's disgust, several Afghan miscreants were caught deserting from the Shah's regiments, and others deliberately hamstringing the English's ammunition-carrying camels. The criminals were hailed back to Caubul and brought before Macnaghten. But he refused to punish them, offering by way of excuse that the Shah's advisers had told him that the men were of good repute and that they could not possibly have committed the crimes of which they stood accused. The suspicion that His Majesty was involved in the troubles began to harden.

The difficulties experienced in clearing the pass meant that the envoy's departure was put off until November 3. His wife took to calling on several senior ladies to inform them that virtually all the country was quiet, that the chiefs were responding well to the political agent's negotiations, and that a peaceful settlement was likely. She did not tell them that Sir William had been warned by at least three different Afghans not to ride out, as was his custom, in the early morning and late evening, or that three other men had sworn on the Koran to kill him. But everyone knew.

Those days in Caubul seemed like an unending and ever-deepening trial of endurance. Military officers in search of orders were sent by General Elphinstone to Sir William and back again. No one seemed to know what was happening; no one seemed to be in charge. Everyone was irritable, and absurd quarrels broke out at all hours between the most placid of people.

Perdita, like the other ladies who were to travel with the envoy's party, had had everything packed in time for the first departure date, and so the house seemed like some demented entrepôt, stacked with trunks and boxes, many of them opened by the servants in search of some vital piece of equipment or clothing. She knew that the mess exasperated Captain Thurleigh, who had an insatiable desire for neatness and order, but she could not help it. Their always uneasy truce became spiked with unspoken argument.

The only event that lightened the days for Perdita was the arrival of a *dawk* from the Punjab. One of the letters she was handed was from Charles Byrd. It seemed to her almost incredible that the mail should get through to Caubul as though nothing had happened, but the knowledge that Charles at least was safe helped her to fight her terrors.

Every caller who came to the house strengthened Perdita's anxiety, even Lady Macnaghten and Captain Lawrence, the envoy's military secretary, who always tried to reassure. Lady Sale came once to tell her of Sale's wound and another morning that the brigade had lost ninety men. Then Aktur begged permission to talk to the lady-sahib. She went out onto the veranda to talk to him wrapped in a huge black and red shawl, for it was growing very cold. He told her that he would not be able to work for her any longer.

"But why, Aktur? Have we displeased you in some way?"

"Of course not, lady. But it is difficult for me to leave the city each day to come to you. And something terrible is going to happen. We do not know what, but you should be on your guard. Something will happen."

When he had gone, Perdita sent a note over to the Mission to warn Captain Thurleigh of what her groom had said, but she received no answer.

When her unwelcome and reluctant guest returned to her house for dinner, he told her, "These Afghans love a drama, you know. We discussed your note, but it is Sir William's opinion that the young man is bored with working and was making an excuse to leave your service."

But next morning, they were all awakened at dawn by a tremendous commotion and the sound of firing from the city. Worried and frightened, the English dressed. The soldiers stood to arms. Everyone waited anxiously for news.

At seven it was confirmed that there was an uprising in the city but that it was not thought to be serious; at nine, that Captain Johnson's house had been sacked and his treasury plundered; at ten, that Sir Alexander was by the grace of God safely in the Bala Hissar; at twelve, that the first message had been a lie and that no one had seen him and that the worst should be assumed.

The troops had been standing to since dawn. When no firm, clear orders had come by eleven, Brigadier Shelton sent Sturt to the city to discover what he could. Later in the morning, Perdita heard that Sturt had been treacherously set upon and knifed at the Lahore Gate and that Shelton's men had marched into the Bala Hissar.

She went as soon as she could to Lady Sale's house, where the wounded man had been carried, to see if she could help. Mrs. Sturt could not leave her husband, but her mother came out for a moment or two to thank Perdita for her concern. She said, "He has been stabbed deeply in the shoulder and side and on the face. His nerves have been affected by the wound, and his mouth will not open. His tongue is swollen and paralyzed. He cannot speak or take any liquid. He is in the greatest agony, and he looks ghastly and faint from loss of blood." She covered her eyes for a moment and said in a more broken voice than Perdita could have believed her capable of, "The choking sensation of the blood in his throat is most painful to witness."

"I can imagine," said Perdita, remembering Aneila's dying agony. "Please tell Mrs. Sturt that if there is any help I can give, she has only to send a servant over, and I shall come."

They shook hands briefly, and Perdita went home to find Captain Lawrence on the veranda talking to Captain Thurleigh. Lawrence broke off when he saw her to greet her courteously, but Thurleigh impatiently dragged his attention back to the matter at hand. Perdita heard him say, "Never mind that now, George. What the hell is happening?"

"We cannot be sure, but the Shah has sent a message that Burnes is safe. Apparently he went to consult the *wazir* at the beginning of the outbreak."

"But you told me yourself that you did not see him there this morning. I don't trust the Shah one inch. If you ask me, he is behind all this trouble."

"Bosh, James. He may be weak, but he is not a scoundrel."

"I would not be too sure of that." Then he turned to Perdita and demanded coldly, "Where have you been?"

"Only to visit poor Mrs. Sturt," she said, startled by his tone.

"Well, do not go outside cantonments, and tell me where you are going within. I have guaranteed your safety to your husband."

"Of course," she said, and went into the house.

Later in the day, Lawrence was back with the news that the Shah had sent another note to confess that he had not seen Burnes all day and did not know where he was but that if the insurrection were not over by the next morning, he would burn the city.

"I suppose that is something," said Thurleigh.

"How can he? The houses are all mud," said Perdita.

Thurleigh answered impatiently, "It's been done three times before now. You throw shells into each house individually, and they burn enough before the mud roof falls in and smothers the flames."

Perdita retired to the edge of the room and listened to the two men without volunteering anything.

"But why haven't the troops been sent in?" asked Thurleigh.

"It's not as easy as all that," answered Lawrence. "The streets are all so narrow and the houses so well built for defensive operations that our fellows would be massacred if they went in. One of the Shah's regiments has already been cut to pieces."

"Well, if something isn't done soon, those devils will assume that we are utterly supine, and the whole country will rise. We must take the town, even if only to put the women and children in the Bala Hissar. That's the only place where we could possibly hope to keep them alive. What on earth is the matter?" he asked as Lawrence gestured toward the back of the room.

"You must be seriously worrying Lady Beaminster. Please do not misconstrue Thurleigh's words. Our case is not so desperate as all that. We shall of course be able to protect you all." He smiled kindly at her.

"Oh, don't be ridiculous, Lawrence. She's intelligent enough at least to see the truth of our situation. Don't insult her with pretense."

Almost too surprised to speak, Perdita just managed to say quietly, "Thank you, Captain Thurleigh. I must say that I prefer not to ignore our probable fate, though I am grateful, Captain Lawrence, that you wished to spare me anxiety." She went out to find the children, wanting to spend as much time as she could with them and hoping that if the worst came, they would at least be killed outright and not have to linger in agony like poor Sturt or in torment like Lieutenant Loveday at Khelat.

But when Annie asked, "Where is Papa?" Perdita could not control the tears that seeped from her eyes.

She hugged the girl and whispered, "I wish I knew. Oh, Annie, I wish I knew."

She was awakened at three the next morning by the drums beating the troops to arms. Throwing a shawl around her shoulders, she ran out into the hall to find Thurleigh coming out of his room buttoning his breeches. She averted her eyes and said, "What is it? What is happening?"

"How in God's name should I know? Stay here. Keep the servants calm, and I shall come back when I can. Oh, and stop that damned child from yowling."

Perdita hated him at that moment. She did not wait to see him go but ran to the nursery where Annie had been awakened by the noise and was wailing for her. Charlie was standing on his bed looking out the window at the rushing men and horses thundering toward the gate.

The passing torches threw weird flashes of light into the room, and in one she saw excitement on his flushed little face. She wanted to drag him from the window, bury his face in her breast, and tell him that war was not exciting and killing was not honorable, that he must not enjoy it or it would destroy him. But she could not. She took some comfort from the feel of Annie's warm, compact little body clutched to her own, straining to hear the shouted words that echoed past the walls. First it was, ". . . from the Seeah Sung. Yes, hundreds."

And then, "Well, so much for Macnaghten's views of the peace."

"What happens to the women? Someone must st—"

"Oh, Lord, here they come. Ready, lads."

Then a wild shout. "But there's Europeans with them. It's the 121st!"

"It can't be. Hold up the torch. By God, it is!"

At that, Perdita stood up, and with Annie still clinging to her she walked to the front door. She opened it and stood on the veranda as unconscious of the impropriety of appearing in public in her nightgown with her hair hanging down her back as of the icy cold of her bare feet, to watch the regiment ride in, pennants fluttering, spurs and bits jingling, guns thundering past on their iron wheels. Through the spurt of pride, she looked fearfully for her husband. When she saw him riding erect at the head of his men, she bent down and whispered absurdly, "Everything will be all right now, Annie. Papa is back."

She waited there in the cold, hoping that he would come back to the house, but soon it was clear that he must be with his men. Reluctantly she went back into the hall, closing the door behind her, to warm her feet and the child's and then persuade the two of them to go back to bed and sleep.

She herself slept almost as soon as she had closed her eyes and for once did not awaken until her ayah came to open her curtains. She dressed hastily and ran to the dining room, hoping to find Marcus. He was not there, so she had to make polite conversation to Captain Thurleigh, who had looked up surprised at her precipitate entry. But in a very few minutes they heard Marcus greeting the butler, and a moment later he came in. Perdita could not stop herself from going to him and putting her arms around him.

He patted her back perfunctorily and said, "My dear, don't. I have not had a bath or a change of clothes since we marched."

She had in fact been aware of a most peculiar smell as she embraced him, but she said as she stepped back, "What does that matter compared to your safety? Marcus, I am so—" Dizzy with relief that he was safe, unwounded, and back with her, she could not find a word to express herself.

He smiled as though he knew and said, "Would you send for some breakfast while I change?"

"Of course, Marcus."

He patted her again and said over her shoulder, "James, I'll tell you all about it when I get back." He left them.

They sat in silence for some time until Thurleigh said without thinking very much, "He looks none the worse for it."

"No. Almost as though he had enjoyed it," answered Perdita, wondering how that could be possible.

Thurleigh said more sharply, "Perhaps he is just happy to be back with—" He stopped himself, then said, "Back at home."

"Perhaps," she said. She looked up to see the *khitmagar* coming in from the kitchen quarters. She gave him orders for the lord-sahib's breakfast in her now fluent Hindustani.

When the man had gone, Thurleigh said, "I hope he is hungry."

For the first time Perdita smiled at him in genuine, friendly amusement. She said, "Well, I expect he is, but even if not, he will understand why I ordered it all."

Thurleigh smiled at her without antagonism, as though recognizing that she, too, was a human being with feelings like his own. He was just beginning, "You know, you are—" when Marcus walked back in, bathed, shaved, and dressed in a clean uniform. They both smiled at him, and Thurleigh begged for news while Perdita brought a cup of tea.

"It was frightful," said Marcus as he sipped the scalding liquid. "Montieth's men had been badly mauled when we got there, and we soon saw why. We could see no one as we entered the pass, but they were there all right." He paused to cram some kedgeree into his mouth. Perdita and James Thurleigh waited impatiently while he swallowed it and took another gulp of hot tea.

"Well, come on, man," said Thurleigh. "What, then?"

"James, give me time. I haven't had a real meal for days."

"Sorry, old man."

"Well, they were there, all right—behind every rock and in every chimney all the way to the heights. They were hidden with their guns pointing down on the column. They seemed to wait until we were fairly entangled in the pass, and then they opened fire."

"Yes," urged Thurleigh, still burning with impatience.

"We could tell where they were from the flashes of their matchlocks, but it was next to impossible to hit any of them. And they just went on pouring their fire down on to us."

"How did you get through, then?" asked Perdita.

"Flankers, really," he said, carrying another loaded forkful of kedgeree to his mouth. They watched him chew and swallow.

"The column was ordered to press on without slackening speed, while companies were detached to left and right. They engaged the Afghans, and we marched on until we came to a devilish wall of stones they must have erected the night before." He paused, then caught sight of James's expression and put the fork down. "We rushed it though, James, and for some reason they did not even try to defend it. As soon as there was a gap, Davis lashed his horses and took the guns through at a gallop. It was a magnificent sight, Perdita, those blacks of his flying through, their manes streaming and their mouths showing red while the guns crashed and careered behind. I don't wonder the tribesmen kept away."

"Oh, *shabash* Davis!" cried Thurleigh, banging his fist on the table in frustration. "I wish I had been there instead of trapped here with these fools and women."

"It must have been hard to come back," said Perdita thoughtfully, "after winning through like that."

"Yes. Lots of our fellows were angry that General Bob selected us to come back to protect the envoy. But I was pleased," he said, and smiled at her. "By the way, James, is it true that Macnaghten is paying those fiends again?"

"Yes, but not as much as at first."

"I see. Well, I hope to God it's enough to keep them quiet while we take the women through. Never mind, dear," he added, noticing Perdita's pallor. "Tell me what has been happening here." But he did not wait to hear, turning to James to say, "I could hardly believe it when we heard that there was a rebellion in the town and none of you did anything about it."

"That is not quite fair," answered Thurleigh, "though Burnes is dead. We know that now. Poor fellow! He never got his chance to show how much better he could run this country than Macnaghten."

"But why has nothing been done? Why haven't you taken the town?"

"Several reasons, but you'd better get them from Lawrence; he believes 'em. I don't. Oh, very well. One, it is difficult to see what kind of operation could have been mounted in that rabbit warren of a town with cover for enemy marksmen everywhere you look. Two, the uprising was not thought very serious at first. Don't look at me like that, Marcus. Remember last year when all that fuss turned out to be unnecessary? Three, the general thought it inadvisable. I ought not to tell you this, perhaps, but he wrote to Macnaghten explaining his dilemma over the propriety of entering the city and then said, 'We must see what the morning brings and then think what must be done.'"

Marcus dropped his head into his clasped hands and groaned. Then he said, "With an old woman like that at the head of the army, we are lost. Has no one ever told him that a commander must be decisive?"

Thurleigh interrupted. "Possibly. But I imagine they also told him long ago that it is essential for a general to be able to ride—or at least walk. Yes, you need not look so skeptical; the general is confined to his sofa with the gout."

"If they had to choose an ancient, they at least might have chosen one who knew what he was doing. Why on earth did he have to be a Queen's officer? Experience must have told them by now that in the East you must have commanders who know the East."

"He fought at Waterloo. Presumably that is why Wellington sent him out here."

Perdita could remain silent no longer.

"Should you not both be with your chiefs? If our situation is as desperate as you suggest, surely you should be doing something useful." She saw the surprise and anger with which they received her intervention and rushed to apologize. "Forgive me. I suppose I am too anxious to be rational. I shall go and see the children."

As she closed the door behind her, Marcus was already getting up.

"She is right, you know, James. I'll see you later, old fellow."

The desperation of the situation became clearer and clearer. Lieutenant Eyre, who was the Deputy Commissary of Ordnance, disposed all the guns he had around the perimeter of the cantonments, but even people with the least military intelligence could see that they were pitifully inadequate to withstand an attack and quite useless against the sniping, skirmishing Afghans, who proceeded to surround the commissariat fort.

The young officer in charge of its defense sent a stream of notes to the general reporting on his position and begging for reinforcements. General Elphinstone appeared to think the request quite reasonable, for he ordered two companies of the 44th to reinforce it. Unfortunately they had to pass a fort owned and defended by Mohammed Sharrif, one of the most belligerent of the Afghans, on their way to the beleaguered garrison and were cut to pieces by his sniper fire. Both captains were killed; their men straggled back to cantonments dispirited, wounded, and demoralized.

Later in the day another attempt was made, this time by the cavalry, but again they were turned back. It came to the ears of the commissariat officers that the party had been given instructions to evacuate the fort. They hurried to the general to point out the absurdity, the foolishness of abandoning all their stores to the enemy when the supplies kept within cantonments were sufficient for only about three days. General Elphinstone saw the point and agreed to send strong reinforcements to the inexperienced and obviously panicky lieutenant guarding the fort. But other officers present, led by Captain Bellew, pointed out the dangers of such an exercise and made so many helpful and unhelpful suggestions that their courteous commanding officer wavered first one way and then the other, as though quite unable to make himself rude enough to adopt any policy proposed by one faction if it were disapproved of by another.

The result of it all was that the fort was evacuated in the early hours of the following morning. Later in the day the spectators in cantonments watched bitterly as the enemy swarmed over the fort's walls, only to emerge carrying off the precious supplies of grain, spirits, wine, beer, and all the arrowroot and sago for the sick.

Lady Sale had taken up her usual position on the flat roof of her house, clinging to one of the chimneys. She invited Perdita to join her to watch the shameful sight. Together they looked down on the plain, watching attacks on the forts commanded by Captains Mackenzie and Trevor. They wondered what was to be done to stop the escalating trouble. It was all too obvious to both Perdita and Lady Sale that if a force strong enough to fight through to the forts were sent out of cantonments, there would not be enough troops left for defense.

Perdita was thinking what she would be doing if she were Mrs. Trevor when Lady Sale said urgently, "Look! All is well, Lady Beaminster." She craned forward and saw coming through the main gate a party of Trevor's native troops escorting the family, each adult carrying one of the children.

They were all soaked to the thighs, having had to wade through the river, and their faces were gaunt from lack of sleep and anxiety, but there was triumph in their bearing. To have brought eight children from the fort just as the Afghans breached its walls was a feat to be cheered.

That small success raised the garrison's spirits for a while, until failure piled on failure dashed them again. With each exhibition of English supineness and muddle, the Afghans increased their daring, and the morale of the defending troops fell still further. They had no confidence left in their invalid general. They all knew that he would listen to any advice, even from the most junior officer, and was quite unable to make up his own mind. His gout had recently become very bad, and he was unable to walk or ride.

Understanding how useless he was, he sent for Shelton, who had been quartered in the Bala Hissar since the beginning of the troubles. He also sent letter after letter down through the passes to Sale, begging, ordering, and cajoling him to return at whatever cost to save the Caubul army. Macnaghten did the same, but as the days went on, wearing down the spirits of the beleaguered English, it became horribly obvious that for whatever reason, Sale was not coming.

Very few people ventured to criticize him in his wife's hearing, but more than one considered that his refusal to obey the order to come to their rescue was tantamount to cowardice and desertion. He had a strong brigade with him and several guns, all safely ensconced behind the high walls of Jellalabad, while at Caubul his colleagues, not to speak of his wife and daughter, faced imminent defeat and very probably death.

Every day seemed worse than the last. Food became scarce, and as the weather worsened daily, the lack of firing became acute. The commissariat officers did their best to buy food and fuel from the surrounding villages, but even when the prices were reasonable, the villagers and their convoys of vital produce were harassed and attacked by tribesmen.

Perdita, struggling to keep the two children unaware of their plight, warm, and fed, thought she could have kept her equanimity better if she could have had peace at home. But no house containing James Thurleigh could offer that.

Their brief moment of alliance just after Marcus's return

from the pass might never have existed. Perdita could feel Captain Thurleigh's irritation whenever she entered a room where he was talking to her husband, and from the bleakness in Marcus's eyes as he watched them, she knew that he could feel it, too. When they were all three together, he seemed to withdraw from both James and Perdita, and they were left to converse spikily with each other. Perdita used to wait avidly for the sight of James Thurleigh descending the steps from the veranda so that she could go to find Marcus blessedly alone. Then he would seem gravely glad to see her, and they would be able to talk.

On November 16, Thurleigh left the house immediately after luncheon, and Marcus was off duty until the evening. Perdita was sitting peacefully with him in the afternoon, and for once he was almost frank about his fears for the future. Perdita had told him a little of her own when they were interrupted by Thurleigh. She tried not to show him the anger he displayed so openly to her, and she was glad when he told Marcus why he had come.

It seemed that Shah Soojah wanted to negotiate with the rebels to put an end to the fighting. Perdita said, "Thank God. Then there may be some hope for us all."

Thurleigh answered bitterly, "Don't depend on it. I believe that the chiefs would take any agreement as a sign—yet another sign—of weakness on our part, pretend to agree, and then, once our defenses are relaxed, attack with all the men they can muster. Sir William has demanded to see a copy of any terms before Soojah signs, so we may get away with it. But, you know, the best news is that the Afghans are fighting among themselves. If Macnaghten can divide them properly, we'll be able to rule them once again."

"Isn't that rather risky?" asked Perdita. "Did any of us believe at the outset that the tribes would unite to the extent they have now?"

James Thurleigh glared at her, and Marcus quickly changed the subject to the more acceptable, if equally important, one of the garrison's dwindling supplies.

"Perhaps we'll start eating the dead camels. At least that would be better than suffering the stink of their rotting carcasses," answered Thurleigh. Perdita felt sick.

The situation grew desperate as November ended. Officers

no longer worried about letting their men see how little hope they had of victory, or even of survival. One morning when an encouragingly large consignment of grain reached cantonments, the colonel of the 5th Native Infantry said gloomily, "It is needless, for they will never live to eat it."

Everyone knew that Brigadier Shelton was urging General Elphinstone to decide on a mad retreat to Jellalabad, while Sturt, now partly recovered from his terrible wounds, was begging the old gentleman to move the entire garrison into the Bala Hissar, which at least could be properly defended. It was common knowledge that Shelton always pretended to be asleep during consultations so that he would not have to answer difficult questions; that Captain Bellew raised objections and difficulties to every plan proposed; and that the general would no longer order out any of the troops unless he could persuade Macnaghten to take responsibility for it.

Creeping despair and a conviction that they would all die or at best be made prisoners and slaves had seized almost all of the English when at last a loophole seemed to open. Akbar Khan, the fighting second son of the Dost, arrived at Caubul and assumed leadership of the chiefs of all the tribes with whom the envoy had been attempting to negotiate. His terms were stiff and humiliating but at least guaranteed the garrison a safe retreat out of his country.

When the news leaked out, Perdita and most of the other ladies felt astonished relief. To get out of the hated country at last, with an escort of tribesmen to see them through the passes! In the sudden exhilaration that attends any release from paralyzing fear, they set about packing up again. The idea of such a long journey in the cold, sleet, and snow of the last few days was unattractive, but most of them believed it would be worth it. Perdita sought out all the warm furs and skins she could find for her family and servants and gave orders for the best arrangements for packing up the furniture and silver she had brought with her.

Marcus warned her that with so many of the camels dead, it was unlikely that she would be able to take it all. Cheerfully enough, she revised her plans and had some of the less favored pieces chopped up for firewood for the last few days in Caubul. Once again the house became really warm, and the Beaminsters found themselves immensely popular.

Visitors called at all hours to sit over Perdita's fires, talking now hopefully, now in despair, about their prospects of survival. Notably absent from these almost jolly gatherings, though, were the politicals, who seemed to be avoiding their friends and military colleagues. One or two officers remarked on it, but the general opinion was that they were working out the details of the march and the Afghan escort with the chiefs.

The true reason for their absence did not become clear until December 23, when Sir William was treacherously murdered by Akbar Khan and the English discovered what he and his assistants had been plotting. Captain Trevor fell, too, leaving his wife with the frightening prospect of getting the eight children back to India alone. The rest of the English officers who had accompanied the envoy to his meeting with Akbar were taken prisoner. Disgusting details of what was done to the poor men's bodies began to circulate around cantonments. Macnaghten's hands had been cut off, and his head, and his legs. The head was paraded through the streets of Caubul, and the trunk hung from a meat hook in the Char Chouk.

It was with some shame that James Thurleigh admitted to Beaminster that his dead chief had been trapped by Akbar into breaking faith with the tribes. Once they had reached agreement with Macnaghten, Akbar sent him a secret message, offering infinitely more attractive terms in return for a personal subsidy and a promise of British support for his own campaign against the other chiefs.

Thurleigh saw Marcus's expression of horror and hurriedly said, "I know. I knew what you would say. But look at it from his point of view. Akbar proposed our waiting until the spring before attempting the passes, quite apart from helping us retrieve our honor."

"Honor? By breaking a treaty?" demanded Marcus angrily.

"I think," commented Perdita in a dry voice but with almost equal anger, "that *pride* would be a more appropriate word."

This time she did not wait for their response but left them

and wondered whether to have everything unpacked yet again or to leave the cases and boxes and trunks as they were. She wished she had not been so profligate with the furniture. Now it looked as though they might all be stuck at Caubul for months longer, and the weather would become far worse before spring.

But eventually, on January 6, the Caubul garrison marched out of its expensive cantonments. The last days had been hideously cold, and everyone had been hungry; even the officers and their families had been cut to half and then quarter rations like the sepoys and camp followers. Rumors about the finally agreed treaty circulated as usual, and everyone who heard them was loud in condemnation of the terms. General Elphinstone had agreed to pay fourteen and a half lakhs of rupees for safe conduct through the passes to Peshawar, leaving six hostages to guarantee their behavior and six of their guns.

Few but he were disposed to trust the word of Akbar Khan. It was universally agreed that the Commander in Chief should have ordered the six guns to be spiked so that they at least could not be used against the retreating army. But General Elphinstone for once stuck rigidly to an opinion of his own: the six guns formed part of a treaty; it would be dishonorable to do anything but hand them over in proper working order.

"I wonder why he does not leave Vincent Eyre behind to help them fire the damned things," said Thurleigh furiously when he heard.

He was far from being the only man to doubt the good faith of the tribesmen. Sergeant Deane, who had married an Afghan and so had innumerable friends in the city, reported that he had heard that the column was to be attacked by ten thousand Kohistanis at Tizeen and then by all the Ghilzais at Soorkhab. But his information was dismissed.

Lady Sale's servant, Mohammed Ali, warned her to beware of treachery, and Perdita's erstwhile groom, Aktur, forced his way into the cantonment once more to deliver a similar warning. She said in her halting Pushtu, "I will tell the sahibs, but I think they will march even so."

He looked at her with an intensity in his black eyes, saying urgently, "If that is so, do not ride with the other memsahibs but among the *sowars*. And wear these." He presented her with an unsavory bundle containing what he called *neemchees*, a kind of sheepskin jacket, and coarse turbans.

"That sounds like wise counsel, Aktur. But what of my children?"

"They must wear the same and go nowhere near the *palkees* or camel panniers. They must ride with you."

"But they are too young. It is nine times ten miles to Jellalabad alone."

"I know it. But ride they must. There are coats enough here." Then he went, reiterating his warnings, which Perdita repeated to Marcus later in the day.

He said dispiritedly, "I can well believe that the Afghans will attack us, for a more treacherous set of scoundrels I have never set eyes on. We must march as soon as possible, and the southern route is impossibly long and probably just as dangerous. But there is nothing to be done. We must go as soon as we can. And may God have mercy on our souls."

Eighteen

Perdita had never been so cold or so afraid. She was half lying, half sitting in a kind of nest of *poshteens* and *neemchees* she had made in the snow when the column halted to bivouac for the night. Marcus, on his way to see to his men, had urged her to take the children at least into a tent that had been pitched for the officers' families. But remembering Aktur's advice, she had insisted on camping among the troops at the head of the column, in spite of the children's tearful protests and wailing demands for their ayahs and their beds. As Marcus walked away, she called, "Come back when you can. We shall be warmer all together."

He waved in what she took to be agreement, and so she persuaded the children to lie down in their eccentric and distasteful bed and settled down to wait for him. All around them were noisy animals, worried officers, men straggling in and trying to find their companies, and hundreds and hundreds of camp followers trailing their babies and their baskets, getting in the way, and causing unutterable muddle for the soldiers.

As darkness fell, the sky to the west of the bivouac was lit with an orange-red glow that was unpleasantly reflected in the moonlit snow. Perdita asked a passing officer of the 121st what it could be, and he called despairingly, "It's the cantonment burning. They started the sack even before the last of our fellows got away." He strode off, leaving Perdita to try to ease her aching back and wait.

Once she was sure that the children were asleep, she took her arms from around their shoulders and then half turned awkwardly to scoop up a mound of snow under the sheepskins to make a backrest. The relief she felt as she leaned against it was almost piercing, and she believed after all that she might survive until Marcus returned.

He came nearly an hour later with Captain Thurleigh, and she persuaded them both to add their sheepskin coats to her nest and lie down close to the children. Thurleigh hesitated, but the cold was so intense that he saw the sense of it and lowered himself down between the layers of skins.

Marcus watched him and then said, "Perdita, my poor dear, are you very uncomfortable?"

She summoned up a smile and said, "Not so bad. If only there were some water! But any thirst is better than staying in Caubul, so I am not complaining. How far have we come?"

The two men looked across the heap of coats that covered them all, and Thurleigh said roughly, "Above five miles."

The horror of it silenced Perdita. They had ninety miles to go and in a whole day's cold, painful marching had only achieved one eighteenth of the total. There was no wood for camp fires and no fresh water, and the baggage train was in such disorder that no food had been distributed. She and the children had dined off biscuits soaked in sherry, the only liquid available.

"At least it is helping them sleep," she said aloud.

"What, dear?"

"Oh, I am sorry, Marcus. I was thinking aloud, that at least the sherry I gave the children is helping them to sleep."

He found her hand under the furs and squeezed it. "And you, too, I hope. You will need all your strength when we reach the pass tomorrow."

"Shall we reach it tomorrow at this snail's pace?"

"We must."

When the gray dawn came, releasing them from the necessity of pretending to sleep and trying not to move in case they should inadvertently wake the others, all three adults were unsure whether they had actually slept at all. But at least they were warm, except for their faces, which were pinched and reddened from the cold. Perdita brought one of her hands, warm from the nest, up to brush something from her eyelids and discovered that her eyelashes and brows were frozen hard. She was trying to thaw her face, wincing in the pain, as she saw the others struggle out of their coverings.

Marcus said, "I have to see to the men. But I'll try to find some breakfast for you and the children and discover when we're to march."

"Thank you, Marcus," said Perdita, resolutely trying to keep down the panic that seemed to rise in her throat like vomit.

When he came back, his face was unhappier than she had ever seen it. She started to get up, saying, "Marcus, what has happened?"

He said, "This is a catastrophe, the worst mess anyone could have imagined. The rear guard did not reach the bivouac until two this morning—that was what all the commotion was. Most of the baggage train has been lost, and with it the entire commissariat. But worse, far worse—" He broke off and actually groaned. Before Perdita could urge him to tell her the worst, Thurleigh walked up and gripped Marcus's arm above the elbow.

"There is nothing to be done now, old fellow, except see that the march is pushed forward with all speed, to get the living to some kind of shelter."

Perdita said forcefully, "Will one of you two please tell me what has happened?"

"Most of the Indian troops have suffered severely from frostbite, Lady Beaminster. Many of Marcus's men are dead."

"From cold?" asked Perdita.

Marcus said bitterly, "They were not allowed to wrap leggings around their boots as some of us wanted, and they had no bedding. Some of them took off their clothes to burn as fuel in order to feel some warmth before they died. The camp followers are in worse condition, if possible. There are bodies all over the road; they just lay there and died."

"Ayah," came Charlie's sleepy voice from beneath the *poshteen*. Perdita gestured her husband to be silent. "Ayah, bring my clothes," he said imperiously in Hindustani.

Perdita answered in English. "Ayah is not here, my son. And you are wearing your clothes. Look. We are on our way to Jellalabad, remember? Annie, here, let me help you to sit up."

"Breakfast, Mama. What is for breakfast?" asked Charlie.

"I don't really know, old boy. Marcus, did you—?"

"Oh, yes," he said, feeling in his pockets. "Johnson has given me some Caubul cakes and tea for you all. But didn't you tell me that you had some raisins and *ottah* in your saddlebags?"

"Yes, but if we are marching at only five miles per day and the army has rations for only five days if they do not get lost, we will need those supplies before we reach Jellalabad."

"I don't think it right to take Johnson's food while you have your own," said Marcus.

Perdita was so angry that she actually felt the blood warm and pounding in her cold cheeks. With some difficulty she said, "I cannot fight. But I am trying to insure that the children reach Jellalabad alive. And if that involves keeping the food I brought in spite of all official reassurances that rations would be provided, I will do it."

Marcus, who had never seen her so definite and was in any case too worried, cold, and exhausted to argue, handed over the flask of tea and the collection of flat, grayish-brown pancakes and went back to his company.

Before the orders were given to march at about half past seven, groups of Indians began to struggle through the encampment, carrying bundles and squalling children. They stumbled past Perdita's bivouac, one child tripped over the tether of Perdita's yaboo.

She picked him up and called to his mother, "Where are you going? Have orders—?"

The woman called back with none of the obsequious deference Perdita was accustomed to from Hindus. "No. But any fool can see that death awaits all who stay for the sahibs' orders."

Seeing the sense of that yet knowing that to push on toward the pass without military protection was tantamount to suicide, Perdita set about packing up, ready for the column to move off. She started to roll up the sheepskins, directing the children to put on their coats and tighten the wrappings around their legs. They simply looked at her, puzzled, until she realized that both had always been dressed by their ayahs. Neither had any idea how to put their own arms into the sleeves of a coat.

Perdita knelt down in the snow, soaking the skirts of her gown to dress the two children, talking gently to them as she did so. Charlie's normal exuberance was dimmed, and Annie's eyes were dilated with fear. Perdita hoped they did not understand quite how precarious was the army's situation, and she forced her voice into calm.

They were all waiting by the fretful, stamping ponies who had had no fodder since the previous day when Marcus rode up. He said, "The order of march is to be reversed today. We are to form the rear guard under Brigadier Anquetil, and the 5th and the 54th will form the advance with the Shah's 6th—what's left of it—and four guns. Will you ride with them or with the rest of the ladies in the center?"

"With the advance, Marcus," she said, determined to follow Aktur's instructions.

"You will not be alone. Lady Sale and Emily Sturt will be with you. We march at eight. Oh, and take care of the ponies' hooves; they probably have ice embedded there. Do something about it. I can't stay."

She watched him ride off to join the rear guard and set about trying ineffectually to do something about the ice in the ponies' hooves. It was rock-solid and obviously caused them some discomfort, but she had no idea what to do.

A sapper sergeant who was passing saw what the matter was and came to help her. He knocked the ice out with a chisel and mallet and roughly bade her mount.

"I'll put the children up, ma'am."

"Thank you, Sergeant. I am afraid I do not know your name."

"Deane, ma'am."

"Well, thank you, Sergeant Deane. I wish I had something to give you."

He touched his cap and said, "Never mind. Good-bye."

He went on his way, and Perdita urged the children forward to join the advance guard. As they went, their yaboos stumbling over the bodies of men, women, and children that littered the area, Annie called, "Mama, I don't like it. Why can't I sit in a *khajava* like Maria Jamieson?"

"Because it is safer to ride, Annie. It is not comfortable, but it is safer. Come, let's trot to get warm. Heels down, knees in. Come on. That's right. Not so fast, Charlie. We mustn't outstrip the column. Look, here's Lady Sale. Good morning."

"If it can be called so," she answered. "Have you had breakfast?"

"Of sorts." They smiled at each other, knowing well the danger they faced and the privations they would suffer but sharing a determination to get through.

The column moved off at a walk. Within thirty minutes Perdita heard firing and, looking back, terrified, saw the tribesmen pouring down toward the rear guard and the remaining baggage. It was hard to see what was happening, but sepoys came running past the column toward the straggling camp followers who had anticipated the march and were clogging the route and making a steady, soldierly advance impossible.

Lady Sale, whose expression of disgusted irritation showed exactly what she thought of the proceedings, directed her daughter's attention to the increasing numbers of Afghans riding on both flanks of the column. All she said was, "So much for fourteen and a half lakhs' worth of protection."

They pushed on toward the pass, Perdita's mind full of fear for Marcus fighting with his men at the rear. She tried to keep the children amused and not too afraid and thought that Lady Sale probably disapproved of such young children riding in the van, but she was not going to relinquish the position unless she had to. When trouble came, she wanted them to be mobile, not trapped in unwieldy camel panniers that could be tumbled in the snow if their camel were shot, like so many of the women and children.

It shamed her that she could so coolly think of the possible fate of the party in the center, of women with whom she had shared the last two years, some heavily pregnant, others having only just given birth and now ludicrously clad in their nightgowns under the rugs and furs with which they covered themselves. But overriding all her training and all her conscious wish to help others was a furious instinct to survive, to defend her own and let everyone else do as they would. She did not like it, but she would not fight it.

A young galloper came riding past Perdita, threading his way as quickly as he could through the muddle of men, horses, guns, women, and frightened camp followers. Perdita and Lady Sale watched as he rode up to General Elphinstone's party. He dismounted, saluted, and handed something over to the general. The note must have been very short because Elphinstone read it quickly and beckoned to two of his officers. The three of them talked for some time, the colonel vigorously, the younger man shaking his head and pointing toward the column. Elphinstone turned his head from one to the other, as though he were a spectator at a tennis game. Perdita said with feeling, "It is tantalizing not knowing what they are saying."

Lady Sale answered with contempt, "Frustrating, indeed! Knowing how supine and bigoted this command is, I expect they are making some ridiculous decision that will end in the loss of hundreds of lives."

"If only your husband were here, Lady Sale!"

"He would be if he could. I expect that he is still pinned down at Jellalabad and could not risk having the brigade cut up. Better a strong British force at Jellalabad than that." Her ladyship's overly severe tone suggested to Perdita that the general's wife, too, had some doubts about her husband's absence from this fighting retreat, and so she held her peace.

Lady Sale put her spurs to her pony's sides, saying over her shoulder, "I am going to find out what is happening. Wait there, Emily, with Lady Beaminster."

Perdita quietly asked how Emily's husband was faring; he was now back on his feet but obviously suffering from his wounds. His wife was describing something of his courage and determination to do his duty in spite of what he thought was the cowardice and stupidity of many of the senior officers, when her mother returned.

"The messenger was from Brigadier Anquetil. It seems that the rear is being harassed by tribesmen and the guns are at risk. Anquetil requested reinforcements."

"And?" prompted Perdita, more afraid for Marcus than for the guns.

"It is considered that the road is too choked for a sufficient force to get through. We are to press on. The lack of management and military sense of this operation is shocking. Why can't Shelton send some men from the center?"

The three women looked back, the two younger thinking about their husbands, the elder of the incompetence and supineness she saw all around.

Charlie said, "What is happening to the guns, Mama?"

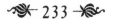

"The tribesmen are trying to take them from our column, Charlie."

"Well, Papa will stop them, won't he?"

Perdita tried to smile encouragingly, but she could no longer bring herself to tell soothing lies, and so she said, "We must all hope so. Now, come along you two. Back to the column."

The small party followed her, and they rode on to Boothak, where once again the column was halted and more messages were brought up. They learned later that General Elphinstone decided at Boothak that the rear was in real danger of being cut off. He ordered a halt and sent back all the troops that could be spared, and two of the guns. Perdita was torn between an instinct that said to her, "Ride on, ride on or you will perish," and a horrible fear of what was happening to Marcus. If she had not had the children to see to, she might have ridden back herself, so great was her anxiety.

She helped the children off their ponies and set them to running up and down, around and around, anything to keep them warm and lively, while she and the other women looked back to try to make out what was happening. They saw Brigadier Shelton take possession of some of the nearer hills and keep the enemy in check for at least fifty minutes before retiring. Perdita and Lady Sale were watching in reluctant admiration when they saw what they took to be a messenger riding down from the Afghan troops.

As he came nearer, they saw he was one of theirs, and Lady Sale soon recognized him as a Captain Skinner, with whom she was slightly acquainted. They waited, wondering what was happening this time and when the column would be able to move on again, when they heard that Skinner had been to talk to Akbar Khan himself.

The Khan, who had been with his tribesmen all that day, had apparently expressed his regret for what was being done but had said that the column was attacked only because it had left the cantonments too early without waiting for the escort he had promised. He now offered to provide not only men to protect the column but also food and ammunition if the general would halt the column and not push on through the Koord-Caubul Pass that day.

To Lady Sale's hardly disguised fury, the general acquiesced and ordered a halt.

Perdita, who was becoming almost as forthright as the general's wife, said, "We cannot have moved even as far as we did yesterday. This is absurd."

Emily Sturt said, "But it will be worth it if we are given proper food and something to keep warm with."

"If," said her mother with something very like a snort. "I expect it is Bellew who has urged this halt."

"Well, Mama, at least the firing has stopped and those savages are keeping away from our people," said Emily.

Perdita left them to their disagreement and set about preparing another bivouac, feeling bitterly resentful that the English should have suffered so much at the hands of the Afghans and were now forced to waste half a day's marching time waiting around for them to do as they chose. It seemed worse than absurd for the commanders to believe the word of a man who had already murdered Sir William, broken agreement after agreement and promise after promise, and watched his soldiers killing the English all that morning without intervention. Either he was in favor of the murders, or he was without control over the tribesmen. Whichever was the case, there was no point in waiting around for his promised escort.

She hoped that Marcus would be able to leave his men sometime that night to see her and the children. Trying to drive all fear from her voice as usual, she made Charlie and Annie snuggle down into the *poshteen* bed, early though it was, and gave them a little *ottah* and a handful of raisins each while she told them stories.

By the time her husband arrived, her voice was aching with cold and effort, and she was glad to be able to keep silent for a while as Charlie questioned his father closely as to what had happened during the day. Marcus told the children one version, making it sound as much like a retelling of the story of St. George and the dragon as he could, and then in French he gave Perdita the reality.

"We have lost four guns. Two were spiked by the 44th as the Afghans overcame them, and two more had to be abandoned—six-pounders. The poor horses could not drag them any farther through this infernal snow."

Perdita tried to lighten his unhappy face with a small joke. "Until today I had always thought of the infernal regions as being hot. Well, perhaps it will be better to freeze than to burn for our sins."

He acknowledged her attempt with a brief, hard smile and said, "That's right, keep your courage up, my love. We shall get through only with courage."

"I know," she said. "Courage and Akbar."

"I would not put much faith in him. I know the general believes he means to give us food and an escort through the pass, but do not rely on it. I am worried about your going through in front—"

She interrupted. "But, Marcus, Aktur—"

"I know what he told you. And you must do as you think best. We have only the slimmest chance, and I do not believe one part of the column will be much safer than any other. But what I do say is that if there is trouble, remember Lieutenant Davis, who—"

"Took his guns through at a gallop," supplied Perdita thoughtfully. "Yes, Marcus, I shall remember." She saw that he was gathering his horse's reins preparatory to remounting and said, "But you will be back tonight, won't you?"

"If I can."

She did not see him again for hours, and when he finally arrived, it had been dark for some time and snow was falling. Once more she had refused to join any of the other women in the only tent and had spent some time rigging up a shelter to keep the children's faces clear of snow. She had just lain down herself, the end of her turban covering her nose and mouth, when she heard at least two men crunching through the snow. She made out a tiny, flickering light coming toward their little camp. Very quietly, so as not to awaken the children, who had eventually succumbed to sleep, she called, "Marcus?"

"Yes, my dear." His voice sounded thinned by exhaustion, and when he came closer and she could see his face in the uncertain light of his lantern, she was shocked by his pallor.

She said, "What has happened?"

He seemed unable to speak, and it was Thurleigh who

answered for him. "Beaminster has been trying to teach the men to bivouac like this for warmth, but it is an uphill struggle. They cannot understand that the animal warmth generated by all their bodies together will protect them far better than each man keeping his clothes to himself."

The two men added their own sheepskin cloaks to the makeshift bed and eased themselves into it, feet inward. One of them must have kicked Charlie, for he half stirred and mumbled, "Ayah, is it morning?"

This time Marcus spoke, and the child relapsed into sleep.

It was a colder night even than the one before, or it seemed so to Perdita, and although she slept for a few hours before dawn, Marcus found himself jerked awake every time he began to relax into sleep. He felt tormented for his men, many of whom he had had to leave wounded and dying beside the road at the mercy of the Afghans' knives. But there was nothing more he could have done for them. They could not be carried through with the baggage train because what was left of it was in chaos; the camp followers were dying more quickly than even the sepoys.

He was haunted by the sight of one tiny Indian girl, who could not have been much younger than little Annie, kneeling by the side of the road quite naked. She was alone and would be dead by morning. But even if he picked her up and asked Perdita to look after her, there would be a hundred others like her, and he could not take them all.

He shut his eyes and tried to sleep once more. Even apart from his frantic and overstimulated brain, there was the noise to keep him awake. Camels bellowed; horses and yaboos neighed in pain and hunger; children cried; and all around, men of both races groaned and cursed as the cold bit into their flesh, and the fear and certainty of death bit into their minds.

Only dawn freed him from the torment of lying still, and the resumption of hostilities gave him a chance to take some mind-numbing action.

Despite Akbar's promise of protection and an end to harassment, it was clear to everyone that the array of tribesmen drawn up between the camp and the entrance to the Koord-Caubul Pass was hostile. Officers struggled out of their makeshift tents and bivouacs all around, calling to their men and trying to instill some kind of order. Many of the sepoys were so frostbitten that they could not pull the triggers of their muskets, and more than one of the cavalry had to be lifted on to their horses, too stiff to mount.

But Major Thain put himself at the head of the 44th and, joined by Marcus Beaminster and Captain Lawrence with some of the 121st, made a spirited charge at the assembled Afghans. As usual, they dispersed under the threat of organized attack, and the brave force was cheered as it returned to the encampment.

Perdita assumed that the column would march immediately, taking advantage of this small victory over the enemy, but no orders were given. Seeing Captain Thurleigh riding past at almost eleven o'clock, she hailed him and begged for news.

He pulled his horse to a halt for a moment, sympathizing with the fear on her face, and shouted, "The Sirdar is said to be having the pass cleared of hostile Ghilzais, and we are to wait. We are trying to get some order in the column so that the fighting men are not encumbered with this rabble." He waved his hand toward the struggling mass of humanity and animals all around him in the snow.

"What did Uncle James mean, Mama?" came a voice at Perdita's elbow.

She squatted down in the snow beside the children and tried to explain. "We have to ride through a narrow passageway between these high hills—through there. And there are bad men there now who have to be moved away before we can go through. So we have to wait."

"Mama, I do not like it," said Annie, pinched and pale with hunger, fatigue, and cold.

Her face reminded Perdita all too easily of Aneila's at the end, and she hugged the girl, whispering, "Nor do I, Annie. But we have to put up with it so that we can go home. Now," she went on more briskly, "when we ride into the pass, we must go as quickly as we can. Stay close to me, and when I tell you to, you must make the ponies gallop really fast."

"But I hate galloping," Annie protested, her voice trembling on the edge of a rare whine.

"I know you do, Annie, but it must be done. Promise me." She smiled gaily, as though they were negotiating over some game.

The child said reluctantly, "Very well."

She stood up again then, trying to shake the snow out of her skirts, which had now been damp and half frozen for two days. She gave the two children another exiguous ration of the food she had brought and poured them each a drink of sherry, once again the only liquid that could be found among the broken cases and baggage scattered around the bivouac. She herself accepted a tumblerful from Captain Sturt and downed it like any trooper, feeling no ill effects, only a momentary warmth.

Shortly after that, at about midday, the order to advance was given, and the column began to move into the gloomy defile that had obsessed the thoughts of nearly everyone. In spite of an escort of Afghan chiefs who rode in advance, almost all the Europeans were afraid of what they would suffer on that bleak road.

Perdita and the children rode with Lady Sale and Emily Sturt; Marcus, farther back, led his demoralized sepoys and James Thurleigh rode with the general and his staff. To Perdita, as to nearly everyone else, the pass was a fearful sight. Almost no sun penetrated its narrow depths, and the cracked and creviced rocks rose steeply on either side of the road, across which poured a tumultuous winding torrent. The ponies had to pick their way through it again and again as it crossed and recrossed the road. On the third or fourth time Annie's yaboo stopped halfway across and refused to budge in spite of angry or encouraging slaps and the child's tearful urging.

Perdita slipped off her own animal, gasping as the cold of the icy water soaked through her skirt and boots. She gave Charlie the reins of her pony and told him to lead it through, while she took Annie's with both hands above the bit and, facing the reluctant beast, pulled hard. At last it picked up one foot and then another; she turned around and led it out of the river, slipping badly at the edge where the stiller water had begun to freeze. Her ankle bent sickeningly; although grimacing with pain, she went grimly on up out of the water. She turned to wring as much water out of her skirt as she could before it froze, and then remounted, urging the children to catch up with Mrs. Sturt.

About half a mile farther on, firing started, and she remembered Marcus's description of his previous fight there. Murderous fire poured down on them, and Perdita shouted to the children, "Now! Gallop! Follow Mrs. Sturt. I am behind you. Go on! Whip him with the reins, Annie."

Bullets were whizzing past them, and she could not believe that they would get through unhurt. Seeing that Annie could not make her pony follow Charlie's, Perdita scooped the child up onto her own horse before her, and together they galloped through, ducking absurdly as the iron rain whipped past.

Perdita saw Lady Sale sway and made as if to stop, but the indomitable woman cried, "No, no! Go on! I shall do well enough."

The fierce little river impeded them time and again as it wound across the road, but they all splashed through, urging their mounts with complete recklessness and disregard for the treachery of loose stones and sudden troughs.

The pass was five miles long, and when Perdita finally burst through into the sunlit valley at the end, it was almost impossible to believe that she had survived. Breathlessness bowed her forward over Annie, her ears rang, and blood pounded through her body, but they had gotten through. When she had fought her lungs into almost regular breathing, she raised her head to see Charlie, his eyes sparkling and his cheeks bright red, riding up beside Emily Sturt, who said, "Lady Beaminster, are you hurt?"

"No, Mrs. Sturt, just winded for a moment. Where is your mama?"

"She is here, too. One bullet entered her arm, but she says the others damaged only the *poshteen.*"

They all dismounted and waited, getting gradually cold again, for their husbands and friends to struggle through, powerless to help until the dazed and wounded people appeared at the mouth of the defile. Emily thought she saw Sturt for a moment but decided she had been mistaken when he did not emerge. Then came the general's party almost intact, with Thurleigh winding a handkerchief around his left wrist. Perdita went toward him to help, half afraid he would order her out of the way, but he did not. He held down his hand for her to secure the improvised bandage and said, "Marcus?"

She shook her head. Then, seeing from his expression how he had translated her gesture, she made herself speak. "Nothing yet. But none of his men are through yet, either, so we may hope."

He came at last, swaying in his saddle, supported by a *subadhar*, who headed over to Thurleigh in relief. This time Marcus had been wounded in the knee and seemed to be in bad pain, for his face was greenish white under the dirt, and he had bitten deeply into his bottom lip.

Together James Thurleigh and Perdita helped him off the horse and laid him on a pile of sheepskin coats. Perdita turned to her children and said, "Charlie, please go to Mrs. Sturt and ask if she has any of that sherry left for Papa. Annie, come here and hold Papa's head for me."

They did what they could to make Marcus less uncomfortable, which was not much, until Charlie came back with a bottle and the news that Captain Sturt was badly wounded.

"Worse than Papa. He can't speak, and there's lots of blood. He's making a horrid noise."

Perdita put her hand to her eyes, unable to stop tears of horror—horror that the child should have to see such things, and horror that poor Sturt should suffer so much again. The tears seemed to be welling up more and more quickly under her fingers, and hard as she tried to stop crying, she could not. She felt her arm gripped hard and heard Thurleigh's voice, harsh. "Stop. There is a time and place for such nonsense. This is not it. Do something for your husband."

Nineteen

By nightfall, Dr. Brydon had found time to dress Marcus's wound, having roughly dug out the ball. He took Perdita to one side and said, "It will be painful, but he is not in danger, except for the fever." Then he told her quickly of some of the others who had survived, and more who were dying, before hurrying to attend to as many of them as he could.

Sturt was dying, he told her, and Maria Jamieson was already dead, although two of her children had gotten through alive. The sepoy leading their camel had marched doggedly through the pass in spite of his wounds. Mrs. Trevor still lived with seven of her children, and young Mrs. Mainwaring had heroically walked most of the way, carrying her child and struggling over the bodies of men and cattle as she went. Little Mary Anderson, Annie's best friend, had been taken by some tribesmen, as had some other children Perdita did not know. It was thought that nearly three thousand died in those five miles.

Perdita's mind could hardly take in the horror of it: so many men and women she had known were murdered, their bodies left to rot in that charnel house of a pass. And the children—they had had to watch such things, dying in pain and terror or, worse perhaps, taken captive by their tormentors. In the face of such carnage, to have survived unhurt seemed almost shameful; and yet the determination to live burned in Perdita still.

The sufferings of the living were not at an end. As night fell, the firing continued, and the survivors lay down in the snow, colder than ever, hungry, many of them hoping that they would not awaken again. As usual, Thurleigh joined the Beaminsters as soon as he could leave the general's side, and as usual they made their *poshteen* bed and tried to sleep. This time they were afraid to lie in a circle in case someone accidentally kicked Marcus's wounded leg, and so Perdita arranged them in a row with Marcus at one edge, Thurleigh at the other.

Perdita had the satisfaction of seeing the children sleep almost at once, exhausted by their wild and shattering ride, and soon afterward she dropped into an uneasy doze, punctuated by nightmares and the sound of screams and groans that seemed part of the dreams. She was awakened by a convulsive start from Marcus, lying beside her, and she opened her eyes to see a young boy in Afghan dress kneeling over him. She was struggling out of the skins that covered her, hampered by her wet and clinging serge skirts, when Marcus screamed penetratingly.

Seeing the moonlight gleam off a knife in the boy's hand, Perdita lunged at him and grabbed his right wrist. He must have been only twelve or so, and although he was wiry and strong, with her superior weight she managed to roll him onto his back on the ground. She dared not turn to see to her husband, for the boy squirmed and kicked at her violently.

All around her she could see Afghan men and children running through the camp, slashing and stabbing at the wounded and the dead. Some of the sepoys and their officers tried to fight the tribesmen off; others lay apathetically, allowing themselves to be killed or hacked, as though too battered by the horrors they had suffered to care whether they lived or died.

Perdita heard Thurleigh's despairing voice. "His eyes, dear God, his eyes!"

Suddenly she understood what the boy beneath her had done to Marcus. Quicker than thought, impelled by hate and terror, she knelt astride him to keep him still. Taking her hand from his wrist, she wrenched the knife from his hand. He writhed between her thighs, shrieking curses. She drove the knife into his chest, pushing hard through the tough leather of his *neemchee.* The blade slid in quite easily, and the body stilled. She could not believe that killing was so easy and wrenched the knife out again to drive it back into the boy, and again once more.

She felt a man's hand on her shoulder and heard a rough English voice saying, "Enough! Enough, ma'am! The wretch is dead."

Dazed and sick, she allowed the man to help her up off the corpse. He bent down to pick up a handful of snow and used it to wash the blood off her left hand. She raised the right and in the thin light saw that it was dark with blood: sticky between her fingers and horrible under her nails. She looked at the hand as though she did not know what it was. Then her eyes dilated.

"Marcus?"

The man turned her around, and she saw her husband lying with his head in Captain Thurleigh's lap, blood all over his face.

The children were huddled under the *poshteens* looking at their father, both in tears but neither making a sound. Perdita turned back to the man and at last recognized him.

"Sergeant Deane, thank you. Please find Dr. Brydon or any of them, and tell him to come."

Watching him go, she realized that all the raiders had left the bivouac.

She went back to her family and waited for the doctor to arrive. When he came twenty minutes later, she saw that he was shaking with fatigue, and his fingers fumbled with the clasp of his bag of dressings. He did what little he could for Marcus. Thurleigh laid him down and took his hand.

Perdita looked at them in silence, nearly every feeling beaten out of her by what she had seen and done; she wanted to lie down in the snow, undisturbed, and sleep for the rest of time. She tried to remember what it had felt like to be alive before this war, and her mind fixed on Charles Byrd. Her conviction that she could get her family safely through to Jellalabad had dwindled to nothing, but through her despair she felt a longing to see Charles once more. Dying there in the snow would cut her off from him for eternity. The failing spark of her strength flickered once more, and she tried to nurse it back into flame.

"Captain Thurleigh, I think we should keep watch now. Have you a weapon?"

"Of course, but you had better take this." She held out a smeared hand, into which he put the cold, hard weight of a revolver.

"It is not cocked. Do you know how to fire it?"

"Yes," she said briefly, remembering that Marcus had taught her during the winter when Thurleigh had been away in Jellalabad. She turned to the children and persuaded them to lie down again. Charlie's eyes were fixed on her face; he seemed unable to close them.

"Mama, Mama, why is Papa crying like Captain Sturt?"

Perdita stroked his forehead, wincing at the sight of the dried blood on her fingers. Making her voice as calm as she could, she tried to soothe him.

"He has been hurt, Charles. We must all be as quiet as we can so that we do not disturb him. Lie down again. I'm coming in beside you, Annie. There is nothing to frighten you now. Lie down."

They obeyed, but she was afraid that they would not sleep. She herself sat beside them and spent what was left of the night straining to see if anyone was approaching in the murky moonlight, bitterly reproaching herself for sleeping earlier and asking herself how any twelve-year-old child learned the cruelty necessary to do what had been done to Marcus. She had known that blinding was a traditional punishment for any ruler overthrown in Afghanistan or an enemy defeated, but the reality of it far outstripped even her most grotesque imaginings. She thought it would have been less evil to kill than to maim him in such a way.

Morning brought the usual shambles and uncertainty. Just after dawn there was a tremendous commotion as most of the fighting men and practically all the camp followers started to move off toward the next pass. Individuals were grabbing ponies or camels where they could. Perdita lost no time getting the children up, rolling up their *poshteens* and strapping them to the ponies. Then she helped Thurleigh get Marcus into his saddle.

With his face set in vicarious pain, Thurleigh said, "I cannot stay. I must go to Elphinstone. Will you take his reins?"

"Of course. Marcus, can you stay in the saddle, or shall I find a place in a *khajavah* for you?"

He made a ghastly effort to smile in the direction of her voice and said, "I'll stay on."

"Very well. But you must tell me if I go too fast, or if you want to stop. Now, Annie, you must ride with Charlie today so that I can help Papa." She lifted the child up in front of Charlie, detaching her clinging hands as gently as possible.

Then she gave her son strict instructions to take care of the little girl.

They rode off, joining the milling force that was straggling across the valley. As they passed the small tent in which the surviving English wives had spent the night, she saw piles of Indian corpses. It was not until much later that she learned that the poor wretches had tried to force their way in to share what warmth they could. Being repulsed, they had simply lain down outside and died.

Perdita and her family had not ridden half a mile before an order rang out to halt. They were beside a group of English-women being carried in camel panniers. One of the women threw her child down into the snow in despair. Perdita shared some of the woman's feeling and muttered, "Oh, Christ, what now?" unaware that she was blaspheming.

As usual, ignorant chaos reigned. Some said that the whole force was to be turned around; others that still more dangers awaited them between the valley and Tizeen; yet others that Akbar Khan was genuinely going to provide them with an escort and food this time. Messengers, both English and Af-ghan, came and went. No one took any notice of a party of tribesmen riding down on the right of the column until they had seized the bridles of Perdita's and Charlie's ponies. A few sepoys raised their muskets, and one or two even fired, but their shots were so wide that no one was hit.

Perdita was too frightened to speak and looked wildly back at Marcus, only to realize that he could not help her, that she was now responsible for him as well as for the children.

He said painfully, "What is it, Perdita? Why are we riding away from the column? Who is firing?"

"Oh, Marcus," she began, "they are taking us—" She stopped, hearing wild shouts and the crunching of a pony's hooves in the snow behind them. She narrowed her eyes against the painful glare and then said, "Marcus, Captain Thurleigh is coming."

"Thank God," he answered. But the tribesmen had heard him, too, and two of them detached themselves from the raiding party, wheeled around, and thundered down toward him. He took aim with his revolver, but before he could cock and fire it, they were on him and had snapped his hands behind his back, roughly tying them with harsh cord.

They were driven quickly away from the column. Horrific pictures flashed one after another through Perdita's mind: of poor Lieutenant Loveday's starved, beheaded body at Khelat-y-Ghilzai; of Colonel Stoddart in the mad Nasrullah's unspeakable prison; of young Mrs. Smith running for her life among the rocks north of Candahar. Although the previous night the thought of lying down to sleep and never waking again had held some comfort, now the idea of dying filled her with terror, and at the thought of what the tribesmen might do to the living bodies of her children, bitter bile rose in her throat. She choked it down and at last found her voice. "Where are you taking us?" she said in Pushtu to the man who had seized her bridle. "What do you want of us?"

He turned and from under the coarse blue turban seemed to smile like a fiend.

She shuddered and was grateful for the sound of Captain Thurleigh's English voice. "Do not give them the satisfaction, Lady Beaminster. What is coming will come, and all we have now is our pride."

Marcus said once more, lost in his fog of blindness and pain and shivering under the weight of his damp and icy clothes, "What is happening?"

Thurleigh answered in a calm tone, almost as though he were delivering an official report. "A group of tribesmen has overpowered us and seems to be taking us away from the valley into the hills. We do not know what they want with us, but they have shown us no violence."

"Why us?"

"God knows," answered Thurleigh, but for him, as for the other two adults, that was the question that remained: What had they done, or what could they offer, that they had been singled out so terrifyingly? A little later, as though answering one of the others, he said, "I don't think it can be ransom, for how could these ignorant savages understand Marcus's position? If they were kidnapping for money, they would surely have taken one of the senior officers. No, it must have been a random choice. But for the love of God, why?"

"Perdita?"

"Yes, Marcus."

"Have they hurt you?"

"No. Neither me nor the children." She turned back to

look down the valley, but the struggling, intractable column was now hidden from her by a spur of the hills. She sat back in the saddle and tried to think of nothing but the sight of the man leading the children's pony, who appeared to be entertaining them, making faces at them and whistling. She had once heard that all Afghans love children, but after what she had seen on the retreat, she could not have believed that the affection could encompass the children of their enemies.

Then a more frightening thought seized her: She herself had killed an Afghan child. Could these men be from his clan? Were they taking her and her children to some tribal stronghold to exact a terrible vengeance for his death? Common sense returned in time to prevent panic from taking control of her, and she asked herself how any of the boy's family could know who had killed him or even that he had been killed unless they had witnessed the scene, in which case they would have taken their vengeance then and there.

They rode on for four hours in increasing fear and discomfort. Perdita's eyes burned with tiredness; all her joints seemed to ache with cold and exhaustion. Her icy clothes stuck to her body. She felt degraded with the dirt and blood that soiled her.

Then, as the ponies climbed the last few yards toward a squalid-looking mud village on a small plateau high in the mountains, she deliberately looked around her to try to find some peace of mind before facing what was to come. To her surprise she found that she could see a certain beauty in the landscape. The little village might be poor and mean, but the mud of its walls had dried to a calm beige that echoed the snowless slopes of the bald mountains above it. The snow on the plateau and dusting the higher slopes was dazzlingly white, and the bright sun picked out silver lights on the bare, fastigiate trees within the village walls. A frozen river was stilled by its icy imprisonment, and a bird sang somewhere. There was peace there, and a strange loveliness.

Perdita turned to face the village and said to James Thurleigh, "Now we shall know. That must be the headman." They both looked toward the turbaned man who was waiting for them. As they came nearer, Perdita could make out his dress and features. His grayish-white turban was wound above a broad brow, creased and burned brown.

His eyes, as hazel as an Englishman's, were narrowed against the glare and seemed to her to express the loathing of her race that she had come to recognize in Caubul. His mouth looked as full and sensually cruel as the Dost's. She kept her eyes on his as her captor helped her to dismount and waited for the Khan to speak.

Without moving, he said in slow, carefully enunciated Pushtu, "Welcome. We have food for you. Come."

Warily she translated what he had said for James Thurleigh and, leaving him to help Marcus, turned to the children. They were happily standing by their escort, carefully repeating a series of words that he was teaching them. Mystified and extremely frightened, Perdita led them behind the headman into one of the bigger houses.

They walked into a grimy, littered compound, in one corner of which an old woman tended a large, steaming iron pot on a primitive mud stove. The man gestured toward a low doorway on the left and said, again very slowly, "We have little room. Go in. Food will be brought to you."

They went in obediently and found a bare, windowless room, dimly lit by an oil lamp. There was a small ragged carpet on the floor but nothing else in the room at all. Perdita turned back to the door to ask for the *poshteens* from their ponies. One of the brigands who had brought them to the place nodded and ducked down through the compound door.

While they waited, Perdita looked questioningly at Captain Thurleigh.

He shrugged and said, "God knows. They don't appear to be hostile, but these tribesmen are treacherous bastards." He paused, then went on. "I beg your pardon, Lady Beaminster. What I meant was that it is impossible to trust any of them. We all know that Akbar Khan has betrayed every promise he made. Still, if they feed us, that will be something. Perhaps they have taken us for ransom, after all. If so, they must keep us alive for that. Who can tell?"

Only moments later a man arrived with the bundles of sheepskin coats, followed almost immediately by the old woman carrying her iron pot. She dumped it unceremoniously onto the floor and departed without a word. A savory scent issued from it in wreaths of steam. Perdita felt saliva spurt into her dry mouth. Her clenched stomach ached for the hot food. The children darted toward the pot, but she stopped them.

"Captain Thurleigh, do you think it is safe to eat?"

He looked at her and, having settled Marcus by the wall, walked to the tantalizing pot, bent down to smell its contents, and then dipped in his hand. He ate a little and then smiled. "As far as I can tell, it is only mutton and rice. Very greasy but wholesome enough."

She released the children, who dug their hands into the mess and crammed their mouths with the first warm food they had had since leaving the cantonments. Perdita then filled her hands with the sticky rice and went over to squat on the mud floor beside Marcus. She tried to make him take the food, but he was so weak and dispirited that he could not make the effort, and so she fed him, rolling the rice into small glutinous balls and picking out bits of meat and pushing them into his mouth. Only when he said, "No more now," did she herself eat.

Never had she imagined that there could be such pleasure in swallowing something as unpalatable as the congealing rice and mutton fat from the bottom of the pot.

Later, when the children slept and Marcus had lapsed into a kind of half-consciousness in his corner, Perdita looked at James Thurleigh, more worried by his physical proximity than she had ever been while they camped out in the open sharing the dangers of the last few days. Now that they were under a roof of sorts, she found herself deeply embarrassed by him. She longed to ease her stays, which felt as though they were biting into her, to strip off her sodden clothes, and somehow try to dry and warm her body. She needed desperately to relieve herself.

He was in much the same state but lacked most of her shame. Making an unspecific apology, he went to the farthest corner of their room and turned his back on her. She could be in no doubt about his purpose and closed her eyes and tried not to listen. Nevertheless, in spite of his example, she made herself wait until he was asleep before following it.

Twenty

They had all been awake, hungry and stiff from lying on the hard floor, for what felt like hours before they heard someone at the simple lock on the outside of the door. The room was pitch black, for the lamp had long since run out of oil. Perdita held the children's hands firmly.

The door opened outward, and they could see a square of brilliant light for a moment before most of it was blocked by the stooping figure of a burly tribesman carrying another dim lantern. He said in the slow, clear Pushtu the headman had used, "Come now. Outside." His voice seemed to hold no belligerence. Nevertheless, Perdita felt her pulse pounding, and the back of her knees were clammy with the sweat of fear. She tried to reassure the children, but her voice croaked and would not shape the right words. She managed only, "He wants us outside."

It was Thurleigh who said, "Well, let us go. We have to know sometime. Let it be now. Come, Marcus." He put his hands under his friend's arms and hauled him up. Then putting Marcus's left arm across his own shoulders, he helped him limp out into the daylight. Perdita followed with the children, her mind now mercifully blank.

The light hurt her eyes, and she whispered to Charlie and Annie, "It is too bright. Keep your eyes closed, and it will not hurt so much."

They stood in a row, one truly blinded, the others unable to see for the moment. Perdita was trying to focus through the glare and fizzing in her eyes, when a voice said, "Lady-sahib, do not fear. There are no Ghilzais here, and my father will protect you."

All she could see silhouetted against the sun was the outline of a man in shaggy trousers, loose tunic, *poshteen*, and huge turban, but something in his voice broke through her bruised mind. She said quietly, "Aktur?"

"Yes, lady-sahib."

"What? I mean, why? What has happened?"

He started to move toward her, and she felt the children

shrink nearer to her legs. She also sensed Thurleigh tensing on her right. She said quickly to them in English, "Do not be afraid. It is Aktur, my old groom. I do not know what is happening, but we should not be afraid."

He came to her and took the children's free hands, squatting down to their level, and repeated in English, "Not afraid, not afraid," through his gapped and chipped teeth.

They recognized him at last, and their tense, white faces relaxed infinitesimally. Aktur looked up and went on slowly and clearly in his own language, "My father's village is poor, but we shall give you what we have and keep you here until the snow is gone and it is safe to send you over the mountains to the English at Jellalabad. At night we must keep you locked in that room, and you must not leave the compound."

Perdita found her voice again. "Aktur, why are you doing this when your people hate us and all your country wishes to drive us out?"

He straightened up and said, "We owe you our honor. Without you the man would still live, and our family's *izzat* would be gone. And you are beloved of God. After what I saw at the grave of Baba Shah, I could not let you die." She was silent, and after a while he said, "My mother will bring you food." He gestured to the old woman by the mud stove and turned away.

James Thurleigh said in agonized frustration, "What did he say? What is going to happen?"

"Nothing. They are going to protect us." She saw his expression of scornful disbelief and tried to explain. "He once saw me having an epileptic fit, and because of that, he thinks that I am favored by his god. My uncle once told me that many primitive people have such ideas."

"But that cannot be all. What else did he say?"

"That his father's village has very little, but they will share it with us and protect us until spring, when they will take us over the mountains to safety. We must promise not to leave the compound, or they cannot guarantee our safety, and they will lock us in at night."

She could not bring herself to tell him the rest: that months ago she had bought their lives with that of Lieutenant Flecker, who had died in the dust at Gandamack because of what she had told these people. That was her guilt. She would have to carry it alone.

Gradually, their clothes and sheepskins dried out, and they began to learn to live in the village. It was very hard at first for any of them to accept the dirt and smells that surrounded them and to believe that they could survive on a diet that consisted mainly of flat, unleavened bread and water, supplemented occasionally by preserved vegetables and once or twice by rice greasy with fragments of mutton. They learned to live with the sun and eventually to sleep soundly on the hard mud floor almost as soon as darkness came.

In the beginning their astonished gratitude for life and disgust at its condition monopolized their minds, but once they became used to security again, their lack of occupation began to fret the adults. They could not ride or hunt; they could not even walk outside the mud walls that surrounded the headman's house and courtyard. Marcus alone was too ill to feel the want of activity, succumbing to a recurring fever that left him weak and drowsy. It was clear to his wife and to James Thurleigh that he suffered from continual and excruciating pain in both his knee and his punctured eyes.

The children spent most of their first week in the village clinging to Perdita's skirts, as though afraid to leave her for a moment, but in time they came to trust their uncomfortable safety and began to stand on the edge of games played by the Afghan children and eventually to join in. As the weeks wore on, Perdita became used to the sight of them playing some kind of tag, or rushing about with an irregularly shaped leather ball in the snow, their cheeks reddening with exercise and the sharp, cold air, or squatting in a corner of the courtyard learning a game of skill that looked rather like jackstraws.

Watching them, she could not banish the memory of the child who had mutilated her husband, whom she herself had held pinned between her thighs and stabbed until he was dead. He had looked so like these other boys, these children who were initiating her son into their games, that sometimes she could scarcely contain her hatred.

Often she would turn away from the exuberant shouts of the children to try to make Marcus less uncomfortable, wishing desperately that there were more she could do for him. Her desire to palliate his pain was such that she could look with equanimity on the sight of James Thurleigh cradling her husband's head in his lap, stroking his brow, and talking softly to him, and she would move out of the room to give them some privacy.

Aktur, who sometimes disappeared for days at a time, brought her news now and then, and all of it added to the weight of fear and hatred that she carried. It seemed that almost the entire British Army had been massacred about thirty miles from Jellalabad in the Jagdallack Pass in front of a barricade of thorn trees and bushes built across the narrow pass. Perdita passed the intelligence on to Marcus and James, but she suppressed the rest of Aktur's story, believing that it was given to him in malice by his informants, for it could not be true. He had told her that when the sepoys made a gap in the painful structure with their bare hands, groups of mounted officers had ridden over them to reach the gap and fled, leaving their men to suffer death and dismemberment. Some of the men had even shot at their departing officers, but several got away.

But whatever the truth of their escape, it had done them no good, for they were all butchered. Aktur said that he had heard a rumor that one man had reached Jellalabad, but both he and Perdita considered it unlikely. She said, "But we cannot be the only ones left alive. That cannot be possible."

He answered, "No. I told you of the prisoners of Akbar Khan. They are said to be safe and in good health."

"Did you tell me? Who are they?"

"Married ladies and their families and some officers. And there may be others like you in villages in the hills."

"Aktur, have you paper and pens I could have?"

"Paper? No, lady-sahib. We have no need of paper here. What do you want with paper?"

She turned back to Marcus and James without speaking. She had wanted to write down everything she remembered, not only to absorb some of the time that seemed to trail onward like the raveled wool of some vast celestial spindle, but also to try to understand what had happened. The more she thought about the events of the past two years, the more unbelievable they seemed. Yet they had happened.

An army of one of the two most powerful nations on earth had been defeated and massacred by groups of undisciplined, uneducated tribesmen. Nearly seventeen thousand men, women, and children had been killed. She could not understand why it had been allowed to happen. The cruelty and waste of it defied analysis, and yet she needed to understand it. And she needed to blame someone. She recognized the uselessness, even wickedness of that, but she sometimes thought that if she could work out whose fault it had been, she could rest more easily or look at Marcus's scarred face without such tingling horror and guilt.

The sight of his pain, which she could do so little to alleviate, was almost unbearable. She wanted to ask him continually how he felt and if he were any better, but she understood that the impulse was rooted in her own selfish wish for comfort, and so she rationed herself. But there were times when she thought something in her must snap if they had no relief: the prospect of months more of this powerlessness, this frustration, was unendurable. Yet it must be endured. There was nothing else to do. Once or twice she caught herself thinking that their life must be easier for Marcus than for herself. He at least had the tangibleness of pain to deal with. After a time she could recognize the thought beginning to form in the uncontrollable mists of her mind and would shut it off from the rest of her, knowing that nothing could be worse than the pain he suffered or the unbearable knowledge that he would never see again.

She tried to discipline herself to sit by him while James Thurleigh slept, talking gently of what they would do when they reached India once more, but she could see that even that sometimes distressed him, and she would search for other things to say. It seemed terribly important to talk of something other than their present situation or the horrible past or the question of what the villagers really meant to do with them. Often she wanted to say, "It will be all right in the end. I know that we shall get back. And I am sure the doctors will be able to do something about your eyes." But that would have been an insult to the way he was enduring his pain. She might nurse her own absurd hopes, but she would not commit the cruelty of adding them to the load he carried.

Instead, she invented wishes and interests for herself and talked of those; of places in India she pretended she wanted to see in order to try to force him to talk to her. She hoped that if he became used to answering her questions about Agra and the Taj Mahal or Delhi and its Red Fort, she might one day get from him a truthful answer to the questions she could not ask. "Tell me what it feels like to be you, wounded like that, deprived of so much. Do you think you will die? Are you afraid to die—or to live? Tell me what it feels like."

It seemed to her that some days she went on and on, her voice prattling like a machine, until she wondered that neither Marcus nor Captain Thurleigh cried out in anger for her to stop. Then she would stop herself, only to listen to the silence and watch Marcus suffering.

Her husband was dimly grateful to her for keeping his mind away from the pit of despair. He knew that he was not responding adequately to her efforts, but he thought she must know how thankful he felt, because it was so obvious to him. In the same way, he never said anything to James to thank him for the solace of his physical comforting. To feel James's hands holding his head was as sure a way of keeping back from the brink of the pit as having to answer Perdita's questions. But for much of the time he was too ill to know anything of what they both did for him.

It was at those times that Perdita would leave him almost entirely to James Thurleigh and search for something to occupy herself elsewhere. She had tried to help the women at their various apparently unending tasks around the compound, but they would not let her. She used to watch the girls leave to fetch water twice every day and would beg Aktur to let her go with them. Invariably he answered, "No, lady-sahib. It is not fitting or safe."

"But, Aktur, I wish to go. To walk outside would mean so much."

But he would never allow it, and so she watched the procession leave every morning and evening, each girl muffled up against the snow in a coarse black woolen blanket over her red or purple tunic and trousers, carrying an elegant plain clay pot on her shoulder. The picture they presented was magnificent, their brightly colored clothes set off by the brilliant snow and the translucent blue sky, their carriage so graceful under the burdens they carried. Once Perdita said as they came back, tired but uncomplaining from their three-mile trudge, "Aktur, why do you not have a well dug within the compound instead of sending them so far every day for water?"

"There is water in the river. How do we know that there is any here for a well? Besides, we have always done it so. What else have the women to do?"

Having felt the crushing weight of the boredom of living in his village with no purpose, Perdita could say nothing more. None of the women of his clan could read or write; none of them traveled outside except to join a husband from another village. Reason told her that he was right: there was nothing they could do except keep themselves and their men and children clothed and fed. Yet it troubled her that the women toiled so hard and looked so much older than their husbands. Aktur's father was a fine, upstanding eagle of a man; his wife, a bent, wrinkled, exhausted old woman who appeared to labor unceasingly.

Now that she understood the harshness and poverty of their lives, Perdita could also understand the legendary and much-mocked Afghan liking for money, and indeed the rapacity of the tribes who held the passes. But understanding did not bring acceptance. It seemed to her that their lives need not be so difficult; that there would be easier ways to provide the necessities of life and to leave time for the pursuit of civilization and gentleness.

But then she would ask herself how much civilization her own people showed or why the Afghans should be gentle with a foreign army that had invaded their country, whatever the spuriously legal excuse they gave for it. Her mind seemed like a cage of wild animals prowling angrily around and around. As soon as she persuaded one uncomfortable thought to lie down, another would rise and snarl in its place.

She came to hate the village and the life they had to lead, and by the middle of February she realized that Captain Thurleigh hated it, too. She did not know what kind of thoughts tormented him, but she saw their effect and tried to sympathize.

Her efforts were clumsy, though, and her words were so

irrelevant to his concerns that he hardly heard them, saying only, "What was that you said? Leave? I expect they'll let us go in the end. If they had other plans, they'd have done something by now. No, I think you can take it that we're being allowed to live." The sneer in his rough voice was too obvious to miss, but she could not understand it. She had no way of knowing that he saw the promise of life as something shameful.

When he had seen Marcus and his family carried off, James had ridden impulsively in pursuit. He had had little hope of saving them, but he had not wanted to let Marcus die alone. Now it seemed that he had bought his own life by deserting his post, and the shame of it ate deeper into him every day.

He had watched angrily as his friend's children became assimilated into the life of the village children and Perdita talked with increasing fluency to the headman and his sons. To James Thurleigh she seemed serene and without conception of her disloyalty to her country in her treatment of its enemies. Then she came to talk to him for the first time in days and blurted out what he took to be a demand for reassurance. Bitterness seethed in him; once again he tried to blame her for her husband's condition and his own desertion. That he could not made his angry shame worse and flung back on him the full weight of despair.

The next morning Perdita went as usual to fetch their meager breakfast as soon as the door to their room was unlocked, leaving James Thurleigh to deal with the unspeakable latrine jar. When she came back carrying a pile of flat, grayish wheat cakes and a water jar, she saw him standing outside the door, staring out at the mountains with a pistol in his right hand. She understood at once and ran to stand in front of him. With her hands full of food and her blue eyes blazing with anger, she said, "How dare you?"

He looked down at her and said unemotionally, "I have to." Then, seeing her look of uncomprehending anger, he went on, "I am a deserter. It is a matter of honor."

The stupidity of it, the wickedness, held her mute for a full minute. Then she bent down to put her burden on the filthy ground and straightened up to say bitingly, "If you think it more honorable to shoot yourself here, causing God knows what trouble, than to live to help me get a blind man and two children safely through eighty miles of enemy-held mountain passes to Jellalabad, you must be demented. And better dead."

Then she turned from him, hardly caring whether he lived or died, to take the food in to Marcus. She tried to put the incident from her mind as she fed him, soaking the unappetizing gray bread in water for him and coaxing him to eat it. As usual, he stopped her after a few mouthfuls and said, "What were you and James quarreling about?"

It was the first sign he had made that he was aware of anything outside his own suffering body. Perdita wanted to lie soothingly but was too relieved to know that he was sane to shut off the real world from him, and so she compromised.

"He is ashamed because he thinks that in riding after us to save us from the tribesmen, he deserted his post. If we had all died, that would have been acceptable and he would have been an honorable man, but because he is still alive, he sees himself as a coward and a deserter. I tried to make him see reason."

"Be gentle with him, Perdita. You are so strong."

The absurdity of it shook her. That the sneering, arrogant, hateful man who could shrivel her always shaky confidence with a look should need gentleness from her was patent nonsense, but Marcus had asked for it. She lowered his shoulders back against the mud wall and put down the cup she had been holding before saying, "Very well, Marcus, I will try."

She stood up and walked back to the courtyard, blinking in the sudden light. There had been no shot, and so she was not afraid of what she might find. The first thing she saw was the revolver lying in the dust. She picked it up gingerly, only to find that it was not cocked. She thrust it into her waistband. Then she said as kindly as possible, "Captain Thurleigh?"

He was sitting in the corner formed by the compound wall and that of their room, his hands clasped around his calves and his head resting on his bent knees. She walked over to him and put her hand on his shoulder. She saw with distaste that her skin was grimy and her fingernails torn and full of God knew what filth. A louse ran out onto her hand from under his collar, but she barely noticed them now.

"Captain Thurleigh?"

He raised his head then, and she was shocked to see that his eyes were red and the dirt on his face streaked white by tears. His magnificent face seemed pinched. He looked beaten. For the first time she felt pity for him and a twisting kind of desperation. As much as she had always disliked him, she had relied on his strength and his knowledge to take them safely back to the army. Now she knew there was no one but herself to do that.

He leaned forward and scrambled onto his knees, pressing his face into her dirty and stinking skirts and gripping her body. She heard him say, "Oh, God, what will become of me?"

She put both hands on his rough, caked hair, feeling yet another louse under her fingers. Pushing her disgust away firmly, she said, "Don't weep, James. We shall all live. When we get to Jellalabad, all will be well. You will rejoin the regiment. No one will think that you have deserted. There are truly times when life is worth more than honor."

As though that word had triggered something in him, he dropped his arms and withdrew from her. Turning his head away, he got up and said in a barely audible voice, "I beg your pardon, Lady Beaminster." And he walked away.

She stood looking after him and wondered how they were all going to live cramped in their one room for another two months after this. She saw Aktur and waved to him. He came up to her, and before he could speak, she asked, "Aktur, what is the news?"

"Nothing new, lady-sahib. They say that at Jellalabad the general has refused to make a treaty with the Ghilzais and that the *feringhees* were rebuilding the walls when an earthquake hit them. All their walls were thrown down, but when Akbar came to take the fort, they had been built up again."

Taking a deep breath to steady her voice, she said, "Then, Aktur, do you think we could leave soon? If the division is safe in Jellalabad and the tribesmen are preoccupied with the earthquake, would it not be better if we went now?"

"The cold and the snow will stop you."

"But if we wait for the spring, it will be worse. There will be rain, and all the rivers will flood. We would have to wait until May at least, and then it might be too late. The English might have left Jellalabad. I think you should send us now."

He looked at her as though weighing what she had said against unvoiced arguments of his own. The fear that lived just below the surface broke through again. Perdita remembered the endless broken promises of men of his race and was afraid that she might have aroused his anger.

He said abruptly, "I go to speak to my father and my brothers."

Five days later they marched, with Aktur as their guide, carrying provisions for ten days. He thought that it would take them only half that time to reach the fort, but none of the adults was prepared to risk another march like the last. They all wore the *poshteens* they had brought from Caubul, and heavy black blankets the headman had given them for cloaks. He had also provided torn strips to replace their tattered leg wrappings.

In the end Perdita and James Thurleigh parted from him with regret. Filthy, uncomfortable, and verminous his village might have been, but it had provided sanctuary. Now that they were setting off across wild mountains, expecting to face bands of vengeful Ghilzais, they knew how to value that safety. And now, too, they were certain of it, as they had never been when they had lived under his protection. He said, "My son will take you as close to Jellalabad as possible, and he will show you the rest of the way. He tells me you have no ammunition left for your guns, so take this."

Perdita waited, expecting to be offered a long *jezail*, but he presented her with a smallish, heavy goatskin bag. She handed it to Thurleigh, saying to the Khan, "We thank you for this, but also for your hospitality and for the risks you have taken for us." Then she turned to Thurleigh to say, "He says we have no bullets for the revolvers. Are those the right sort?"

"Yes. By God, do you realize where—"

Perdita cut in hastily. "They must have come from the passes. I know. But do not say anything now, *please*, Captain Thurleigh."

"Don't you understand? These scoundrels must have been

looting the bodies of our men. They probably killed them, too."

"Of course I know. How do you suppose Aktur has been getting his news if he were not joining the other Afghans down there? But we cannot stop that or change it. We can only accept that they are helping us and be grateful for their help. Will you reload both guns?"

"Of course." She handed him hers, took the leading rein of Marcus's pony, smiled at the children who were sharing one provided by the chief, and led them out of the compound gates.

The view in front of them was breathtaking: rank after rank of mountain peaks glittered under a sun that blazed in a sky as pale and clear as enameled glass. A mile and a half away across the plateau, she could see the river where the women went for the water, and above it the magnificent sight of a frozen waterfall. The air was so clear that even from that distance she could make out the great ice stalactites that hung from its black rocks and the curtains of ice that spread downward into the still liquid pools.

As they rode nearer, she pointed out its glories to the children, saying, "Just imagine, Annie, when the spring comes, all that will be water again, pouring down into the river. Perhaps we shall be back in Simla by then. Do you remember it at all?"

"I do," said Charlie proudly. "There were monkeys there that came into the dining room to eat the fruit."

Perdita laughed, and Marcus smiled when he heard the sound. She said, "Yes, how clever of you. There was one who came in one morning. Do not look so frightened, Annie. It was only once."

"I don't remember that," said Marcus, sounding almost happy.

"Well, it must have been after you left. Yes, it was that last summer before we joined you, just after Charlie's second birthday."

"Ah, I see. And how much do you remember about Simla, Annie?"

"Not very much, Papa. But I don't think it was as cold as Caubul."

"No, it was not. And much more beautiful. There is a

little valley up above the town, so lovely you would hardly believe it could be real, with flowers and a lake. The flowers . . ."

Perdita could hardly bear to listen, understanding that Marcus was trying to see it again with his memory as he never could with his eyes. She had not known that he thought like that about places, and she glanced back at Captain Thurleigh to see what he made of it.

He was riding a little behind Marcus, and she saw him watching her husband with a smile of frightening tenderness. She had no way of knowing that he was remembering the last time they had seen that valley.

They had ridden there one morning when Marcus was smarting after a quarrel with his mother. As they reached the valley, he had said, "James, I am sorry to burden you with my low spirits. But you are the only one who understands."

"Of course I do, my dear," James had answered, leaning over his saddle to ruffle Marcus's hair as he had done all those years before, when Marcus had been a scared and homesick junior officer. They had dismounted and tethered the horses in the shade.

Then, much later, as James had sat with his back propped against a warm, smooth rock, he had looked down at Marcus lying beside him on the ground, his head on James's thigh, and had said, "Better, old fellow?"

Marcus had looked up, his brown eyes unshadowed, and said, "I feel clean again."

James remembered vividly the feel of Marcus's lips as he traced them with his fingers. He remembered how he had said something like, "You must not let them worry you so. While I am with you, nothing can happen to hurt you." Marcus had answered simply and with complete confidence, "I know."

James Thurleigh shuddered at the thought of the hurt he had not managed to prevent and looked around for something to help control his feelings. He looked up at the sun far to their left and said angrily to Perdita, "Jellalabad lies directly to the east. What is this savage doing? We must be heading almost due south. Tell him we know what he is up to."

"James," she said pacifically, "we must trust him. I assume he has a reason."

"Oh, I'm sure he has," he answered, heavily sarcastic. "But ask him what it is."

"Very well." She handed him the leading rein and spurred her pony forward. After a short colloquy with Aktur, she rode back and said, "He says there is a Ghilzai fortress in the way. We must go around it to avoid trouble. I believe him."

Thurleigh only shrugged, but by the end of that day's march even he accepted that once again they were heading in the right direction. Aktur led them along barely discernible tracks way up in the hills to avoid any possible collision with Akbar's forces or stray looting parties on their way to or from one of the richly strewn passes.

They slept that night in the shelter of a vast overhanging rock and were up and moving off just after sunrise. All that day and the next they met no one; the holiday mood of the first morning's ride persisted. It was very cold, but no snow fell, and the sensation of traveling home, unhindered and unencumbered, was so powerful that even James Thurleigh succumbed and ceased to frown.

On the evening of the fourth day, when they had made their bivouac and shared out the ration of dried fruit and bread, Aktur said slowly to Perdita, "Jellalabad lies just over those hills there." He pointed directly opposite the declining sun, which had dyed the sky and the mountains a deep orange-gold. "Tomorrow I must leave you. But if you follow this track, it will take you across the hills and you will see the fort."

"Must you leave us?"

"Yes, lady-sahib. I must go to my people. I cannot ride into the *feringhee* camp."

"I see."

She turned away and hunched down under her coarse blanket, ashamed of herself for wanting so much more from this man, to whom they all owed their lives and who had probably risked his own to help them. She told herself that if Jellalabad were really only on the other side of the hills, nothing could go wrong. And she had no reason to doubt his word. Nevertheless, she dreamed horribly that night and in the morning could only just prevent herself from flinging herself down in the snow to catch his stirrup and beg him to stay with them.

Instead she thanked him formally for what he had done on her own behalf and that of the others. He answered only, "Go with God." Unsmiling, he turned his yaboo and rode away, leaving them alone in the wilderness of rock and snow. They watched him ride away until his tiny dark figure dwindled into nothing in the distance.

"Come," said Perdita briskly, "we have only twenty miles now. Just over those hills, and then we shall see the fort. Charlie, roll up that blanket. That's right. Will you do Annie's, too?"

"Mama, why did Aktur go?"

"He had to get back to his village, Charlie. We shall be all right now."

"Yes, I know," he said, but he kept looking back. "Does Uncle James know the way?"

"Yes. And so do I. This track goes all the way to the fort. Aktur said that we had only to follow it and we would get there."

It was not until about midday, judging by the height of the brazen sun in the sky, that anything untoward happened. There was a distant, ominous rumbling sound, a closer crashing of rocks, and then a peculiar, heavy stillness. Just there the track ran around a high, craggy mountain. Less than a hundred yards ahead, it turned out of their view.

"Another earthquake," said Captain Thurleigh into the silence. "Wait here, and I'll find out what damage has been done to the road."

"Be careful," said Perdita involuntarily as he rode toward the bend. He had hardly been out of sight for three minutes before the sickening noise came again. Into the silence that this time seemed even more eerie than before came the screams of an animal in pain. Perdita thrust the leading rein at her son, saying, "Charlie, take Papa's rein. I must see what has happened."

She rode nervously around the bluff to be confronted by the evidence of a small rockfall. Scars on the mountainside above the track showed where the stones now strewn about it had come from. There was no sign of James Thurleigh or his horse, although its screams became more distinct with every step her own pony took. She urged it forward and soon saw what had happened.

A vast boulder, obviously detached from the rocks above, had pinned the pony against a rocky wall above a tiny depression just below the track. Perdita dismounted, took out her pistol, and cocked it, walking forward to take aim at the poor creature's head. It was not until she stood over it that she saw James.

He, too, lay half under the rock. One of his arms was free, and he was jerkily feeling about him, touching and rejecting the rocks in a desperate search for something. Perdita carefully uncocked the revolver and knelt down.

"James, James, can you hear me?" she said, taking that searching hand in her own.

"Perdita," he said, gasping for breath, "I can't find my gun."

"Don't worry. I shall shoot the poor pony for you, and then we'll get you out of there."

His hand grasped hers strongly, and he said, panting slightly, "No, you cannot. And, anyway, my back must be broken." He gasped again and went on. "I can't feel anything below my waist. You will have to shoot me. But you must do it first, before the pony, so that Marcus will hear its screams after the shot and think you missed."

Perdita recoiled in horror. To kill in cold blood someone who was not an enemy, who did not threaten the life of anyone she loved, was not possible.

Seeing her hesitation, he whispered in desperation, "Sweet Christ, you must do it."

Looking down at his agonized face, she made herself imagine the alternative. She could see that he was right, that she could never shift the vast boulder to free him. If she left him, he would die, anyway, but not quickly. He would have to wait as the inexorable effects of exposure ate into his resistance, suffering pain that she could see from his face already tormented him. Even if he had been an enemy, she could not have found it in herself to consign any human to that hell.

"Perdita, please!" he begged in anguish.

"Hush," she said as she used to say to Charlie in his babyhood. "I will do it for you." She felt his hand relax and looked at his face with terrible pity. Sweat stood out on the grayish skin in large drops, and deep lines had been scored from his mouth by the pain. There could be no shrinking in the sight of his nightmare. She used both hands to recock the pistol. Then she took his hand again.

His heavy eyelids lifted once more, and the dark eyes looked into hers. He must have felt the cold muzzle on his skin, but he gave no sign. He said, "Don't tell Marcus. Don't ever tell." She tried to smile at him and shook her head.

"I won't," she said. Then, forcing herself to keep looking into his eyes and smiling at him, she pulled the trigger.

Bitter vomit rose in her throat, and her breath broke on a dry, gasping sob. She forced her eyes away from the reddening snow and lifted the weapon once more to put the pony out of its agony.

Then she stood up, her knees shaking and the sickness making her stagger. She tried to make herself walk past James Thurleigh's shattered head to take the life-saving blanket and food from his pony's saddle. Jellalabad might be only a few miles away, but they could have lost the right path and take days to reach it. She could not gamble with the children's lives to save herself this horrible task.

When she had struggled back on to the road with the half-unrolled blanket, she saw that the hem of her dress was dabbled in blood and so were her hands.

"It is the pony's," she said aloud, and walked back to her own animal. He shied at her approach, and so she did not attempt to mount him but took the reins and led him back to the others.

As she rounded the bend that hid Marcus and the children from the scene, she saw Charlie waiting for her. His face was greenish-white and his eyes stared. She was sad to find that her voice shook as she said, "It is over, Charlie. The poor yaboo's legs were broken. But I have shot it now, and it is out of the pain forever." She put her free hand on his head to comfort him. But then she saw that her hand was bloody, and when she moved it, the pale blond hair was stained as well.

When they reached Marcus, she went straight up to him, took his hands, and said, "He was dead, Marcus. The rocks caught him and must have killed him immediately. He had hardly bled at all, and so it must have been quick."

"Are you sure he is dead? How could you tell?"

"I listened to his heart, Marcus, and held the gun to his lips, and there was no breath to mist it. He was dead, my dear."

"There were two shots."

"I know. My hand was shaking so much, I did not kill the poor pony the first time."

"Yes, I heard it scream," he said, his quiet voice in horrible contrast to the shaking of his hands. She wanted to touch him, but the knowledge of James's blood on her hands made that impossible. All she could do was watch as he brought the trembling under control. Then he spoke to her again. "My poor dear, you should not have to do such things. Do you want to rest?"

"Rest? No, no," she said more violently than she meant. "We must reach Jellalabad before dark."

She helped Charlie onto the pony and saw Annie's eyes widen at the sight of blood all over her hands. Perdita said carefully, "The poor pony was badly wounded, Annie. Don't look when we pass the place. It is a sad sight."

"Yes, Mama," she whispered, and obediently closed her eyes. Charlie, who was capably directing their mount, looked firmly ahead all the way along the track to the rockfall and then seemed to his mother to look sideways at the bodies. She prayed he would say nothing to alert Marcus.

As his pony paused, Marcus said, "Is this the place?"

"Yes."

"I can smell the blood."

"I wish I could have buried him, Marcus, but the rocks are too big to move."

"I know you would have if it had been possible," he said.

After that they rode on in silence. There were no more tremors, and in due course the track brought them to the edge of the hills above the fort. When they emerged, dusk was falling, but they could see the flag flying bravely from the ramparts, its bright colors challenging and welcoming.

"There, Marcus, there is Jellalabad! We must get down before the light fails. Come. Oh, look, children, the sentries are hanging lanterns on the walls."

Twenty-one

They reached Jellalabad, but it provided only comparative safety, for the fortress itself was under intermittent but fierce siege by Akbar's men. Nevertheless, the spirits of the defenders were high, and they greeted the Beaminsters' arrival with wild triumph.

They delved into their meager supplies of food and clothes in an outpouring of generosity. There were no Englishwomen there to share their gowns with Perdita, but one of the regimental tailors contrived a kind of skirt for her from several pairs of trousers, and officers rushed to offer her their spare shirts and coats. For the first time since the retreat began, she was able to strip off her filthy, ragged clothes, bathe, and scrub the vermin from her skin and hair.

She did the same for the children and Marcus as soon as they had been examined by Dr. Brydon, who was the only man to have survived all the fighting in the passes and who had reached the safety of the fort to bring its defenders news of the catastrophe. Then together they burned all the bloody, frightful clothes, even the sheepskins that had saved their lives. As Perdita watched the flames and thick, choking smoke, she tried to believe that the fire could wipe out her memories as easily as it exterminated the filth she had carried with her.

In time the horrors retreated just far enough for them all to cope with the life they now had. The doctor assured Perdita that the children had suffered no physical harm and that their fears and nightmares would cease in time. Marcus's leg was healing as well as could be expected, and although there was not even the tiniest hope that he would ever see again, he was learning to live with his blindness. She watched him sometimes talking to Sale's officers about the war, showing none of the desperate, aching horror she had expected him to feel, and he seemed happy to walk with them on the walls of the fortress as they told him of Akbar's frequent assaults and the measures they had taken to defend it.

Full of admiration for his courage, she tried to learn from him and convince herself that she need no longer be constantly on guard against an unexpected attack. But it would take time. She still jumped violently at any sudden noise or unexpected touch, and the men around her learned how to warn her quietly of their approach.

To them she was a heroine, and they would have done anything for her. Any survivor from the hell of the retreat would have been cherished, but a lady, and one who had led her blinded, wounded husband and two small children through the mountains to safety, was more than just a survivor. She gave them hope for their own wives and children and the others who still lived in captivity in one of Akbar's forts to the north. She seemed to be a symbol of the ultimate victory for which they all prayed.

Marcus, overhearing them talk one day, thought back to the impossibly shy, flinching woman he had married and was astonished to think of what she had achieved. With no help from him or James, she had led them all to safety with decisiveness and a courage that no woman he could think of could have matched. He, who had once had to protect her and teach her how to live in his world, would now depend on her for the rest of his life, and he knew that he could.

How long that would be was still in doubt, for there was no escaping the knowledge that the defenders of Jellalabad, however high their spirits, were still cut off from their own people and would have to continue to fight for their survival. By then they knew that a new army had been raised in India under the command of General Pollock and that its purpose was retribution as much as rescue. They had been informed that it was on its way, to their relief, but weeks passed and there was no sign of its arrival. Supplies became very short, and raiding parties had to be sent out day after day to round up the enemy's sheep and cut grass for fodder, while messengers were dispatched almost as often to General Pollock, begging him to bring the new force as quickly as possible.

The runners hid their messages to and from Pollock in the most surprising places, knowing that they faced death if they were caught by Akbar's men. Many got through. Because of them, Sale knew that the army of retribution was waiting at Peshawar. With their help he sent plea after plea for help, explaining the situation of the desperate garrison in an attempt to rouse their impatience and make them move.

Charles Byrd, too, was in Peshawar, waiting in agony for word of Perdita. He had been in Lahore when the first news of the Caubul catastrophe reached the Punjab, and he had turned back at once, reaching Peshawar, the nearest he could get to the Afghan frontier, by early February. There he had heard of the survival of a group of married officers with their wives and children, and he made himself believe that Perdita and her family were among them. When the actual list of prisoners was promulgated, he was left to face the assumption that the Beaminsters had died in the retreat and that her body was one of those that he had heard lay in stinking, rotting heaps in the passes, mutilated and looted of anything of value by the blood-happy tribesmen.

When General Pollock arrived with his army, Charles begged to be allowed to march with them—a gesture the emptiness and absurdity of which did not escape him. They could not let him, of course, and he was on the point of leaving the Punjab and India when one of Sale's secret, crumpled messages was brought in with the news of the Beaminsters' miraculous survival.

A friendly officer on Pollock's staff who knew of Charles's connection with them came as soon as he could to Charles's lodging near the bazaar to tell him the story. At first he could hardly take it in.

"The Beaminsters? Lord Beaminster? And Perdita, his wife?"

"That's right, Byrd. And two children. They reached Jellalabad two weeks ago."

To his shame, Charles felt the first tears since childhood springing into his eyes. He gritted his teeth in an attempt to stop them and felt the muscles in his face and neck shudder with the effort, but the tears were forced out, and his breath broke into one uncontrollable, gasping sob. He turned away from the British officer, his whole being flooded with a tearing, overwhelming relief. He felt the man's hand grip his upper arm and controlled himself enough to say, "Thank you for that. She has a father, you know, in Simla. Has he been told?"

"Not yet, old chap. We only got the message this morning, but it will be sent on."

"I'd better go. I'll take it."

"That's mad, Byrd. It'll get there much faster by the usual channels. But you can always follow, unless you want to wait here for them. They're bound to come through Peshawar once the siege is over."

The temptation to stay was powerful, but he knew that he could do little for her there, and he would hardly be able to attach himself to the Beaminsters' party as they traveled back to Simla. Whereas if he were already there, he would be able to see her often and might be of some help. He stayed long enough in Peshawar only to write letters to her and Marcus, to scour the town for any clothes and preserved delicacies he could find, and to persuade the friendly staff officer to add them all to his baggage when the army eventually marched up the Khyber Pass. Then he left to ride at breakneck speed across the Punjab, following the runners who had taken the news to Simla.

Pollock's army left Peshawar on March 30, fought their way successfully and bloodily up the Khyber Pass, and marched out onto the plain of Jellalabad on April 16. The garrison that had waited so long for them and fought so bravely to hold their beleaguered position played the new army in with an old Jacobite melody.

Perdita, standing on the walls with Marcus and a group of Sale's officers, rather liked the tune and turned to Havelocke to say, "I haven't heard that before. What is it called?"

He looked down, and she was surprised to see a smile of dry mischief on his usually severe face. " 'Oh, but ye've been lang a'coming.' "

The wit and the fantastic relief of it combined into a spring of laughter that bubbled up in Perdita, and she hugged Marcus's shoulders in delight.

Six weeks later, having exchanged their makeshift clothes for the ones Charles Byrd had sent them, the Beaminsters reached Simla. The instant the carriage stopped outside Whitney House, Perdita lifted the children down, called a servant to help Marcus, and ran into the house.

Her father caught her in his arms and hugged her in an

embrace that felt like safety itself as he said to her over and over again, "My dearest child. Perdita. Oh, my dear child."

He released her only as he saw Marcus being helped up the steps and went to take the servant's place. Perdita watched him speaking gently and encouragingly to her husband, and felt her burden slip a little.

A familiar, deep, slow voice said, "Perdita."

She turned her head toward the shadows at the far end of the hall and held out her hands. "Charles?"

He walked forward and took her hands and kissed them.

Looking down at his bent head, remembering through everything the misery of his departure, she said, "You didn't go."

"How could I when I knew what was happening?"

Marcus, too, recognized the voice and came limping toward them, supported by Edward's stalwart arm.

"Byrd?"

"Yes, Beaminster," he answered, still holding Perdita's hands.

"I'm damned glad you're here, Byrd. Those things you sent up to us from Peshawar—it was really very good of you to take such trouble."

He held out his right hand, and Charles shook it firmly, trying to say something but finding that the sight of Marcus's wounds made anything he could think of banal, trivial. All he could manage was, "It was so little, but all I could think of that might help."

"It helped. To feel clean, clothed, and fed like that had become something of a dream by the time we got your boxes, eh, Perdita?"

"Yes, Marcus," she said simply, but her eyes and her smile told him that his gifts had mattered to her.

It was a profoundly emotional moment. The four of them stood there in silence, as though unable to find a way of breaking it. Then Charlie said imperiously, "Mama, Annie and me are very hungry. When's luncheon?"

The pattern broke, the adults laughed, and life seemed to reform around them all. Edward started to urge his son-in-law forward again, saying over his shoulder to his grandson, "It's ready now. And we'll all have it together today in the dining room." He turned to his daughter. "I thought you'd prefer that to banishing them to the nursery today, Perdita."

"Thank you, Papa. I don't think I could have done that, after—I mean, just now." Charles put an arm around her shoulders and gave her a brief comforting hug before letting her go to pick up Annie and carry her toward the dining room.

It seemed very strange to Perdita to be sitting at a smooth, polished table once again, drinking claret as smooth as butter from stemmed crystal glasses and eating thin slices of chicken in a delicately spiced, creamy sauce from flowered porcelain plates with silver knives and forks. The contrast brought the memories she was trying to bury rushing back, and she found it difficult not to cry out. To steady herself she said something to Charlie and then noticed that he and Annie had forgotten the weeks at Jellalabad and had reverted to the manners they had learned in the village. They were pushing the food into their mouths with their fingers. Marcus, too, had some trouble finding the food on his plate to cut it up and forking it to his mouth without dropping bits into his lap. Conventional table manners seemed so unimportant after the events of the last months that Perdita could not rebuke the children, but she looked apologetically toward Edward. His smile and gestures made it very clear that he understood.

None of them talked very much. There would be questions later, but for the moment he was content simply with the knowledge that they were all safe. Their gaunt faces and a certain wild, bruised look in Perdita's eyes, as much as the tenseness of her smiles, gave Edward some idea of what must have happened to them all. He had heard reports of the retreat, and it horrified him that his daughter and the children should have had to witness such things. For Marcus he had tremendous sympathy, but he was, after all, a soldier, and such risks were part of his chosen way of life. But for Perdita, who had been frightened almost into imbecility by infinitely less, he was seriously worried. He and young Byrd would just have to try to help her relax and forget what she had seen.

During the days that followed, Edward and Charles Byrd did their best to create an atmosphere of normality while Perdita and Marcus did their best to respond, but both found it difficult, for with relaxation came a whole army of troubling emotions. Perdita came to feel that she was cut off from her father and Charles by what had happened, and she was angry, too, that they seemed not to understand that. She realized that when they talked of unimportant things or laughed at trivial pleasantries they were trying to help, but it felt like insensitivity. Longing to talk of what had happened, she did not know how to start and could not believe that either of them would understand. Frustrated and unhappy, she tried to concentrate on helping the children and Marcus over their own difficulties of adjusting back to normal life.

Once the first euphoria of return was gone, they were all at a loss to fit into the life they had known before the war. They had become used to spending all their energies to stay alive, working out how to conserve their food and organize their clothes for enough warmth to prevent death from exposure. It seemed impossible to either that they should once again spend their lives in visits, pleasure parties, and polite conversation. Marcus had his blindness to battle with, as well as the difficulty of coming to terms with what had happened. Perdita ached for him as he tried to learn his way about the house, feeling gingerly along the walls and coming to grief all too often as he misinterpreted one of the sounds, scents, or touches that he had to use for signposts. Each time it happened, she would be there to help, and he clung to her as the only safety in his dark world.

One morning Perdita was just leaving the breakfast room with Edward when they heard an ominous crash from the drawing room. She left her father to run into the long, sunny double room.

"Marcus, are you hurt?"

He was standing by the little golden table between the windows. It had once held a beautiful plain Chinese vase, whose celadon glaze had picked up the green in the silvery silk rug on the floor. But now the broken porcelain was scattered around Marcus's feet like the petals of a dead flower. One of his hands gripped his stick so tightly that his knuckles stood out sharply under the skin; the other covered what had once been his eyes.

"No, just vilely clumsy," he answered. "Whitney?"

"Yes, Beaminster, I'm here. Don't even think about the vase. It is easily replaceable," he said, looking at the pretty shards with regret.

"I am most desperately sorry. I—I was just feeling it, trying to see what this house looks like: smooth, lovely as I remember it, civilized. And then I stumbled or something. I shall keep my hands to myself from now on."

Edward walked over to his son-in-law and took his arm.

"My dear boy, don't talk like that. The vase is of no consequence. Your doing whatever you want to find your way here matters far more. We all know—" He stopped, thought for a moment or two, choosing his words carefully, and then said, "We all know how difficult it must be for you, although we can only imagine what it must feel like."

Marcus said formally, "You are very good." He turned his head as though searching for his wife. She went to him immediately, and when he felt her touch and smelled the scent of the rosewater she had used ever since their return, his hands relaxed. She led him to one of the sofas and talked gently to him. Edward left them to go in search of Charles Byrd.

He found him in the cool library trying to come to grips with his work. Charles looked up as the door opened, and seeing Edward, he closed his books and laid down his pen.

"Charles, I'm sorry to disturb you, but it's important. Would you take her out somewhere this afternoon?"

"Of course, sir, if she'll come; but every time I've tried to suggest such a thing, she's refused. She seems to want to spend every minute with Beaminster or the children."

"I know, but it can't go on. She hasn't been out of the house since they got back. She looks terrible; I know she's not sleeping. If she can't lay down responsibility for them all and try to learn to forget what has happened, I am afraid she will be really ill."

"That's what worries me, too. She seems so locked in, as though you and I hardly exist for her. And she won't talk about any of it, although he will. She may need some persuading to come with me."

"I'll get Beaminster to help," said Edward, and went to find him. As soon as they were alone, Edward explained what he wanted.

Terrified at the idea of being without her even for a few hours, Marcus nevertheless understood and, suppressing his instinctive protests, said, "Yes, I'm sure she should get out for a while. Ask Byrd to take her somewhere where there are flowers. Hush, now. I think that's her step."

They both turned toward the door, and it was indeed Perdita who opened it. Marcus held out his hand, and when she had taken it, he said, "Your father has just offered to take me for a drive this afternoon so that I can get out for a while. Will you be all right? You could always ride somewhere. I expect Byrd would take you."

Edward watched her immediate recoil and quickly said, "There isn't room in the curricle, or I'd ask you to come with us, but you won't mind, will you? Beaminster badly needs to get out of the house for a spell."

"Of course not. Marcus, I am so sorry that I didn't realize."

He smiled and shook his head.

"Don't be silly, Perdita. But ride with Byrd; it would do you good."

It seemed too exhausting to argue when they were both so set on the plan.

"Very well," she said apathetically. But later, when she was riding beside Charles away from the house, she wished she had refused.

Protected in Whitney House, she had not realized that the Simla season was in full swing around her. She was appalled by the number of people who greeted Charles and tried to waylay them both. She recognized very few, but everyone seemed to know who she was, and they all wanted to say something about the war.

They were full of congratulations for her escape and apparently sincere concern for her health, but she found them horrible. She had felt cut off from her father and Charles by their ignorance of the things that had wrenched her out of the cocoon of their old comfortable life together, but now it seemed that the Simla set who greeted her so curiously stood on the far side of a deep, dramatic chasm, and she looked at them with fear and incredulity.

They were so like their predecessors in dress and manner that behind every one she could not help seeing the ghosts of the dead. Maria Jamieson, who had once stood just there by Stirling Castle in just such a buttercup-colored promenade gown and leghorn bonnet, had been thrown out of a camel pannier into the snow, shot, and then set upon and mutilated by tribesmen armed with knives. These people, with their smooth faces and hands, their eyes empty of everything but trivia, knew that men and women had died, but they did not know how. Fears they had, but they had never seen their most nightmarish fears made manifest.

Their compliments filled her with disgust and their questions with terror. Before she and Charles Byrd had even reached the edge of the town, she whispered to him, "Charles, I can't bear this. Will you take me home?"

"Hang on a little longer, Perdita. We'll be out of the town in another ten minutes, and then there won't be any more people."

Her blue eyes darkened, and she said, "I hate the way they look at me."

"It is only because they know a little of your story and are full of sympathy."

"They know nothing," she answered, and turned her head away.

Charles looked sideways at her pale, set face and wondered how he was ever going to break through to her. Like her father, he was convinced that she would have to talk about what had happened to her before she could come to terms with it and lose the brooding despair that he could see in her eyes. But he was sure, too, that any probing on his part would drive her further into silence.

He found it almost unbearable to have to watch her like that, longing to help yet unable to reach her. Sometimes he thought that if he seized her and awoke some physical response in her, she might be shocked out of her frozen isolation, and he had an idea that her father felt the same. But some quality of her silence made her inviolate, and he could not touch her.

He had decided that it would be useless to take her to the

falls, in spite of their joint memories of the valley, because it would be full of picnic parties and promenaders, and so they turned off the road up a steep path to the left, toward a tiny upland plateau he had discovered. It had no river or waterfall to excite the curiosity of the Simla visitors, and no one ever went there.

When they reached it, he helped her dismount and, with a strange sense of déjà vu, tethered the ponies and urged her to walk with him to the far end of the little meadow, where white roses fountained up the gray rock of the mountainside. Perdita seemed to breathe more easily now that they were alone, and he thought that she looked around with pleasure. But when she had reached out to pick a spray of roses and held it to her nose for a moment to inhale its sweet, sad scent, she looked at him helplessly and said, "Oh, Charles. It is all so lovely, but I have no place in it anymore."

Very much at a loss, he walked toward her until they were only about a foot apart. He did not touch her but said quietly, "Why not, dear?"

This time she tried to speak but could find no words. The roses dropped to the grass, and she brought both hands up to cover her face. He put his hands gently around her wrists and pulled them down. She let him do it but said, "You see, I can't talk even to you. It's as though there is an abyss between me and everyone else. I am cut off from anyone who was not there."

"There are bridges, Perdita, that can cross anything." He looked at her bent head, knowing that if he said the wrong thing now, it would take him weeks to get back to the position they had reached. He kept his hold on her wrists.

"What is between us is enough to build any kind of bridge if we want it enough." She looked up, and he was shocked at the despair in her tired blue eyes.

"Help me, Charles. Please help me."

At that he released her wrists and gathered her into his arms. "I'll help you, Perdita. Trust me."

She let him hold her, and for a few blessed moments the snow and ice and blood she saw everywhere were blocked out.

He murmured softly, "I love you. I can help you if you will let me. I love you so." Then her moment of peace ended.

She stiffened and withdrew from him. He let her go but took her left hand in his right. "Let's walk a little."

"All right," she said, and took a deep breath. "Oh, Charles, it is so wicked of me to behave like this when no one has done anything to me, but I can't make myself stop. There is Marcus, who suffered all that so bravely, while I, unwounded, can't pull myself together. There is nothing to fear anymore, but I can't sleep. All four of us are safe, but I weep all the time over nothing. I feel so weak."

"My dearest, even if nothing was done to you, what you have seen is enough to stop anybody sleeping; and you must be so tired that of course you cry. But weak? Only physically, Perdita, from privation and anxiety. No one who has done what you did could be described as weak."

She stopped and rounded on him, her sad eyes dark and angry. "What do you know of what I did? What can you possibly know?"

Taken aback by her sudden passion, Charles could only say doubtfully, "Only what Beaminster told me last night after you'd gone to bed. My dear, don't look like that. He told me that without you, he and the children would be dead; that it was your courage and endurance that kept them all going. And your forethought in making an ally of that groom of yours. I have known very many women in my life, but none who could have done what you did."

She shuddered and turned away from him. But he caught the glint of tears on her cheek. Concerned and deeply puzzled, he walked on a little way. Then he turned back to where she stood looking up toward the hills, her upper lip clenched between her teeth and her hands gripping each other.

"Perdita, tell me, please tell me."

She shook her head dumbly. Then she released her lip, and he saw that she had actually bitten into it, that there was a smear of blood on her teeth.

"I can't, Charles. Don't you see? Don't you understand? Unless you were there, you can never know what happened. No one who was not there can begin to understand."

Mastering a sudden, equally angry retort, he took off his gloves and pulled out his handkerchief to wipe first her tears and then, very gently, the blood from her cut lip. He peeled away her yellow kid gloves so that she could feel the warmth of his hands and said, "Perdita, I know that I left you in Caubul when you were so frightened, and that while you faced hell in those passes I was safe in Lahore, and because of that I have no right to speak to you of anything that happened in Afghanistan. I understand that by leaving you to suffer alone I have forfeited any position I might have had in your regard, your life. But you must believe that I want only to help."

She heard real grief in his voice, and somehow that broke through her own. Aghast at how she had misled him, she poured out words of apology.

"Charles, Charles, that wasn't what I meant. You must believe me. I never even thought such a thing. I used to wish desperately that you were with me so that I would not be alone, that I could rely on you to tell me if I was right or wrong. But all the time I was also glad that you weren't. No one who saw what happened could ever have wished another human soul to be there. You can't think I blame you for not being there."

His voice was hoarse, and she saw him blink once, twice, as he answered, "What else could I think?"

She leaned forward against him and put her arms around him, one hand stroking the back of his neck, wanting now to comfort him for what she had only just understood. Then she let him go and went to sit on a flat, sun-warmed rock at the edge of the valley. When he joined her, she said, "Charles, there is such an immense distance between the person I was when you knew me and what I have become now that I don't think I could explain to anyone who was not there how it happened. The gulf *is* too wide." His tense features relaxed a little and she went on. "You have always been so independent, so untouched by the things people say, that I did not imagine you could have thought such a thing." She was relieved to see a trace of his old mocking smile slide into the green eyes that had always been so expressive.

"Well, I have never felt like this before. I haven't any practice. I'm sorry, dear," he said, slowly coming to understand that his unhappiness had reached her as his concern and care never had. He tried to go further. "I suppose it is because I have felt so guilty for leaving you."

She was touched by that, too, for she of all people knew what guilt could do, and she let her head droop sideways onto his shoulder. He put his arm around her, and they sat, silent and at peace for once, until a growing coolness reminded him of the time.

"Come on, Perdita, if we're to reach Simla by dark, we must go now."

She got up quickly, remembering Marcus and her children, who had been out of her thoughts for the first time since their escape. Charles bent down to brush the bits of grass and fallen rose petals from the skirt of her habit. Then he fetched their gloves and went to collect the ponies.

Twenty-two

Marcus, who was waiting for her in the hall trying not to resent her absence, realized at once that something had happened to help her. The sound of her step was lighter, her breath was quicker, and her voice no longer dragged. He almost thought there was a smile in it as he felt her kneel by his chair and heard her say, "Marcus! Have you been back long? I hope you haven't been waiting for me."

He put out a hand to touch her face. Charles, who was standing behind her, had to clench his fists to stop himself from reaching out to push that trembling hand away. He had never forgotten—could never forget—the sight of Perdita's face when she had discovered her husband's homosexuality. It seemed outrageous that this man who had rejected her so painfully should touch her now.

Marcus sensed him standing there, or deduced his presence from the small sounds he made, and said, "Byrd? That was good of you. Thank you for taking her out for me."

It took a supreme effort for Charles to say only, "Not at all. I enjoyed it." But he could not watch them anymore, and thanking Perdita for her company, he walked away to his room, resolving to move out of Whitney House as soon as he could.

He had leased his old bungalow when he first arrived at Simla but had yielded to Edward's pressing invitation to stay at Whitney House. They had been glad of each other's company, and Charles had come to have enormous admiration for his host, but now he would have to go.

When he announced the decision at dinner that evening, he could not but be glad of the sudden shock on Perdita's face. But when Edward urged him to stay, he said, keeping his eyes on her face, "It's very good of you, sir, but I think I ought to move back to the bungalow. For one thing, it might make me do more work."

"Of course, Charles, whatever you wish. But I hope you will continue to look on this house as your home and not desert us completely."

"I could never do that," he answered, looking away from Perdita to her father. "You have been so good to me, sir. I can never thank you enough."

"Nonsense. I was glad to have you here," said Edward, wondering very much what had happened that afternoon. It was clear, even in Perdita's current state, that whatever she felt or did not feel for her husband, she loved Charles Byrd. In spite of that, Edward did not think she would ever leave Beaminster, and he would have been disturbed if she had.

He had been furiously angry when he discovered from Charles Byrd the truth about her husband's friendship with James Thurleigh, but in the face of Beaminster's appalling injuries, the anger had died. Looking at him now, Edward wondered how he could have been so unaware of his son-in-law's true nature. It seemed so obvious and explained so many things that had puzzled him—Beaminster's very presence in India with a commission in a dull, middle-class regiment, his choice of so unlikely a wife, his mother's extraordinary acquiescence in that choice—and he cursed himself for his blindness.

He looked carefully at his daughter and thought that her face was at last beginning to come alive again. Blessing Charles Byrd silently, he believed she might now be able to overcome whatever it was that troubled her so much.

But that night he heard her crying in her room. Seizing his dressing gown, he went quickly in to her and, standing by her bed, said gently, "Perdita, is there anything I can do to help?"

She sat up, blew her nose, and apologized. "No, Papa. I am sorry I disturbed you. It is perfectly stupid to weep like this now, but I can't stop."

"The war must have been very frightening indeed, and I can understand that it will take you time to forget, but it is over now. Nothing like it will ever happen to you again. You are safe now. I promise you that, my dearest child."

"Papa, I wish I were a child again. Then you could change my fears with a word like that. But there isn't anything you can say that would alter what happened in Afghanistan. When I become more accustomed to the memory of it all, I shall be better."

He thought that in spite of what she said and her thirty-two years, she looked very childish in her white frilled night-gown, her hair hanging in thick plaits on either side of her face. But she was far too pale, and there were enormous dark circles under her big eyes. He kissed her brow, and she smiled at him with some of the old sweetness.

"I am glad you were here for us to come home to. I don't think I could have gone on alone for much longer."

He let her go and put one strong, square hand under her chin.

"Perdita, I think you could do anything at all. It is clear from what Beaminster has told me that without you, he and the children would have died."

Her swollen eyelids dropped, and she said wistfully, "Has he said anything to you of James Thurleigh?"

"Only that he died in a rockfall on the road to Jellalabad. It must have been horrible for you to find him like that," he said, thinking that perhaps that was what worried her so. "And Marcus must be sad to have lost so old a friend. But you must not look so tragic, Perdita. Your safety and Charlie's will more than make up for that."

She looked at him in surprise. It seemed amazing that he should not have known.

"But he loved him. Marcus only married me so that he could stay in India with James Thurleigh."

Edward seized the opportunity to try to repair some of the damage her husband must have done to her. "Young men, especially soldiers out here, often have such sentimental friendships. They believe that they would die for each other as gladly as they would die for England. They think that no warmer passion could possibly exist than the comradeship between them. But the day almost always comes when they discover what it is like to love a woman."

Perdita shook her head.

"Not Marcus. He loved James."

"As much as Charles Byrd loves you?"

"I don't know. I didn't know you knew. Yes, I think so. I don't know," she repeated, confused and anxious.

"Well, don't worry about it now. You and the children and Marcus are all alive, and that is what matters most. Try to sleep now."

The next morning, Perdita spent an hour with the children before the adults' breakfast was served in a small room off the hall. When she got there, she found both Edward and Marcus waiting for her. She hurried to hand her husband a cup of tea, guiding his fingers into the handle. He thanked her and asked, "Did you sleep well, my dear?"

"Not very, Marcus. I seem to remember too much. You?"

"Better than before, I think," he said with a little smile, "though it often seems hard to believe that we won't wake up on a cold mud floor with that dreadful jar in the corner." His smile broadened, and she thought he looked genuinely amused.

"I suppose in the end we may be able to laugh at a lot of it."

"If we don't, we shall never be able to forget the rest."

"That sounds very sane, Marcus. And very brave. Oh, I am sorry, I'll do that." She leaned forward to take his cup and refilled it. When he had finished that and eaten most of a thin piece of bread and butter, he sat back. Perdita put down her own cup.

"What would you like to do today, Marcus?"

"Your father has to go down to Sabathoo for a couple of days and has invited me to go with him. I think I would like to go, if you have no objection."

"I? Good heavens, no. When do you expect to return?"

"Probably in about three days' time," answered her father. "Would you care to come with us? The children would be quite happy with the servants, and Byrd could keep an eye on things if you would like to come."

"I think not, thank you. I need to spend more time with the children. And in any case, Charles is moving into his own house today, isn't he?"

"So he is. Well, that's probably just as well if you're going to stay here without us." He turned to Marcus. "Will you be ready to go in about an hour, Beaminster? I'd like to get there while it's still light."

"Yes, of course."

They both left the breakfast room, and when she was alone, Perdita made herself eat a small piece of buttered bread. It tasted like raw cotton, and she found it very hard to swallow, but she gradually choked it down and finished her tea. Then she went down the passage toward the day nursery at the back of the house.

Passing the library, she glanced through the open door to see Charles sorting his books and papers into a vast box. She thought him oblivious to everything but his packing, but as she stood in the doorway he lifted his head and smiled at her. When she smiled back, he got up from the table and came out into the hall to her.

"Will you ride with me again today, Perdita?"

"I meant to spend the day with the children. I have neglected them in seeing to Marcus."

"Nonsense," he said robustly. "They are happy enough with their ayahs, and you must have time to yourself occasionally. Let me take care of you for a while. Ride with me this afternoon? If we leave directly after luncheon, we'll avoid everyone else."

Remembering what he had given her the day before, she could not resist the temptation, and so she nodded.

"Good. I'll order the ponies for three o'clock. It will be very stuffy, but that will be better than riding in a crowd."

"Thank you, Charles," she said, and went on to find the children, who greeted her with demands for stories and favorite games.

As she played with them, she was pleased to see how much they at least had recovered. Their faces had already filled out again, and she thought that they must be beginning to forget. But when at last she picked herself up off the floor to leave the nursery, Charlie clung to her legs and Annie wept.

Perdita could not bring herself to leave them like that, and so she sent one of the servants with a message to Charles and ordered her luncheon to be served in the nursery with the children's.

They were all three settling down at the round table in the big bay window when Charles appeared at the door of the nursery. Perdita saw him and said at once, "Charles, I can't leave them. I'm sorry." She was relieved when he smiled.

"I know. But will you let me eat with you here instead?"

"Of course," she answered, and sent one of the servants for another chair.

Charles sat down beside her and proceeded to entertain the two children with wildly apocryphal tales of his adventures around the world. Perdita listened in growing amusement and watched the two children's faces light up with interest and excitement. During a pause she said, "Charles, it is easy to see you're part of a large family. I haven't seen these two so well entertained before. Don't you miss your brothers—and your mother?"

"Occasionally. But the gap they left was filled when—" He stopped, remembering the hovering servants.

"What's a gap, Uncle Charles?" asked Annie, interested.

"An empty space, Annie. Like the space that is left when someone you like very much is far away."

"So will there be a gap here when you go to your house?"

"I hope so. Will you miss me?"

"Oh, yes. Even Mama doesn't tell stories like yours."

They both laughed, and Charles said, "Perhaps Mama will bring you to my house so that I can tell you some more. I hoped that she would come and see it today, to help me arrange all the things I have bought for it, but she says—"

Charlie interrupted truculently. "Mama is going to take us riding this afternoon."

"Couldn't we all go together?" suggested Charles, thinking that if Simla became accustomed to the sight of him with her children, there might be less scandal if he were seen alone with her.

The children considered and then agreed, and later they all went to Annandale, where they were quickly accosted and questioned about their experiences. This time Perdita parried the curiosity better, and when the questions became more than she could bear, she turned them aside by speaking of all the thousands who had died. Her questioners were always shamed into silence by that.

Charles watched her and started to think that in spite of having to share her, the afternoon was not quite wasted; every step she took back into ordinary life was helping her. But once she turned to him in desperation and he saw what the effort was costing. Quickly he rounded up the children and took them all home.

The next day was better. Charles called at Whitney House and persuaded Perdita to ride with him without the children, and although the lowering sky presaged rain, she agreed to go up to the small, empty meadow of their first ride together.

She was silent as they rode past the last houses.

Hoping to bring some relaxation to her drawn face, Charles said, "I really like your father."

She turned to him, quickly smiling. "So do I. I'm glad that you had a chance to know him."

"He is very generous, isn't he? And very good company. When I arrived here, incoherent with anxiety for you, I don't know how I'd have carried on without him."

"Charles?" she said.

"Yes?"

"Why did you stay and wait for us? After what you said at Baba's tomb, I thought I would never see you again."

"I know. And I meant to stay away. But when I heard what had happened, I couldn't." He said nothing more until they turned off the road up to their valley. Then he went on. "It seemed to me then that I ought to have forced you to leave with me or to have stayed with you. I knew how frightened you were. I think I even knew that some terrible catastrophe was going to overtake the army. But I was so damnably jealous of Beaminster that I left you to face it all alone."

"Oh, Charles."

"When the news began to trickle through—when we heard of the deaths and the shocking, stupid, wicked shambles of it all—I began to feel as though I had murdered you myself."

The sudden jerk of her hands pulled her pony to a halt; surprised, Charles stopped, too, and backed his animal until it stood beside hers. "What is it, Perdita?"

For some reason his words made her think that the chasm was not quite as deep or as wide as she had thought. Gathering up her courage and her faith in his feelings for her, she turned to say, "I did murder someone."

He was so surprised that he stared at her, mute and unmoving. But she kept her eyes on his and then said deliberately, "I killed three men, Charles."

"You went through a war. Men are always killed in war." He dismounted and came to stand at her stirrup, looking up at her. "It isn't murder in wartime, Perdita."

She put one of her hands down to take his and said, "One of them was."

"Come and tell me about it," he said, leading her pony and his own up the last few yards into the small green valley. "Tell me about the other two first."

"One was the Afghan who put out Marcus's eyes. He was only a boy, Charles, and I killed him."

"How?" Somehow it seemed important now to make her tell him everything, any detail she remembered.

"He had a knife, and I took it from him and stabbed him again and again." Her voice was dully neutral, and her eyes were blank. His first reaction was horror that she should have had to do anything so terrible; his second, admiration that she had done it.

"He was your enemy; he had just blinded your husband. Surely his death doesn't torment you?"

"Not really, although he was only a child."

"And the other? Who was he?"

"James Thurleigh."

Completely astonished, Charles protested, "But he was killed in a landslide after an earthquake. Your husband told me so."

"It didn't kill him; it only broke his back and trapped him. We couldn't have moved him, and he asked me to do it. I am still glad for him that I did, but I can't forget that he was Marcus's dearest friend and that I killed him. I can't look at Marcus without remembering that and asking myself what he would say if he knew."

"It must have taken great courage, Perdita," said Charles quietly. "And if Marcus knew, he would be grateful."

She turned on him suddenly. "Don't tell him. Promise me you won't tell him. He mustn't know."

"Hush, hush. Of course I won't tell him. And the third?"

She had just begun to tell him about Lieutenant Flecker when the first of the rain began to fall, but she hardly noticed it. Charles did, but he was too relieved to hear her speak at last of the things that troubled her so badly to mind getting wet. He listened to her account of the rape of her groom's sister and its sequel, and when she was silent again, he said without moving, "Perdita, that was not murder, either. You could not have known what the girl's family would do, and you cannot be responsible for their barbarism."

"But it was only because of his death that we are alive now. I bought my life with his death."

"Not knowingly. Oh, my lovely, lovely one, you must not torture yourself for that. Come, you must be wet through; let me take you back now."

She looked upward, vaguely, as though only just aware of the rain that had been pouring down and soaking through their clothes. She brushed her hand across her eyes and got up. She hardly noticed that her dark blue skirt clung to her legs; she had been so much wetter and colder that this seemed nothing. But Charles noticed.

"Perdita, you will catch a most dreadful chill. Will you come to the bungalow to dry off? I'll take you home later."

"All right," she said, too exhausted by the effort of speaking what was on her mind to think of anything else.

They rode in silence back to the town and up to his little bungalow. The storm had kept everyone else indoors, and so they met no one on the way. When they reached the house, he said, "I'm afraid it's in a shocking mess. The servants have not arrived yet, and I've only half unpacked."

"I don't mind mess, Charles," she answered, preceding him into the house.

He took her into the drawing room and put a match to the fire that was already laid.

"Sit by that, my love. I'll just stable the ponies; I shan't be long."

When he left, she stripped off her gloves and the soaking jacket of her dark blue dress and dropped them on the floor with her veiled beaver. Then she went to open the shutters to let what little light there was into the room. She stood in front of a looking glass to see if she could do anything about her hair. It was very wet, and so she took out the pins and went to sit by the fire, brushing out the knot with her fingers and drying the ends of her hair.

It had not struck her that she was breaking the most serious of all the conventions: she was alone in the house of a notorious rake with not even a servant for propriety. But despite his reputation, he had never seemed like a rake to her. She knew only that she was with a friend, a man she loved and who had heard what she had done without turning from her in loathing. She shook the rain out of her hair and waited for him.

When he came back, he noticed at once that she had opened the shutters, as though to announce to everyone in the houses nearby that his was occupied. He rather liked the innocence of that but nevertheless went to shut them again before he lit the candles, saying, "With these we don't need what's left of the daylight, and the shutters will keep out the damp. My poor Perdita, are you very wet?"

She looked up, smoothing the golden brown hair out of her eyes, and smiled. "I'll be all right, Charles." He came to kneel on the floor beside her and brushed the long hair out of her eyes. He held her face in both hands and kissed her. To his delight, he felt her lips move under his and her hands touch his back. When he pulled away a little to look at her, she said, "I didn't know it could feel like that, Charles."

"Nor I. Perdita, you know that I love you. Will you let me show you how much?"

Suddenly everything seemed very simple, and so she nodded.

"I love you, too, Charles."

He kissed her again, more urgently, and as she responded, he started to caress her. She brought up her hands to still his, but he said, "Let me love you. Perdita. I need you so much."

There was nothing in his voice or face to frighten her, and nothing to remind her of Marcus's unhappy attempts. She brushed his face with her left hand and gave herself up to him. His long and varied experience had taught him how to be gentle with her and to awaken in her the passion that surged in him. But nothing he knew had prepared him for the importance of making love to a woman for whom he cared so deeply.

At one moment he saw her looking up at him, puzzled. He stilled himself and asked anxiously, "What is it, love?"

"Charles?"

"Yes, I'm here. What is it?"

"I—I . . ." She couldn't put into words the feeling she had of wanting and owning the whole world. She could only say his name again. He kissed her gently, lingeringly, and slowly brought to her the unimagined, unanswerable pleasure he wanted her to have.

Afterward, as he lay with his head on her heart, she slowly stroked his smooth, fair hair. When his erratic breathing slowed to a soft, quiet rhythm, she said huskily, "Charles, I never knew what it all meant until now."

"I'm glad, love," he said sleepily.

She lay quietly by the crackling fire, more at peace than she had ever been. She felt that she had been immeasurably enriched. There was no shame, no embarrassment anywhere in her mind. Charles had shown by every word and gesture that her body was right and that whatever she had done and said was what he wanted because it was said and done by her. It was as though he had freed her forever.

She lay there with him for an hour or more before he awoke, not really thinking of anything except that she loved and was loved. The memories of war had been pushed as far away as those of her difficult, damaged husband. She was Charles's, and he was hers.

When he awoke, the fire had died down and cast only a pale red glow on their faces and limbs. In the dim light he raised his head from her breast and kissed her.

"Oh, Perdita." He looked down at her lovely face and traced the hollows beneath her eyes and cheekbones. "I suppose I ought to take you back now, before your household begins to worry."

She smiled and let her arms drop away from him. "But I will see you tomorrow?" There was no anxiety in her voice; she was sure at last.

"Of course. Whenever you want me, I'll be there."

She went back to Whitney House with him in a mood of profound peace that lasted all through the evening she spent alone, that gave her a night of uninterrupted sleep without dreams, and that took her through the next morning in a state of astonished happiness.

The first hint of a snake in her Eden came when she went to the nursery to have luncheon with the children. They greeted her as exuberantly as usual, but soon Charlie asked, "Mama, where is Papa?"

"At Sabathoo with Grandpapa. Well, no, not exactly," she

amended, looking at her little watch. "They will be driving back now."

"But does Grandpapa know the way? Papa cannot see, you know."

"Yes, Charlie, I know."

"But why didn't you go with them? What if Grandpapa gets lost?"

"Grandpapa won't get lost," she said almost sharply, as the thought of all her responsibilities came rushing back into her mind, banishing the peace. "He knew the way between Sabathoo and Simla long before I ever came to India, Charlie, and long, long before you were born. He will look after Papa for us all."

"Well, when will they be back?"

"In time for dinner, I expect."

"Can we stay up, please, please, Mama?"

"Yes, Annie, of course you may."

They seemed satisfied, left the subject alone for the rest of the meal, and were quite happy for her to leave them then.

She went to change out of her morning dress of pale yellow muslin and looked anxiously out the window, hoping to see a break in the low clouds or a slackening of the heavy rain, but both looked well set in. Rejecting the riding habit that had been laid out, she asked her maid to fetch a dress of delicate rose levantine that Charles had once admired, and she dressed to receive him in her father's drawing room.

Charles came soon after three, very wet, and saw at once that something had happened to disturb the mood of the previous day. Annoyed that the rain made it impossible for him to take her away somewhere, he sat on one of the sofas near the fire and waited for her to tell him what had happened. But she did not speak, only looked into the flames with an expression of wistful regret that worried him. After a few minutes of growing anxiety, he took her hands and made her face him.

"Perdita, something has happened. What is it?"

"Yesterday was outside time for us, Charles."

He waited, but when she did not explain, he pressed her. "I don't know what you mean."

"Don't be angry, Charles. It is very difficult to say."

"I'm not angry, love, only very worried. You looked so

happy when I brought you back yesterday. What has happened?"

"I've remembered who I am. Yesterday I wasn't thinking of anything except you and what you meant to me. But this morning, when Charlie reproached me for letting Marcus go away without me, I remembered that I am his wife. Although every bit of me yearns to be with you, Charles, I belong to him."

"That's not very fair to me, is it?"

When he saw the tears on her lashes, he was sorry he had spoken so roughly, and he took out his handkerchief to catch them.

"I'm sorry, Perdita. I didn't mean to do that." He smiled ruefully. "I have never been in this situation before. I don't know how to go on."

Forgetting for a moment that any of the servants might walk in, she leaned forward and rested her head on his shoulder. She was still holding his hands, and so he could not reach out to embrace her.

"Charles, I feel as though everything in me will shrivel and die if I am not with you. But he needs me more than you do. He is blind, and—and I killed his . . . James."

"You can't let that bind you to him. He never should have married you; he had no right."

Perdita lifted her head and drew back.

"But he did, and he is the father of my child. He could never live alone now, and I am his wife."

There was no answer to that. Charles looked at her, his heart feeling as though it were being gripped in an inexorable vise and squeezed quite dry. Trying to keep the pain from his face, he said, "Do you regret yesterday?"

"How could I? What you gave me then will be with me always."

"Oh, God, Perdita, I feel as though I shall love you to the end of time. You can't—"

"I must."

"You won't make me go away, will you? You must at least let me see you."

Her hands moved in his, and her feelings were as clear as though they were painted on her face.

"Of course, Charles. I don't think I could bear it if you went away now."

Twenty-three

That night, just as she was drifting off to sleep, Perdita heard the door of her bedroom open. Something in her was forced into a desperate, mute protest, but she made herself call softly, "Marcus?"

"Yes."

Perdita heard nothing more except for the sound of their breathing and knew that he was waiting by her door. She got out of bed and went to shut the door behind him. Then she touched his arm.

"Marcus, my dear, you've no dressing gown. You must be so cold. Come here, come to bed." She helped him in and pulled the quilt up around him.

When she had gotten in beside him, he gripped her hand and said despairingly, "I couldn't put it on. Isn't that stupid? A grown man feeling around for his dressing gown, finding it, but getting himself so tangled up in it that he could not put it on."

Perdita could think of nothing to say that would comfort him, and so she turned very gently to kiss him. His other hand came up to her shoulder and turned her back onto her pillows. Lying back as he buried his ruined face in her breast, she stroked his hair. She was trying to find words to tell him that with practice he would learn to put on his clothes, when he said, his voice choked, "I hated being in Sabathoo."

"But Marcus, why? Was Papa—I mean, did Papa say something to distress you?"

She felt his head shake. Then he said painfully, "You weren't there. Without you I am so afraid. I have tried to pretend it isn't so, but I can't anymore. Cold frightens me; so does heat; the feel of a strange hand guiding me; the sound of voices, of dogs barking, a whip cracking, horses' hooves. Everything terrifies me when you are not there. Oh dear God, Perdita, I need you so much."

The irony of his words was bitter. All the time she had longed to give him just what he needed now, he had shut her out; and now that he wanted it so desperately, she had found someone else who could give her all the things she needed, yearned for, that Marcus could not give. But as he had told her years before, there is a bond between people who have fought and faced death together that cannot be broken; and now, as Marcus lay in her arms, she could feel the strength of that bond, the bond that had once kept them so far apart. So, pushing all thoughts of Charles out of her mind, she said again and again, knowing that it had to be the truth, "I shall be there, Marcus. Always. I shall always be with you."

His hands began to move over her, and he started to make love to her. Despite the anguished protests of her heart, she recognized his need for what it was: a longing for deep, physical solace to drive away the terrors that besieged him. She could not deny him that.

When it was over, he lay back beside her without a word and was almost instantly asleep. She lay awake, listening to his breathing and to the tick of the clock, hour after hour.

At first she tried to make sense of what had happened to them all, but that was fruitless. She tried instead to turn her mind to deciding what she must do to make some kind of life that would be possible for them. Gradually it became obvious that she would have to take Marcus and the children away from India. There was no place in the Company's army for a blind, lame man, and without the regiment, Marcus had no place in India.

That a return to England would deprive her not only of the man she loved but also of her father could not be allowed to weigh in the balance of Marcus's need. Besides, he had responsibilities in England, responsibilities that would one day belong to Charlie. It was only right that she should take them back there. But as three o'clock struck, she turned her face into her pillow, crying silently, How can I do it? Everything I care for is here. I hated England. What will happen to my father if I go now that Aneila is dead? Must I really give up everything just because a savage Afghan child drove a knife into my husband's eyes?

She hardly recognized the answer that her other self provided, but its meaning gradually calmed her wild protests until she understood it and accepted it: not because of his eyes but because in spite of everything, you love him, too. And he needs you now. Then she slept.

The following morning, as soon as Marcus had gone to his dressing room, Perdita went into her father's room. He was standing near one of the long windows while his bearer knelt to put on his shoes, and he looked up, very surprised at her precipitate entry.

"What's the matter, Perdita? Has something happened?"

"No, nothing. But I think I've got to take Marcus back to England," she burst out.

Edward looked carefully at her and then dismissed his servant. "Come and sit down, Perdita, and tell me what this is all about."

Taking a deep breath to calm herself, Perdita spoke more slowly. "The regiment won't have Marcus back now, and James Thurleigh is dead. There is nothing left for Marcus in India. But at Beaminster there must be all sorts of things he could do. From what Juliana told me, he owns most of the county and has hundreds and hundreds of tenants. Surely he ought to be there? And he might be happier."

"And what about you? Will you be happier there, Perdita?"

When he saw the expression on her face, he was about to apologize, but she forestalled him.

"I don't think that can be part of the equation, Papa. Beaminster is Marcus's home, and one day I suppose it will be Charlie's. I have no right to keep them here, away from it, just because . . ." She faltered. He prompted her gently. "Because?"

"The idea of England fills me with despair; living with his mother, with terror; and losing you—I wonder how I shall bear it. But I can't see an alternative."

"What does Charles say about all this?"

"Yes," she answered indirectly, "there's that, too. But he knows I can never leave Marcus, and he must understand." She raised her eyes, and Edward saw just what her decision was going to do to her. He wished that he could dissuade her, but she was so obviously right that he could not even protest.

Perdita watched a deep crease force its way between his

eyebrows and waited to hear what he had to say. When it came, it surprised her in its simplicity. "I shall miss you terribly."

She put out her hands to him in an involuntary movement, and he took them in a hard grip.

"Papa, couldn't you come with us?"

"Oh, Perdita dear, no. My whole life has been spent here in India. England would be an exile for me now. I couldn't adjust to that at my age. And my work is here."

"Then what shall we do about Annie? I love her, and she and Charlie are so accustomed to one another now that it would be cruel to separate them."

"You must take her, if you will. There's no question. A man of nearly sixty, alone, with a four-year-old daughter! It wouldn't do, and you were right when you told me that she needed a mother. She seems more yours than mine now. Beaminster seems fond of her, too."

"Yes, he is. Oh, dear, he must be dressed by now. Papa, I'd better go before he trips over the breakfast table. And I haven't told him any of this yet, so please don't mention it."

"Of course not. But wouldn't it be easier for you if I suggested it to him so that the final decision could come from him?"

Perdita shook her head. "I don't think so, Papa. I think the idea of making such an important decision would worry him too much at the moment. I'll tell him, but . . ."

"Yes?"

"Oh, nothing. I was going to ask you to tell Charles, but that's cowardly. I shall have to do it."

But she found it very difficult. Telling Marcus had been unexpectedly easy, and the children were wildly excited, although Annie kept asking worried questions and Perdita had to reassure her endlessly that there were no tribesmen in England, and that the mountains were only hills, and that no one would hurt her there.

Charles came every day to read the newspapers to Marcus, amuse the children, talk to Edward, and be with Perdita, and every day she resolved to tell him but found she could not. Even the worry that one of the children would let the news leak out to him could not force her until Edward told her that he had secured berths for her on a steamship leaving Calcutta in the middle of September, only seven weeks away. She knew then that she could wait no longer and asked Edward to read to Marcus so that she could be free to talk to Charles alone.

When he arrived in the middle of the morning, she took him to the library, where no one else ever went. They sat down in the deep green leather armchairs on either side of the empty grate, and Charles said, "You're leaving."

"How did you know?"

"I couldn't think of anything else that would bring that expression of determination and anxiety to your lovely face. And I suppose I have been expecting it." He looked straight into her eyes. "But it doesn't make it easier." Then he laughed, and the bitterness she heard in the sound made her wince. "Nemesis is a clever bitch, isn't she?"

"Charles, don't."

"That first summer here, when I decided to have you, I planned it all so cleverly. I would work on you gradually through the summer until you were ready, like an apple so ripe that it needs only a touch to fall into the picker's hand. And then I would take you, just before I left Simla so that our one magnificent moment wouldn't be muddied by emotion."

"Charles, please don't."

He brushed aside the hand she had put on his arm, as though to restrain him.

"I thought we should both be able to enjoy a nice wallow in sentimental sadness that way. And now this is what I have done to us both." He laughed again without a vestige of amusement.

"You once asked me if I regretted what happened, Charles. Do you regret it?"

"As you said to me, how could I? Perdita"—his voice changed, losing its saw-sharp edge—"you took me into a world that had never existed for me."

The bitter anger had died out of his eyes, and he smiled more gently at her as he put out an unsteady finger to brush a tear off her dark eyelashes.

"Don't weep."

She tried to smile back at him as she shook her head.

"It's only because it seems such an unjust waste. Cruel. Will you go back to America?"

The sudden change of subject took him aback, and he looked around the cool, book-lined room before he answered slowly, "I don't think so. If your father will have me, I think I might stay on here for a while. When . . . when do you sail?"

"The middle of next month. Papa has taken berths for us, and he thinks we should leave here next week. We'll stay in Calcutta with the Macdonalds, old friends of his, while everything is packed and crated up. He is to come with us, but I expect he'll come back here when we've gone."

"A week. One week to last for a lifetime."

Twenty-four

Calcutta, November 1842

My dearest Perdita,

Leaving your father last month was a bitter wrench: not only because he is my last link with you but because I have come to care for him so much. But I could stay no longer; the book is done at last, and my mother has written that my own father is ill. I sail for Virginia next week.

We are to dock at Southampton, where I change ships, and I wish I thought I would be able to see you, if only for an hour. But I do not suppose you will come. But write to me care of the shipping office, if you will, so that I know that all is well with you.

I do understand why you had to go with him, in spite of what I said to you. Write that you forgive me.

Charles

Beaminster Abbey, February '43

My dear Charles,

There is nothing to forgive. Leaving you like that almost pulled me into two pieces. I am glad that you understood.

We both miss India terribly and are finding this new life hard to bear. I have never lived in such a house. I suppose it must be ten or more times the size of Whitney House, and that always seemed huge to me. And my ignorance and stupidity fret my mother-in-law into the most awful anger. Marcus left England while he was still only a boy, and so he is nearly the same case.

I think it is the size that appalls me most. The oldest part of the house was an abbey (obviously), and the family seems to have been adding to it ever since they were given it by Henry VIII. But it is beautiful: the whole

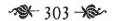

amorphous pile has been built of the same local stone, a pale golden color that sits very well against the green. I had forgotten that lush, wet-looking greenness of this country, or perhaps Norfolk was never the same. Looking out at the lawns here, I sometimes think that they must be deep tanks of some imaginary substance—half liquid, half soft, resilient matter. Pay no attention, Charles! I only write like this because there is no one here to talk to. My mother-in-law is impossible; Juliana is too preoccupied with her own affairs; and Marcus— Marcus is trapped in his memories.

Sometimes I long for him to talk about what happened, to find out whether he thinks James's death was my fault, so that I can exorcise it and leave that great burden of guilt and fear and memory behind. But he will not talk, and if he ever hears the children speaking of Afghanistan or "Uncle James," he stops them, as though if no one ever says anything more, we can pretend that none of it ever happened. If I could only see his eyes, I should know, I think, what it is that he truly thinks. And if he still had his eyes, I might be able to force him to speak, but in the face of that injury I cannot. Oh, Charles, how shall we ever forget what happened?

The only thing that seems to give Marcus any pleasure at all is the knowledge that I am with child again. But I think the thing that keeps me from despairing is the memory of what you said to me that day in Simla. I, too, Charles . . . until the end of time.

Perdita

August '43

My dearest Perdita,

I suppose that I am glad for your sake about the child, but I confess to bitter jealousy. She or he should have been mine. Forgive me, dear, I will not write anything like that again.

I told you, I think, that my father was ill. Well, I

reached home just in time before he died. It is a sad thing to write, but I could never forgive what he did to my mother, and the sight of her face after his death, almost as though she had been freed from some intolerable weight, makes dutiful mourning impossible.

But since then I have begun to understand your difficulties at Beaminster. I have had to take over his estates, and I know nothing of tobacco. It is absurd that my brother Robert did not inherit; he is far more fit to run the place than I. I miss my traveling life, and the temptation to hand over the reins to him and take ship somewhere becomes stronger every week.

Charles

November '43

Charles, my dear,

I do not know if this will reach you because I expect your roving nature has pulled you away from Virginia by now, but I had to write. I was sorry to hear about your father, but I envy you your freedom to leave Virginia whenever you want. We shall be confined here forever.

It might not be so bad if Marcus and I and the children could live alone together, but that is not allowed. Marcus and I have been allotted bedrooms in one of the modern wings overlooking the gardens down to the lake, and my morning room is on that side of the house as well, but the nurseries are at the other end of the older part; and we have to take our meals with absurd ceremony in the hall, surrounded by everyone from the chaplain to my mother-in-law's pathetic cousin and any visitors she has summoned. I know that I should stand up to her; for the moment it is *my* house, after all, not hers. But as I still do not understand how everything happens, or how to give all the orders that seem necessary, I find that I cannot.

Sometimes, when I look around at this house and think of all the people who work for us here, I remember that five of us shared one tiny, windowless room for nine weeks. The contrast makes me despair. When that happens, I escape from all the things I am supposed to do and retreat to the library, where I know I shall find Marcus. It is a lovely, peaceful room—long and low with faded old velvet chairs and worn curtains—and it has become our refuge. They always light a fire there first thing in the morning to stop the damp from harming the books, and so it is really cozy—the only place that is. The books are a wonderful selection, and would keep anyone occupied happily for years. Sometimes I try to read to Marcus, but too often I can tell from the way his hands twist and he bites his lip that he is not listening. Then I am afraid that he is back in Afghanistan and thinking of James.

His mother is forever sending agents and men of business and bailiffs to talk to him and ask for orders, and he hates it so. They all know so much more than he about what needs to be done that the whole procession seems like an empty travesty—cruel, almost. I try to stop her, but all she says is that both he and I have to learn to carry out our responsibilities. I suppose that one day we shall learn, but it seems an idiotic way to spend our energies in a world where people are killed by the thousands on the whims of statesmen pursuing their own political obsessions.

The children, though, are truly beginning to forget. They no longer wait helplessly if they drop something, or call imperiously in Hindustani for the servants. And Annie has even stopped hating this English food. At first, I think, that was her greatest difficulty—porridge and vegetables and bland, nursery meals. Poor child!

I wish that I knew where you are, Charles. Then I could picture you, working on one of your books, perhaps, and feel that there really is a life beyond Beaminster Abbey. Papa's letters help, too. I need you both so much.

Perdita

Hong Kong, December '44

My dearest Perdita,

Your letter of thirteen months ago has finally caught up with me. As I read it I wished I could be with you to help. But the only solution I could suggest would be the one I have perfected: escape.

Why not try, Perdita? Must you remain in Dorsetshire? If it is so uncongenial, and if Beaminster has nothing to do except give orders to men who know just what they should do, why not take him to London? His position must entitle him to sit in your House of Lords. Could he not do something there? It would not be so complete an escape as mine, but it might alleviate what you suffer now.

You have written nothing about the child, Perdita. Tell me about it (her? him?) and that you are happy.

Charles

London, January '46

Dearest Charles,

I do not know if this will ever find you, because your December letter took so long to arrive that you have probably wandered away somewhere else, but I have to write.

I did as you told me and took Marcus to London, and at first I thought he would be still more unhappy, because he hated to go among strangers and could read nothing of what he needed to learn. But now it is better.

There are still many people at Westminster who remember his father, and Marcus's affliction makes them all very good to us. I have had to learn all about blue books and government papers of all kinds and read to him by the hour. We write his speeches together, and sometimes I even feel as though I, too, were involved in his work. We both believe that we might one day be able to do something to make this government think twice about going to war, and if we can do that, then all our labors will have been well rewarded. We are learning to become masters of army constitution and foreign affairs, but we are still novices, and one day we shall make a mistake that will make Marcus a laughingstock. So far that has not happened, I think.

You asked about the child. We decided to call him Richard; people say that he looks like me. I think he will be more like my father. I hope so. Papa seems to have a much happier nature than either of us.

Perdita

Virginia, November '46

Dearest Perdita,

Your letter followed me to Hong Kong and now has caught up with me here. I hope that you had all the letters I sent in the meantime.

I came back to see to the publication of my empires book, long delayed, I know, but there have been many misfortunes at the printers. My father would have been astonished that I had ever finished it. Even when he was dying, he told me that I was a good-for-nothing, always running away from the difficult or demanding. For months I was so angry that I would not even think about what he said. But now I have the answer I would have liked to make, and I present it to you, the only person I can trust to understand. Yes, I do run away— but not from trouble or hardship. I run from boredom, confinement, and the threat of having to pretend to feelings I do not have.

Yes, you are right again. I shall be leaving here very soon. Robert and his wife look on me with pitying scorn, but my mother has always understood—as you do.

Yours always, Charles

London, January '47

My dear Charles,

The parcel with your book has arrived, but no letter. Is all well?

I read the book with interest, as you will suppose, but so much of it is beyond my understanding. It sounds foolish, but I never knew how wise you are. Reading the book, I could not prevent myself from wondering how you ever came to love me.

Where are you now? Reports of almost every country in the world are so violent that I fear for you. I find myself saying "what if" and "if only" too often. Please do not stop writing to me. Your letters bring you back to me so vividly that without them I do not know how I should go on. The days when the letters come always seem full of sun, even when the clouds are black and thick and the rain pours down as heavily as on that day in Simla. I know we should not spend our lives looking back, but I cannot help remembering.

Perdita

The Cape, June '47

My dearest,

I am glad that you remember. It is something that should not be forgotten. I am back here to finish the China book, and I hope it will impress you as much as *The Management of Empires*, but you are a goose: You know perfectly well why I love you, and it has nothing to do with books.

The efficient and virtuous Robert is organizing everything in Virginia, and so I have taken up residence here. I am considered something of a freak by the Boston matrons; they are all happy to come out to the Cape in the summer, but to leave the warmth and comfort of their redbrick houses for these wooden ones by the shore, where the wind whistles in winter and the ocean crashes up on to the beaches, seems mad to them. But I like the space, and no one troubles me here. I am fixed here for a while, and I promise not to go anywhere without telling you first. May I come to London soon?

Charles

London, November '47

Dearest Charles,

I cannot prevent you going anywhere in the world you want, and I should never try. But I am glad that you are avoiding the most dangerous places at the moment.

I think London could be dangerous, too. Is it very selfish of me to want to keep on as we are? If we met again, we might lose our peace. . . .

P

The Cape, February '48

Very well, Perdita, I accept your prohibition, but only because I know too well the suffocating frustration of being made to do things and see people I would rather avoid.

If that sounds too emotional, it is because my mother (even she cannot quite understand) is trying to marry me to a young cousin of hers—a serious, black-haired child called Emily. She is almost beautiful in a restrained, Bostonian fashion, and she can talk sensibly of things that matter. It is possible that had I met her ten or fifteen years ago I would have succumbed, but I know too much of myself by now. I have no inclination to exchange this paper love affair for the drab realities of domestic matrimony. I know that I would be driven mad by the imprisonment of it—and my "infidelities" would distress her. I dislike hurting people, and I would always hurt her.

But the only real regret I have in resisting the temptation is that I shall never have a child of my own. Strange, is it not, how such atavism is presented to the most unlikely subjects?

I have finished the last volume of my China work, and I expect the printers will have done their part in time for me to send you a copy for your birthday.

Dear Perdita, I do not know how I would arrange my life if I did not have you in it.

Always yours, Charles

My dear Charles,

It is weeks since I received your last letter, and perhaps you have been wondering why I have taken so long to answer. The truth is that it aroused an explosive mixture of emotions in me that had to be separated before I could write.

At first I suppose it was jealousy that consumed me—not of your Emily, who sounds a charming girl—but those "infidelities." Then once I had found a way to be rational about what I have in fact known must be so, I discovered a passionate wish that you should have what I have found with Marcus. We have become so comfortable together, and I have learned to value that highly. I do not suppose that I shall ever again be as happy as I was that day in Simla, but nor shall I plumb the depths I should have known had I gone away with you and then learned of those "infidelities" or come to realize that I was confining you in the way you fear so much.

Marry her, Charles. I know that you will always want to escape, but it is good to have an anchor—and children. I do not understand what "atavism" means, but if you could feel for a child what I have with Richard, you would know that a little imprisonment is worthwhile.

Perdita

The Cape, April '49

Ah, Perdita, Perdita—I love your honesty—and thank you for that jealousy. It is a compliment I will treasure that you still feel like that seven years later.

I do envy you your Richard, and when I am tired or sorry for myself, I envy you and Beaminster. But, Perdita, you and I are not the same despite what we shared. It would never suit me to be anchored as you are.

It is a good thing that you were strong enough to resist my childish importuning. Do you know that verse of Keats?

Bold lover, never, never canst thou kiss,
Though winning near the goal—yet do not grieve;
She cannot fade, though thou hast not thy bliss,
For ever wilt thou love, and she be fair!

It is good to be able to write that I shall always love you.

Charles

London, September '49

My dear Charles,

Do you not find it curious to look back and remember how intensely we felt and how amused we can now be about it all?

I longed for you in quite a new way recently, for help with my poor Charlie. He has become so uncontrollable in the last year that we have had to send him away to school. I hate the thought, but when I found out what he had been doing to Annie, I had to send him away. I found her once with the most shocking bruises on her arms, and when I questioned her, she eventually told me that he had made them. At last the whole story came out —years of teasing, bullying, and actual physical hurt. She hates me for sending him away and insists that none of what he has done to her merits such punishment.

But, Charles, what could I have done? Apart from what he did to her, which was bad enough in all conscience, I am so afraid of him turning on Richard. He is so young and so happy that it would be cruel to make him afraid. I suppose that is the difference between them: Richard has never seen the dreadful things that Charlie and Annie saw when they were so young. Perhaps it is only surprising that Charlie has done nothing worse yet.

It is this kind of thing that I wish I could talk of to Marcus. He was there in Afghanistan, too, and he could help them both, I am sure. But he will not. The burdens of memory are still with us, like the huge packs those poor sepoys carried, and we will carry them until we face what we did and what was done to us.

There is yet more talk of war with all those rebellions last year. The complainers are certain that some predator will soon threaten us or our possessions. I pray that they are wrong.

Perdita

Venice, April 1850

My dear,

In spite of your advice, I escaped once again and left my mother and the unfortunate Emily to their regrets, to come here in search of another book. The late rebellion, which concerned you so much, provides a splendid excuse: Venice, so ravishingly beautiful, was once fantastically powerful for so small a place; yet now it is abjectly crushed beneath the feet of another imperial power.

I wish I could show this island to you. Occasionally, in spite of Keats's words, I dream of a time when we shall meet again, but . . .

Charles

London, November '50

My dear Charles,

It is so good to be back here, working with Marcus, that I can almost forget my fears for poor Charlie. And Marcus is glad, too. The secretaries we found for him are clever, of course, and can do all the reading and writing he needs, but he says that he needs me, too. We talk of everything now except the past, and it is hard sometimes to remember how aloof he once was. But I still wish he would break his silence about the war. I believe that until he knows the truth and accepts what happened, there will always be a barrier between us. But I dare not risk breaking my promise to James Thurleigh. It is cowardly, but I could not bear it now if Marcus were to turn from me in hatred for what I did to James.

He is very dear to me, Charles. I would do anything if I could be sure it would make him happy.

Annie has made several sketches of him, and they are such remarkable likenesses that I am sending you one. Most of the time he looks as content as she has shown him, but there are still occasions when the old pain returns, and I cannot seem to do anything for him.

Perdita

London, January '52

Dear Charles,

No letters from you. Have I offended you by writing so much of Marcus? Or have you simply escaped again?

Life continues here much as it was when I last wrote. Marcus says that Russia is still frightening the war party, this time because of Constantinople. They seem to think that the existence of Russians there threatens India once again. Where will it all end? What will happen next?

Please write to me, Charles. I need you, too.

Perdita

Venice, March '52

Perdita, my dear,

Of course you have not offended me. I cannot think what has happened to all my letters—perhaps they are tumbled in a ditch somewhere in Europe after an accident with a mail coach. Perhaps the Austrians think I was writing sedition. Who can tell?

I am nearly finished here and find the city and lagoon very oppressive. It is strange that a place as beautiful as this can be so melancholy and stifling. I thought of going home to write up all the notes I have made, but in the end I decided to return to India. I wrote to your father to ask if he would see me, and I have his reply here. I leave as soon as I can get a ship and will be in Simla soon.

Still yours, Charles

London, August '52

My dear Charles,

I think that this is the first time I have truly envied you your freedom. To go back—to see Papa again! You must know how much I miss him. Will you try to persuade him to come here, Charles? His latest letters have worried me, and I wish I could go to him. He writes often, and Marcus and I fancy that we can almost hear him talking when I read his letters aloud, but it is not the same, and I am afraid of his growing old in that country. Not that I would not live there if I could. I miss that, too, in a way I had never expected. Will you tell me everything, from the moment of your arrival at Calcutta? I want to hear the birds, smell the scent of the flowers, see the colors, that light, all the things that are so different from their English counterparts.

Please persuade Papa to come here, if not to stay, then just for a visit. If he came overland, it need not take too much time.

Perdita

Twenty-five

Simla, February '53

Perdita, my love,

You see that I have reached old Simla at last. I was afraid too much might have changed and I would not be able to see the places we knew. It is true that the town has grown—with rather ramshackle houses for the most part—but enough is as it was. The hills are exactly the same, of course, and so is the air. I had forgotten what a contrast there is between the stuffiness of the Plains and this clear, brilliant air (from which you will have gathered that so far we have escaped fogs and snowfalls—there is plenty of snow, but it is not falling now).

Your father, too, is just as I remembered him. He says that he has slowed down and that he creaks at the joints, as though he is an old piece of furniture. It is true that he looks older and he does seem tired, but his conversation has all the old vigor, and his welcome of me was as generous as the day I arrived here from Peshawar all those years ago.

We do not talk much about that time, but he has shown me all the letters you have written to him since. He has kept every one and has his favorites in that inlaid mahogany box you gave him beside his chair in the library so that he can reread them whenever he wants. He picked out several for me to read.

He also showed me the portrait of Richard that you sent him last year. As I looked at it, an extraordinary idea presented itself to me for the first time. I can't think why it never occurred to me before. Perdita, am I wrong? You have told me how much the boy means to you, but very little else about him. . . .

Perdita put down the letter and picked up a miniature of her younger son, which stood before her on the desk. As she looked at it, noticing once again the delicately cut lips and the greenish eyes as much as the shape and structure of the face, she asked herself once more the question that Charles had not quite put into words: Was he Richard's father?

Suddenly she could not bear him to think that she had deliberately misled him, and so she found a pen and, without stopping to think very much, wrote:

My very dear Charles,

I do not know. When Richard was born, I knew that it was possible that he was your son, but I had no way to be certain. As he grew into childhood, people said that he looked like me, and I let myself think they might be right and told you nothing.

But more and more I have wondered. In many ways he seems like Marcus; they share a peculiar gentleness and that tremendous, undeviating loyalty that Marcus has always shown but that I have only recently come to understand; and they are such good companions. This may sound sentimental, but it is not meant to. When Marcus lapses into one of his bleak periods, when I cannot reach him at all and I am so afraid of what he suffers, Richard can almost always wake him out of whatever thoughts are gripping him.

Yet he is like you, too, Charles. He has a joyousness about him that seems quite foreign both to Marcus and to me; it reminds me of you as much as his imperviousness to doubts and shyness—his rather engaging certainty that life will go his way.

I wish I could be sure. All I know is that Richard is the most lovable child—and very happy in his life. None of us will ever be sure, but in all legal and practical ways he is Marcus's son. And Marcus loves him. Charles, you must see him if you wish, but I beg you not to speak to either of them about what might be. You know that I loved you, and the thought that he might be your son gives me great happiness, but it is a happiness that we must keep to ourselves. Marcus has been hurt enough for three lifetimes. Do not make him suffer anymore.

Perdita

She folded her letter, sealed it, and directed it to Charles at Whitney House, marking it to go via the express Suez route so that he would receive it as soon as possible. Then she rang for one of the footmen to take it at once to the offices of the Peninsular and Orient Line.

Once the man had gone, she tried to forget it and turned to her other letters. When they were dealt with, she remembered other things she could do to keep her thoughts at bay and sent for the housekeeper to give her orders for the following week.

There were to be a series of breakfasts for Marcus's colleagues, and a large formal reception for the leading members of the opposition and their wives, and it was essential that everything should be arranged perfectly. As she waited for Mrs. Ramsden, Perdita thought how incredible such an occupation would have seemed to the pathetic Miss Whitney of the rectory at Fakenham. Looking back across the years, she remembered her conviction that her life had ended with her mother's death and that when she had sailed from England, she had believed herself worth nothing and had even wanted to die. Terrible things had happened to her since then, but it was no longer those that she saw; it was the discovery of her father that seemed to shine out of the past, with all the good that had grown from it. It was he who had first taught her that she could be lovable, just as it was Marcus's need that had shown her her own strength. Because of the way they—and Charles—had taught her to value herself, she knew that whatever happened in the future, she would never again despair. She would be able to deal with whatever fate did to her.

She wanted more, of course, all kinds of guarantees of safety for the children and for the three men that she loved. And above everything else, she longed for Marcus to be different, to be able to be her lover as well as her husband and friend. Her years with him had given her so much that it seemed ungrateful to want from him also the kind of love Charles had given her; but at last she had learned not to be ashamed of wanting it. Marcus—

A knock at the door interrupted her meandering thoughts and brought them back to her task of insuring that everything went correctly when she received Marcus's guests.

Mrs. Ramsden was the last and most capable of a series of housekeepers, and Perdita knew that she would do exactly as she was told, but that she did have to be told. Nothing could be left to chance.

"And please insure that Rusham does not include any lilies in the vases this time," she ended. "You know how the scent disturbs his lordship."

"Very good, my lady," answered Mrs. Ramsden. "I did tell him last time, but I shall make sure now."

"Please do. His lordship has enough to bother him without unnecessary annoyances like that. Oh, just a moment," she added as the plump, soberly dressed woman rose to leave. "Where is Miss Annie today? I didn't see her at breakfast."

"I believe she's in that studio of hers, my lady. Sarah said that she had a tray in her room and went straight off to paint. Shall I send one of the maids to fetch her down?"

"No, don't do that. I shall go up myself. Thank you, Mrs. Ramsden."

Perdita followed her housekeeper out of the elegant octagonal room where she had her writing table and went on up to the attic rooms. A year earlier, when it had become clear that Annie had exceptional talent, Perdita had given her a room of her own to paint in, and she knew that the privacy it afforded was highly prized. She rarely violated it but was worried enough about Annie to do so now. Ever since Charlie had been sent back to school at the beginning of term, she had been unnaturally quiet, and her pallor and thinness reminded Perdita frighteningly of Aneila in the months before the consumption took hold.

When she reached the door of the studio, she knocked briefly and went in without waiting for an answer to see Annie dressed in a long, cream-colored linen coat working at a large canvas in the cold north light. She held a brush in her right hand and a palette knife in the left, and she was peering closely at her work. She seemed unaware that there was anyone else in the room. Perdita stood silently by the door, watching.

Annie's eastern blood was obvious in her inky black hair and huge dark eyes, but her father had bequeathed to her both height and a warm complexion. Perdita thought she looked splendid in the severe linen coat, although her hair was bundled back untidily and already there was a streak of carmine paint across her left cheek.

"Annie?"

At the sound of the voice, the girl looked up and quickly turned her easel to the wall. She put down the knife and brush and came toward the door, wiping her hands on a messy rag.

"Good morning, Perdita," she said gravely to her half sister, who had long since ceased to be "Mama."

"I did not mean to disturb you, Annie. Please don't stop for me. Is it going well?"

"Well enough. What can I do for you?"

"Why, nothing. I came to see how you are and to ask whether I could see the picture."

To her surprise, Annie blushed deeply and shook her dark head.

"But, Annie, you have always let me see your work. What is the matter?"

Aneila put her hands into the pockets of her long coat.

"You won't like it, Perdita. It will hurt you. And I don't mean to do that or want to. It is just something I had to paint." The staccato sentences were so unlike her that Perdita began to be seriously worried. She walked over to the easel and without asking again swung it around under the fanlight. At first she took in little of the subject matter in her recognition of the extraordinary advances in technical competence that it showed.

"But, Annie, it is going to be very good, much better than *The Charge*. I like the way you have painted those snowy rocks."

Then she looked more closely and began to understand. The canvas, which must have been about six feet by four and a half, showed an almost photographically exact representation of the scene in the mountains behind Jellalabad when she shot James Thurleigh. There was the man under the stone and the scrambling pony pinned down in front of a woman who leveled a revolver at them. Perdita was distressed to see that Annie had given her an expression of furious hatred, and she was about to speak when she looked again at the figure under the rock and saw that his face was

Charlie's. Without turning her head she said sadly, "Oh, Annie."

"It is his nightmare," she answered in a dull voice. "I started it after he went back last time. He had only just told me about it. I thought if he saw it with his eyes instead of his mind, it might go away."

Perdita lost her own shocked hurt in the desolation of Annie's voice and went to hug her. "Come and sit down." They sat side by side on the model's couch, and Perdita held her half sister's hands in a firm clasp.

"Did he tell you why he dreams that dream?"

The bent head shook slowly. Perdita stroked it gently.

"He may have forgotten, but I will tell you. Do you remember the ride to Jellalabad in the war?"

"Not really," she whispered, "only the cold."

"There was a small earthquake on the last day, one of a series of shocks, and James Thurleigh, whom you and Charlie called Uncle James, was caught by a fall of rocks loosened by the tremor. I left you and Charlie with Papa behind a bluff and rode to see what had happened, and I found Uncle James and his pony trapped. It was impossible to move them, and they were going to die. Not quickly, but of cold, starvation, and whatever wounds the rocks had caused. He begged me to shoot him so that he did not have to suffer that. I had no choice, Annie. He died holding my hand.

"When it was over, and I went back for all of you, I found that Charlie had followed me. For a long time I hoped that he did not see what had happened, but now I know that he did."

"Mama." Something in Annie's use of that long-abandoned name touched Perdita deeply.

"Annie, for years I felt guilty. I told myself that I had killed Papa's dearest friend and that I was wicked for it. But then I learned to understand. There is nothing on earth wicked if it prevents the kind of suffering James would have had if I had refused to do as he pleaded."

The studio door opened at that moment, and the butler came in, panting after the unaccustomed climb up to the attic. Perdita looked at him, angry that there had to be an interruption at that moment.

"Yes, Hobson, what is it?"

"Mrs. Fawcett has called, my lady."

"Well, tell her that I am not at home," she said with rare asperity.

"I did, my lady, but she was very insistent and asked if she could wait until you returned."

Without thinking of anything except getting rid of the butler, she said, "If it is so important, please ask her to come back this afternoon. Oh, tell her . . . three o'clock."

"Very good, my lady," he said in a voice heavy with injured dignity.

Perdita waited for Annie to speak again when he had shut the door, but she was silent. Perdita tried again. "Annie, I wish terribly that I had known of Charlie's fear long ago, so that I could have explained it to him, told him what happened. But I am sure he knows, really, that I would never hurt him."

"Then why did you send him away? I know he was always in trouble. But why did you send him to that horrible school? He hates it so much."

She had not quite said, "But you hurt him every time you make him go back," but the words seemed to be there between them. Without letting Annie's hands go, Perdita said, "You know that we had to send him, Aneila. I know he does not like it much, but Annie, don't you remember the things he used to do? He is so much calmer now, and kinder. Isn't that worth a little unhappiness?"

The bent head lifted, and Perdita saw that there were tears sliding out of the big dark eyes, the first tears she had known Annie to shed since her childhood. She did not sob or cry out; she just wept and wept.

"You see, I love him," she said.

At that Perdita took the girl in her arms and rocked her, murmuring, "I know you do, dearest. And he loves you, even if he doesn't often show it. But he will learn to, Annie, as you will both learn to love other people. I know it seems now as though no one else will ever be as important to you as he is, that nothing will matter so much for the rest of your life, but it isn't so. I promise you that. I know it from my own life."

As they sat there, Perdita wondered whether this perhaps might be the end of it; whether all the memories of the war's cruelties could be finally buried with this revelation of Annie's. She felt as though the burden she carried were lightened as they sat together, surrounded with the smell of sized canvas, paint, turpentine, and linseed oil.

But her new happiness was short-lived. The following morning, her footman brought the letters to her little writing room, and she saw that there was another addressed in Charles's writing. Never before had he sent letters in such quick succession. With fingers trembling in quick anxiety, she broke the seal to read:

Simla

My darling,

Your father died last night. The doctor assures me that he was not ill—just old and very tired.

I know that the news will be a great shock to you, but if you had seen him, you would not have been able to be too sad for him. It happened on the evening we were both to dine at Government House. He decided not to go at the last minute—he said he was too tired—and so I went alone. When I got back, there was still a light burning in the library. I went in to have a word with him and try to persuade him to go to bed.

He was sitting in that big wing chair to the left of the fireplace, and the fire had died down so that there was just a dim, red glow lighting his face. He had your writing box on his knee and a pen in his hand. For a while I thought he had just fallen asleep over the letter, and it was not until I went to take the inky pen out of his hand that I understood.

He looked so peaceful, Perdita, that he could have felt no pain or fear. When my time comes, I shall be pleased if I can die like that—in my own home, unafraid, writing a letter to you.

I do not think there is anything else I can tell you. The lawyers will be writing to you soon, but I wanted you to hear the news from someone who truly cared for him, and I wanted you to have his letter as quickly as possible. Don't grieve too much, my dear. He had spent his life well and had fewer regrets than most men.

Charles

It was some time before Perdita could bring herself to open the other piece of paper. Pictures of her father flashed through her mind faster and faster, and she ached all over with the knowledge that she had lost him completely. It hurt badly that she had spent the last few weeks believing him to be alive when he was not. Although she could accept rationally what Charles Byrd had written, her whole being felt flooded with grief.

When she could control herself, she picked up her father's last letter, but when she unfolded it, for a moment or two she could not read the words. She brushed the back of her hand against her eyes and looked down again.

The whole piece of paper was covered with her name, spelled differently each time, as though he had been trying to force his dying mind to focus enough to tell her something he wanted her to know. Prdita, Perdata, Perdy, Perdi, Pertada. The writing was shaky, and some of the words ran off the sheet. Through the tears that rushed inexorably to her eyes, she felt the love of which he had been trying to tell her, and she whispered with a breaking voice, "Papa, oh, my dearest dear, my dear Papa," until the knowledge became just bearable.

She folded the two letters together and searched for a handkerchief. The door opened, but she heard nothing until Marcus's voice reached her.

"Perdita, my dear, what has happened?"

"What?"

"Has something happened to you? I felt just now as though you were calling out. I came as quickly as I could. What is it, my love?"

"Papa . . ." She couldn't speak, but she was so grateful that he had come.

"Tell me."

"He is dead."

Marcus found his way to her chair, let his stick drop to the floor, and put his hands to her face. She felt his thumbs

gently wipe the tears from under her eyes as his fingers cupped her face. It was the first time he had touched her for years except when he needed her help. He said in a voice that seemed to come from miles away, "Oh, my dearest child, I am so sorry. I know how much you cared for him."

Tears welled up again.

"But I never told him so, Marcus."

"He knew."

"I wish I had told him. I could so easily have written it. I wish I had never left him there alone."

Marcus moved his hands to her shoulders and helped her to her feet. She found herself leaning against him with his arms wrapped tightly around her and his lips on her hair. Very quietly he said, "My darling, I know how much it cost you to leave him to bring me home. And I have always honored you for it. I know—" He stopped, finding it almost impossibly hard to break a reserve that had grown nacre-hard around his deepest feelings. But her need was of overwhelming importance, and so he tried again.

"I know that I have never told you all the things I ought to have said, but I hoped that you knew them, anyway."

Perdita was so moved by his touch and the thought of what he might be trying to tell her that she could not answer.

"When we married—" Marcus stopped again, the difficulty of what he wanted to say silencing him. Perdita felt his hands tighten on her back. He tried once more.

"When we married, I did not know how to love you, and for a long time afterward I did not understand what was happening to me. It was not until I realized what you had done for James Thurleigh that I began to learn what it was I felt, what I had felt for a long time." He felt her stiffen in his arms, but at last he knew how to say it. "I had always wondered about those two shots, you see, because I did not understand how you could have missed an animal at such close range. And then Charlie came to tell me what he thought he had seen. Then I understood, Perdita, and I was so grateful, so desperately grateful that you had enough courage."

Feeling his arms securely around her as he spoke, Perdita laid her head on his shoulder in complete trust.

"It was terrible, Marcus. But I knew that I had to do it. I

have wanted to tell you about it so many times, but he made me promise never to let you know what really happened." Her voice dropped so that he had to strain to hear what she was saying. "And I thought the truth might make you hate me."

Marcus could feel her heart beating fast against him. He said at last, "I never hated you, Perdita. I could not. I loved you then. And I love you now."

The rest of her burden slid away, and another life began.

AUTHOR'S NOTE

There can be few things more absurd than a bibliography in a novel such as this, where historical and topographical fact has to be adapted to fit into a fictional setting, but there are some debts that need to be recorded.

Anyone who has read Emily Eden's wonderful *Letters from India* (1869) and *Up the Country* (1860) will see at once how much I owe to them. The journals of Fanny Parkes, published in 1850 as *Wanderings of a Pilgrim in Search of the Picturesque*, have also provided much invaluable background detail about the voyage to India and the life an Englishwoman could expect there, as have the letters of Honoria Lawrence quoted in Maud Driver's biography (1936).

J. W. Kaye's *History of the War in Afghanistan* (1859) is the standard Victorian work on the First Afghan War, but most of the detail I have used has come from Alexander Burnes's *Mission at Cabool* and the eyewitness accounts written by the few survivors, particularly: Lady Sale's *Journal of the Disasters in Afghanistan*, Vincent Eyre's *Military Operations at Cabul*, and G. R. Gleig's *Sale's Brigade in Afghanistan*. Of more modern works, the most interesting analysis I have found of the political background to the war is J. A. Norris's *The First Afghan War* (1966), and it is that book that drew my attention to Napier's marginal invective in his copy of Eyre's account, which is now owned by the India Office Library.

Where historical characters, such as Emily Eden, Florentia Sale, and John Colvin, speak, I have used their own words as much as possible. Where I have had to invent, I have tried not to misrepresent either their attitudes or their actions at the time. Apart from such historical characters, the facts of the invasion and occupation of Afghanistan and the subsequent retreat from Kabul, all the characters and events are imaginary. There were no Beaminsters, Whitneys, Fletchers, Jamiesons, Fullers, Fleckers, Byrds, or Smythams, and no Europeans except Dr. Brydon reached the fort at Jellalabad, but other people did live and die in such places in such a way, and their journals and letters are eloquent testimonies to what they endured.

In the matter of the spelling of Indian, Sikh, and Afghan

names, I have not used modern transliterations, preferring to give readers some idea of the way early Victorians would have pronounced the words. I have followed Kaye, who wrote in his preface: "I have written all the names in the old and vulgar manner, most familiar to the English eye, and, in pronunciation, to the English ear; and I believe that the majority of readers will thank me for the barbarism." Thus, Kabul becomes Caubul; Ranjit Singh, Runjeet Singh, and so on.